T0094561

OUT OF WHACK

SUSAN X MEAGHER

OUT OF WHACK

THIS TRADE PAPERBACK ORIGINAL IS PUBLISHED BY BRISK PRESS, BRIELLE, NJ 08730.

COVER DESIGN AND LAYOUT BY: CAROLYN NORMAN

EDITED BY: LINDA LORENZO

FIRST PRINTING: OCTOBER 2014

ISBN-13: 978-0-9899895-5-8

By Susan X Meagher

Novels

Arbor Vitae
All That Matters
Cherry Grove
Girl Meets Girl
The Lies That Bind
The Legacy
Doublecrossed
Smooth Sailing
How To Wrangle a Woman
Almost Heaven
The Crush
The Reunion
Inside Out
Out of Whack

Serial Novel

I Found My Heart In San Francisco

Awakenings: Book One
Beginnings: Book Two
Coalescence: Book Three
Disclosures: Book Four
Entwined: Book Five
Fidelity: Book Six
Getaway: Book Seven
Honesty: Book Eight
Intentions: Book Nine
Journeys: Book Ten
Karma: Book Eleven
Lifeline: Book Twelve
Monogamy: Book Thirteen
Nurture: Book Fourteen
Osmosis: Book Fifteen
Paradigm: Book Sixteen
Quandary: Book Seventeen

Anthologies

Undercover Tales
Outsiders

ACKNOWLEDGEMENTS

My name's on the cover, but it takes many people to produce a novel.

Blayne Cooper spent a day helping me kick around ideas well before I wrote a word. Then Peyton Andrews, Cheri Fuller and Nancy Jean Tubbs gave me feedback on the first draft. Each of them provided much needed insights.

Linda Lorenzo worked under a very tight deadline to do her usual bang-up job of editing.

As always, my wife Carrie's contribution in producing the book was easily equal to mine. She's the key to my writing—and my happiness.

CHAPTER ONE

A LOUD RUMBLE MADE Darcy look up sharply, only to realize it was her own stomach making the racket. She was knee-deep in quarterly projections, but her stomach wasn't shy about reminding her she hadn't stopped for lunch.

Just leaning back in her chair felt like a coffee break. She looked at the clock. It must have stopped. It couldn't possibly be seven o'clock. Swiveling around, she saw the quiet street bathed in the ugly orange of the streetlights. Damn, if she kept working this hard, she'd be pulled out of the office feet first.

Half standing, she saw Harry still plugging away in his office. He must have seen her pop her head up, because he twitched his hand, calling her in.

"Hi," she said, seeing the mess of paper on his desk. As busy as she was, Harry was at least twice as swamped. And three times as anxious. Running a small accounting office in an unfashionable part of Brooklyn was about to kill them both. How did the partners at the big firms do it? The pressure must have destroyed their souls.

"You can't stay this late every night," he said, frowning at her.

"I don't. I didn't come in at all yesterday."

"It was Thanksgiving," he grumbled. Stopping to lean back in his chair, he regarded her for a second. "I didn't have time to ask about your day. Did you spend it with family?"

"Not this year," she said, hoping he didn't press for details. "How about you?"

"Yeah, yeah," he said, something on his desk tearing his attention away. "The usual group. Along with some joker my older daughter's dating." Whatever had diverted his focus disappeared. He fixed her with an unblinking gaze. "You're on salary, Darcy. I know we agreed you'd take flex-time when we're not so busy, but I have no idea when that's going to be."

"Don't worry about it. I'm not even keeping track of my hours any more. We'll figure something out."

Harry's bushy gray eyebrows almost met when he frowned. She guessed he'd been a good-looking guy when he was younger, but working close to a hundred hours a week had taken a toll. Although Harry was probably only around sixty, no one would have doubted him if he claimed seventy-five.

He ran a shaky hand through his thinning, gray hair. "That's not fair to you. You need to keep track of your time."

She sat down in the single side chair that barely fit in his cramped office. "Harry, I've been here for six months, and I've already racked up three hundred hours of overtime. It's silly to keep track of it any longer. I'll take days when I can and we'll call it even."

He let out a long, heavy sigh. She sure hoped he made a lot more money than she did, 'cause he was working himself to an early grave.

"Sometimes I wish you hadn't applied for the job." A short, wry laugh bubbled up, a strangely happy sound that always caught her by surprise. "If you were a jerk, I wouldn't mind treating you like this."

"I don't mind," she assured him. "I don't have much of a social life yet. It's not like I'm canceling plans to work."

"You're gonna wish you were back in Jersey."

"Nah. I'm glad I made the move. I've always wanted to live in New York, and"—she ordered her face into the brightest grin she had—"here I am!"

"Yeah," he scoffed. "Stuck in a two-man shop in Gravesend. Just where every young CPA wants to wind up."

"I'm not young," she insisted, but he was right about the uninspiring location, if not her age. She'd always wanted to work for a big firm and live in an apartment in Manhattan—with an expansive city view. But she'd finally faced the facts and took the only job offered —this tiny spot near the southern tip of Brooklyn, with a small, featureless apartment four miles away in Kensington. The only pleasant surprise of the whole experience was learning that a load of lesbians had moved into Kensington in the last few years. Maybe one day she'd be home in time to meet one of them.

"You're a good accountant, Darcy. Too good for this place. I wish …" He trailed off, his once handsome features drooping into defeat.

Harry was a hell of a nice guy, and that made up for a lot. If you were going to be stuck in Gravesend, it helped to share the office with a guy who had a heart.

"I wish we were both partners at a Big Four accounting firm, making seven figures. I also wish I was thirty and gorgeous. I could go on all day," she added, grinning, "but we're here so we might as well make the best of it."

"You're too sharp-eyed to not see how pretty you are." He laughed softly. "You know, that's the reason I keep telling Barbara not to come by the office. She would *not* like me hiring a pretty young girl."

"So I'm not going to get to meet her until I'm older and weathered?"

"Go home," he said firmly, a small grin peeking out. "Get yourself a decent meal and relax."

"Not if you don't go too."

"I will." He looked down at his desk, his attention already back on whatever he'd been working on. "I've got to wait for someone to stop by. Then I'm out of here."

"Do you want me to get something for you? I'm happy to."

"No, Barbara's waiting dinner for me. Go," he said shooing her out with a gesture.

"You win. See you in the morning." His attention was locked onto his work by the time she'd crossed the threshold.

Darcy went to her desk and collected up her gear. She'd been roller-blading the four miles to work, but the dusting of snow they'd gotten the day before was a pretty good sign she'd soon have to pack up her blades for the winter. It was only ten stops on the F train to the office, so taking the train wasn't going to be bad. But she knew once the blades were in the closet, she wouldn't get any exercise at all. There was just no damned time for it.

She shrugged into her jacket, slipped on her gloves and slung her huge pack onto a shoulder. Blading home without something to eat was very unappealing. If she ate first, her dinner would be digested enough by the time she got home to let her go right to sleep.

After stepping out of the storefront onto the mostly deserted street, she looked up as the elevated rumbled overhead. People made fun of Jersey for being loud and dirty. They'd obviously never been to Brooklyn. Or at least her part of Brooklyn. With luck, work would calm down around Christmas. Then she could explore her new home and see the Brooklyn that everyone raved about.

She lugged her stuff down a few blocks to a bar on Avenue X. She'd been there several times, and knew they could produce a good meal—if they were in the mood.

Darcy entered the dark space, pleased to find only six other patrons. There was usually only one bartender and one guy in the kitchen, and they seemed to work slower when it was crowded. It was a Russian place, and most of the patrons were Eastern Europeans. But she liked that it was different—very different from her suburban Jersey home. She'd moved to see a different kind of life. And this spot was about as different from Marcello's Molto Pasta as you could get.

She'd been there often enough to know the sukhoi gribnoi soup was good and hearty, with an earthy, intense, mushroom flavor. Probably dried mushrooms, if she had to guess. Tonight it was delivered quickly, and the thick soup satisfied her so thoroughly she wasn't in the mood to blade home. So she hoisted her gear onto her back and trudged through the cold, passing the office on the way to the subway. The lights were still on. Maybe Harry needed a little boost to pull his butt out of that chair. As she fumbled with her keys, she noticed the blinds were closed. That wasn't like Harry. He liked to show how little there was in the office to steal—not that they had a crime problem. This part of Gravesend was quiet, mostly residential.

When her key slid in the lock and it snapped open, Darcy felt a chill race down her spine. The office was quiet, deadly quiet, but it didn't seem naturally so. More like someone had stopped what he was doing and was waiting her out.

A large part of her wanted to back out and give Harry a call to remind him to pack it up. Pausing in the doorway, she forced herself to admit she was still skittish about being in an unfamiliar city. She had to stop letting her imagination get the best of her.

Stepping all the way in, her heart almost stopped when she saw a large gun pointed right at her head. Blood pounded in her ears with each beat as she took in the scene. Harry was tied to her chair, his face a mass of bruises, blood trickling from the corner of his mouth. A very large man with a shaved head, beady eyes, and a black leather coat that nearly hit the floor held what she now recognized as a Walther PPK in his gloved hand. Not a big gun at all. It just looked bigger when it was pointed at you. *Fuck*. When a guy carried James Bond's weapon, he was making a statement. Her mother had always said you could read the message a guy was trying to send by the weapon he carried. This thug wanted people to fear him. He was one hundred percent successful.

"You work here?" the goon asked, his heavily accented English pegging him as Russian.

"I was just ... leaving."

"You are not. Sit." He pointed the gun at the straight-backed chair next to her desk.

Her knees were shaking so hard she could hardly make the ten-foot trip. If not for the years of lessons she'd learned from her mom, she might have tried to run. But she'd learned much about firearms and the criminals who carried them. This guy was a pro, not some two-bit burglar. When you were facing down a pro, you had to follow orders while trying to think your way out of the situation. Being a hero might make you famous—but only in the obituaries.

Now that she was sitting right next to him, Darcy saw that Harry was unconscious. What in the hell was going on? "We don't keep any money here," she said, her voice betraying her fear. "We've got nothing but old computers and accounting files."

"You've got more," the thug said, his voice strangely soft and smooth. "You've got my money."

"I don't … I have no idea who you are. We're accountants, not bankers."

"You've—got—my—money." Now the gun was about six inches from her temple. One round and she was dead.

"Tell me what you want and I'll give it to you."

Harry mumbled something as his head moved slowly. The thug grabbed him by the hair and shook him so violently that Darcy almost screamed.

"I want my money now!" he shouted, bending over so his thick lips were right at Harry's ear.

"Only for Viktor. He's the boss …"

The thug slugged him in the gut, forcing all of the air from Harry's lungs. He gasped, struggling for breath, his face flushing an unnatural shade of red. Before he could begin to take another breath, the thug hit him again, catching him right in the solar plexus. Harry sat bolt upright, his eyes bugging out grotesquely. Then he shivered, just once, and collapsed, his body hanging loosely from the rope tied around his chest.

Darcy could barely breathe. Fear clutched at her chest so heavily it hurt. Then she heard a soft splattering sound and looked down to see a trickle of urine hitting the carpet. "You killed him!"

"He killed himself," the guy grumbled, completely unconcerned. "He was weak." Now he turned to Darcy, his flat grey eyes locked on her. "Open the safe."

A thousand thoughts rolled through her head. She had no idea who this guy was, but Harry was willing to give his life to defy him. That either meant Harry also didn't know him, or there was someone he feared more than this guy. "I can't," she managed to say. "I don't know the combination."

The safe, a big, old clunky thing, sat in the corner, cemented into the floor. She'd seen Harry hurriedly closing it once in a while when she'd entered in the morning, but he never touched it when she was sitting at her desk.

"Yes, you do," the guy said, his voice a gentle purr. "You don't want to go where Harry is, do you?"

"No! You can have the whole office! I'll give you the keys to my apartment! Whatever you want! But I don't know the combination." She was shaking so hard she was afraid she'd lose control of her bladder. Not that wetting herself was her paramount concern. Living had shot to the top of that list.

He reached over and caressed her cheek for a second, then pulled his arm back at lightning speed and clocked her, catching her right on the chin.

It was true. You really did see stars when someone punched you. Then the pain made its way through her nerves and she almost vomited. Her eyes fought to focus, but he was a wavy, moving image that wouldn't stay still.

"I don't know it," she mumbled, the pain so great it felt as if her head would explode.

"What hand do you use?" he asked, getting right into her face.

Still struggling to see, she fought to understand his question.

"Right or left?"

"Right," she said, confused and slow.

7

"Everyone lies." He grasped her left hand and pushed it back until she screamed in terror. Then a bone cracked, the sound a sickening thud. Pain radiated up her arm, competing with the throbbing in her head until she fell forward and vomited onto the bottom of his coat and all over his shiny, black cowboy boots.

She was on her knees, bent over when one of those boots caught her right in the ribs. Too stunned to move, in too much pain to cry out, she fell to her side, clutching her battered body.

He reached down, grabbed her by the hair and pulled her to her knees. Then a wallop to the side of her face snapped her head back.

"You ruined my boots!"

Darcy spit blood down her shirt as she tried to get control of her body. She didn't have time to feel. She had to think!

He spoke as if he was talking to himself. "Women can't take pain, so you are telling the truth. I must kill you."

"No! You've got to …" She fought with every bit of mental acuity she still possessed. "Viktor! Call Viktor!"

"You know Viktor?" He got down on his knees so his face was right in front of hers. "How do you know Viktor?" His head tilted like an interested puppy's.

"He's the boss," she said, mimicking Harry's claim. "He won't want you to kill both of us."

"Ha!" He patted her on the cheek, then stood. "Viktor would not care if I killed everyone on the block. You know nothing but … me. That is bad for you." He put his hand on the weapon, cocking it.

"No! Call Viktor. Tell him you're about to kill everyone who knows about his money. No one but me knows this system. It'll take months for a stranger to figure out what's going on."

"*You* don't know what's going on," he scoffed. "Harry was not so stupid to tell you."

8

"You're right. I didn't work on Viktor's books. But I know Harry's system and all of his passwords. I can figure things out much, much faster than an outsider. Doesn't Viktor want things done quickly?"

She had no damned idea who Viktor was or whether he used Harry as a bookkeeper. But she didn't have any other reasons for this goon not to waste her.

He shrugged his ridiculously broad shoulders, then took out his phone and hit a button. "Trouble," he said when it was answered. "Harry's dead." His Cro-Magnon brow furrowed. "No, I didn't kill him. He died." His beady eyes settled on Darcy, as if he were daring her to contradict him. "He wanted *you* to tell him to give it to me." He stared at the wall, looking like he was about to snap off a smart reply. "He's not in charge. *I* am." His head turned and he scowled at Darcy, like he was angry she was hearing him getting chewed out by the boss. "Yes," he barked. "I beat him up. Is that against the law now? He's an old, fat man. I gave him a lesson to show him he has to obey all of us." His voice lowered. "Harry's no problem. A girl's here. She's seen too much. I will kill her."

"No!" Darcy cried, yelling at full volume. "I can help you figure out the books. We're running custom software that's ten years old. The company that customized it is out of business. You'll never figure it out without help!"

The thug listened for a few moments, then held the phone to Darcy's ear. "Speak," he demanded.

"I'm Harry's co-worker. I don't know who you are and I haven't worked on your books. But I know this system. I can figure it out ... guaranteed."

A harsher voice, equally Russian said, "Why should I trust you? You are a liability."

"No, I'm not. If Harry's been doing your books you must need to ..." She hesitated. Criminals probably didn't like to be called criminals, but she didn't have time to sugarcoat this. "You must need to make things look legitimate. I don't care if you're laundering money, selling heroin to children or smuggling women to Shanghai. I can help you sort things out. I swear no one else will be able to. This system is *ancient*."

"Let me talk to Sergei."

"Please, please don't tell him to kill me. I'll do anything to be able to walk away from this. Just let me try."

"Sergei," he said, clearly finished with her.

She looked up into Sergei's emotionless eyes. "He wants to talk to you."

Sergei put the phone up to his ear and listened. "I don't know. Yes, maybe she lies. But maybe not." He looked at her critically. "I can fix that. Yes. Got it." He hit the End button and grasped Harry's limp hand. He concentrated, lines forming on his brow as he worked to force the lifeless fingers together. Then he leaned close, slammed his arm against Darcy's mouth to muffle her screams, and dragged the nails down her cheek, ripping strips of skin off.

Fear and pain and revulsion rocked her. Then he stood, looking very pleased with himself. "Your skin is here." He shook the lifeless, pale hand still dangling from his paw. Then he pointed at the floor. "Your blood. Harry's blood." His ugly face slowly showed a grin that somehow made him even uglier. "You keep your mouth shut and help us or you go to jail. For murder."

"But I didn't ..." She snapped her mouth shut. Never argue!

"The local captain is ours. If we tell him you did this—no one will argue."

"I'll do whatever you want. I *swear* it."

"I will send someone for the books. You will tell him everything. Someone else will come to open the safe."

Be helpful. Make yourself useful! "I'll ... I'll leave a note with all of the neighbors, telling them a water pipe broke and we have to break through the wall to fix it. Harry is good ..." Her heart flew to her throat and she almost vomited again. *Poor, poor Harry.* "Harry *was* good friends with Konstantin in the barber shop next door and Hagop at the dry cleaner on the other side. They'll wonder about the noise if you have to blow the door off the safe."

"What else?" He cocked his head again and the resemblance suddenly hit her. He looked just like a pit bull. A slate grey pit bull.

"Nothing. I'll be here to reassure the neighbors. And I'll work my butt off to show whoever you send how to decipher our system. You'll be good to go in a week or two."

"You will finish in three days."

She gazed into his cold, blank eyes. "And you'll let me live if I do?"

"Of course." He laughed, the sound so sinister it made her skin crawl. "I don't *like* killing. It's my job." His laugh grew even more harrowing. "I kid. I like it too." He slapped her on the head, rattling her brain again. "I won't kill you if you do what you say. If you don't … you will go to visit Harry." He leaned over and spoke right into her face. "The cops do as we say. They are not your friends. They are mine."

The phone in Harry's office began to ring.

"That's probably Harry's wife Barbara," Darcy got out, still seeing double. "She'll call the police when he doesn't come home. She's …" She started to sob, thinking of the poor woman warming a dinner that would never be eaten. "She's waiting for him."

"She will wait a long time," Sergei said, blithely tossing off the comment.

"But the police will come. They'll have the whole place sealed off as a crime scene. We won't be able to work. You won't be able to get the safe open."

"You think in funny ways," he said, laughing at his own joke. "The police are my puppets." He put his meaty hands in the air, moving them like he was playing with marionettes. "I decide when the police come." Darcy stared at him, stunned as he strolled out without a word. Was he really going to let her live? She stood, then sank back into the chair, so woozy she was certain she'd faint. But she managed to reach the lever for the blinds, opening them a crack, hearing, then seeing a huge black SUV start and glide down the street.

She was numb. That was the only word for it. Thoughts and ideas weren't processing normally. There were shorts throughout her electrical system. The only thing that was constant and reliable was the pain. Never having broken a bone or been hit in the face, she was completely unfamiliar with the way the pain infused every part of her body, rolling through it in waves.

It took a while, but she finally managed to stand and shakily make her way to the safe. She'd never attempted to open it; curiosity wasn't something that motivated her. But Harry had told her the combination on her first day of work. He'd also made it clear she was only to use it if something happened to him. He'd been so earnest that day, so reticent to share the information. But she'd memorized it, hoping she'd never have the need to open it. She turned and caught a look at Harry—grey, lifeless, battered. A guy who'd worked like a dog his whole life to wind up dead at some low-life's hands.

Darcy's fingers were wet with perspiration, her nerves so shot she could barely recall the six simple digits. But she finally heard the satisfying "click" as the tumblers aligned. The door creaked noisily as it opened. Stunned, she fell to the floor, landing on her butt. It took a second for her brain to register the sensations that shot up from her beaten body. A scream burst from her, as tears filled her eyes. Blinking, she was finally able to focus at the dozens of stacks of hundreds, all neatly lined up.

Her brain was going to burst. Thoughts raced through her head, a complete jumble. She'd successfully stood up to a stunning threat. Not because she had guts. She'd never fool herself into believing she was brave. But she was a planner, a strategist. She was breathing at that moment because the combination to the safe had been her only card, the one thing she had to barter with. Her mom had always said that brave people got the headlines, but the strategists got the win. There was no way in hell she was going to give away her only chip, only to have Sergei kill her after he got the money.

So much money! Suddenly, the situation fell into focus. Her only chance was to take the money and get out of town. She'd call the police and tell them what happened. Then, when she was certain they believed her, she'd come back and testify against Sergei and Viktor and the whole bunch. Those bastards were going down!

After dumping her skates, helmet, knee guards and wrist guards onto the floor she started, one-handed, to pile the money inside her bag. There was so much of it the big bag was almost filled. But she'd need cash to hide out until this was all over. Yes, Sergei would be angry she'd outsmarted him, but he would have killed her whether or not she knew the combination, and whether or not she took the money. At least now she had a fighting chance. She paused for just a second and looked up towards the heavens. Her mom would be proud of her for still being alive. That meant everything.

Darcy thought she'd known pain. But she didn't have even a vague acquaintance with what pulsed through her body with each breath. Putting the pack on her back was a little bit of hell, but she'd managed. Now the town car she'd hailed delivered her to the corner opposite her building.

Her mom had been a cop in Jersey City for over twenty-five years, and she'd routinely shared the tips and tricks of the trade with her daughter. But they'd never discussed how to tell if your apartment was being watched. Tears rolled down her cheeks as she stood there, the pain in her ribs feeling like she was being stabbed with an ice pick. At least her wrist didn't hurt as much. And she'd almost forgotten about her chin. Pain clearly had an order that had to be followed and the ribs were the winners.

She somehow managed to get into the building and take the elevator to the fourth floor. After entering her apartment, she dropped the bag, relief flooding her. But it was temporary. She had just a few hours—at best—before someone checked the files and got her address.

Her eyes slammed shut and she cursed loudly. She hadn't thought to take Harry's computer! Why hadn't she destroyed her own personnel file? If she'd done that they'd be chasing their tails!

Darcy gingerly perched on her desk chair, self-loathing filling her. The only way to fix that was to go back. But there was no way in hell she was going to do that. Her careless mistake might just have cost her life. Stupid, stupid, stupid! All she could do now to protect herself was to put her own files onto a flash drive, then reformat her hard drive. At least then they couldn't go through her contacts to find other people to terrorize.

After staring at her phone for minutes, she finally pressed the button for Harry's home and waited. His deep voice asked her to leave a message, but she hung up. You couldn't leave a message telling a woman her husband was dead.

Embarrassed to admit how relieved she was that she couldn't speak to Barbara, she called her uncle. Danny was a cop on Long Island, and even though he wouldn't know anyone in Brooklyn, he'd help her through this. Danny was a rock.

The phone rang and rang, then went to voice mail. *Shit!* She hung up and turned on her computer. Checking her calendar, she saw that Danny and his new girlfriend were on a cruise. Their boat was due back to Bayonne the next day. *Great!* The one person she could rely on was unreachable until morning.

After dumping all of her files onto a flash drive, she sat in her chair and spun around slowly, looking around the apartment she'd so lovingly decorated. It wasn't much. She wasn't the type to fool herself about her circumstances, but it was the first place she'd been able to call her own since she was … thirty-one? Thirty-two? A long time, any way you looked at it.

Even though many of her things had meaning, she couldn't take them with her. She got up, gasping in pain, and went to her bookcase where she removed the one thing she couldn't replace. A blue leather album, created in fits and starts through the years. It wasn't much, but it was all she had that she truly cared about. She managed to get the zipper to the pack open and stuff it in. While it was open, she took out a few hundred bucks and shoved the money into her pocket. Then she grabbed the warmest jacket she had, put the damned pack back on and walked out, stifling the tears that so desperately wanted to come.

The emergency room was relatively quiet on this late Friday evening. As she sat in the oddly still room, listening to other poor souls stoically bearing their pain, she tried to keep her mind focused on the very immediate future. Finding a place to hide was number one on her list—after getting something for the pain. A splint of some kind for her wrist wasn't a bad idea, either. Once the ribs calmed down she was certain it was going to hurt like a bitch.

Finally, a nurse called her name and she went to a small examining room where she fought to get out of her clothes and into an open-backed gown. After a while a harried young doctor came breezing in. "Hi … Ms. Morgan," she said, looking at the forms Darcy had filled out. "What's brought you here tonight?"

"Roller blading," she said, holding her throbbing wrist up. "I ran into a tree." Wincing, she pointed at her ribs. "I think I broke something here too."

Instead of looking at the obviously broken parts, the doctor stood close and shone a tiny light at her face. "What about this?" she asked, touching near but not on the gouges.

"No idea." Darcy started to shrug, then her ribs reminded her that was a very bad idea. "I guess the bark cut me?" She tried to put herself in the mindset of someone who'd run into a tree and probably hadn't looked in the mirror. "It stings a little." She lifted her hand and touched her face. "Ouch! I didn't even realize I'd cut myself."

The doctor held her wrist in her hands, then gently touched all along the swollen skin. "I'd expect to see scrapes or broken skin here." She pulled the gown aside to peer at her ribs. "And this is a single point of contact. More like someone kicked you than the kind of injury you'd get from slamming into a tree." After putting a hand on Darcy's shoulder she said gently, "Who did this to you?"

"A maple ... or an oak! I was blading home from work, in the dark. I was going through Prospect Park and stumbled on something in the path. Next thing I knew I was on the ground."

The woman sighed then shook her head. "Are you married? Living with anyone?"

"No. I live alone." It was still hard to say that. After eight years of round the clock caregiving to someone so dear to her ...

"I can't make you admit someone hurt you, but we have mandatory reporting requirements for domestic violence."

"Call an arborist! I was assaulted by a tree!"

"Fine," the doctor said, sighing. "I can only get the police involved if you've been injured with a weapon or you've sustained significant burns. But I know you didn't run into a tree, Ms. Morgan. I can get a social worker involved ..."

"I appreciate that. I really do. But I just need a splint on this wrist and some tape or something on my ribs." She tried to adopt her most sincere expression. "No one hurt me. This was self-inflicted." That was true, in a way. If she'd simply given Sergei the combination when he'd asked for his money she'd be dead by now. But other than a gaping hole in her head, she wouldn't have another scratch.

Darcy sat in a twenty-four hour diner just a block away from the hospital. How had we hit the twenty-first century and still not figured out a way to fix broken ribs? Not even a bandage for the incessant throbbing. Once the doctor had convinced herself Darcy had been beaten, she seemed to lose interest, or maybe she'd just checked out emotionally. It had to be hard watching people voluntarily go back to dangerous situations.

Darcy had stopped at the pharmacy and had her prescription filled, but she was afraid to take one of the powerful pain pills just yet. First she had to get to safety. The only thing that made sense was to get in a car and go. It didn't matter where. Just drive until she reached some place where the Russian mob didn't have any control. Maybe a nice Amish settlement in Pennsylvania. But she didn't have a car, and there wasn't any place to buy one at one in the morning. All she could think to do was to stay at this all night diner until the used car places opened. It wasn't going to be fun, but when you didn't have many options it didn't do much good to whine.

Trying to take her mind off her troubles, she leaned back in the booth and listened to the woman behind her. Her mind flashed to the game she and her mom had played when she was a kid. They'd listen to one side of a phone conversation, then make up a whole imagined life for the person. They'd try to be as outlandish as possible, assuming espionage, treachery, murder and every other kind of crime just because some lady said she was running late.

The woman's voice was soft but perky and bore some kind of accent. Maybe California? She sounded a little West coasty.

"Yeah, it is late. My sleep schedule's all screwed up. That last trip to Japan was tough on me. I'm going to do nothing but sleep on the boat." A long pause. "Sunday afternoon. I'm flying to Frankfurt tomorrow, then I'll get on the ship the next day."

Darcy listened attentively, guessing the woman was some kind of travel professional.

"Uh-huh. They call this a shake-down cruise. Just crew and a few people from the travel industry. I think I'm the only one writing a

17

feature." She paused for a minute. "*Road Trip Magazine.* What's it like to be on a cruise ship with no real passengers."

Ahh … a writer.

"No, I'll be gone for a whole month, Mom. The cruise is a week, then I'm going to Bavaria for a week, then the Rhône for a week and the Black Forest for a week. Once I get home, I'm taking at least a month off. I don't care *who* calls with a job."

Must be nice to travel for a whole month.

"I wish I was settled. But I've been in my apartment fewer than four days in the last month. The only people happy about that are my downstairs neighbors. I bet they think they got the world's quietest upstairs sublet. Little do they know I stomp around half the night when I've got insomnia."

Ooo, insomnia sucks. Not as bad as a broken wrist, fractured ribs and a sore jaw, but it still sucked.

"I won't be able to call when I'm on the cruise, but I'll give you a buzz when I'm back on land." A pause. "I know I don't have to, mom. But if I have a minute, I'll call." The woman let out an exasperated sigh. "And just when would I have had time to find someone to date? I don't know where the grocery store is yet. Give me time to get settled!"

She sounded so annoyed. Darcy almost turned around and told her to enjoy every moment of having your mother care for you. Once she was gone …

"I know you're just worried about me," the woman said, making Darcy smile. "And I promise I'm going to join the Park Slope food co-op or volunteer somewhere. I'm going to find someone to love this year, and I know it's easiest to find someone when you're doing something you're into. I'm not going to waste my time on another head-case like Sam."

She laughed, the sound so happy it warmed Darcy's heart. "Yes, Mom, I'd like to have a grandchild for you to spoil too. Nothing would make me happier. But I'm not going to do it alone. I need to find some sucker to join me on that adventure." She laughed again, and Darcy almost teared up at hearing this woman so clearly enjoy talking to her mom. You could learn a great deal about someone by how she treated her family. It wasn't as exciting as espionage or selling government secrets, but it was heartwarming.

"Okay, I'll let you go. Tell Dad I'm going to find the best mushrooms in Germany for him, but I'm not sure I can bring them back. You know how picky the guys at customs are. Love you both. Talk to you soon. Auf Wiedersehen."

Darcy was buoyed by listening to this perfectly normal conversation from a perfectly normal-seeming woman. No threats, no punches, no breaking bones. Not even a kick to the ribs. She sat with her chin in her hand, idly watching the TV that hung over the donut case. The sound was off but the pictures were sensational. They always were, even on the very late news. A picture caught her attention and suddenly every nerve was alive. A photo of Harry, looking twenty years younger. A banner headline read "Brooklyn Accountant Murdered." The crawl under his photo said the police were seeking his employee, one Darcy Morgan. Then her picture, the one she'd given Harry for the file appeared. Her hair was shorter, and it wasn't a great likeness since she'd taken it herself and hadn't been able to get the angle right, but it looked enough like her to have even a mildly observant person make her.

What in the holy fuck had happened? She was supposed to have until tomorrow to go through the books!

Shaking, she got to her feet and went to pay. It was a cold night, but she was going to have to spend it in Prospect Park. She couldn't afford to be seen on the street. Any street.

As she got to the register, her booth neighbor was right in front of her. Darcy had been so stunned at seeing her own face on television that she hadn't noticed her getting up.

Trying to use her uninjured hand to pry her wallet from her left front pocket was slow going. How had she never noticed how much your ribs moved? The woman turned and gave her a darling smile. "You look like you could use a hand. A left hand."

"Yeah," she said, immediately tongue-tied. She'd always been clumsy and shy around women—especially straight women. Something about them made her clam up or stutter like a dope.

"Let me help you." She reached into Darcy's pocket and extracted her wallet. "There you go."

"Thanks." Darcy gave her a dumb-looking smile, unable to say another word.

"You've got quite a bruise under your chin. And those scrapes on your face look really sore." She winced noticeably, as if she could feel the pain herself. "Did you fall?"

"Yeah. Roller blading." She held up her wrist. "Broke it."

"Yeah, I know," the woman said, laughing. "That's why I took your wallet out." Her smile dissolved as concern filled her face. "Are you okay?"

"No, not really." Darcy almost let it out, telling this obviously compassionate woman she was in trouble, but she couldn't afford to do that. Until she spoke with her uncle, she had to keep up the lie. "I'm a little worried about getting home. I just left the ER and I'm woozy."

"I'll give you a hand," she said without a second thought. "Do you live in the Slope?"

"Yes. Yes, I do," she said, thrilled at the thought of having someone to walk with. The police wouldn't be looking for two women walking together.

"I'm Center Slope. How about you?"

"Me too," Darcy lied. If the woman could just accompany her to Prospect Park she could duck in and find a quiet space where she could shiver in silence. "By Prospect Park."

"I'm on Prospect. Let's do it."

It was hard to get her feet moving. Her brain wasn't sure what was more terrifying, being found by the police or having to converse with a cute woman. "I'm not sure I remember how to get home."

"What street do you live on?"

"Uhm, First," she said, knowing the streets were numbered before they switched to names.

"Great. I'm at Fifth. You'll just have to go a few more streets. Think you can manage?"

"Yeah, I think so."

She gave her a smile so warm and friendly it made Darcy's knees weak. "If you can't, I'll help you. Don't worry about a thing."

They exited and started to walk up 7th Avenue, but there were so many cars speeding by Darcy's skin crawled. "Let's cut over. I like the side streets better."

"So do I. I don't think I'll ever get tired of looking at these gorgeous old brownstones." They crossed 7th Avenue, then started over 10th Street, walking slowly to accommodate Darcy's shuffling gate.

"I'm usually a little better at conversation," she said, even though that wasn't entirely true. "But I'm really hurting."

"What did you do?"

"Hit a tree when I was roller blading home."

"From work?"

This was working. She could answer specific questions without being too tongue-tied. "Uh-huh. It's a four-mile trip. Four point two to be exact."

"Wow. That's very adventurous."

"Eh … I don't know about that. I just like being outside."

"I'm an outside woman too. I start feeling cooped up after just a few hours in my apartment."

A police cruiser started rolling down 8th Avenue, seeming like he was checking out every person who passed. "Look at this balcony,"

Darcy said, stopping well before the busy avenue. "Wouldn't you love to have a place like this?"

"Who wouldn't? But I'm barely able to afford my one-bedroom. I lucked out and found a sublet that the co-op board didn't require reams of applications for. I consider myself very lucky."

"I bought my place," Darcy said, already missing it. "But it's small too."

They'd made the turn onto Prospect Park West, and after just a few minutes were standing in front of a four-story building. "I didn't catch your name," Darcy said, smiling as well as she could.

"Tess. And you're …?"

"Darcy."

"That's a nice name. I don't think I've heard that for a woman before."

"I haven't either. My mom picked it out of a baby book. She just liked it."

"Your dad didn't get a vote? My mom was stuck on Tess, even though it wasn't on my dad's list. But she claimed she got two votes because she had to do the heavy lifting."

"No dad involved. I've never met him," Darcy said, feeling just a touch of sadness. It was hard to miss something you'd never had.

"You seem okay now," Tess said. "Like your head's clearing."

"I guess it is."

"Well, I'd better get inside," Tess said. "I don't have a coat warm enough for this weather." She stuck her hand out to shake. "It was nice to meet you, Darcy. I hope your injuries heal quickly." She pulled her phone out and said, "Give me your number. I'm going to give you a call in the morning to check on you."

"Uhm …" She couldn't afford to give out her number. Tess would see her picture on TV and call the cops. All of her scant options paraded in front of her. None of them were good. It had gotten colder and she found herself shivering. If the police didn't arrest her in the park, she might freeze to death. A police car cruised down Prospect Park West, slowly shining a light at the benches along the boundary. "Do you have a car?"

"Huh?" Tess looked at her like she was beginning to question her sanity.

"I was thinking of getting one, but I don't want a big hassle with parking."

"Oh. Right." She shook her head. "Can't help you. I don't have one."

One option gone. Darcy swallowed and chose the only path she could think of that would give her the most safety. But it would also cause the most harm. She was sure she'd regret it in the morning, but she had damned few choices. "Could I come up and use your bathroom?"

Tess smiled, but began to look wary. "You just live four short blocks away. Can't you make it?"

"I really wish I could, but I can't." She'd never been so forceful with a woman. Apparently it took fear of imminent death to make her open up and be decisive.

"Mmm, I wish I could be more hospitable. But I don't know you very well …"

"I really, really hate to do this," Darcy said, lifting her shirt to show her Beretta stuck in her waistband. "But I need to go up to your apartment." She swallowed, her nerves about to make her jump out of her skin. "I'm really sorry, but I have to."

CHAPTER TWO

SHE'D BEEN IN OVER three dozen countries, some of them steeped in danger. But Tess had never been more afraid than she was at that moment. Slowly, they walked up the four flights of stairs, with Darcy's plodding gait and heavy breathing making her skin crawl.

Who in the hell was this woman? She'd looked so normal at the diner. Clean, well dressed, a gentle smile, charmingly shy. All of her injuries seemed exactly like those of someone who'd had an accident. But they weren't. No one pulled a gun on you because they'd run into a tree. Someone had hurt this woman—and there was no reason to assume the person who'd done it had come out any better—if they were alive.

Tess tried to swallow, but she didn't have enough moisture in her mouth to manage it. She'd never had any formal training in self-defense, but before a trip to some dicey parts of Latin America, she'd taken a kidnapping prevention course the State Department recommended. The instructor had drummed into them that the smartest action was to go along with whatever your kidnapper demanded *and* to show you were too terrified to be a threat. He'd stressed that repeatedly—don't make your kidnapper think he had to watch you every second. Sometimes they killed you if they thought you were more trouble than you were worth.

But what could this woman want? She seemed so unhappy about forcing her way inside. Like she truly felt this was her only option. What could make her so frightened? With a sickening feeling that lodged right in her gut, Tess had a good guess. Someone meaner and much more powerful had scared the crap out of her. That meant mean and powerful people would find *her* if they found Darcy.

They'd reached her apartment, the unit right at the top floor landing. There were three apartments down the hall, but she'd not met, seen or heard another soul during her few days in the place. Leave it to her to find a relatively soundproof place in Brooklyn. Next time she was going to look for paper-thin walls and nosy neighbors.

Her hands were shaking when she got the door open, then Darcy pointed at the chair. "Sit down."

Tess did, knowing the next few minutes would decide her fate. If Darcy wanted to kill her and … what? Steal her identity? Whatever she wanted, it was going to happen now.

"I need scissors and … a sheet."

"Scissors are …" She tried hard to think, finding her nerves made the simplest questions remarkably difficult. "Tool box on the floor of the hall closet. Sheets are in a box in the bedroom."

Darcy stood behind her and put a hand on her shoulder. "Get up and walk slowly to the closet. Get the tool box and find the scissors for me."

Tess followed instructions to the letter. But the tool box her father had made for her was so stuffed with things, she had to dump the contents on the floor.

"Hand me those zip ties," Darcy said. "And the duck tape."

"These?" She held up a pack of black plastic strips, each nine or ten inches long.

"Yes. And the gray tape."

She stooped and picked them up, then handed them to Darcy.

"Back to the living room. I don't need the sheet now." Tess felt something press against her back, assuming it was the gun. Sweat trickled down the sides of her chest and she almost begged to use the bathroom. Stress always made her kidneys work overtime.

"Sit and put your hands behind your back."

The chair was small, and her arms fit around it relatively comfortably.

25

"Cross your wrists."

If she was going to kill her, she didn't need to tie her up. Maybe this was a good sign?

Tess crossed her wrists, then felt the plastic touch one wrist and then get snugged around both of them. She couldn't see how Darcy was doing this with one hand, but it sure wasn't taking her long. She must've had experience. Great. A career criminal. Maybe that was best. In her class they'd said the biggest danger was amateurs who got scared quickly. Hopefully, Darcy was cooler than she looked.

A ripping sound made Tess flinch, then Darcy's hand was in front of her mouth applying a strip of tape. Tess's claustrophobia started to kick in and her heart raced, full-tilt in seconds. But then a soft, soothing voice was right next to her ear. "Don't be afraid. I'm going to tell you everything that happened. Then you'll understand why I had to do this."

They sat close, Tess in the chair, Darcy on the sofa. Tess was pale and shaking with fear, and Darcy felt sorrier for her than she did for herself. But this would be over tomorrow for Tess. For herself … she had no idea when or if the nightmare would stop.

She'd told Tess the whole tale, from the moment she met Sergei until the present. "I'm just stuck on why they got the cops involved tonight. We had it all worked out that I'd help them figure out the books. I was sure I had at least a day or two to prove I wasn't out to screw with them."

"Mmm moog here honee."

"I can't tell you how sorry I am to do this to you. I swear I won't hurt you. I just need to be safe for a while until I get this sorted out. I'm going to take the tape off—as long as you'll be quiet. I can't afford to have you scream."

Tess shook her head rapidly, indicating she wouldn't. Darcy ripped it off fast, knowing it would hurt less that way.

Wincing in pain, Tess's eyes blinked rapidly. Then she stared hard at Darcy. "Did you leave the safe open?"

"Uhm …" The scene flashed in her mind. She didn't remember closing it, but she also didn't remember leaving it open.

Tess obviously wasn't in the mood to wait for her to think this through. "You took their money! They sent someone over to check the place out and saw that the money was gone. That's a killing offense."

"I had no choice!"

"I'm sure they care deeply about your limited options." Her glare was so heated, Darcy's skin felt hot.

For a minute, Darcy let Tess's words sink in. That was the only thing that made sense. Tess was clearly perceptive. And a perceptive person would know that whoever was gunning for Darcy would grab Tess too. She had to reassure her, to make her see it wouldn't hurt her to allow Darcy to stay for a while.

"My uncle's a cop in Suffolk County. He's out of town tonight, but he'll be back tomorrow morning. As soon as I can get hold of him, we'll figure out what to do next." She put every bit of confidence she could summon into her voice.

Despite being terrified, Tess still showed some fire. "If you're not going to hurt me, why'd you show me your gun? Just because it's pretty?"

"Uhm … good point. I've never shot anyone, and I don't plan on it. But you wouldn't have let me come up if I hadn't … made you." She'd never been more ashamed of herself. Dragging an innocent victim into this was the most self-centered thing she'd ever done. But if she hadn't, she knew she wouldn't have a self to center.

"If you were really innocent, you'd call the police. The whole force isn't corrupt."

"I know that. But if you'd seen how confident Sergei was …"

"Then call the FBI!"

An electrical charge made every body part tingle. "Great idea!" She grabbed her phone, then stared at it as she pondered the suggestion. "They'll be able to trace the call." She looked over at Tess. "And they're not too fond of kidnappers."

"Then call the police," Tess urged, her voice softening a little as she leaned forward to look into Darcy's eyes. "Call police headquarters. Tell them the local guys in Brooklyn are in with the mob."

"I will ... I think. But I've got to talk to my uncle first. Just give me one day. I'll pay you ... ten thousand dollars for one day."

"I'll pay you a thousand to leave. You can go to a hotel."

Darcy's temper started to rise. She must not have been making herself clear, but she didn't have any better way to make her case. "I can't be on the street! My picture was on television!"

"I'll help you come up with a disguise. You can wear my sunglasses and a hat."

"That's a super idea," Darcy said, trying unsuccessfully to hold her temper. "I've got pain shooting through every part of my body and I'm not thinking straight. It's cold out and I've got nowhere to go. You know there aren't any hotels around here. I'd have to go to downtown Brooklyn and I'm sure as hell not able to walk."

"Call a black car," Tess said, clearly trying to make it sound easy.

Darcy looked at the clock near the door, her energy almost tapped out. "I'm not calling a black car, I'm not going to a hotel, and I'm not going to wander around all night." She knew she sounded irritated, but Tess didn't seem to understand her life was on the line. "I need to take a pain pill and get some sleep. If you'll just give me a few hours, I'll get out of your hair." She looked at the sofa. "I'll sleep here and you can go into your bedroom."

"I just have that," she said, indicating the sofa.

"Why did you rent a one bedroom if you're not going to buy a bed?"

"Oh, you're a kidnapper *and* an interior decorator. Will you shoot me for not getting around to buying a bed yet?"

"I'm not going to shoot you! Jesus!"

"Then put the gun away." Tess glared at her.

"I can't do that. I might *have* to shoot you." She knew there was nothing Tess could do to make her pull the trigger, but she couldn't afford to lose her edge, however dull it was.

Tess sat up straighter and spoke in a soft tone. "I want to help you, Darcy. I do. But my boyfriend comes by after he gets off work. He … works at a bar. They're closing soon …"

Darcy shook her head. "You don't have a boyfriend. You want one, but you don't have one now. I heard you talking to your mom."

"Fuck! You're a kidnapper and an eavesdropper!"

"Yeah, I guess I am." All of a sudden, she couldn't keep it together. Everything hit her at once and she started to sob. "I'm so sorry. I really am. But I watched my boss die, I got beaten, then I threatened an innocent woman with a gun. And I'm in so much damn pain." She leaned to the side, the only position she could be in that helped a little. Then she rested her head on her hand, wincing when her sore chin made itself heard. She wasn't usually a crier, but this horrible day had stripped away all of her defenses. And having Tess sitting there, glaring at her, made her feel as creepy as Sergei. "I keep thinking of what Harry's wife is feeling. Not only did she lose her husband, but they've probably convinced her that I killed him. That has to make it so much worse."

"Call her," Tess urged. "If you didn't do it, let her know."

"I'm afraid to. If the police are involved, they might be able to trace my call. I can't risk it."

"Don't cry," Tess said after Darcy had dampened both sleeves of her shirt. "You'll get this figured out."

"I'm trying to. I swear I'm trying to," Darcy sobbed. "If I could just get some sleep …"

"Look. Let's agree that you didn't kidnap me. I'll leave and you can stay—with my permission."

29

"I don't think it works that way."

"Of course it does!" she said, suddenly perky. "If I don't press charges, they've got nothing. Come on," she pleaded, her pale eyes so earnest. "My arms are starting to ache from sitting this way."

"I don't want to keep you tied up," Darcy admitted. "But I have to be clear—you can't leave."

"I get that." Tess's gaze was so calming. It was also filled with not only honesty, but empathy. Maybe she really did understand.

Darcy wasn't at all sure she was doing the right thing, but she got up and cut the zip-strips. "I'm trusting you," she said, putting as much meaning into her words as possible. "I'm trusting you with my life."

Tess stood and rubbed her pink wrists. "You need to get some sleep. Let me get you a T-shirt." She started down the hall, then stopped. "Do you want pajamas? I'm only a couple of sizes bigger than you are. I probably have some that will fit you."

"No, thanks. But a T-shirt would be nice. This shirt makes me sick when I see the blood on it."

"If you're a killer, you're a really bad one." Tess gave her a sincere-looking smile, then went to her room. When she came back, she handed Darcy a T-shirt. "Give me your blouse and I'll get the blood out of it."

Darcy looked up at her like she'd offered to perform a magic trick. "How do you do that?"

"Hydrogen peroxide. It works on every human stain."

"Every *human* stain?"

She stuck her hand out, waiting for the shirt. "We give off all kinds of liquids. Think about it."

Darcy got her blouse unbuttoned, but struggled to get it off her shoulder. Surprisingly, Tess gave her a hand, easing it off quickly. "Do you need help with your bra?"

"Yes," she said, blushing. "But I'm not going to make you my servant. It's bad enough you have to sleep with me."

Shrugging, Tess went toward the bathroom. "I shouldn't have been so lazy about getting a damn bed. My mom always chides me about procrastination."

Tess sat on the tub, watching the peroxide soak into Darcy's blood stains. She knew she should be frightened, but her fear had almost completely disappeared when Darcy cut her loose. Killers didn't do that. Nor did they turn pale at the sight of a few drops of blood. But now that she wasn't terrified, she was pissed. Really pissed. No one had the right to drag an innocent person into whatever shit they'd found themselves in. But even through her anger, she couldn't honestly think of what she'd have done differently if she were in Darcy's shoes. *If* she was telling the truth. That was a big if. Darcy didn't seem like the type to kill her, even if she was involved with gangsters, but desperate people did desperate things.

As Tess exited the bathroom, Darcy looked up guiltily. She was in the process of putting Tess's laptop, keys and cellphone in a paper shopping bag. "I'm sorry. But I can't risk you calling the police when I'm asleep."

"Great. That's just great." Tess strolled past her, going into her bedroom to root through boxes to find a pair of pajamas. She didn't like wearing them, but she wasn't going to sleep half-naked with a gun-wielding stranger. After she'd changed, she went back into the living room to find Darcy standing in the door of the bathroom.

"Do you have an extra toothbrush?"

"Toothbrush? You have mobsters coming for you and you're worried about plaque?"

Clearly mortified, Darcy just nodded.

"If I have one, you're not getting it." She might have to let her stay, but she didn't have to be nice.

"Okay," Darcy said, her hangdog look making Tess feel a little guilty. "Uhm ..." Darcy pointed at the double-deadbolt. "Do you only have one set of keys?"

"Figure that out for yourself. You won't shoot me for being standoffish, will you?"

"No," Darcy said, her voice even quieter. "I know this isn't my business, but when you have this kind of deadbolt, you need to keep a key right by the door. In case of fire, you don't want to be rooting around in a smoky room."

"What in the hell are you talking about?" She put her hands on her hips and stared. The woman was a lunatic!

Darcy looked at the door. "You have to have a key to get out ..."

"I *live* here! Don't you think I know how to get out of my own apartment?"

"You asked what I was talking about ..."

Damn, she was getting slower by the minute. Maybe she was on the verge of passing out. One could hope. "I meant that it's a little strange to have you holding me at gunpoint while lecturing me about fire safety. There's a slight disconnect there."

"I won't shoot you and you know it. But I can't let you go and I can't leave."

"So I've heard." Tess went to the sofa bed, tossed the cushions on the floor, and pulled out the bed. The sheets were already on it and she went back to her bedroom to grab her pillows.

Darcy was looking at her with a sheepish expression. "I don't have the strength to push it, but I need the sofa to be in front of the door."

"Why? As you pointed out I can't get out without a key."

"You might be able to get the keys away from me while I sleep. I wish I could trust you, but I can't."

"Great. Allow me to rearrange my furniture for you."

As soon as the sofa was blocking the door, Darcy put the paper bag under her pillow and lay down, fully dressed. Tess was exhausted,

32

having not slept for over twenty-four hours. You'd think a travel writer would have a good way to deal with jet-lag, but she always had a tough time when going from West to East.

She sat on the chair, glaring at Darcy. The bed looked less inviting with a kidnapper lying in it. Maybe she'd go lie on the floor of her bedroom. At least she'd be alone.

As she sat and stewed, she watched Darcy fall asleep in seconds, even though the lights were still on. Tess gazed at her for a minute, trying to figure out what was true and what wasn't.

Despite the story she was trying to sell, Tess knew next to nothing about Darcy. It was hard to even tell how old she was. Probably around forty, but it was tough to get a bead on someone when she was in a lot of pain. Her color wasn't good—her skin almost grey, with dark circles under her light brown eyes. Her hair, a nice shade of chestnut, probably looked good when it was clean, but now it was a mess, with most of it back in a ponytail, but hanks of it askew. It looked like someone had dragged her around by it. She shivered. Maybe someone had.

Darcy twitched like a dreaming dog, her arms and then her legs jerking and bending. Every time she moved, she whimpered in pain. That was tough to listen to. But Tess couldn't afford to feel sympathy for this woman. She was at least a kidnapper, at most a killer. Tess grabbed her pillow from the sofa, piled up the cushions and took the whole bundle to her bedroom. Better to sleep on the floor than with a murderer.

Groggy, confused, and hurting, Darcy fought to go back to sleep. But something kept tugging at her. Opening her eyes, she spied Tess trying to ease the Beretta from her waistband. Grabbing onto her hand, she found herself fully awake and furious. "One fucking night! I'm going to give you ten thousand dollars for one night on your damned couch!"

"I don't want your money! I want you out of my apartment!"

Unable to control her temper, Darcy shouted, "I know what you want. But I don't want to die! Isn't someone's life—even a stranger's—worth a little inconvenience?"

"No, it's not. You should call the police. That's what an innocent person would do."

Darcy hauled herself out of bed, cursing under her breath as the pain slammed into her. "Fine. I understand my life doesn't matter to you. But it matters to me." Now deadly calm and determined, she went into the kitchen and grabbed the duck tape. "I don't want to do this," she said as she stood by the sofa, "but you've given me no choice." As soon as Tess saw the tape, she tried to make a break for it. But Darcy was strong and had taken more self-defense courses than she could count. She knew how to render an attacker helpless—even while wracked with pain. A knee to the gut kept Tess pretty well restrained, then Darcy leaned over her and got both arms under control. "Stop struggling!"

"Fuck you!" Tess tried to roll away, but Darcy pressed more of her weight into her, making her gasp for breath.

"I do *not* want to hurt you. But I'm going to tie your hands. Stick them out."

Darcy was amazed when the tension left Tess's arms and she compliantly held them in the air, wrists crossed. She went from total submission to snarkiness to trying to steal a gun—with no warning. It was hard enough to understand why people you knew well did things. Damned impossible with a frightened stranger.

Despite the cast, Darcy could use the exposed fingers of her left hand to help get the duck tape wrapped around Tess's wrists. "Now your feet." Darcy had to take her knee off Tess's gut and was rewarded for that momentary lapse by catching a knee to the face, right below her eye. Blinking back tears, she jumped onto Tess's thighs and finally got the squirming feet secured. Darcy was so intent she hadn't even tried to stop the pounding blows to her back, nor the unceasing screams that made her ears ache. As quickly as she could, she turned and slapped another piece of tape over Tess's mouth. Still she screamed, but it was muted. No one would hear her unless they were right outside the door.

Panting from exertion and pain, Darcy ground out, "I'm not going to wind up in prison for the rest of my life just because you're inconvenienced!" Now she had to decide whether Tess's screams had summoned the police. At this point, it hardly mattered. She'd never make it if she had to run.

Darcy stumbled over to the chair and sank down into it. "God damn it," she said, more wrung out than she'd been after Sergei had finished with her. "Why can't you just let a few hours pass?"

Tess could only glare at her, eyes now filled with hatred. What a difference a few hours made. Tess had been so perky and kind-hearted when they'd met in the diner. Strawberry blonde hair with an attractive wave to it that just ticked her collar. Pale eyes that were either blue or green—Darcy hadn't noticed then, and now it was hard to tell in the dim light in the apartment. They were about the same height, maybe even had the same frame, but Tess was stockier. No, that made her sound fat and she wasn't. Maybe fleshy was the right word. Or voluptuous. *That* was the word. She had the kind of body pin-up girls in the 50s had. The kinds of curves that Darcy had never laid her hands on —but had always wanted to. In addition to a gorgeous body, Tess's face was symmetrical and very sweet-looking. Wholesome, actually. The type of girl an All-American boy would want to take home to meet mom. But she had a mean streak that frankly surprised the hell out of Darcy.

It didn't take long, probably just thirty seconds, for Tess to settle down. She started trying to talk again, but Darcy couldn't guess what she was saying. Given the fear she saw building in her eyes, she was probably asking to be allowed to speak.

"Do you want me to take the tape off?"

Tess's head nodded dramatically.

"Are you going to scream again? Not that it did you any good. Your neighbors aren't going to win the neighborhood watch award."

Tess let out some sort of grunt and Darcy got up and stood over her. "I'll take it off, but if I have to put it on again—it's staying on."

Another rapid head nod.

Darcy ripped it off, feeling bad when tears came to Tess's eyes. "Shit, that hurts!"

"I know. And I'm sorry."

"Look," Tess said, clearly trying to speak calmly. "I can't have you do that again. I'm claustrophobic and I'll have a full-on panic attack if you do."

"I don't want to have to tie you up at all." She thought of her reason for having to do it, finding her temper spiking again. "I wouldn't have touched you if you hadn't tried to get my gun!"

"I was lying in my room, trying to decide if I believed you. I don't. Innocent people don't carry guns around with them." Her scowl grew darker. "I'm supposed to believe you're this dedicated little accountant, but just an hour after a stranger beat you up you're brandishing a gun at me. Accountants don't pack heat. So I decided to take it away from you."

Darcy tried to collect her thoughts while staring at this strangely forceful woman. A woman who could send her to an early grave. "I have a gun because I grew up around them. My mom and I belonged to a shooting club. She was a cop. A good one. And she taught me to keep a weapon in the house for self-defense."

"I'm sure she'd be very proud of you," Tess sneered. "Given how you have to *defend* yourself." She held up her bound hands and shook them.

"Was I supposed to let you take my gun? Then what? Would you have shot *me*?"

Tess turned her gaze toward the windows, refusing to make eye contact.

36

"It's not so easy, is it. What would you have done when you had the gun?" She got up and went to stand over her. "If I fought you for it, it could have easily gone off. How would you have felt if you'd killed me?"

"It would've been self-defense," she snapped, eyes blazing again.

Darcy's voice grew more gentle. "I didn't ask if you'd go to jail. I asked how you'd feel." She sat on the edge of the bed, only slightly wounded when Tess immediately scooted as far away as she could. "You should never hold a weapon you're not ready to discharge."

"So you would have shot me if I hadn't let you come upstairs?"

"I wasn't holding it," she reminded her. "And, no, I wouldn't have. I would have run. I would've been caught, but I couldn't have shot you. Your life is worth as much as mine." She shrugged, gasping when the pain in her ribs bit her. "Probably more."

"Answer this one. If you're so close to your mom, why haven't you called her? Your photo's on TV as being a suspect in a murder and you haven't made a single call. That's not the sign of an innocent woman."

"My mom's dead," Darcy said, suddenly missing her as much as she ever had. "On Monday it'll be seven months."

"Sorry," Tess said, sounding pretty sincere. "What about other people? Friends? Lovers?"

"I don't have many," Darcy admitted, shame coloring her cheeks. Why was it so hard to admit how disconnected she'd become?

"I'm sure it's hard to make friends when you have to put a gun to their heads to make them hang out with you."

Darcy could feel her control slipping away. She missed her mom, their life together. She missed New Jersey and the routine, but predictable life she'd fashioned. She missed the friends she'd lost over the years. And, most of all, she missed having one single person to talk to right now. Instead, she had a furious woman glaring at her. Insulting her. Taunting her.

It was stupid trying to explain yourself to a stranger, but Darcy couldn't let that last comment go unchecked. "My mom got sick and I had to quit my job to care for her. Your friends don't stick around when you can never go out with them and all you want to talk about is your mom's illness."

"That sucks," Tess said, her voice softening a tiny bit. "But that doesn't give you the right to take me hostage. Your mom would be ashamed of you."

"She would not! She'd be proud of me for staying alive!"

"At an innocent stranger's expense?" A pale eyebrow rose, taunting her.

"Do you have kids?"

"No, of course not. Do you think they're hiding in a box?"

"People get divorced. They have ex husbands …" She shook her head. "If you had kids you wouldn't ask that question. My mom wouldn't want me to hurt you, but she'd be more than happy to have me borrow your apartment for a few hours to *save my life*!" Her voice had gotten so loud the neighbors might call the police because *she'd* alerted them.

"Would she have been proud of you for working with those goons? I know you were involved. They'd have no reason to hurt you if you weren't."

"I would *never* disgrace my mother by being involved with mobsters." Tears flowed once again, and she was powerless to stop them.

Suddenly, Tess's hand was on her leg, patting her gently. She had to use the back of her bound hand, but it was a surprisingly kind gesture. "Come on now, don't cry. Uhm … I know you don't have any reason to believe me, but if you want to go back to sleep, I'll behave myself."

"I don't … I can't trust you. I'd better stay awake until I can talk to my uncle."

"I promise," Tess said. "Really. If half of what you've told me is true, you've had a tough year."

"It's all true," Darcy said, looking down at her. "I wish to God I'd made it up, but it's the damned truth." She went to her bag, removed a banded stack of hundreds and put it on the coffee table. "I know your freedom is worth more than money, but here's …" She counted ten bills, then gauged that it was about ten percent of the total. "Ten thousand bucks. You can buy yourself a nice bed."

"That's no better than Monopoly money. The police are really good at tracing stolen cash."

"I doubt they know about it. Who's going to tell? Not the criminals, and I'm pretty confident Harry's wife didn't know about it. All they'll see is an empty safe. They'll have to guess what was in it."

"Great. So your money's good. You don't have to give me a dime if you'll untie me."

Darcy thought about it for a long time, then said, "I'll untie your feet. But I can't trust you enough to free your hands."

"I guess I don't blame you," Tess said. "If someone tried to steal my gun I wouldn't be happy."

Darcy looked at her, unable to figure out what she was thinking. She was *very* hard to read. And *very* unpredictable. "I'm not happy. I'm very much not happy."

Tess gazed at her for a minute. "Part of the reason I wanted your gun was because I don't believe you. But I'm also worried about the guys you're afraid of. If I could've gotten rid of you, someone wouldn't do to me what they did to you."

"Can't blame you for that," Darcy admitted. "But you don't have to worry. I won't hurt you, but I'll blow the brains out of anyone who tries to get in here."

"Very reassuring. I'm sure I'll drift right off to sleep now that you've made me feel so much better."

"I mean it, Tess. I'm a good shot and I'm not afraid to use my weapon. Anyone who shows up here is looking to kill me, and I'm not going to let that happen."

"I'll lie down and be quiet," Tess said. "I'm not sure I believe you'd kill a visitor, but you're not antagonistic to using your strength. I don't want that knee in my gut again."

"And I don't want to put it there again," Darcy said, slowly lowering herself to the bed. "But I will if I have to."

CHAPTER THREE

DARCY SLEPT FITFULLY, NOT used to sleeping with another person, or with broken bones. She woke, unable to relax again, at seven. After stealthily taking Tess's computer from the bag she'd put it into, she checked on her uncle's ship and saw that it was already in port.

Tess was sound asleep, so Darcy snuck out of bed, trying mightily to avoid grunting and moaning in pain. After going into the bedroom, she used Tess's phone to call her uncle. Relief flooded her when he picked up the call. "Danny," she got out before tears took her breath away.

"Darcy? Is that you? What's wrong?"

"I … I'm in trouble. Big trouble."

"Hold on. Hold on. I'm just getting to my car."

"Is your girlfriend with you?"

"Huh?" The ambient sound changed and now she could hear him much better. "Why do you want to know?"

"Because I need to talk to you alone. It's important, Danny."

"Okay, okay. She's not here. She took a cab to get to work. Now will you tell me what's going on?"

"So much." She took in a breath and tried to get it out as succinctly as possible. "My boss was involved … somehow … with some Russian gangsters. A guy came to the office yesterday and beat Harry up. I don't know if he had a heart attack or what, but he died."

"Holy shit!"

"It gets worse. The guy, Sergei, beat me up too. He wanted a huge pile of cash he'd parked in the office safe. I'm not sure why, but Harry wouldn't give it to him. Right before he died, he said he could only give it to Viktor, the boss … Then he was gone."

"What the fuck? Jesus, Darcy. What did the cops say?"

"I didn't call them."

"You're shitting me! Why not?"

"Two reasons: one, Sergei assured me they owned the local captain and two, he took Harry's hand and dragged his fingers down my cheek. My skin is under his nails. He set it up to look like I killed him."

"God damn, Darcy. God damn!"

"It gets worse," she insisted. "After he left, I opened the safe and took the money. I haven't counted it, but it filled my gear bag."

"What the fuck? Why'd you do that?"

"I thought I could convince the cops I had nothing to do with Harry's death if I showed them the dirty money. But I also figured I might need it if I had to disappear."

"Okay. Okay." He sounded as panicked as she'd ever heard him. A movement caught the corner of her eye and she gestured for Tess to come into the bedroom. "We'll figure this out."

"I'm putting you on speaker, Danny. There's someone with me and I want her to hear the whole conversation."

"Uhm … okay. But do you really want a friend to hear this? I'd keep things under wraps—"

"She's not a friend," Darcy interrupted. She pressed the button and took a look at Tess. "This next part," Darcy said, raising her voice so her uncle could hear, "sounds really bad. I was hurting last night. I've got a broken wrist, two fractured ribs, a chin that aches like hell, gouges on my cheek and …" She caught a look at herself in the mirrored closet door. "A black eye. The last one's from the woman I kidnapped."

"What. The. Fuck. Darcy, I don't know what you're on, but we can get you help."

"I'm not on anything," she insisted. "Turn on the news. You'll see me plastered all over it. Like I murdered poor Harry with my bare hands."

"Darcy," he said, his voice gentle and artificially calm. "Why did that make you kidnap a woman?"

"I *had* to get off the street, Danny. I was at a diner and I overheard a woman say she was going out of town for a month. She said she didn't have friends or family nearby. I know it was a terrible thing to do, but I thought … I still think I wouldn't have made it through the night if I didn't get off the streets."

"Shit, shit, shit! Kidnapping isn't the way to show you're innocent!"

"That's what I keep telling her," Tess broke in.

"Hi," Danny said nervously. "Are you the victim?"

"Yeah, that's me. Can you come get your niece? I've got to catch a plane to Germany this afternoon."

"This afternoon? Uhm … that's … probably not going to happen."

"Then send someone else!" Tess demanded.

"I'm a police officer," Danny said. "I can't get involved like that."

Tess stared at Darcy, shooting daggers. "Then what am I supposed to do?"

Danny broke in. "Hang tight. I'll call everybody I know to see what I can figure out. Darcy, you turn off your phone and don't turn it back on. Do you have your computer?"

"No, I left it at my apartment."

"Good. They might be able to track you if you use anything that connects to a cell tower or an IP address. I'm going to have to report this call, so don't tell me where you are. I know this isn't what you want to hear … but you need to stay put."

"She promised I could leave today!" Tess shouted.

"Think about it," he said, his voice calm and thoughtful. "How can she let you go when you'll run to the cops?"

"I won't!"

"She tried to take my gun while I was sleeping," Darcy said, ignoring the evil look Tess gave her. "Well you did!"

"And I could have taken it this morning. You were snoring loud enough to wake the dead. You wouldn't have felt a thing. But I didn't because you *promised* I could leave."

"I promised to do my best. That's all I promised."

"This is fucked up, Darcy. Getting a stranger involved was a very bad idea. But you'd better have a safe place to hide if you let her go."

"I don't. I've got nothing."

"I wish to god I could help more, but all I can do is try to find out what's going on. I'll go get a disposable phone and call you back later today. I'll call this number. Is that all right, miss?"

"Oh, sure," Tess said, sarcasm dripping. "No problem. Why don't you come join us? Have the whole family sleep on my sofa."

Darcy ignored Tess's whining and replied, "I'll be waiting. I want this over. I'll talk to anyone … FBI, NYPD brass, the District Attorney, the U.S. Attorney. Anyone."

"Got it. I'll call you back. Until then, stay safe."

He clicked off and Darcy looked at Tess. "If you can figure out where to put me, I'll go. If you can't, you've got to cancel your trip."

"That's how I make my living!" She was so livid her cheeks were as red as apples.

"I'll pay you twice what you would have gotten, and you won't have to do any work."

"Thanks. Thanks for nothing!" She stormed out of the room, and marched down the hall and into the bathroom, slamming the door. Even her shitty plans weren't making the grade. Darcy knew she was screwed. Badly.

As long as Tess was going to sulk in the bathroom, Darcy decided to lie down and try to rest. The entry door was locked from the inside, she had Tess's phone and computer stuffed under the mattress and was reasonably sure she'd hear her if she tried to open the kitchen window and climb out via the fire escape. She was afraid it would be too hard to get to sleep, but the stress was obviously getting to her. In moments, she jerked with that falling feeling she often got as she was nodding off. Then she relaxed and tried to clear her mind.

A funny sound woke her. Something tearing or ripping. Prying one eye open she saw Tess standing at the window, peeling off strips of tape from a dispenser and affixing them to sheets of paper. "May I see what you're doing?" Darcy asked, her voice rough from sleep.

"Get up and look for yourself." Tess slapped the last piece of tape on and stalked out of the room.

It took a while to get up from the sofa, but Darcy finally had her feet under her. After peeling off the sheets, she saw the first window sign read "HELP," the next "CALL" and the last "9-1-1." You had to hand it to her. Tess wasn't the type to sit around sulking. She was what Darcy's mom called a conniver.

There were three big windows in the bedroom, and, as expected, they'd already been papered. Darcy shot a quick look at Tess, sitting at her desk chair, chin braced on a hand. Then she went to the windows and pulled the signs down. These bore a different message. Each sheet contained one letter and they filled each window. The first shouted "KIDNAPPER!" The second "HELP" and the third "ME!" As Darcy left the room she said, "I admire your determination."

"Go fuck yourself. The last thing I need is a kidnapper's admiration."

That hurt. More than it should have. No one wanted to be kicked in the teeth when she already felt like a low-life.

A long time later Tess came back into the living room. Darcy decided to let her break the silence, which she did not. They sat there, not speaking, for a long time. "I don't see a TV anywhere," Darcy finally said when she couldn't stand the stilted quiet one more second.

"I don't have one. I watch movies on my computer."

"Mmm." Darcy could feel the walls closing in on her. With no distractions the small apartment seemed much smaller than it really was. In fact, it was light and bright, although under-furnished. Tess was probably in her late twenties or early thirties, but her apartment made it seem like she was just out of college.

"Can I use my computer?" Tess asked, her voice nearly a growl.

"Sure. But I have to see what you're doing."

Tess glared at her. "So I can't watch a movie without you breathing on me?"

"I'll try not to breathe on you," Darcy said quietly, stung by her sharp words. "But I have to see what you're doing."

After letting out a long breath, Tess turned and faced her. "I've got to get out of here. I'm not a true claustrophobic, but I'm close. Can't we go outside? Just for a few minutes? No one will notice us in the park."

"I don't think I can risk it. I wish I could …"

"You can do anything you want, Darcy. You're the one with the gun." She got up and stalked over to the bathroom, slamming the door after her.

Darcy wracked her brain, trying to think of some way to get a little fresh air. She needed it as much as Tess did. Eventually, she got up and went to the bathroom, knocking quietly. "If you can lend me some sunglasses and a scarf or something …"

The door flew open and Tess actually smiled at her. "I can fix you up. Your own family won't recognize you." She went into her bedroom and returned a short time later with a heavy wool scarf and a pair of aviator-style glasses. "Play around with those," she said, going to pick up their coats.

Darcy thought she looked reasonably anonymous, and with the scarf pulled up over her mouth, you couldn't see the bruise on her chin or the gashes on her cheek. If she kept her hand in her pocket no one would see her cast either.

They were just about to leave when Tess said, "One minute. I've got to pee."

She was in the bathroom forever, but Darcy finally heard the toilet flush. When Tess stood by her Darcy put her hand on the doorknob and said, "I'm putting my trust in you. I really hope you don't let me down."

"I promise I won't say a word to anyone." They exited and Darcy paused before starting to descend. Going down four flights wasn't going to be fun, but she had a feeling the walk up was going to be worse.

Tess stood there, waiting for Darcy. "Go ahead," she said, smiling brightly. "You can make sure I don't take off."

"No, I'd rather follow. I want to be able to duck behind you if we run into someone on the street."

A frown settled onto Tess's face. "I think you should lead. Then you can decide where we go."

"I've already decided. We're walking across the street to the park, then we're going to walk around just long enough to get some air."

"Yeah, but you'd still better lead …"

Darcy shifted so she was behind her and gave her a slight push. As Tess's body moved in front of hers, Darcy saw what had taken her so long in the bathroom. Scrawled across her tan jacket, in lipstick, was "Call 9-1-1!"

Using the crook of her bad arm to cover Tess's mouth, Darcy grabbed her arm and twisted it to gain control as she pushed her back to the apartment. "You have no one to blame but yourself," she groused as Tess unlocked the door. "I was more than willing to risk my neck to make you feel better."

They went inside, where Tess yanked off her coat and threw it onto the floor. "Yeah, you're a giver. You only care about me."

"I didn't say that. I know I'm being selfish. But I … thought I could trust you."

"That's what I thought when I offered to walk you home last night. We're even!" With that, she stormed back to the bath, where she whiled away another good hour, doing what, Darcy had no idea.

Tess lay in the tub, trying to think of an effective way of getting rid of her unwelcome visitor when there was a light knock on the door. "What?" she growled.

"I need to write a letter. Do you have any paper?"

"In my desk."

"Uhm … I don't want to root around in your personal stuff."

Tess climbed out of the deep tub and flung the door open. "You don't mind kidnapping me. You don't mind taking away the only thing I have to entertain myself. You don't mind making my claustrophobia flare up." She'd reached her bedroom and started to paw through her desk drawers. "But looking through my desk is too much for you." She found some thank you cards her aunt had given her. "Here."

Darcy stared at them. "I can't use these. Don't you have anything else? It doesn't have to be fancy."

"What the fuck?" Tess threw them back into the drawer. "Use the printer paper." Darcy didn't react quickly, so Tess slapped her hand onto the ream that sat in a tray.

"That's fine. Can I sit at your desk? My ribs might hurt less if I sit up straight to write."

"I'm not playing this game. You're here against my will. Everything you do is against my will, so do whatever the fuck you want." She stalked away, somehow feeling better in the bath. At least she didn't have to look at Darcy's sad puppy eyes.

After an hour her back and shoulders started to ache from lying on the cold cast iron for so long. Tess climbed out once again and went into the living room, pleased to find it empty. But after just a few minutes Darcy walked in, holding a stack of copier paper. "You're a writer, right?" she asked.

"Yeah. Did you learn that peeping at my stuff?"

"No," she said, her head dropping in shame. "I figured that out when you were talking to your mom."

"Right. Right," Tess snapped. "I keep forgetting you're an eavesdropper."

Darcy held the papers out. "Would you mind reading this? I want to make sure I covered everything Barbara might want to know."

"Who the fuck is Barbara?" Tess took the papers and glanced at them. "Oh. The dead guy's wife."

"Right." Gingerly, Darcy settled onto the chair. She was clearly in pain, but Tess couldn't summon any empathy for her. "Are you going to give me another ten thousand for editing?"

"I will if you want it," Darcy said quietly. Tess shot a look at her, seeing pain and sorrow and … disgust in her eyes. It was obvious she didn't want to be here any more than Tess wanted her, but she had choices. Tess didn't.

"Fine. I'll gladly take your blood money." She started to read and in just seconds found herself carried away by Darcy's heartfelt words. By the time she'd finished her eyes had misted up. Annoyed with herself, she wiped at her eyes with the back of her hand. "This is very effective. You missed a few commas, and you meandered a little in the middle, but I can't think of anything she'll want to know that you haven't told her." She handed the papers back. "But how will you send it if you don't know where she lives?"

"I know where Harry lives … lived," she said, correcting herself. "I figured out the address using Google Maps."

"Very ingenious. Want me to run to the post office for you? I've got nothing planned."

One corner of Darcy's mouth lifted in a very small smile. "We'll figure that out later."

"So if your uncle doesn't call back … I'm stuck here another day?"

Darcy nodded her head ever so slightly.

"Fuck!" Tess shouted, then stormed back into the bathroom. This time she decided to take a real bath, hoping the warm water would help dissipate a little of her anger.

Once the tub was filled and scented with some bath salts, Tess got in and let the warm water soothe her. Thinking back to Darcy's letter, she couldn't hold onto her animosity as tightly as she wanted. Darcy didn't seem like a bullshitter, and the way she'd poured her heart out to the widow really was moving. If that had all been a lie, she was a world-class creep. But she sure didn't seem like a creep. She seemed like a good person who'd been caught up in something awful and didn't know how to get out of it. But she still had no right to pull Tess into her mess. That was undeniable.

Tess emerged from this latest trip to the bathroom smelling like spring. Her cheeks were pink, her hair a little curlier than it had been before. She plunked herself down on the sofa and said, "May I have my computer? I've got to tell the magazine that I'm not going to Germany. I'm going to tell them I have appendicitis. I can't afford to look like a screw-up." Darcy had to sit next to her to make sure she followed through and didn't go to some FBI reporting website. She felt like a creep invading her privacy like this, but she had to do it.

Once that was done, they sat there in silence for another few minutes. The tension and stress had Darcy smelling like old gym socks, especially compared with Tess's clean scent. "I'd like to take a shower, but I've got to have you in the room with me."

"Or what? You'll tie me up again?"

"No. I believe you're claustrophobic and I don't want to make this any worse than it is. But if you won't cooperate you're going to be stuck smelling me. We've got pretty close quarters in here …"

"Fine. Take your damn shower."

Darcy found some plastic wrap and carefully covered her cast, then put her gun in a Ziploc bag, taking it with her when she got into the tub. It was silly to be modest, but it seemed too invasive to strip in front of Tess. She removed her clothing and draped it over the rod, being careful to keep it away from the spray. She'd just gotten her hair lathered up when she heard the tiniest creak. Opening the curtain, she saw that Tess was gone. Stark naked, she jumped out of the tub, making it to the door just as Tess got her key in the deadbolt. Darcy yanked it from her hand, cursing quietly.

"I thought you only had one set of keys."

"I never said that. You *assumed* that. Dumb move, by the way."

Grabbing her by the arm, Darcy led her back into the bathroom. This time she left the curtain open. She felt like a fool, but showering, one handed and naked in front of a stranger wasn't the weirdest thing she'd done that day.

After she was finished, she put on the terry-cloth robe Tess had hanging on the back of the door, then washed her underwear out in the sink. When they went back into the living room, Darcy said, "I know you're angry. I'm not very happy myself. But if you'll work with me to figure out another option, I'll take it. I'll *gladly* take it."

"I could go buy you a car …"

"Alone?" Darcy raised an eyebrow.

"You could go to Penn Station and get on a train to … somewhere."

"And you'll just keep our little secret to yourself. Penn Station won't be crawling with cops looking for me, right?"

"This is *hard*," Tess whined.

"I think that's the point I've been trying to make." She stood and walked to the kitchen. "I need some food. What do you have?" She started to open the cabinets, finding … books.

"I don't cook much. And I don't have a bookcase yet."

"*Much?*"

"I'm never home! If I bought food, it would spoil by the time I got back."

51

"Rice and pasta and tomato sauce don't spoil in a month or two. You live like my grandfather."

"Good. Call him. You two can chat about how ill-equipped my kitchen is. Maybe *he'll* come get you."

"He's dead," Darcy said. "Two months after my mother. In case you're interested, my grandmother died two years before that. Yes, in the last two years I buried every member of my family except for my uncle. Happy?"

"I'm not *un*happy," Tess snapped, in what was probably the meanest thing she'd said.

Darcy whirled and stared at her, unable to reply.

"Don't expect me to feel sorry for you after you've cost me a great assignment."

"No, no, how could I expect you to feel any empathy for losing my three closest relatives in a short time period? That's nothing compared to losing a sweet trip to Germany. Nothing at all." She stormed over to the computer, and started to look up local restaurants. "I'm ordering food. If you want some, speak up."

"Ooo, I get food. Bread and water, or just bread?"

Darcy shoved the computer in front of her. "Pick what you want." She watched her carefully, making sure she didn't leave the ordering page. Then she took the computer back and filled out the delivery and payment information. "It'll be here in thirty minutes. Now I just have to figure out how to keep you from yelling for help when the delivery guy gets here."

"Good luck with that," Tess growled.

Darcy put her head back on the sofa and tried to think. This was getting harder by the minute.

Forty-five minutes later, they sat on the sofa, digging into their food.

"You're very clever," Tess said, clearly even more annoyed. "Putting a sign on the door that said, 'Flu,' along with the money in an envelope was a stroke of genius."

"We're eating, aren't we? If I hadn't thought of that, you'd be whining because you were hungry."

"Thanks. I'm eternally indebted."

"Eat up," Darcy said, pointing at her with a fork. "We've got work to do when we're finished."

Darcy wasn't the type to sit around doing nothing, even when she ached from head to toe. She went into the bedroom, followed by Tess, sat on the desk chair and pointed to the mess of boxes littering the room. "The first thing we're going to do is take everything out of these boxes. I want to see inside every single item, just to make sure you haven't hidden any more keys."

"I've only got two sets."

"Can't trust you. Start with that one," she said, pointing.

"You can't make me," Tess snapped. "I know you're not going to shoot me, so you've got no power."

"Yes, I do. I've got your keys, your phone and your computer. You don't have a morsel of food in here, and if you don't do as I say, you're not getting any more." She leaned forward and caught her with a steely gaze. "I can go three days without a bite. No problem."

"Bitch," Tess growled before she approached the box and dumped it onto the floor. "Just sheets and bedroom stuff."

"What's in that box?" Darcy pointed at a decorative wooden box about the size of a loaf of bread.

"Personal stuff."

"Like keys? Another phone? Open it," Darcy demanded.

Tess rolled her eyes, then opened the box and dumped it onto Darcy's lap. A pink dildo, a bottle of lube, packages of condoms and a small lavender thing that was probably a vibrator fell to the floor.

For some reason, Tess didn't seem embarrassed at all. But Darcy was. Deeply, profoundly embarrassed. "I'm so sorry," she whispered, starting to cry again. "I'm not … this isn't who I am. I've never snooped into other people's things. I couldn't even go through my mother's stuff after she died. It was too invasive." She dropped her face into her hand, sobbing.

"Oh, knock it off. So you know I have a sex life."

"No, it's … wrong," Darcy mumbled. "I'd hate to have a stranger look at my private things. I'm really, really sorry I looked at yours."

"Knock it *off.* You didn't know." She stood there, hands on her hips, looking at the mess. "I guess this is as good a time as any to unpack."

Darcy slowly got control of her emotions. "I'm not trying to be rude, but where will you put things? You've got nothing."

"Hmm …" Tess took a look around. "I usually leave things in boxes until I get a feel for a place. It's easier."

"No, it's not. It's always easier to be organized. Start putting stuff in categories. I'll be right back." She walked into the living room and got the computer. Then she logged into the local big-box bed and bath store and started ordering things. They had same-day delivery for an extra fifty bucks, and she happily accepted the charge. "I'm going to need a charge card."

"For what?"

"I'm buying you a few things. You'll charge them, and I'll pay you back in cash."

Tess scowled, then gave her a resigned shrug. "You've got my wallet. Take what you want."

Tess started to pile her sheets up with the towels. "No, no," Darcy directed. "Those things need some air so they don't get musty. Hand me the sheet. You've got it folded like a two-year-old would."

"Great. My kidnapper's a neat freak."

"I'm organized," Darcy said. "And by the end of the day, you will be too."

And, as promised, by dinnertime, the closet was beautifully organized. Stacking bins held sweaters and T-shirts and underwear, leaving plenty of room for all of Tess's slacks, jeans and shirts to hang above. The storage space above the closet now held neatly folded sheets, towels, blankets and extra pillows. The step-ladder Darcy had purchased would even allow Tess to get the stuff out when she needed it. Why a woman would have a huge storage space above a closet and not own a stepladder was beyond her imagination.

Now that they'd reached some level of homoeostasis, Darcy started to think of the immediate future. Tess knew full well Darcy wouldn't shoot her. And she knew full well Tess would take off in a New York moment if she had the chance. At some point Darcy was going to need some privacy, but Tess would bolt the moment she went into the bathroom alone. Even though Darcy had all of her keys, Tess could easily scamper down the fire escape located just outside the kitchen window.

She pondered the question for an hour, then it came to her like a light bulb going off. Adopting the new, forceful personality she was trying to acquire, she called the local Brooklyn sex toy shop. "Hi," she said, trying to sound friendly and smooth. "I'm into a … scene and I need a few things. Do you do deliveries?"

The woman laughed. "No, we don't. I feel for you, but we're not equipped."

"When do you close?"

"Seven. You've got fifteen minutes to put your scene on hold and get over here."

"Do you … by any chance … pass by Park Slope on your way home?"

"What are you asking?" the woman demanded. "I sell sex toys, I don't trick."

"I wasn't implying that! But my partner and I are really … involved. If you could drop a few things off, I could make it worth your while."

"How much worth my while?"

"An extra hundred?"

"Give me your list. And make it a hundred fifty."

An hour later, Darcy had used her trick again, this time writing "Scene in progress. Leave the box," on a piece of paper she'd taped to the door. The money, including the tip, was in an envelope, attached to the sign. A sharp rap on the door alerted her and she went to the bedroom windows to watch a young woman with dreadlocks leave the building, the white envelope in her hand.

Darcy went back to the door, opened it and brought the box in. As she pried it open, Tess's eyes grew wide as she stared at fur-lined wrist restraints, shiny metal handcuffs, bright red bondage tape, and a hot pink ball-gag now placed on the coffee table. "I know you're not going to like this," Darcy said, "but I'm going to need to use the bathroom at some point and …"

"And what?"

"And I need privacy."

Tess stared at her for a solid minute. "You're unable to take a dump with the door open?"

So embarrassed she didn't trust her voice, Darcy dropped her head and nodded.

"I'm not even going to argue with you," Tess said, seemingly resigned. "It wouldn't do me a damn bit of good. You've got my wallet, my driver's license, my passport, and my phone. Even if I escaped, what would I do? After I turned you in just for revenge, of course."

"Of course. Well, I don't know about you, but organizing the bedroom has me famished. What would you like for dinner?"

56

"Whatever's going to make you use the bathroom really quickly. I will fight you tooth and nail before I'll let you gag me. I'm just claustrophobic enough to freak out if you even try."

"We can negotiate that one when the time comes."

A strangely happy grin came to Tess's face. "Pain meds stop you up. With any luck you won't need the bathroom before your uncle comes for you."

"I wouldn't call that luck," Darcy grumbled. "I don't like my bathroom habits disturbed."

Tess blinked at her. "You sure as hell had better not be waiting for sympathy from me. It's not coming."

Tess sat on the upholstered chair, staring at Darcy who was sleeping in an unimaginably uncomfortable-looking position.

Darcy had all of Tess's stuff in an envelope she'd jammed under her leg, but that was the only thing she'd done to allow herself to nap peacefully. She obviously hadn't planned on napping at all since Tess wasn't in handcuffs. But after dinner Darcy's head kept dropping, jerking her awake for a few seconds before she nodded off again. Now she was sitting at the far end of the sofa, her head drooping so her bruised chin rested on a shoulder. As usual, her gun was in her waistband, the handle sticking up, just daring Tess to take it again. But she couldn't. Having it in her hands might lead to one of them getting killed, and there was no way to guarantee it wouldn't be her.

Not having anything better to do, Tess decided to do a little of her own investigation. Stealthily getting up, she moved over to Darcy's coat and extracted her wallet. She wasn't lying about her name. That was small comfort. She had a credit card, a debit card and forty dollars. Nothing very interesting there. That left the big bag that sat under the credenza.

As Tess tried to tiptoe across the floor a board creaked noisily. Darcy stirred, moaned softly and then was out again. After pausing mid-step, Tess continued the trek when she was sure Darcy wouldn't wake. After unzipping the bag, Tess gasped at stacks and stacks of hundreds. She wasn't good at guessing volume, so she couldn't even begin to figure out how much money was lying at her feet. A whole big lot, give or take a million. Something big and square made the bag bulge, and she reached deeper inside to lift it. A photo album? Puzzled, she sat on the floor and paged through the book. Pictures of a cute baby, held by a very proud and tired-looking young woman were on the first page. Then the baby was being held by that same woman, now dressed in a dark blue police uniform. As Tess leafed through, the little girl soon started to look like Darcy.

Tess sat there, befuddled. If Darcy was telling the truth, she was literally running for her life. And all she'd brought with her was a load of dough and this photo album. Idly paging through, she gazed at photo after photo of Darcy taking lessons in some kind of martial art, a tiny gi almost swallowing her; photos of her at a shooting range, holding a smallish gun while she closed one eye and aimed at a target; more martial arts pictures of her at maybe eight, showing impressive form as she threw an adult onto his back; then a bunch of snaps taken at the beach, probably with her grandparents. On and on, the photos showed her finally growing into a young woman graduating from college, with a scarlet stole and lots of gold braid and ribbons adorning her gown. The final picture, a big 8x10, was of her mother in a more impressive looking uniform. Maybe her retirement? Whenever it was, she looked like a tough, no-nonsense kind of woman. The kind of mother who drummed right from wrong into her kid.

Tess snapped the book closed, then tucked it back where she'd found it. Darcy was clearly the kind of kid she'd never liked. The high-achieving, rock-solid, rule-follower. The kind of kid who was always more interested in pleasing adults than making friends. But ... she couldn't look at those damned photos and picture her murdering her boss. That did not compute.

"What are you doing sitting on the floor?" Darcy asked, her voice rough and low.

"I was going to count your money, but there's too much of it. Are you sure you didn't work at the Federal Reserve?" She got up and went back to sit in her chair.

"No. Just your average mob front. A place for the boss to launder money while some doofus from New Jersey chases her tail doing all the work for the legitimate clients."

Tess watched her rub her neck, then gasp in pain at having to move her arm. This was why it wasn't a good idea to play by the rules. You could waste all that time being a good girl, and still get screwed—hard.

Darcy got up with difficulty, started for the bathroom, then stopped to give Tess a long look. "How long was I out?"

"Not very. Twenty minutes or so."

"Hmm … I'm a little surprised you didn't hit me on the head with a frying pan." She gestured to the gear she'd bought from the sex toy store. "I guess I didn't have to buy all of that stuff."

Smiling sweetly, Tess said, "I don't recall being asked for my opinion. I could have saved you a few bucks, but given how much you've got on you, it's no great loss."

Darcy blinked slowly. The pain pills must have really slowed her down. Maybe she'd never taken anything so strong before. "I appreciate that you didn't knock me out. Really."

It was weird having your kidnapper thank you for not causing bodily harm. "I'm not a violent person. My ex said I could peel the skin off a person with a look, but I've never hit anyone and I don't think I want to start now." She cleared her throat and looked Darcy in the eye. "But I truly want you out of my apartment."

Nodding, Darcy continued her short journey to the bathroom. "I realize that," she grumbled before closing the door.

59

It took until ten o'clock, but Tess's phone finally rang. Darcy picked it up. "Hello?"

"It's me," Danny said.

"Let me put you on speaker again. I want Tess to hear."

He waited for a second or two, then spoke. "I wish I had better news, but things are bad. I talked to a guy who knows a guy in Internal Affairs and he says NYPD knows there's a problem in Gravesend but they don't have enough evidence to clean house. This guy says the mobster you're dealing with, this Viktor something or other, is very well connected and very dangerous."

"That's what I thought," Darcy said. "He sounded like the kind of guy who wasn't worried about a thing."

"Right. I don't know if you've seen the news today, but they have a new picture of you, taken from the security cameras at the hospital you went to. It's really clear, Darce. Anyone who saw you would recognize you."

"I'm so screwed," she moaned.

"I wish I didn't have to agree with you, but you are. They're focusing their search on the area around the hospital. On TV they showed a guy putting your picture up on every lamppost and bus stop. The cops are making this a big deal. A much bigger deal than they normally would for a murder. Someone wants you to go down for killing Harry. Someone important."

"But he wasn't killed! Not technically. He died, but …"

"They can make the evidence show whatever they want if they've got enough crooked guys in the division."

"What do I do? I can't stay here forever."

"I know that, kiddo. But I don't have any answers. I reached out to the FBI but they're not interested unless you've got evidence that would allow them to move against these guys. Just knowing two first names isn't much."

"I'd know a hell of a lot more if I wasn't such an idiot! I should have taken Harry's computer instead of this damn money!"

"But you didn't. Spilled milk, Darcy. Let it go."

"What about the higher ups at the NYPD?"

"I don't have any access there. I'm trying, but I don't know anyone who can get me a meeting. Yet," he emphasized. "I'm working on it."

"Don't you have some friends who work out of Queens?"

"Yeah. Those are the guys I've been talking to."

"Can't they help? Like directly?"

"You know better than that. The NYPD's as hierarchical as any force in the country. You work your division. Period. If my friends tried to bypass the guys in Brooklyn they'd be knocked down like flies."

"That's what I thought but …"

"You're grasping at straws. Understandably." He lowered his voice and added, "They grilled me pretty good about your phone call. They're going to be watching me closely, Darce. I'm going to help, but it might take longer than you want it to."

"Thanks, Danny. I know you're doing your best."

"I sure am. I love you, Darcy. You know that, right?"

"I do," she sniffed. "I'll talk to you later. Thanks."

She hung up and stared at Tess for a minute. "If you're feeling like I am, you're dying to get out of here."

"I was dying ten hours ago. But if we go out, I'll have to wear my coat inside out."

"Right." Darcy nodded, recalling her ruined jacket. "Do you have a roof deck?"

"I think so. I've never checked it out, but the guy I sublet from mentioned that you could see the 4th of July fireworks from the roof."

"Want to give it a try?"

"Damn, yes! Yes, yes, yes!"

"You won't try to send smoke signals to call for help?"

"I will not. I just want to breathe some fresh air and see the stars."

"Okay. We can both use a break."

They got their coats and proceeded up the wide staircase. The overhead light flickered on and off, making the climb treacherous for Darcy, who had a tough time getting her feet to move as high as she told them to. But they eventually reached a big fire door with a wide bar across it. Darcy pushed against it and cold, fresh air blew their hair around.

"Sweet," Tess breathed.

Darcy checked the deck out, noting there was no railing. There was no way this was a permitted deck. She kept her eye on Tess. She seemed like the type of woman who'd go right to the edge, and having another person die on her wasn't going to happen.

Standing a safe distance away from the possibility of falling, Darcy stuck her hands in her pockets and breathed in the cool night air. It was wonderful to be outside—and not have to worry about being found.

They'd been out for a couple of minutes when Tess walked up and stood next to her. She was only about an inch shorter, but she looked up into Darcy's eyes and held her gaze. "I'm convinced you're innocent."

"You are?"

"Yeah, I am. Hearing you talk to your uncle convinced me." Tess put a hand on Darcy's forearm and squeezed it gently. "Not only that, I feel bad for you. I can't imagine how I'd feel if I landed in the kind of hot water you're in."

Darcy could almost see a "but" coming. Something about the way Tess was staring at her made it clear.

"But you're making your problem my problem, and that's just not right."

"I know." Darcy swallowed, feeling a knot growing in her throat. "As soon as my uncle said he didn't have any solid leads ..."

"Yeah." Tess squeezed her arm. "I know he's trying to get you some help, but he made it pretty clear he can't be too obvious."

"I know." She rocked back and forth on her heels, trying to make up her mind. It was still hard to think clearly with everything she had going on in her head, but Darcy knew what the right decision was, and it was time to make it. "I'm going to find someplace else to hide."

"You are?" the delight in her expression hurt, but Darcy couldn't blame her.

"Yeah, I am. I'd appreciate it if you didn't call the cops the minute I leave, but if you do, you do."

"I won't," Tess said, looking up at her with what looked like total sincerity. "I won't call them, and if anyone questions me I'm going to say I …" She smiled, but her expression bore a little sadness. "I'll say I picked you up in a diner."

"No one would believe that," Darcy said. "But I'm really grateful to you for being on my side."

"I am. And I'm being serious about my story. I'll say we hit it off while we were walking home and you stayed overnight, then took off this afternoon."

"Sounds good," Darcy said, a little embarrassed. No one would believe Tess would pick up a battered, shaky woman for a night of fun. But it was kind of her to offer. "I guess I'll …" She looked towards the door.

"I'll go with you."

They walked down the stairs, then opened the door to the apartment. Darcy walked over to the bag full of money. "I can't carry this. It's just too heavy. I don't have the strength." She stuffed six packs of hundreds into her pockets. "Do you have a stocking cap or something?"

"Sure!" Gleefully, Tess ran to her room and came back with a bright red wool cap.

"Nice and unobtrusive," Darcy said, grimacing. She put it on, covering her hair with it. That helped a little. Then she handed over everything; Tess's ID, passport, phone, keys. "I'll leave the money with you. If I don't come back—it's yours."

Tess made a face like a child being offered a particularly despised vegetable. "I don't want stolen money. I'll turn it over to the police."

"Fine. They'll probably give it right back to Viktor, but you should do whatever you think is best. Could you …?" she pointed at the bag. "Hand me the album in there?"

Tess fished it out, then Darcy put it in the paper bag she'd stored Tess's effects in. She started for the door, but Tess stopped her. "Wait. Your pain pills." She grabbed them from the kitchen counter and dashed back to the door.

"No, I shouldn't take them. I need to be clear-headed." She started to walk through the entryway, with Tess stopping her again.

"Where will you go?"

"Not sure." A small smile settled on her face. "We've been through this. If I knew where to go, I'd be there already."

"You can't just wander around. They're looking for you."

"I know that. But I can't hold you hostage any more. It's just not right."

"No, it's not, but …"

Tess looked like she was trying to think of valid reasons to continue the kidnapping. She was *really* hard to figure out.

"Involving you was wrong in every way. I was only trying to save my own skin." She lifted her hand and wiggled her fingers in a goodbye. "I apologize again for screwing up your trip, and, even more for frightening you. I hope you keep the money, Tess. Better you than the bad guys." The light from the entryway shone down on Tess, highlighting her features. Her eyes were blue. Cornflower blue. Darcy fervently hoped they wouldn't be the last pair of caring eyes she'd ever see.

She shuffled down the hallway, with no idea of where she'd go. As her mom had often said, sometimes you didn't catch the breaks.

Just before she hit the first step, she heard a soft voice almost whisper, "Good luck, Darcy. I hope … I hope you stay safe."

Finally free, and damned happy about it, Tess jogged down the hallway, then opened the shade and sat on the wide windowsill in her room, waiting for Darcy to leave the building. It took her a very long time. The stairs were probably really hard to negotiate. The livid bruise that made a huge multi-colored circle on her chest had to hurt like the dickens.

Finally, Darcy exited the building, but she merely stood there for a while. Then she shuffled over to a bench in front of the low wall that encircled the park and sat down. Tess watched her, thinking about what she might do. Unable to use her phone, credit cards, or ID. No ability to run or even walk fast. And the entire NYPD, as well as a nasty group of mobsters looking for her. It was hard to guess who'd be the worse group to find her. The mobsters would probably kill her immediately. Tess closed her eyes, thinking of the money sitting on her floor. They'd want that back. Torturing Darcy to get her to tell where it was would be the obvious tactic. But she didn't believe Darcy would tell. There was a basic decency in the woman that even her crazy gun-wielding actions hadn't obscured. She'd take her punishment. Tess's heart started beating harder. Punishment for what? She *knew* Darcy was telling the truth. She'd been in the wrong place at the right time. And for that, she'd probably go to jail or be killed. She looked so sad, so alone sitting down there, her face as miserable as a lost puppy's. *Oh, fuck. I'm going to go get that goofy kidnapper.*

Darcy took her phone from her pocket, powered it up, and waited for it to get a signal. When it did, she dialed her uncle. "Darcy!" he yelled. "I told you not to use your phone!"

"Doesn't matter. I'm going to turn myself in."

"*What?* Why?"

"Because it's wrong to kidnap someone. I can't do it, Danny. I can't justify it any more."

"Damn it, Darce. If there was any way I could let you come here you know I would."

"You'd lose your job and wind up in jail with me. I wouldn't come even if you offered, so don't feel bad about it. You've done all you can."

"I wish I could do more. I really do."

"One last thing. Could you find me an attorney? I'd like to have someone with me when I go to the police."

"I'll get right on it. When do you want to go?"

"I've already left. I'm on the street. Right in front of Prospect Park."

"Shit! Have you lost your mind?"

"Probably. But I've got to live with myself, Uncle Danny. I can't look at myself in the mirror if I keep some poor woman locked up in a room with me for god knows how long."

"I'll get on the phone right this second and find you a good lawyer. Until then … get on the subway or something. No! A bus. Get on a bus that's going to Coney Island. That'll take an hour."

"Okay." Darcy looked up to see Tess running across the street in her shirtsleeves. "Hold on a sec, Danny." She met Tess's eyes. "What's wrong?"

"Come back inside," she urged, taking Darcy's hand. "I can't throw you to the wolves."

"You're not. It's my decision …"

"Come on. You don't want me to pull too hard or you'll cry again."

She dropped her head, embarrassed. "I have turned into a crybaby."

"Sometimes there's nothing else to do," Tess said, helping her up. "Sometimes the only thing to do is have a good cry."

Darcy put the phone back up to her ear. "Danny? The nicest woman I've ever met is going to let me back into her apartment. I'm turning my phone off. If you have to report this, tell them I was going to turn myself in, but I was too afraid the mob would get me before I could."

"All right. Get a disposable phone and call my throwaway tomorrow at six. I should have some info by then. And Darcy?"

"Yeah?"

"Thank Tess for me. I owe her a big one."

Darcy looked at Tess, watching her shiver in the cold. "I owe her everything."

It took a long time to help Darcy climb the stairs. She'd taken a pain pill that morning, but Tess was pretty sure she hadn't taken another. She'd load her up tonight. If she could rest and heal, she'd be able to cover some ground if push came to shove. Given how tight her body was, it wouldn't take her long to get back into shape. No, she shouldn't have been looking, but women check each other out as often as men do. Maybe a pair of roller blades would be a good investment. If she could get her ass to look like Darcy's … Yeah, that wasn't going to happen. You had to put in the work to look like she did, and Tess wasn't the sort to make fitness her primary focus.

When they got back into the apartment, Darcy was pale and shaking. "I'm not the woman I was two days ago," she said, a tentative smile making her lips curl slightly.

"Come on, give me your coat." Tess took the jacket and removed the packs of bills, then hung it up in the hall closet. While she was in the neighborhood, she went to her nicely organized closet and pulled out a pair of pajamas. Darcy would sleep better if she got out of her street clothes.

"Here, I brought you some PJs," she said when she returned. "Let me help you change."

"You don't need to. Really."

She was terminally cute when she blushed. Like a proper lady from a hundred years ago. "I don't mind. Come on." First, she took the silly red hat off her head, then gently helped her remove her blouse. The bra was next, and Tess averted her gaze as she slid the filmy garment down

67

her arms. She'd already seen her naked and had noticed very perky boobs. No need to gawp at her now. Standing behind her, she held onto the waistband of her slacks with one hand, then eased the zipper down with the other. Darcy's slacks fell to the floor and she stepped out of them. "I can do the rest myself," she said, holding out her hand for the pajamas.

"Go for it." Tess sat down, feeling almost normal. Yes, a stranger was in her bathroom, and they were going to get into bed together soon, but somehow it didn't feel strange. A person could get used to anything.

Darcy came out, looking cute in the red flannel pajamas Tess had gotten for Christmas. "Those are brand new," she told Darcy. "My aunt gives me a pair every year, but I never wear them."

"Thanks. I like pajamas. I'm ... I guess I'm a traditionalist."

"That's how you seem." Tess opened the sofa bed, then pulled the sheet down. "Hop in. I'll get your pills." After she grabbed the bottle and a glass of water, she carefully read the label. "It says you should take two." She shook the bottle. "You're overdue. If it was me, I'd take four."

"Tempting," Darcy said. "I slept about an hour last night."

"You'll do better tonight."

Darcy accepted two pills and washed them down with water. "Thanks so much, Tess. You have no idea what this means to me."

"Yeah, I think I do. You owe me your life." She put her hand on Darcy's silky hair and ruffled it, then looked at her hand in puzzlement. Darcy gave off a vibe that made Tess want to take care of her. That was a vibe she'd have to resist. Darcy had more troubles than Tess could even begin to tackle.

Darcy looked up, big brown eyes so earnest it took Tess by surprise. "I do. And I'll do whatever I can to repay you."

"Uhm ... just one thing. If you get caught, tell them you had the gun on me the whole time. I don't want to go to prison for being your ... what do they call it?"

"Moll?"

She had a cute sense of humor when she wasn't scared to death. "Accessory. I don't want to share a cell with you. I've got my limits."

"It's a deal." She looked around, clearly puzzled. "Could I have my gun? I don't expect anyone to break in, but I always sleep with it close by."

Tess went to the table by the front door and gingerly picked it up. "You won't be all groggy and take a shot at me, will you?"

"No. I'm under control even when I'm under the influence. I'll put it under the bed just to be safe."

"Thanks. I'm a little freaked out by guns."

"I'm a little freaked out when the other guy has one and I don't. Learned that from Sergei."

"Don't think about him." She sat on the edge of the bed, put a hand behind Darcy's shoulders, and lowered her. "You're safe here and you're going to sleep much better. I guarantee you'll feel better tomorrow."

"I already do," she said, her eyes failing to open fully when she blinked.

"Do you mind if I use my computer? I watch movies to put myself to sleep."

"I don't mind," she said, her voice soft and sleepy. "But if you lured me back up here just to turn me in …" She started to shrug, then winced. But this time she recovered in seconds, acting like she'd barely noticed the pain. "Oh, well." With that she fell asleep.

Damn, those drugs worked fast.

Tess went to her room to change into a long-sleeved T-shirt. She usually slept in just that, but for Darcy's sake she left her panties on. After getting into bed, she sighed in satisfaction. Her beloved computer was right where it belonged, on her lap, and she checked the queue on her movie service. A new one about a love triangle in Vietnam in the 1950s was next up. Fantastic. Movies set in countries she'd traveled to always caught her interest. Nothing better than lying in bed, trying to recall if the place looked like it had when she'd been there. It was even more fun when she knew she could leave the house in the morning. *Ahh, freedom.*

CHAPTER FOUR

DARCY WOKE SLOWLY, THE cobwebs taking a very long time to clear. Even with the drugs, she'd woken a dozen times. Turning her head, she found the space next to her empty. In a flash, her heart started to beat faster and the skin under her arms prickled with perspiration. Then it hit her. Tess wasn't going to turn her in. She was certain of that. When she moved, a rustling noise made her look down to see a sheet of paper on her chest.

"I'm at the grocery store. Hurrah! I never knew how much I looked forward to running errands. Be back soon ... without the coppers."

That was pretty cute. *Tess* was pretty cute. Feisty, determined, open, willing to say what was on her mind ... the type of woman Darcy had *never, ever* been attracted to. She started to roll over, then remembered she couldn't. Fully awake now, the stiffness from lying on her back all night combined with the pain of a dry, sore throat. She must have been snoring like a bear! They'd have to get online and buy Tess a bed. The poor woman needed some privacy—and quiet.

Thinking of Tess made her squirm with discomfort. Now that they were ... what? Friends? That was going a little far. But they weren't enemies. More like reluctant roommates. No matter what term applied, Tess wasn't antagonistic any longer and Darcy was going to have to deal with her like she would any really attractive straight woman. The kind of woman who turned her into a blithering idiot. She was awkward enough around lesbians she didn't know well, but at least they shared a sexual orientation. Straight women, on the other hand, were a different species. A species that made her question every single thing she did. It was exhausting.

The key jiggled in the lock and Darcy struggled to sit up. "Good morning," she said when Tess crossed the threshold.

"Hi! It's a beautiful day out."

Darcy turned to peer out the window, seeing flat, grey skies with what looked like a storm looming in the distance. The trees were swaying, their bare branches thrashing against each other in the wind. "It is?"

"It's fantastic."

Tess looked like a whole new woman. Obviously she needed fresh air to bloom. Her eyes were bright, her smile luminescent. She seemed to glow with vibrant health and boundless energy.

"It must be cold. Your cheeks are …" *Was it okay to talk about how she looked? Or was that being too forward?* "Pink," she finished weakly.

"It's a little brisk, but I love it." She carried a pair of net bags to the counter. "After breakfast I'm going to go over to the park and do cartwheels."

"You can do that?"

"No," Tess laughed. "But that's what I feel like doing."

"I'd love to go outside." Darcy smiled at her, trying to show she was merely teasing. "But you've got me trapped here …"

"We'll go up on the roof later." She doffed Darcy's too-snug coat and her own gloves and tossed them onto the chair. "I've got bagels and eggs and granola and …" She peeked into a bag. "Orange juice. Does any of that work for you?"

"All of it does. No coffee?"

Tess turned and looked at her blankly. "I didn't think of it! I don't drink it, but I should have asked you." She grabbed the coat and started for the door. "There's a Starbucks on Seventh Avenue. Be right back."

"No! I'm fine. Really. It's optional."

Tess walked over to the bed and looked into Darcy's eyes. "Don't lie. If you're used to coffee, it's not optional."

"But you just went out …"

"I *loved* going out. And I'm going to love going out again. What's your poison?"

"I'll take a regular cup of black coffee."

"That's all? Are you sure?"

"That's what I get, but not what I love."

"Be wild, Darcy. Live it up a little."

"Okay," she said, feeling a little excitement brewing. "I love any of those wintery drinks. Like a peppermint mocha or the gingerbread thing. I'm not sure they have them yet. They're seasonal …"

"Got it," Tess said, playfully tugging on a hank of Darcy's hair. "You want something that tastes like candy, but has caffeine."

"Yeah," Darcy said, smiling up at her. "I guess that's what I like. I hardly ever have one … too many calories and too much sugar … but if I'm—"

As Tess started to walk out the door, she turned and winked. "I'll be back before you're finished rambling. And … thanks for the coat. I can't zip it, but it's warm."

Darcy stared at the closed door for a minute or two, marveling at the difference in Tess's personality. She was the sweet, thoughtful woman Darcy had heard on the phone that night at the diner. All of her grouchiness, all of her bitchiness was completely gone. She wondered if it only came out when she was stressed, or if she was simply unnaturally perky because of her freedom. Time would tell, and the way things were going, they would have more of it than they wanted.

A half hour later, Darcy was sitting up in bed, with a very pleased look on her face. Tess watched as she enjoyed her peppermint mocha with every bit of pleasure a giant cup of coffee could bring to a woman. Darcy was obviously the kind of person who could enjoy the heck out of something simple. That would make living together much easier.

"Oh, I forgot something." Tess jumped up and went to the kitchen, then pulled out the items she'd bought at the pharmacy and waved them in the air. "First, a toothbrush. Then, I looked up how to treat broken ribs. It said you should be icing them through the day." She turned and scowled playfully. "You're a bad girl, but I have an ice bag for you now."

"Yeah, they mentioned that at the hospital, but it's hard to demand that your hostage take care of your bumps and bruises. It was all I could do to keep you from jumping off the fire escape."

"And I got you something to help keep to your bathroom schedule."

"Oh, thanks. I think I'm going to need that. I've never taken pain-killers like this before. It's a new and not very pleasant experience."

Tess filled the bag with the few cubes she had. Keeping the trays full wasn't what she was best at. "Pull your shirt up," she instructed when she returned to the sofa.

"That's going to be cold," Darcy said tentatively.

"But it'll feel better." She reached down and pulled up Darcy's pajama top when she didn't move quickly enough. "Oh, wow. Those ribs must hurt something awful." The big Technicolor circle looked worse than it had the day before. Icing it earlier would have helped but …

"Awful about covers it. But I hate to be cold."

"It'll help with the pain. Then you're going to take your meds and do some coughing exercises. I read about those too. You don't want to get pneumonia."

Darcy winced when Tess put the bag on her huge bruise, but she settled down after a minute and relaxed against the cushions. "That feels better already." She let her gaze slide to the kitchen. "Maybe you'd better fill those trays again. I think I'm going to do this often."

Tess got up and went back into the kitchen. "The good news is you should feel better in a month … or two." She turned and gave Darcy a sympathetic smile. "By then your black eye, the bruise on your chin and those gashes on your cheek should be all gone. You'll be good as new."

Darcy held up her casted wrist. "This is supposed to be better in a month or two also. I can hardly wait for the new me."

Tess walked back into the living room and sat on the edge of the bed. "I think you're being incredibly brave. If I had the injuries you do, I'd be whining like a little bitch."

"I doubt that. You seem pretty stoic." Her expression grew tender and her voice took on a softness Tess hadn't heard before. "Why'd you let me come back?"

Tess let out a heavy sigh. She'd asked herself that same question a hundred times and had come up with the same answer again and again. "I believe you. I can't let someone be killed or jailed because a bunch of people screwed with her. That's just not fair."

"Life isn't fair," Darcy said softly. "It's random, and sooner or later you're going to have something really awful happen to you. Nobody escapes the bad stuff."

"You've had more than your share in the last few years. I didn't want to add to the list." She reached over and fluffed Darcy's hair, pushing the heavy strands off her face. Seeing her flinch like she'd been pinched reminded Tess to back off her usual physicality. Buttoned-up people like Darcy just weren't used to it. "You've had a bad … What did you say? Two years?"

"More than that. For the first couple of years, my mom didn't need live-in help. But eight years ago I had to give up my apartment and move in with her. Then my grandmother fell and broke her hip about"—she scrunched up her eyes as she thought—"three or three-and-a-half years ago. She and my grandfather moved in with us." Sheepishly, she looked away. "I nursed both my mom and my grandmother for a year and a half. All we did was go to doctors."

"Your grandfather couldn't help?"

"Alzheimer's," she said, a resigned sigh leaving her lips. "I had to keep an eye on him and answer the same question ten times in a row while keeping my mom and grandmother comfortable." A wistful smile settled on her face. "I dreamed about going back to work—during tax season—for a vacation."

Tess ruffled her hair again, ignoring Darcy's flinch. "You're a good person. A *very* good person for doing all of that. And I can check on your story the next time your uncle calls, so you'd better not be jerking me around."

Darcy's cheeks turned pink in seconds. "I'm not! I swear. It's … important to me to always be as honest as I can. That's why I need to tell you something."

"Now what? The CIA's after you too?"

"No, nothing like that." Her hair had fallen into her eyes again and she gazed at Tess through the chestnut strands. "You need to know that I'm gay."

Tess sat up straight, letting that information settle. "You are?"

"Yes, I am. I hope that doesn't change anything between us, but I decided I had to make that clear." She looked at the space beside her. "Given that we've been sleeping together … I thought you should know."

God, she was adorable! She knew it wasn't playing fair, but something about Darcy made her want to mess with her. "Gosh, I don't know about this. Should I put those handcuffs on *you* before we go to bed? I'd hate to have you pawing me while I sleep."

"I would never …!"

She was so cute when she was outraged. Something about her reminded Tess of a Victorian—all prim and proper and full of moral precepts. "I'm kidding, Darcy." She looked over at the items on the coffee table. "But I will point out you knew just what to order from the sex toy store. Are you kinky?"

"No!" Now even her neck was pink. Ears too. "I'd gone into the store a month or two ago and saw they had all kinds of things."

"What were you doing in the store?" Tess asked, getting a surprising amount of pleasure from torturing her. "Buying things for all of your girls? I bet you have to beat them off with a stick."

"I don't!" If embarrassment could kill, Darcy was a goner.

"Come on. You're telling me women aren't throwing themselves at you? You've got a gorgeous face, cheekbones for days, beautiful eyes, a good job, and a charming sense of humor."

"I do?" she asked, cocking her head.

"You do. So … what's the deal? No girlfriend? 'Cause if you have one, she's going to be pissed you haven't called."

"No," Darcy said, her eyes shifting down. "I haven't had one in a very long time."

"Because of your mom?" Now Tess felt like a jerk for taunting her about this. It must have been impossible to take a woman home when your mom and your grandmother and your grandfather were filling the house, all needing constant care.

"Mmm, not really. I had a girlfriend …" Her eyes narrowed again. It was cute how much thought she seemed to put into getting the facts straight. "Eight years ago. But she got tired of … how did she put it? Being outside of the circle."

"The circle?"

"Yeah. She wanted to meet my mom and … you know."

Tess gazed at her for a minute. "Your girlfriend hadn't met your mom?"

Darcy swallowed, her throat moving as she nervously shifted her body. "I wasn't out to my mom."

"Really?" Tess asked gently. "Why?"

She was charmingly flustered as she squirmed under Tess's questions. "I wasn't sure how she'd take it. We were close—really close —and I didn't want to risk losing that."

"Poor girl," Tess said, unable to stop herself from touching Darcy. She seemed so fragile, so in need of care and support. As she stroked her arm, she said, "I bet it's hard for you to take risks in any area of your life, isn't it."

"Yeah," she said, nodding. "I guess it is."

"Does your uncle know?"

"He's never said anything, but I think he's guessed. He's not as … rigid, I guess, is the right word, as my mom was."

"I think you should tell him. It'll take a weight off your shoulders."

Darcy looked up at her and let a small grin show. "Maybe I'd better get a girlfriend first. At this point, I'm only gay in my imagination." She cocked her head and gazed at Tess. "Why are *you* single?"

"That's a recent development. And one of the main reasons I relocated. Moving three thousand miles away saves you from ever running into your ex."

"Were you married?"

"No," she said, thinking of how they'd barely been able to agree on what to order for dinner. "We were a long way from marriage, but it was still hard to break up."

"Wanna talk about it?"

Darcy was exactly the kind of person you could pour your heart out to. Tess was sure of that. But she had enough on her plate. She didn't need to hear the usual heartbreak story. "No, I'm okay. It's only been a couple of months. I'm sure my memories of Sam will fade pretty soon."

"I hope so. If you want them to, that is." She smiled as her eyes filled with tears. "I keep hoping that I can stop the recent memories and think back to when my mom and my grandparents were all healthy."

"Ten years gives you a ton of bad memories. I was with Sam less than a third of that."

"Three years is a pretty long relationship," Darcy said. "Emily and I were only together for a year and a half, but it took an awful long time to get over losing her. And we weren't even living together. My mom would have noticed."

Tess smiled at the way she'd said that. Darcy tossed off little comments that were fairly silly, but she didn't always indicate she was joking. She seemed like the kind of person who didn't want to commit to a joke if she wasn't sure you'd think it was funny. "Sam and I got enmeshed pretty quickly. Probably too quickly. You were smart to take things slowly."

"Not according to Emily," Darcy said, her eyes reflecting deep sadness. "I was an idiot. She could have helped me when I was struggling. But I was too chicken to tell my mom about her." She slapped her forehead with her left hand, then winced. "I don't know what hurts worse," she said as she rubbed her forehead. "Jarring my wrist or hitting myself in the head with plaster. This just isn't my day."

Tess regarded her with sympathy. The poor woman probably hadn't had many good days in over ten years, and now she was on the run after having done nothing more than show up for work. That sucked in a major way.

After icing Darcy's ribs, and a gruesome bout of coughing exercises that seemed so painful they brought tears to her own eyes, Tess was ready to head outside again. Normally she walked a lot. A whole lot when she was traveling. But she'd never been so jazzed about walking around what looked like a fairly boring park. The acres of barely-green grass and trees with very few leaves still called to her like the sirens, and she had to go.

"I'm going to explore," she said as she started to put Darcy's coat on. "I haven't spent much time in the park yet."

"Have fun. Hey, uhm … I'm going to need some clothes. If I buy things online can I use your credit card?"

"How much do you need? I'm not very flush."

"I don't know … A couple of hundred dollars?"

"I'd better check."   She went to her computer and looked at her balance. "How much were those closet organizers? I was too mad to care at the time."

"A hundred and ten dollars."

"Mmm … I'm nearly overdrawn, and my credit card's on autopay. I've got to get those expense reports done."

"What?"   Darcy acted like she'd said she had to bury the bodies she'd just offed.

"I'm a little behind on my expense reports. I get reimbursed for what I spend on my trips, but it's such a pain to do the reports. I tend to wait until I'm broke, then turn in a bunch all at once."

Darcy's right hand twitched. The left tried to, but the cast prevented it from doing much. "Give me your receipts. I'll do it."

Tess rolled her eyes. "I'm not as organized as I should be. This last bunch is really a mess."   She was embarrassed to say exactly how much of a mess it was.

"This is what I'm good at."

That hand twitched again, like it couldn't wait to grab hold of paperwork. The woman was clearly telling the truth about being an accountant.

"Hand it over."

Reluctantly, Tess went to her desk, grabbed the sack she'd stuck all of her receipts in, and handed it to Darcy. "Most of the receipts are in Japanese."   Taking in a breath, she added, "I don't speak Japanese."

"Wow."   Darcy pulled out a handful of papers, which barely made a dent in the sack. "How long were you gone? Three years?"

"No, just a month. But I went to at least a hundred restaurants, stayed in thirty different hotels, and took in every cultural sight I could find. It adds up," she said, shrugging.

"How were you ever going to do this? It's really a mess."

"That's why I haven't started. I did make a note on the back of most of them though. Not all of them, but …"

"Go have fun," Darcy said shooing her away. "I'll get them organized, then you can show me the form you need to submit." She looked up, a bright smile lighting up her face. Now that Tess could look at her without wanting to strangle her, she could see just how pretty Darcy was. The pain pills must have been working too, as her color was better. Her eyes even had a twinkle in them. Was that from the thought of filling out an expense report? That was freaky! "I'm going to take off before you come to your senses."

"Don't rush," Darcy said, dumping the whole mess onto the coffee table. "This will take hours."

By the time Tess returned, Darcy had finished categorizing everything and was ready to start calculating totals. She just had to make sure the form was what she anticipated. "Almost ready," she said, looking up at Tess's pink cheeks and sated smile. "You look like you had fun."

"Nice park. Really nice. Not full of attractions like Central Park, but it was quiet and tranquil. I'm going to like hanging out there this summer."

"Do you have the expense form on your computer?"

"Yeah. Give me a second."

When she took off the coat and tossed it onto the chair, Darcy bit her tongue. People could live moral lives if they were messy. It wouldn't be easy, but she was sure it could be done.

"How did you get everything into piles? I'm sure I didn't make notes on at least a dozen receipts."

Feeling proud, Darcy said, "I studied them. The ones from hotels had a distinctive look, even though I couldn't read a word on most of them. And the ones from restaurants had a look too. There were always a number of items on the receipt and some of them had grease stains or watermarks. The pre-printed ones looked like they'd be for an attraction, so that's where I put them."

"Good enough for me."

"I assumed hotels would offer receipts in English for their American guests."

"Not the places I stayed on this trip. I was waaaay off the beaten path. My article was on hidden Japan. I bet some of the spots I stayed in never get Americans."

"How'd you communicate?" Darcy could barely imagine having the nerve to go to an area where you not only couldn't speak the language, but also couldn't read the characters that made up the language.

"Oh, I just figure it out," she said breezily. "People want to help you when you're traveling. I played charades all the time on this trip," she added, chuckling. "And I ate things I would never have chosen if I could have read the menu. I had to close my eyes sometimes, but that's part of the fun."

"I will never close my eyes before eating something," Darcy stated. "My stomach turns if I find a hair on a plate."

"How about eyes floating in soup?" Tess giggled as Darcy felt the color drain from her cheeks.

"You're kidding."

"Not even a little. I had tongues, little feet, maybe a heart … all kinds of organs looking back at me. You've got to learn to just steel your nerves and give it a try."

"No, you really don't," Darcy assured her. "You order something you've had hundreds of times and inspect it carefully. If there's anything even slightly out of line, you send it back."

"You wouldn't make it as a travel writer, Darcy. Trust me on that."

"And you wouldn't make it as an accountant. Trust *me* on that!"

Darcy sat with the computer on her lap, carefully making decisions about what to buy. She'd been at it forever, and Tess was at the end of her rope. Grabbing the machine, she settled it onto her own lap and went to her favorite clothing site. "You're going to want to travel light. So buy these slacks. They're some kind of polyester that dries in a few hours. And the wrinkles fall right out of them. I've worn these on a twenty-hour flight and still looked neat when I got off the plane."

Darcy looked at her, a half smile on her face. "You clearly know what I should buy. Why didn't you say something earlier?"

"Because you were so friggin' intent. I thought you were enjoying yourself."

"Well, I do like picking out new things. But I'll admit it takes me a while."

"Go into my room and take out a pair of Travel Light slacks. Try them on and let me see how they fit."

"Because …?"

"Then I'll know what size to buy you."

As Darcy got up there was a hint of a wry smile on her face. "Things that should have been obvious. I'm still off my game."

In a few minutes, she was modeling Tess's slacks. "They're a little big, but not too bad," Darcy said, doing a slow turn.

Tess was going to say something about how only Darcy's bubble-butt was keeping them from falling to the floor. But Darcy was so skittish about things, she didn't want her to faint from embarrassment. The woman had a fantastic ass, though. That was indisputable.

"Just as I thought. I'm two sizes bigger." Tess put two pair of the slacks, one black and one blue in her shopping cart. "Now a couple of shirts. I like this one," she said, turning the computer around. "Dries in a snap and resists stains." She gave Darcy a long, assessing look. "I think the light blue and the salmon would both look good on you."

"Okay. I trust your judgment. I'm usually a ten in blouses. I've got long arms."

"Not very. But your shoulders are broad. I'll get you a white one, too. Then you'll be set." She went to check out, then scrolled over to another site. "It's only going to get colder, so you need some thermal underwear. Really thin stuff that won't be bulky under your clothes."

"I assume you have a supplier?"

"I do indeed. I'll add some quick-drying underwear too. Bikini, boy-short, or granny-panty?"

"Bikini. High-cut is my favorite, but I can compromise."

Tess smiled at her. "You'll have to. They just have regular bikinis. I'll get you black. Three pair should do it. And a great bra that's as supportive as an underwire, but really soft. You'll love it." She started to assess Darcy's breasts, but figured that would make her faint. "Medium? It's very stretchy fabric."

"Sure. Medium's fine."

"Then we're good. Oh! Socks. I like wool."

"Wool? Really?" She made a face. "I hate scratchy things."

"Good wool socks aren't scratchy. I'm buying you two pair."

"Just two?"

"Two is plenty. You can wear wool socks for a week or two between washes. They're perfect for travel."

"I put my feet in your hands."

"Not sure that's where I want them, but I get your point." She quickly checked out and slapped her hands together. "All done. Now what?"

Darcy gave her a long, assessing look. "How about taking a few thousand dollars and depositing it into your account? I'm worried about you being overdrawn."

"Hmm …" Tess thought about it for a minute. It was *clearly* dirty money. But the criminals couldn't claim it and the police would just put it in an evidence room for a while then … Who even knew what they'd do with it? "Screw it. Why look a gift horse in the mouth?"

"I'm pleased," Darcy said, looking exactly that. "I have visions of the dirty cops taking the money and using it to buy women and drugs. I'd much rather you had it."

"Just a little bit," Tess warned. "I don't need much. But I want to be able to front you money if you need it."

"You can put under ten thousand into the bank without trouble, but we'd better keep it well below that. How about seven thousand?"

"Sounds great." She got up and grabbed the coat. "I'm still loving running errands, so let me at it." As she put on a pair of gloves she said, "Do you need anything else?"

"Uhm, yeah. My uncle told me to buy a disposable phone. Is that too much trouble?"

"Not a bit. I'll be home, with dinner, by six. How about a big chicken parm sandwich?"

"You're talking Jersey now," she said, with a big grin. "I haven't had one since my grandfather dragged me to a place he used to love. Let's do it."

Tess returned right on time and Darcy grabbed the bag that indicated it was from an electronics store. "Sorry to be so aggressive, but I promised I'd call my uncle at six." She wrestled the phone out of the box, but her stomach fell when she realized it had to be charged before it would work. Holding up the battery, she said, "I screwed up. I should have asked you to get this first thing this morning."

Tess took a look. "It won't be charged for hours." She patted Darcy on the shoulder. "Use mine. If he's got a disposable, it'll be fine."

"No, I don't want to take the risk. He'll be worried, but he'd want me to do the safest thing. I'll wait until tomorrow."

Together, they got their dinner ready, then sat on the sofa in the living room, eating their messy sandwiches. "I thought about it a little more," Darcy said as she wiped her mouth with a paper napkin, "and I think it's been eleven years since I've had one of these. They're really good."

Tess's eyes narrowed slightly while they slid up and down Darcy's body. It was an unnerving habit, but one that seemed very natural for

Tess. Darcy would have given a lot to have just a little of her boldness, but it was too late to develop new personality traits.

"I bet you never eat junk. You can't be in the kind of shape you're in if you gobble down chicken parm sandwiches on a routine basis."

"I feel better when I eat healthy." She pushed her plate further away, inching it across the coffee table. She wasn't ready to confess that was one of her tactics to avoid overeating. Having to commit to grabbing another bite of food after you'd clearly finished had stopped her more times than she could count. "I'd gained a little weight after working for a few years. Too much takeout food and not enough exercise. Since then, I try to eat at home as much as possible and avoid sugar and processed foods. And bread. And pasta. And pizza. It's simple when you pare down your choices."

Tess's grin covered her whole face. "If I gave up half of those things I'd lose"—her chin lifted as she looked up at the ceiling—"fifty pounds."

"You couldn't weigh more than a hundred forty!"

"I wish," she said, her grin now impish. "I eat gobs of sugar. That's why I'm worried about working more in Europe. I love pastries and bread and chocolate—all things you're not submerged in around Asia."

"Is that why you moved to New York? To be closer to Europe?"

"Pretty much." She reached over and pulled Darcy's plate close. "You're done, right?"

"Uhm ... yeah."

Amazingly, Tess picked up the other half of Darcy's sandwich and took a big bite. "I love eating off other people's plates."

"Why don't you weigh fifty pounds more? You've knocked back a good thousand calories tonight."

"Ooo ... You're one of those people who know how many calories are in things." She stuck her tongue out. "I hate people who know that. Ignorance is bliss." After taking another bite, she added, "I'm blissfully ignorant."

"But you're a human. Calories expended have to equal calories consumed or you gain weight."

"So they tell me." As if to show how little she cared, Tess took a huge bite, then licked the spicy tomato sauce from the remaining sandwich. "Delicious." She got up and took the plates to the kitchen. After opening the wastebasket she tipped the remains towards the bin, then caught the last of Darcy's sandwich and popped it into her mouth. As she started to wash the dishes, she hummed a tune, clearly happy.

If Darcy had just eaten one and a half chicken parm sandwiches she'd not only be toting up the calories, she'd be planning on what to cut out the next day, as well as how to increase her exercise to even things out. Clearly, one of them was a little more extemporaneous than the other.

When Tess finished, she filled the ice bag and brought it to the sofa. "Time for your treatment. When you're numb, we'll do more coughing exercises."

Darcy looked up at her, seeing what had to be true concern. Empathy. Tess was a hell of a good person. Not many people would help their kidnapper feel better. "Thanks." Darcy took the ice bag and held it to her ribs. They still hurt something fierce, but the ice definitely helped. Having someone care about her helped even more. "Hey, I did a little shopping while you were gone and found a bed I think you'll like." She pulled the laptop over and started to open it. But Tess put her hand on the lid, holding it closed.

"Gotta be honest. I didn't fail to buy a bed because I procrastinate —even though I do. But I'm only subletting for six months. The place came furnished and ..." She trailed off.

"You're afraid to buy a bed if you have to move it again?"

"Partly." She shook her head briefly. "But I can't really afford a bed. And that's the truth."

"You can't?" Darcy stared at her. A bed wasn't a huge expense.

"Not really. You saw my bank balance. I'm barely going to be able to cover my rent."

"But … why'd you move to New York? Anywhere else you lived had to be less expensive."

"Oregon," Tess said. "And yes, it was significantly less expensive. But I've always wanted to live here." Her expression was neutral, like she was explaining something inconsequential. Darcy couldn't imagine how upset she'd be to confess she couldn't afford a bed to sleep on. A good night's rest was vital!

"I have no idea how you earn your living. Do you get paid a salary …?"

"I wish!" She laughed, a real, hearty, head-thrown-back laugh. "Half of the time I just get my expenses covered. Last year was pretty bad. I only made about forty thousand bucks for traveling over two hundred thousand miles and being away from home for something like"—she closed one eye—"two hundred and forty days."

"You can't live here on forty thousand dollars!"

Tess simply shrugged. "I guess we'll see."

"That's it? No way of earning more money?" Darcy's heart had begun to race. What kind of crazy life-plan was this?

"Not really. Things tend to work out. You've just got to take the plunge and see what happens."

"No!" Despite the pain, Darcy stood, then clasped the ice bag to her ribs. "You don't take a plunge that you aren't sure you can afford!"

"Calm down," Tess said, chuckling. "Your blood pressure's gonna make you pass out. If I can't make it, I'll move. Or get a roommate. Or two. Or sell my blood. It'll be fine. Really."

"I'm buying you a bed." Darcy opened the computer and tried to type with one hand, while standing.

Tess got up and took the computer from her. "Fine. Anything to keep your pulse out of the red zone."

Darcy stood over her when Tess sat back down. "Go into the search history and look at the last link. Yeah, that's the one."

Tess smiled up at her. "This looks nice. I didn't know you could buy a bed over the internet."

"You can. I read about the guys who started this company. If you don't like it after thirty days, you can return it. They'll pay the freight."

Tess patted her on the leg as she started to type in her payment information. "I should have known you'd find one with all sorts of guarantees. I don't know you well, but that's one thing I'm already certain of."

"Pay for the expedited delivery," Darcy said. "Then we'll buy you some sheets and pillows. I'm going to be the only houseguest you've ever had who's going to furnish your apartment."

Wrinkling her nose, Tess looked up again. "And I hope the only one who pulls a gun on me to be my decorator."

Tess struggled to carry her folding desk chair up to the roof deck. Darcy was behind her, but that was cold comfort. The woman was still in so much pain she wouldn't even have been able to break Tess's fall, much less catch her if she took a wrong step.

After cursing when she kicked the front of a stair, Tess reminded herself to call the maintenance guy to tell him about the light that kept flickering off and on. Darcy could barely pick her feet up high enough to climb the stairs. She clearly needed all of the light she could get.

Finally Tess pushed open the fire door and dropped the chair to the deck. "Whew! I'm out of shape. I should lift some weights or something."

"I could help you if you want to start. I don't mean to brag, but I'm … competent when it comes to working out."

"Wow," Tess teased. "You're quite the braggart, throwing around your competency." She opened the chair and held her hand out with a flourish. "Your throne."

"I can stand," Darcy protested.

"I know you can, but I want to be up here for a while and you're not bursting with stamina. Come on." She patted the seat. "It's calling you."

Even in the dark, Tess could see Darcy roll her eyes. But she complied, wincing audibly when she sat. "Sitting down hurts more than getting up. I wonder why?"

"But it feels better once you're down, right?"

With a warm smile lighting her face, Darcy looked at her. "Right. This helps. Thanks." She wrapped her arms gingerly across her stomach. "Cold."

"It's a little chilly," Tess admitted. "I want to stay, but I'll walk you back downstairs if it's too cold for you."

"No, I like seeing the stars. That's worth a little chill." Slowly, she let her head drop back until she was gazing up at the heavens. "Have you ever been camping?"

"Camping?" Tess was walking carefully around the perimeter of the building, seeing what she could make out from this new perspective. "Yeah. With my family, friends, different tours. I love to camp. Why?"

"I've never been," Darcy said, sounding a little dreamy. "But I bet I'd like it. I'm crazy about looking at the stars."

"Star," Tess said, chuckling. "You can barely see one in Brooklyn. You've got to get far out of town to get a dark sky."

"I haven't traveled much," Darcy admitted.

"If you love stars, I'd recommend Mauna Kea in Hawaii or nearly anywhere in New Zealand. There are lots of other good places, but those are spots you can get to easily."

"I'm not sure it'd be easy for me." Her head moved slowly as she gazed up at the heavens. "I'm not a traveler. But I wish I were."

"All you have to do is buy a ticket and take off. It's not hard."

Darcy lifted her head and gazed at Tess for a few seconds. "I plan my trips to the grocery store more carefully than that." She let out a self-deprecating chuckle. "Have you always wanted to travel?"

"I guess I didn't think about it as travel *per se*. More like ... living. My parents love to explore, so travel was always part of my life."

"So you thought you'd turn it into a career?"

"Not really. That's ascribing far too much thought to my plans."

"But you majored in journalism, right?"

"Uh-huh, but it hadn't dawned on me that I could make a living writing about places. I was going to major in English or creative writing, but I got good feedback from my professors when I wrote about places I'd been. One of them suggested I'd be a good travel writer." She shrugged. "That sounded good, so I switched to journalism. But I *sucked* at news stories. I'm interested in people, not events."

"I can see that in you," Darcy agreed. "I bet you also like not having a rigidly structured job."

"You've got that right. I've never met a rule I haven't tried to at least bend."

Darcy was watching her carefully—probably worried that she was too close to the edge. "You must have driven your parents crazy."

"No way." Tess moved closer to let Darcy relax her guard-dog watchfulness. "My parents are the biggest rule-breakers you'll ever meet. This apple didn't fall far from those trees."

"Interesting. What do they do for work?"

"More things than I can name. But my dad's mostly a mushroom hunter and my mom ..." She thought of how to describe her mother's eclectic skills and interests. "I'd say she makes most of her money by selling crafts. She's super creative."

"A mushroom hunter? Your dad does that for a living?"

"Uh-huh. Among other things."

"You know what? I don't think I've ever met anyone who didn't have a pretty standard job." She laughed softly. "When people joke about accountants being boring, they're not entirely wrong."

"You're not boring." Tess playfully tugged on a hank of her hair. "You've had my heart racing like crazy a few times in the last two days. Boring people don't do that."

"When I'm not running for my life, I can get into a rut. That's why I moved to Brooklyn. It was time to shake things up."

"But I bet you didn't count on having some pretty slimy characters shake the stuffing out of you."

"No, I didn't." She sounded defeated when she added, "Maybe I should have stayed in Jersey."

Tess patted her head, then went to stand near the edge again. It was fun to see how close she could get without chickening out and backing up. "I don't know much about Jersey, but isn't that where the mobsters live?"

"I never met one. We're the Garden State, you know, not the organized crime state."

"Don't be touchy," Tess teased. "I'm not dissing your state. But maybe you should have moved to … Utah or something if you wanted to live in a safe place."

"Now you tell me. Where were you six months ago?"

Tess thought for a moment. "New Zealand, if I remember correctly. And the stars there put these few little twinklers to shame." She moved over close to Darcy again. "I hope you can use some of your money to travel when this is all over. I'd like for you to see a little bit of the world."

"I'd like that too. I think I've been to … four, no five states."

"Total?"

"Yeah. Like I said … I haven't traveled much."

"Damn, Darcy, you can get to a different state if you just drive a few hours in any direction."

"I know. I just …" She closed her eyes for a few seconds. "By the time I was earning good money and had some vacation time built up I had to quit."

"Because of your mom's illness?"

"Uh-huh. I thought I had everything in order." She ticked the items off on her fingers. "I had my master's in accounting, and I'd earned my CPA license. Then I worked my butt off at a good, small firm until I was supervising a group of ten junior accountants. I had a girlfriend who I was serious about and a sweet apartment." She snapped her fingers sharply. "And I had to give all of it up."

"What did your mom have? You haven't said."

"Really?" She nodded. "Right. I guess we were a little busy when I first told you about her."

"Busy is a nice way to put it," Tess said. "It sounds much better than 'I was holding you at gunpoint.'"

Darcy looked a little abashed, but she seemed to realize she was being teased. "I'm not sure what my mom had, but it was some combination of scleroderma, Parkinson's, and lupus. She had four specialists arguing about her diagnosis for a full ten years."

"What? How can that be?"

"The symptoms overlap and there aren't great tests to rule out any of the diseases."

"Still …"

"Hey, don't look at me to defend the medical profession. For the first year they were pretty sure she had a pinched nerve that caused the numbness and tingling on her left side. Then the ball started rolling downhill and every specialist in town tried to prove the other guys didn't know what they were talking about."

"Damn, that sounds horrible. There was never …" She wasn't sure how to ask this delicately. "Even after her death they couldn't tell …?"

Darcy nodded. "If I'd let them do an autopsy they probably could have given me a definitive answer. But what good would that have done then? I was so sick of doctors building up her hopes and trying new medications that, in the end, I didn't give a damn what had killed her. Whatever it was, it was relentless."

"I'm really sorry." Tess stood next to her and put a hand on her shoulder. "And I'm sorry you've had such a tough time of it."

"It was tougher for her," she said, sounding defensive again. Her mom must have been a goddess. "I just had to watch."

"I know. But it's hard to watch too." After gently patting Darcy's cheek, Tess moved back to the east side of the roof where she could look at the blackness of the big park. "I barely know you, and it hurts to watch you struggle to move around."

"It *was* hard to watch her suffer and die," Darcy admitted. "Maybe that's why I was so fixated on doing whatever I needed to do to stay alive that first night. After that experience with my mother, I value my own life more than I ever have."

Even in the dark, Tess could see the determination in her eyes.

"I haven't had much of a life for a long time. Now that I've gotten another shot at making the life I want, I'm not going to give it up without a fight."

Tess moved back to stand by her. "And I'm going to help you." She put her hand out and Darcy shook it. "That's a promise."

CHAPTER FIVE

IT WAS LATE WHEN they got back to the apartment. Darcy glared at the sofa, dreading another night of pain. Tess must have seen her, for she immediately said, "You didn't sleep well, did you."

"Not very. I think I'd do better if I were sitting up, like in a recliner. The next time I kidnap a woman I'm going to slyly inquire about her furniture before I pick my victim."

Tess was looking around the room, slowly taking in all of the options. "How about if I use all of the cushions to prop you up?"

"That might help, but there won't be room for you."

"We'll cross that bridge when we come to it. Get ready for bed and we'll see what we can do."

A short while later, Darcy was almost sitting up in bed. All of the sofa cushions were propped around her, holding her up. Now Tess stared at the bed, her hand raised to stroke her chin. "I think I've got it." Decisively, she lay across the foot of the bed, occupying the space Darcy's feet should have been in. "Yep. This works." Then she got to her feet and went to her bedroom.

Darcy frowned unhappily when Tess returned with another blanket.

"I'm fine," Tess declared. "I've got as much room as I'd normally have, just with a different orientation." She lay down again and tucked the blanket around herself. "Wake me up if you need to change positions." Sitting up again, she looked Darcy in the eye and said, "Promise?"

"Yes, I promise. Thanks," she said, feeling a catch in her throat. It didn't matter that Tess didn't own a recliner. She was the nicest, most thoughtful kidnap victim in town.

Darcy had a better night—in that she awoke only nine or ten times. But she was going to have to figure out a better way to sleep. Someone had to have worked this out, and she was going to get on the internet and piggyback off someone else's painful experience.

Tess was not lying at her feet and the bathroom door was open. Darcy was just about to call to her when Tess nearly skipped into the room. "Great! You're up!"

"I think I am," Darcy said, trying not to whimper. "Can you give me a hand? I've gotta pee in the worst way."

Tess pulled her feet so they hung over the edge of the bed, allowing Darcy to shift her weight and make standing up more bearable. "I've got news," Tess said. "Hurry up."

"Hurrying isn't what I'm best at, but I'll give it a try."

"Pee in the shower," Tess said. "Then you don't have to sit down and get up."

Darcy stopped mid-stride. "Pardon me?"

"You heard me," Tess said, giggling.

"I might move like a wounded bear, but I haven't been reduced to living like an animal." She almost sniffed like they did in the old movies, but thought that was an overreaction. "I'll make it fast."

A few minutes later, Darcy emerged. "Mission accomplished … in the proper receptacle."

Tess had brought her desk chair into the living room. "Try this one. It's taller."

After sitting with a bit less pain, Darcy looked up and smiled. "Every little improvement helps. Thanks. Now I've got to call my uncle. Can you hand me the phone?"

With a slight frown, Tess went to get the phone from the kitchen. "Here you go. But make it snappy!"

Chuckling, Darcy dialed her uncle's disposable phone. It rang and rang, and she finally ended the call. "He must be at work. I'll guess I'll try at six tonight."

"Super. My *news*," Tess said dramatically, "is that I spoke with an old friend who works at *The Times* and he hooked you up with a reporter in the Metro section who's sharpening her knives just waiting to hear your tale about police corruption."

"You told her about me?" Darcy was instantly planning on what to pack and how much money she could take with her.

"Not anything specific." Tess put a calming hand on her shoulder while she bent over enough to look into Darcy's eyes. "I know you can't be too forthright. And I'm not about to give them any info the DA might try to squeeze out of them. All I did was ask my friend who the best investigative reporter on the Metro beat was. I said I had an acquaintance who had some dirt on the police department."

"Whew." Darcy took deep breaths, trying to get her heart rate to slow down. "I'll try to calm down and not see Sergei's big gun every time the slightest thing happens."

"I understand," Tess said, the fierceness in her voice surprising Darcy. "If I'd been as close to being murdered as you were, I'd be a mess." She bent further, her face just inches away. "Really."

"That means a lot to me," Darcy said, her voice breaking with emotion. "One of the worst parts of this whole thing was when I couldn't convince you I was innocent." She blinked the tears from her eyes. "Somehow that was worse than Sergei."

Soothingly, Tess stroked her hair, making Darcy wish she could nuzzle against her hand like a puppy would. "I'm sorry," Tess whispered. "I feel really bad about that. My one opportunity to possibly save a woman's life and my reaction was shit."

"I threatened you with a gun, Tess. Don't make it sound like I was lying on the street, bleeding, and you kicked me out of your way."

Tess's voice was soft and filled with emotion. "Even when you had a gun on me, I had a tough time believing you'd use it. You just didn't seem like a criminal." She took in a long breath. "I basically threw a tantrum because I couldn't do what I wanted." Still staring at Darcy,

Tess sat on the upholstered chair next to her. "I wouldn't let myself think of how terrified you were. I just focused on myself and I truly feel bad about that." Reaching out, she took Darcy's hand. "That's not the person I try to be."

Darcy looked down at their joined hands. When you had a friend, even the worst situation wasn't insurmountable. "You're a good person, Tess. I frightened you, I invaded your space, and I hurt you professionally. That's nothing to sneeze at."

"Your life was in imminent danger," Tess said, her frown increasing. "That trumps everything."

"How about this?" Darcy asked. "What would you have said if I'd told you the whole truth? No gun. No threats. Just the truth. What would you have done?" She waited patiently as Tess considered her answer. But Darcy already had a very good idea of what it would be.

After her pretty blue eyes closed, Tess said, "I would have helped you. I probably would have let you stay in my apartment while I went to Germany." She blinked. "Nothing about you seemed like a killer. It was only the gun and losing my freedom that freaked me out."

"I knew you'd say that," Darcy said, deeply ashamed of her choices. "I screwed up."

"You were panicked. You were in terrible pain. You weren't thinking straight."

"All true. But that didn't give me the right to do what I did." She squeezed Tess's hand when she noticed they were still linked. "And I apologize for everything. Sincerely."

Tess let go of Darcy's hand, then ruffled her hair as she stood. "Forgiven. Totally. Now let's have some breakfast. Another candy-flavored caffeine delivery vehicle?"

"God, yes," Darcy said, letting her head lean back in joyful anticipation.

After they'd eaten, Darcy dictated while Tess typed a detailed recreation of the night Harry died. They worked on it for an hour, making sure it was pithy, yet detailed as possible. It would have been easier to talk to the reporter, but Darcy wasn't willing to do that. If Tess's referral was good at her job, she'd be able to write a compelling story—even without an interview. Once they were finished, Tess printed it off, put it into an envelope, and got ready to make a run to the post office. "Should I go over to Manhattan or Queens to mail this to *The Times*?"

"Don't bother. Knowing the letter came from Park Slope doesn't give away much. Besides," she said, her voice gentling, "I don't want you to be gone that long." As soon as the words left her mouth, she regretted them. What a dopey thing to admit to!

But Tess didn't seem to think that was an odd thing to say. She patted Darcy's cheek, the one that didn't have scratches down it, and said, "Good point. We'd miss lunch if I did that, and I hate to miss a meal. I've got a hankering for a good salad. How does that sound?"

"That sounds perfect. Just perfect. Load mine up with vegetables. Any kind. But no croutons or cheese. And make sure the dressing's on the side." The mere fact that Tess hadn't embarrassed her for her childish dependency added to her growing list of top-notch traits. Finally bringing in a salad didn't hurt either.

After lunch, Darcy could tell Tess was getting antsy. She was clearly used to being very active, and sitting around with nothing to do seemed to get on her nerves. "Why don't you go do something fun? Go shopping or to a movie." She took a quick look at the dark grey skies. "Or go for a walk before it rains."

Hesitating, Tess said, "You'll be okay?"

Damn! She shouldn't have let her know how needy she felt today. "Sure. I'll be fine. I'm going a little stir crazy, but it's not smart to go out."

Tess jumped to her feet and nearly scampered for Darcy's coat, which was lying haphazardly on the end of the sofa. "I'll go shopping. If you're a good girl, I'll bring you a treat."

"Just don't make it a treat with hundreds of calories. I'm burning about a third of what I normally do in a day."

"Treats are supposed to be bad for you," Tess teased. "But I'll try to honor your ascetic nature."

Darcy's eyes nearly popped out when Tess leaned over and kissed her on the head.

"Don't get into any trouble when I'm gone. You're prone to it."

"Not until recently. Really."

"I knew that," Tess said, rolling her eyes. "You'd be the type they'd recruit if the Girl Scouts had a women's division." With that, she stuffed the jacket pockets with wallet and keys, then held out her phone. "I assume you don't want me to use this?"

"I'd rather you didn't. But if you need to …"

"No, I like to be disconnected."

"Take some money and buy yourself a new coat," Darcy reminded her. "Unless you want people calling 9-1-1 every time you wear your own coat."

Tess gave her a dazzling smile. "And you're supposed to be the jaded Jersey girl. No one would have called 9-1-1. They wouldn't have even noticed. At best they would have thought it was a weird fashion thing."

"But it's not, so buy a new coat."

Tess sighed, but grabbed a packet of bills from the bag that still sat on the floor. She peeled off a few and stuck them into her jeans pocket. "I'm fully loaded. See you!"

It was dark when Darcy heard a plodding, thumping sound from the stairwell. She was always on edge, always alert for the slightest sound that might signal danger. But unless someone was dragging a body up the stairs … She got to her feet and peered out the peep hole.

Nothing. The thump was replaced by a scratching sound, then she saw Tess standing outside the door. Darcy used the extra keys to open it. "What in the world are you carrying?"

"Half of Brooklyn." Tess bent over at the waist, gasping for breath. "I took a black car home, but getting this all upstairs almost killed me."

"You should have left half of it downstairs. I could have helped you …" She stopped, realizing she couldn't make those kinds of offers for quite a while. "In a month or two I would have helped you."

"Right." Tess gave her a pat as she moved to the chair and dropped into it. "I had a very successful shopping day. Feel free to take everything out. I'm too damned tired to help."

Two of the bags were huge and both advertised a housewares store. Darcy reached into one and pulled out a massive pillow. The biggest she'd ever seen.

"Body pillows," Tess said. "Sixty inches long. The biggest they make."

"Do you think it'll help?"

Tess batted her eyes. "Could it hurt?"

"You've got a very good point. The sofa cushions are a little scratchy." She stopped, then amended, "They're really helpful. My skin's just very sensitive."

"It's okay," Tess said, her cheeks no longer flushed from exertion. "It's not my sofa anyway."

"Right. I forgot that the place was furnished." Darcy opened another bag and took out two pairs of plain, black, lace-up shoes. The kinds of shoes her grandmother started to wear when she was in her eighties. "Uhm … these are … functional. Do you buy everything in twos?"

"No. And I rarely buy different sizes when I do. One pair is for you, and one's for me."

"Great!" It was really hard to be enthusiastic. Why would Tess want them to wear matching orthopedic shoes? Another bag revealed a pair of surprisingly long black skirts. Darcy lifted an eyebrow in question, but Tess pointed at the other bags, clearly urging her to get moving. Drab, shapeless, wool coats bulged from another pair of bags. The last held packages of panty hose and a pair of dark, print scarves. "This is all … interesting," Darcy said, trying to be polite. "Are you getting ready for a trip?"

"I am." Tess stood and stripped out of her jeans, donning the skirt instead. Then she shimmied into a pair of remarkably thick nylons, added the shoes, and wrapped a scarf around her head, effectively hiding every bit of her hair. Lastly she put on the coat and held her arms out. "How do I look?"

"Are you going to … Saudi Arabia?"

"Nope. We're going outside. Both of us."

"I can't! My face is in the newspaper, on TV …"

"True. But no one will recognize you when you're dressed like this."

"But …"

"No buts. You need to get out and move around. I don't want you to get pneumonia from not using your lungs like you usually do. A brisk walk will help you sleep too."

"In a jail cell!"

Tess stood close and put a hand on her shoulder. "No one makes eye contact with strangers in New York. If you dress modestly and look down when you pass people, I guarantee no one will recognize you."

"Wouldn't a parka have been a better choice?"

Tess laughed. "You're just not getting it. Tell me honestly how I look."

Darcy moved back a few paces and really gave her the once-over. "You look … older and … less you. It's a pretty severe look, Tess."

"If you were checking out girls, and saw me on the street, would you give me a second look?"

"Uhm, no. You'd pretty much blend in with the scenery." She smiled as it dawned on her. "You're trying to blend in!"

"You are correct, sir. We're going to look like Orthodox Jews or maybe Muslims or even Amish. Women who try to hide their charms from the general public. Luckily, we're in a great area for this. We'd stand out like sore thumbs in Los Angeles."

"You've really thought this through." She held Tess's gaze for a few extra seconds. "I appreciate all the planning you put into this."

"No problem. I just ran over to Williamsburg and shopped at the stores that cater to orthodox and Hasidic Jewish women. It was funny," she said, laughing a little. "The woman who waited on me couldn't figure out why I was dressed like I was but wanted to buy all this stuff. Then she tried to talk me into something more stylish. But I stuck to my guns."

Darcy ran her fingers across the fabric of the dark grey coat. "You really think this will work?"

"Guaranteed. When women make it clear they're not available sexual objects, men don't look at them. And most cops and most mobsters are men. If we knock them off the list, we have far fewer people to worry about." She picked up the other coat, the color somewhere between mustard and mud. "Yours has big slash pockets. You can put your hand in there and no one will be able to see your cast."

"Sold! Can we go out now?"

"Well, we could, but I've got to have dinner first. I couldn't carry anything else so we'll have to order out. Pizza?"

"We're going to have to go for a hell of a walk if I have pizza."

"No problem. It's a nice night. We can walk all the way to Williamsburg to make sure we fit in. If no one gives us a double-take over there, we're set." She got up to grab her phone. Once it was in her hand she held it to her chest, looking at Darcy. "I have a confession."

"Are the police in the hallway?"

"No, nothing that dramatic. But ... I enjoyed thinking of what to buy and getting it done. I know this is life and death for you, and that's why I feel guilty. But … I kinda dug it." She wrinkled up her nose, grinning slyly.

"Don't worry about it. If I were in your position, I might feel the same." She sighed heavily, thinking of how her entire world had changed so dramatically in such a short time. "I'd love to be in your position."

It took Darcy a long time to get ready. Tess offered to help, but it was embarrassing to have a near-stranger help you put pantyhose on. At least the exercise helped take Darcy's mind off her ribs. Using one hand to pull and tug the heavy material over her hips forced her to focus so intently everything else dropped away. Maybe she could do something difficult while trying to sleep. Anything would be an improvement over the last few nights.

"Are you sure I have to wear the nylons?" Darcy called out from the bathroom.

"Positive. You don't want to be the one bare-legged woman wandering around a Hasidic neighborhood. Sure you don't want help?"

"I want it," Darcy admitted, "I'm just too embarrassed to accept it."

The door opened and Darcy had to stop from screaming. She covered herself with her hands as a flush crawled up her entire body. "Gah!"

"Don't be modest. You've got one hand and you can't bend over. Let's get shakin'."

Before she could stop her, Tess bent to bunch the hose up in her hands. "Ooo, you're very Euro with the unshaved legs," she said, looking up.

Darcy held onto the sink and tried not to die of embarrassment.

Quickly, Tess tugged the stockings into place, slapped Darcy sharply on the ass and exited. Stunned, Darcy stared at the door for a full minute, listening to Tess's melodic laugh. Finally, she collected herself, finished dressing and looked at herself in the full-length mirror on the back of the door. She looked … bland … and older. Not a good combination. But she wanted to go outside, and this look would keep them safer. When she opened the door, Tess was right outside the bathroom, grinning.

"Who looks worse?" Tess turned slowly, like she was modeling in a worst-dressed woman competition. "I think I do."

Darcy took a long look at her. Apparently they weren't going to mention the fact that Tess had not only burst into the bath, she'd slapped Darcy on the butt like they were sisters … or even lovers. The woman had no barriers!

"Well?" Tess asked. "Give me your verdict."

Focusing, Darcy assessed her. "It might be a tie, but if I had to choose, I guess you'd win."

"That's what I thought. Your cheekbones are so awesome you look good without your hair showing. I look washed out. Almost sickly."

Not many people had ever commented on her cheekbones, but Tess had mentioned them twice. Of course, Tess didn't seem to have a filter of any sort, so she said exactly what came to mind, something Darcy's usual friends would never have done. "Maybe we should change scarves. Mine might look better with your coloring."

"No thanks. I want to look as plain as possible." She started to chuckle. "I think I've done it." Handing her phone to Darcy, she said, "Take my picture. I've got to send this to my parents."

Darcy took a few snaps, then Tess did some selfies of them standing together. "One day we'll look back on this and laugh."

"It's pretty funny right now," Darcy had to admit. "Ready to take off?"

"Yeah. Let's do it." They walked down the stairs together, with Tess providing a guiding hand on Darcy's elbow. It took a very long time to get downstairs, but once they were walking, Darcy started to feel better. Or maybe she was just distracted. Whatever caused it, she was happy for the improvement.

It had only been four days, but she could see a huge diminution in her fitness. The first block seemed like two, but that was probably because she was concentrating so hard to make sure she didn't trip. Not being able to pick her feet up as she normally did made her conscious of every step. They didn't speak, and Darcy's mind wandered in many directions. They'd gotten to Grand Army Plaza before Tess said, "You didn't talk to your uncle, did you."

Damn! She thought she was doing a good job of hiding her worry. "No. Danny's as reliable as a hunting dog, so if he's not answering, it's because he can't. And there's no positive reason why he can't."

"Sure there is." She made a face. "I just have to think of one."

"I've been trying for two hours. Good luck."

Tess squeezed her arm. "I'm more optimistic than you are."

"I'd be more optimistic if I wasn't worried that he has a target on his back."

"Even bad guys aren't stupid, Darcy. And it'd be stupid to lean on a police officer too hard."

"I know it's unlikely they went after him. But I can't imagine why he hasn't answered all day."

"I can." Tess slid her arm around Darcy's so they were now walking down the street like two elderly aunts, both trying to keep their balance.

"Thanks," Darcy said. "I'm a little shaky."

"No problem. Here's my guess. Either his new phone isn't working right or he's afraid to use it. Maybe … well, I don't know what could have happened. But whatever happened doesn't have to be horrible."

"I guess not."

"Right. Now we have to decide how he'd try to contact you if his phone wasn't working."

"He doesn't know where I am, so he can't write. My phone's off and I'm sure he wouldn't call yours." A sick feeling hit her gut. "You'd better turn yours off. They might look at every call he's made since the killing.

If they do that, they'll see the first call I made to him the night I kidnapped you."

"Let's give that another name," she said, giving Darcy a half grin. Tess took her phone from her pocket and powered it down. "Let's call it the night we met. When I write a book about this, and you know I'm going to, I don't want to reveal that little detail."

"If you don't reveal that little detail, you're going to go to jail for harboring a fugitive."

Tess stopped quickly, pulling a little on Darcy's arm. "What?"

"Sad but true. You either say I've had a gun on you the whole time or you have to confess to a felony."

"But you're innocent!"

"I know that, and you know that, but you don't get to be the judge and jury. Choices have repercussions."

Tess started to walk again, mumbling, "Fucking repercussions. I was already imagining my book tour."

It took them over two hours to reach Williamsburg. The neighborhood had, in the last decade, gotten a reputation as a hipster hangout. That was true, but it had long been home to sizable populations of people of Puerto Rican, Dominican, Polish, and Italian descent. Tonight, they were headed for the part of the neighborhood where people from a variety of Hasidic Jewish sects lived.

If they could blend in there, they'd gotten it right. It was late, and few women were out on the streets. But the ones they saw were dressed similarly—modest clothing, sensible shoes, wigs, hats or scarves covering their hair.

A group of young men wearing black fedoras walked by, none of them even sparing a glance. As they got closer to a subway stop, more men hustled by, rushing to the train.

"I've got to admit it's nice to have men ignore me," Darcy said, as three guys crossed in front of them.

"Do you get a lot of attention?"

"More than I'd like. I go out of my way to cover up, especially when I'm blading, but a lot of guys don't have any qualms about staring at you like you're for sale." She chuckled. "I don't even have to ask about your experience. Guys must drool over you." She realized how that sounded and tried to backpedal. "I mean … You're pretty curvy and guys …" She slapped herself in the face. "Help me."

Tess took her arm and gave it a squeeze. "It's more fun to listen to you flounder. But yes, I get a lot of catcalls. The stereotype about construction workers is one hundred percent true, in my experience. Some of those guys are shameless!"

"Probably because they're in groups. Guys misbehave more when they have an audience." A group of teenagers came towards them, with each of the kids acting like Tess and Darcy didn't exist. "I think I might dress like this all of the time. It's strangely freeing."

"I'm pretty proud of myself for choosing these outfits," Tess said. "I was going to get us the kind of head covering Muslim women wear but with my pale coloring I thought I might not be able to carry it off. I'm sure there are strawberry blonde Muslims, but they're not the norm."

"I've always wondered if my dad might be of middle eastern origin. My skin tone was darker than anyone in my family."

"I remember you said you didn't know your father, but I didn't realize you knew nothing. Was that …" Tess trailed off.

"I asked a few times when I was a little kid, but my mom made it pretty clear we weren't going to discuss it." She let out a wistful sigh. "I didn't push it."

"Even in the last years? You were together constantly. Didn't it ever come up?"

"Not really." She thought for a minute. "My grandfather would sometimes get a little inappropriate as his disease got worse. One day he asked my mom what ever happened to the guy who knocked her up." She had to laugh, thinking of the look on her mother's face. "All she said was that it wasn't like that and that Grandpa had just forgotten. That was the only time she mentioned my father in a concrete way."

"And you didn't ask."

"No, I didn't. I figured it was her life, and if she didn't want to talk about it …"

Tess pressed their arms together in a kind of hug. "It was your life too, Darcy. If you wanted to know your father, you should have asked."

"I did," she admitted, "but I didn't. After my uncle cleaned out my mom's personal things he gave me a letter he found. It was dated about six months before I was born and was from a guy named Ben."

"And you think this guy might have been your dad?"

"Maybe," she said thoughtfully. "He read her the riot act about breaking up with him without any explanation. It was a really angry letter. I'm not sure why she kept it."

"Give me more info," Tess said. "What were their circumstances?"

"I can't be certain, but it's possible he was a classmate. She was in law school on Long Island, but she quit after her first year when she got pregnant. I suppose my father could have been just about anyone, but law school's pretty tough. I don't think most people have time to go out looking for guys. They tend to date ones they're with all the time."

"That makes sense. What else?"

"Mmm, that's about all I know. She decided she wanted a well-paying job with good benefits, so she looked for a job with a police force. She'd gotten past the first hurdles to being hired, gave birth to me, then joined up when I was just two months old. I think she lived with her parents until then, but I'm not a hundred percent sure about that. I could ask my uncle."

"He didn't know who she was dating?"

"No. He was six years younger than my mom. That would have put him in high school when she got pregnant. I don't think most high school boys pay much attention to their older sister."

"Hmm," Tess mused. "My guess is that she liked the guy but didn't know him very well. Or that he wasn't marriage material. But maybe she wanted to be reminded that at one time he really wanted to be with her, so she kept the letter. Maybe that gave her some comfort."

"Maybe," Darcy said, thinking it through. "As far as I know, she never got close to another guy. I guess that could mean she had a very broken heart, or he turned her off romance completely." She shrugged. "That's why I've never made an effort to follow up. There's a fifty-fifty chance he was a complete asshole."

Tess gave her arm another quick squeeze. "And a fifty-fifty chance he was such a good guy she knew she'd never find another who'd match up."

Laughing, Darcy said, "We're probably both way off. This Ben guy might have been a boyfriend who she didn't want to know she'd gotten pregnant. My father might have been a guy she met in a bar and hooked up with in the parking lot."

"Was your mom a party girl?"

"If she was, it was a very, very well-hidden trait."

Tess hailed a black car that was cruising down Bedford Avenue and they were back home in twenty minutes. The stairs seemed like they'd grown another hundred treads, but there were probably still only about sixty of them.

"Next time, sublet a place on the second floor, okay?"

"It's a deal. Actually, the garden apartment I looked at would have been a great idea."

Darcy dropped her coat on the sofa and settled gingerly into the desk chair. "This is the most comfortable place for me. I wish I could sleep here."

Tess patted her on the shoulder. "It's not getting any easier, is it."

"No, it's not. I thought it'd feel a little better every day but that hasn't been true for the ribs. My wrist doesn't hurt much though. I guess I'll find out how bad everything is tomorrow. I'm going to take my last prescription drugs tonight."

"We'll figure something out. There has to be a way to make this better. Millions of people must break ribs every year. Someone has to have an answer."

"The answer is don't break your ribs," Darcy said. She pulled the computer over to rest it on her lap. "I had an idea on the way home."

Tess came to stand next to her, and took the scarf from Darcy's hair. "I can only take you looking this severe when we're out in public."

"Sorry. I forgot." She was scrolling through Craigslist posts, concentrating fully. "Maybe my uncle used Missed Connections?"

"That's a good idea. Oh. You've got to specify who you're looking for. Go for M4W. Might as well take the obvious route."

Darcy started to drill down, going past the warning for explicit sexual material. "There are hundreds of these," she grumbled. "Do people really go to the trouble of looking for each other just because their eyes met when they passed at the Lexington Avenue exit of Grand Central Terminal at 5:40 p.m. on Monday?"

"They must or people wouldn't bother."

"Who knew the 'R' train was such a hookup spot? I guess that's how I can find a girlfriend. Stare at a woman on the subway, then run home and post a message telling her how hot she was."

"I'm sure that'll work. Let me know." Tess pointed at a longer listing. "What's that?"

"That's me!" She began to read, "Bitsy, sorry we haven't been able to talk. My phone's broken. Drop me a line when you have time." She turned to Tess, relief flooding her. "My grandmother used to call me Bitsy because I was so little when I was born."

She got up and tried to stretch some of the stiffness from her body. Going from no exercise to over two hours of walking might not have been smart.

"He's okay. You were right. His disposable isn't working and he's afraid of putting his new number in the message."

"Do you think it's safe to write?"

"I hope so." She thought for a minute. "I'll send him the number, then, just to be safe, I'll just keep buying disposables and toss them after we talk. Thank god I've got all of that dirty money. It'd kill me to have to spend my hard-earned dollars on stuff like this."

"I don't think of it as dirty money anymore. *I* think of it as a gift that's going to get you out of this mess. *I* think you've earned it," she said, tapping the tip of Darcy's nose.

Darcy let out a heavy sigh. "I feel so much better. Thanks for the cool clothes and the exercise and especially for listening to me blather on. It feels good to talk about all of the stuff I have banging around in my head."

"It's not a hardship. I like being with you. Now get into your pajamas and take your knockout drops."

"If I had them, I'd take them." She shuffled into the bedroom to fetch her PJs. "Next time I kidnap a woman, she's going to be an anesthesiologist."

By the next afternoon, Darcy had another questionable option in her quest for a good night's sleep. She stood in front of a multi-colored lawn chair and gave Tess a doubtful look. "I can't imagine how this will help."

"You've said you feel best in the desk chair. This is similar, but it reclines."

Darcy sat down and nodded. "It's pretty good. But I don't know about the reclining part."

"Give it a try." Tess moved the bar near the seat and let the chair lean back a few degrees. "How's that?"

"Okay, but I can't imagine sleeping like this."

"One more adjustment." Tess let it move back another few inches. "Now?"

"Not bad," Darcy said, feeling some of the tension leave her abdomen. "But my head will fall over."

"No it won't. Trust me," she said with a devilish look in her eyes.

Many minutes later, Darcy sat, fully reclined at an angle that was a vast improvement over the sofa. Her feet were propped up on a moving box, with pillows under her knees and calves. Yet another pillow was behind her neck and both her head and the pillow were fastened, via elastic bandage, to the back of the chair. Tess had to document the look and Darcy agreed that she looked absolutely insane. But she was in less pain than she'd been in for five days, despite not having any more narcotics.

"I'm going to take a nap to try this out," she said, already yawning.

"Sleep tight"—Tess started to laugh—"literally."

Darcy was awakened by the buzzer ringing. "What ...?"

"It's the door," Tess soothed. "I think my bed is here."

"Or mobsters coming to kill us!" Darcy tried to stand, but she was locked into the chair.

"UPS said it was coming today, and this is when the guy usually gets here. I'll go look down the stairwell. If I don't see a big box, I'll run back here and grab your gun."

"Don't go!" Darcy begged, certain that would be the last she'd see of Tess. But just a few seconds later she was back.

"It's the regular UPS guy. He's bringing it up to the landing for me."

"You're sure no one followed him in?"

"Positive. Relax, Darcy. It's fine."

Tess stepped outside again, and Darcy could hear the guy flirting with her. She couldn't blame him, but she was starting to feel strangely proprietary over Tess. That was just short of madness, but you couldn't tell your feelings how to behave. All you could do was control your actions, which she was fully in charge of.

The door opened and Tess started to push a huge box inside. "It's light," she said when Darcy looked at her with alarm. "He's bringing the frame up next."

"You'd better tip him," Darcy advised.

"My sweet smile isn't enough?" Tess started to push the huge box down the hall, looking like a cartoon character. Her smile would have been enough for Darcy, but she wasn't sure the UPS guy was as smitten as she was.

Along with Tess's bed, the UPS guy had brought most of Darcy's new clothes. She decided to try everything on. When she had her clothes off, she looked at herself in the mirror. It wasn't pretty. But it should be documented. "Hey, Tess? Can I use your phone to take some photos of myself?"

Tess's voice sounded like it was right outside the bedroom. "Kinda freaky, but sure. If you want to leave naked pictures of yourself on my phone, I'm sure I'll be able to entertain people with them at some point."

"Not naked," Darcy said. "I just want to document my injuries."

The door opened and a phone poked through. "Have at it. Let me know if you need help."

"I think I've got it," Darcy said as she tried to capture the colors of her bruising accurately.

After finishing, Darcy struggled to get into her new clothes. Everything looked and fit perfect. Light fabric, with a silky feel that would resist wrinkles. The kind of clothing you could leave packed in a bag for a while.

That gave her an idea, and she pitched it to Tess when she went back into the living room. "Given that we might have to leave quickly,

I'd like to put this stuff in a bag and keep it right by the door. Do you have something lightweight for me? God knows I can't carry much."

"Sure. I get carryalls thrown at me all the time. I'll grab a couple." Tess was a real wizard at how to pack a small bag and they soon had toiletries, shirts, slacks, underwear and socks all neatly stored away. Darcy insisted on keeping their new winter coats draped over the bags just in case they needed to make a run for it.

"Are you sure you can stand having our coats lying out?" Tess asked as they stepped back to assess. "I see how you look at me when I leave yours on the sofa."

"Stop being so perceptive and you won't have a thing to worry about."

Darcy was nodding off by nine. Tess had her new bed all set up, and she was bubbling with excitement about trying it out.

"I'm ready to sleep," Darcy said. "Do you mind trussing me up like a Thanksgiving turkey?"

"Not a bit. Will it bother you if I lie in bed and watch a movie?"

"Bother me? I'll be in here and you'll be in your room."

Tess got up and started to drag the lawn chair into her bedroom. "No way. You're tied to a chair and you get very disoriented when you sleep. I've got to keep an eye on you."

"But you've finally got some privacy!"

"Privacy's overrated." She put her hands on her hips. "Put your jammies on. Your evil stepmother has to tie you to your chair for bedtime."

A few minutes later, Darcy was strapped to her chair next to the head of the bed. With her head just a few inches away, Tess spoke softly. "I'll be right here if you have to use the bathroom. Don't worry about waking me up. This dreamy soft mattress will lull me back to sleep in seconds."

"All right." Darcy took in as deep a breath as she could manage. It was divine to be in less pain. "G'night, Tess. Thanks for trying so hard to make me more comfortable."

Tess patted her gently on the head. "You're like having a pet. I've got to do the things you can't do for yourself."

Darcy closed her eyes, determined to rid her mind of thoughts about her discomfort. Thinking about Tess petting her head let her slip past her reality and glide into a fantasy world where she could run and play with all of the other dogs.

On Wednesday morning, Darcy's disposable phone rang. She kept it in her pocket at all times, and she jumped in alarm at the unfamiliar buzz. Fumbling for it, she finally hit the answer button. "Hello?"

"Thank God you checked the classifieds," Danny said, sounding very relieved. "That cheap phone broke after one use."

"Oh, damn. Tess thought there might be a simple explanation for why you didn't answer." She let out a wry laugh. "I was sure you were in jail."

"Not far from it," he said soberly. "I'm in lockdown here, Darce."

"Tell me what's going on." Tess came out of her room and perched on the arm of the sofa, alertly watching Darcy. "I'm putting you on speaker so Tess can hear."

"Got it. The NYPD has a detective trailing me. Since I told them about your first call, they assume I'm going to sneak off to meet you."

"Shit. I'm sorry, Danny. I wish I'd never called."

"Don't be dumb," he growled. "We're family."

"Okay. I wish I hadn't called the way I did. I should have thought of something better."

"No big deal. They haven't been able to nab you by now, so they must not have been able to trace the call."

"Damn," Darcy breathed. "That was close."

"I think you're safe," he said. "Really."

"I'm worried for you, Danny. You're the one who could lose your job over this. They'd love to be able to fire you the year you're going to retire."

"Don't worry about me. I'm being as careful as possible. I'm going to toss this phone after we hang up. In case they search me, I don't want your number in the memory."

"I'm doing the same thing. I'll keep two on hand, and give you the number for the next one every time we talk."

"Great. Uhm … I wish I had better news, but I'm getting no traction at all with the NYPD. The article in the paper seems to have made them even more locked in."

"There was something in the paper?"

"Something?" He laughed. "It's all anyone at work is talking about. You're famous."

"Just what I wanted. I wish I'd thought of another option, but I felt like I had to get my story out there."

"I think it was a good idea, Darce, but it's not going to make things easier for you. Big organizations don't like to be called out in the newspaper. They tend to close ranks."

"Do you think I should hire an attorney yet?"

"Not if you're not considering giving yourself up—which I don't want you to do."

"Neither do I," Tess called out.

"Sounds like your kidnap victim's on your side," he said, chuckling.

"She is," Darcy agreed. "She's also the nicest person I've ever met."

"She's barely been out of New Jersey," Tess said, chuckling at her own joke. "Very little competition."

"It sounds like you're in good hands," Danny said. "My only advice is to hang in there and hope the press coverage breaks something open."

After giving him her new cell number, Darcy hung up. Tess had already opened the paper to reveal the article, which was set off in a block on the bottom of page one. "Special To The Times" the headline read. The text laid out Darcy's story in condensed form, then made her allegations of police involvement with the mob. She and Tess sat side by side, reading every word. When they'd finished, Darcy said, "I think she did a good job of putting my side out there. Now we have to see when and if the NYPD responds."

CHAPTER SIX

THE AFTERNOON WAS SURPRISINGLY warm. Darcy opened the window in the bedroom and sat on the wide sill, just watching people stroll down Prospect Park West. It was the kind of day that made you forget it was December, with dozens of people out walking just to soak up the sun.

Surprisingly, she was content. Maybe even happy. Tess was working on a teaser for a piece she wanted to write about glamping—glamorous camping. She'd been thinking of camping ever since Darcy had asked her about it, and Tess was the kind of woman who had the talent to get someone else to pay for her dream vacations. That wasn't the kind of thing Darcy would ever be able to do, but it was fun watching Tess position herself to get what she wanted.

Earlier that day, she'd read some pieces Tess had written in the last year. She had a real knack for making a place sound like you had to go pack your bags and book a ticket as soon as possible. The way things were going, Darcy would be able to read everything Tess had ever written. Luckily, she was looking forward to that—although it would have been nicer to have been in her own apartment while doing it.

She wasn't sure how long she'd been sitting, but it was twilight and the temperature started to drop. Darcy was just about to close the window when she looked down and saw him. *Sergei.* He was exiting the building right next door and as she fought to get her voice to work he entered their building. "Sergei," she managed in a hoarse croak.

"Fuck!" In an instant, Tess was running down the hall. Before Darcy could extricate herself from the window, her gun was in her hand.

A strange calmness settled over her. She wasn't able to give in to her fears. She had to protect Tess. "If he knocks on the door, I'm going to shoot him," she said, watching Tess's eyes widen. "I don't want to, but he's here to kill me, and I can't let him. I'll shoot him right through the door."

"Oh, shit." Tess was trembling so furiously Darcy thought she might faint.

"You stay in here. If something bad happens, barricade the door with your bed and call the police."

Tess threw her arms around Darcy, not seeming to realize she was squeezing her broken ribs. "Don't let him hurt you," she whispered fiercely.

"I won't."

Darcy walked quietly down the hall and pressed her ear to the door. Because the stairs were marble, it was nearly impossible to climb them and not make noise. But Sergei wasn't even trying to be quiet. Darcy hadn't heard anyone buzz him in, but it wasn't hard to hit a buzzer and say you had a delivery. People were very trusting in small buildings like this.

Sweat ran down her chest and her finger ached from putting just enough pressure on the trigger to allow her to squeeze off a round with another twitch. It sounded like he'd reached their floor. Heart hammering, Darcy had to focus to hear his steps over the sound of her own blood whooshing in her ears. Then his steps seemed to grow more distant. The sound of someone climbing was different from a descent, and he was definitely still climbing. He must have lost count. He'd passed right by the door, and was heading to the roof deck. Then, after a few seconds, probably to catch his breath, his heavy tread started back down. Darcy widened her stance and aimed the gun for where his chest would be. Her hand started to shake with fatigue.

Suddenly, something hit the door with a wallop. She waited, unable to decide whether to fire or not. Then ... silence. She hadn't planned on that. The thump on the door didn't seem like a knock. More like a ... thump. Maybe he'd banged on the door to scare her and was waiting to pounce. Out of the corner of her eye she saw Tess start down the hall. Waving wildly, Darcy urged her to get back into the bedroom. But Tess wasn't great at taking directions. In a few seconds, she was right at Darcy's side.

"What happened?" she asked, her voice shaking.

"I don't know," Darcy whispered, assuming that Sergei could hear. "I'm going to go into the bathroom to get a better angle. You throw the door open. If he's on the right side, I'll have a clear shot."

"What if he's on the left?"

"Then he's got a clear shot at you. Run like hell as soon as you pull the door open."

Tess looked at her, a range of emotions Darcy couldn't begin to name crossing her face. "Promise you won't let him hurt you," she whispered, then put her hand on the key, turned it quickly, and threw the door open.

Darcy let out some kind of squeal when a shoulder dropped into the room from shin-height. "Get your computer and stuff it into your bag. We've got to go. Now!"

Tess started to run, heading for the bedroom. Darcy stepped into the darkened hall and saw not a drop of blood. When the light above her head flicked on, it dawned on her that Sergei had tripped in the dark. His shoulder had struck the door or the wall next to it and his head must have hit something too. Bending, then cursing at the pain, she put her fingers to his neck, regret washing over her when she detected his pulse, strong and true.

If she'd been in her own apartment, she would have put the gun to his temple and blown his brains out. It would have been murder. There was no way to play with the facts. But she would have done it, and not had a moment's regret. With Tess involved ... It was out of the question. The police would link her to the killing and Darcy couldn't

121

allow that. Even though letting Sergei live would probably shorten her own life.

After getting to her feet by using Sergei's inert body to push off from, Darcy walked as quickly as she could to the bedroom, finding Tess struggling into her new skirt. "We don't have time for this! We've got to run!"

"I wet my pants," she said, her lower lip quivering.

Darcy grabbed her and gave her the most soothing hug she could manage. "He's unconscious. With any luck his brains are scrambled, but he might also wake up and start shooting."

"Put on your new clothes and your headscarf. The mob knows you're in the neighborhood, and they're more dangerous than the cops."

Darcy almost refused, but Tess had a point. Besides, Sergei had really taken a wallop. He had a concussion at the very least, and no one jumped up and got right back into action after one of those. She nearly dove into her costume, but she didn't take the time to put on the pantyhose. Fellow believers would just have to mock her for being out of uniform. As they ran for the door, she grabbed the bag of money. It hurt like hell to carry it, but she wasn't going to throw it away at this point.

They reached the street, panting. A taxi slowed down at the corner, its "available" light calling out like a beacon. Darcy held up her hand, then opened the door when he paused. "Going to Queens," she said decisively.

"Airport?"

"No. But close. Head to JFK and I'll tell you where to turn."

"Can't do that. I've gotta have an address."

"189-03 Northern Boulevard."

He nodded, put the address into some automated system and started to drive. Tess was a mess, shaking, pale, and silent. Darcy didn't know what kind of comfort she liked to receive, but when she put her hand down and grasped Tess's cold fingers the grip was immediately returned. They rode through the heavy early evening traffic, neither of them saying a word. Darcy was able to relax—slightly. She'd spent hours thinking of escape scenarios and this one seemed to be working —so far.

By the time they arrived, Tess had calmed down and her color was better. Darcy paid the cabbie, adding a generous tip for taking them out to where he'd never get a return fare. They stood there on the curb in the largely industrial neighborhood. "Why in the hell are we out in the middle of Queens?" Tess asked.

"I hope that's what anyone looking for us will think. I'm going down the block to rent us a car. You stay right here. I don't want your picture to show up on the security cameras."

"No!" Tess grabbed her arm and held her still. "They'll find you in two minutes!"

Shrugging helplessly, Darcy said, "I don't have any options."

"Of course you do! I'll rent the car. No one knows about me."

"And it's going to stay that way."

A fire grew in Tess's eyes. "Darcy, we're in this together. If I rent the car, we'll both be safer."

"I don't think that's true. I really don't. Having only one of us on the radar is much safer."

"But the police have probably flagged your license or your credit card."

"If they have, I'll be able to tell by the way the clerk acts. So if I come out and go in the other direction I want you to take off and walk until you find a cab. Then go … fuck," she grumbled. "I don't know where you should go. But don't go home. Use the cash to get a hotel room and stay there until I send you a message. I'll use Craigslist just like my uncle did. Look for a message from Bitsy."

Tess grabbed onto the shoulders of her coat, holding on possessively. "Please don't go, Darcy. Please."

Leaning forward to kiss her head, Darcy said, "I have to. I've got forty thousand dollars in my pockets. If I have to run, I can hole up some place out here. I'll be fine," she promised, hoping she wasn't lying.

"I'm holding on, but just barely," Tess said, her voice quivering. "I can't make it without you."

Darcy gripped her shoulder. "Yes, you can. You're doing great. I have complete confidence in you." Once more, she kissed her forehead, pressing her lips firmly against the soft skin. "This will work."

As Darcy started to walk, she could feel Tess tugging on her coat. But she had to keep going. This was their best chance.

On the way to the office, she pulled her scarf down a little more and buttoned her coat. After entering the run-down office, with her hands shaking like mad, Darcy went up to a bored-looking young woman. "I need a car," she said, being careful not to look up. The security cameras were usually in the corners of the ceiling.

"We've only got a few. How long do you need it for?"

"A week?"

"I've got a compact you can have. Is that okay?"

"Sure. Fine."

"Do you want the—"

"No extra insurance," Darcy said, cutting her off. She took her license and charge card from her wallet and slid them across the counter. They lay there like ticking bombs for a few seconds, then the woman ran the card through a reader. After checking the license against the name on the card, she typed in the license number and handed both back. Darcy nearly fainted with relief, but she held it together and signed when she was told to. With a shaking hand, she picked up the keys and went to the lot where a very disinterested young man walked around the car and noted all of the scratches and dings. "Sign here," he said, sticking a form in front of her. Then she was free, and a sense of elation came over her so strongly that she nearly floated into the driver's seat. Then she struggled to get the seat belt on, finally letting it snap back into the holder. When she pulled up in front of Tess, a gorgeous smile of relief greeted her. Rolling down the window, she said, "Can you put the seat belt on me? This beeping is about to make me crazy."

"Want me to drive?"

"Yeah. I'll be distracted watching for the cops, who are probably going to be looking for me in minutes."

She'd been pale before, but what little color had been in her cheeks vanished. "They are?" she asked, her voice cracking.

"I think so. They've got technology to track credit card usage. But I figured that even if they got a ping on my card it would take a few minutes to send a patrol car over here." She looked into Tess's eyes. "That's why we might want to hurry."

In a flash, Tess opened the door and helped her out, then got her settled in the passenger seat and clicked the belt into place.

"Where do we go?" Tess asked when she lifted a shaking hand to adjust the rearview mirror.

"Mmm, I have a few options, but it's probably best to head south. Go to the BQE, then back across Staten Island and head for Jersey."

"I know what none of that means, so you'd better be able to substitute for Google Maps, unless you want me to turn my phone on."

"I haven't traveled much, but I know Jersey like the back of my hand."

"Why did we wind up out here?"

"Escape plans. I had three. This was the one that seemed most viable."

Tess's smile was wan but sincere-looking. "I'm glad I was kidnapped by a CPA. If you were like me, we'd still be in Brooklyn ... in a cell."

"I'm only able to relax when I'm organized. Sometimes it's a pain in the butt. Sometimes it's a very good trait to have."

"Today it's very good. Now can you tell me what in the hell happened to Sergei?"

"You know that light that flickers on and off in the hallway?"

"Oh, damn, I never called to report that to the super."

"Thank you for your procrastination. I think he went up to the top, saw it was the roof and started down. I'm not sure if the light went out or if he just slipped, but he fell into the door or the wall. He was out— really out. I'm just hoping his skull is fractured in ninety places and his brains are dribbling out his ear."

"Couldn't happen to a nicer guy." Tess turned and met Darcy's eyes. "I can't summon up one bit of sympathy for him. You live like a violent beast, you die like one."

"I can't argue with you there." She let out a short, bitter laugh. "How did I go from being a peace-loving accountant to a fleeing felon who fervently hopes a guy has brain damage?"

Tess gave her a reassuring pat on the leg. "Circumstances changed. So ... what does the escape plan entail?"

"Not sure. I think we should go south until we find a place that looks appealing. And isolated."

"How about Oregon? It's not south, but my parents live way out in the woods. You can barely find the house if you have a map."

Darcy looked at her, seeing the deep longing in her eyes. If her mother were alive she'd feel the same way. When times were tough, you needed some comfort and no one could provide that like your mom. "If that's what you want, that's what we'll do. Just stay on 278 all the way to I-95 South."

"You're going to have to cue me. These signs have too many confusing things written on them."

Darcy let out a groan as they hit a particularly bad pot hole. "I'm going to offer to pay higher taxes if they'll just fix the damn roads."

"Do you have any idea how long it'll take us to get to Oregon? I've never driven cross-country."

Wincing as the car shook from hitting another dip, Darcy tried to think. "I haven't either, but it's got to take ... four days? Maybe five?"

"Shit. That's a long time to be in this box."

"Yeah." She tried to smile, but the constant jostling had her gritting her teeth. "But it's better than jail—I think."

It took forever to crawl from Queens through Brooklyn, but they finally reached the Verrazano Narrows bridge, her twinkling lights giving off a majestic look as they approached.

Darcy's minute of pleasure at seeing the familiar bridge was shattered when they banged into a pot hole that felt like it would tear the car in half. "Holy fuck," she muttered, grabbing at her chest.

"We're not going to be able to go to Oregon," Tess said quietly.

"Why not?"

"You're not well enough. We need to find a place close by and rest until you're able to be in a car and not burst into tears." She turned and met Darcy's eyes. "I can't do this to you."

"I'm okay. No matter where I am, I'm in pain. It hardly matters."

"No," Tess said, her voice firm. "We're going to stay close until you're better."

Darcy reached over and squeezed Tess's arm. "Thank you."

"No problem. Once you're well, we can start out again."

That probably wasn't going to happen. They'd be caught long before that. But it was a nice delusion.

"Where are we now?" Tess asked. "Should I find a motel?"

"Staten Island," Darcy said. "I don't know a thing about it. I'd rather keep going to Jersey. I'll have the home-field advantage there."

Traffic wasn't much better, but the road was newer, making it less bone-rattling. "Let's get on the Garden State Parkway," Darcy said. "We'll pick a spot that looks good."

The traffic was still heavy, but it moved fast. Darcy let herself daydream about taking the road down the shore when she was a kid, heading to Wildwood or Seaside Heights for those summer idles.

"Atlantic City?" Tess asked when they saw the first sign for it.

"Mmm ... I guess that's a possibility. Do you like to gamble?"

"Not with money." She turned and gave Darcy a smile. "But I don't mind going on an adventure with a fleeing felon, so I guess I'm a different kind of gambler."

Smirking, Darcy said, "You might do better with blackjack."

"What do you think?" Tess asked as they neared the exit. "Stop here or keep going?"

"We might as well stop. I'm not sure it's smart to go to a big hotel, but there are dozens of smaller places to choose from."

As Tess glided through the express lane, a wave of panic hit Darcy like a shot. "How have you been going through the toll booths?"

She pointed at the small plastic device that rested behind the rearview mirror. "That thing."

"Fuck." She slapped herself in the head, hard. "They'll be able to see exactly when we've gone through every booth."

Tess reached up and tried to wrench it from the glass. "Then we'll throw it away!"

"It's too late for that. Take the next exit for Route 9. We'll stay on that for a while, and find someplace to hide."

"Fuck!" She slammed her hand onto the steering wheel. "How could I be so stupid!"

"You?" Darcy said, filled with self-loathing. "I've lived here my whole life! I've been driving on these roads for twenty-five years."

"Don't beat yourself up. I should have paid attention."

"I've had a transponder ever since they started using them," Darcy said, trying to examine the thought process that led her to such a bone-headed move. "I guess they disappear into the background and you forget they're just another way for the government to keep an eye on you."

"You're sounding like my parents," Tess said. "I always thought they were a little paranoid, but maybe not."

They kept going, silently moving along the local road. After a long time, Tess's stomach rumbled loudly. "Are you hungry?" Darcy asked.

"I guess. I alternate between hungry and nauseous."

"I think it's safe to stop. Pick whatever looks good."

"Safe?" Tess's voice was high and strained. "You just told me the cops know exactly where we are!"

"They do ... but I don't think an alarm goes off when we pass through a tollbooth. I think it's more that they can do a search when they link the license plate to me. I'm sure it's not instant." She could see how tense Tess was, just by her posture. "I promise. We can safely stop for dinner."

They drove for just a few more minutes, with Tess pulling into the parking lot of the first diner they saw. As soon as she turned the car off, she let her head fall to the steering wheel. "I want to go home," she whimpered, her voice choked with tears.

Darcy got out and went over to Tess's side of the car. The door opened and Tess got out, then pressed her head gently onto Darcy's chest. "Will you hold me?" she asked, shakily.

"Of course." They stood in the dark parking lot, with Darcy tenderly rubbing Tess's back while she cried. "I'm sorry we can't just keep going until we hit Oregon."

"It's okay." Tess straightened up and wiped her eyes. "I'm a big girl. I can't run home to mom every time something bad happens."

"I'll try hard to make fewer bad things happen."

Tess looked up at the signs in the window, advertising their specialties. "I don't know about you, but I'm having fried chicken. If I can't have my mom, grease and fat are going to have to substitute for love."

Darcy didn't get the fried chicken, but the salad she'd bought was so lacking in nutrition, she wished she had. "Okay, I've thought about where we should go and I think Cape May is a good choice."

"Never heard of it."

"It's right before you cross into Delaware. It's miles from where we got off the Parkway, so they won't be sure of where we are. And there are dozens upon dozens of B&Bs because of birding."

"Birding? In New Jersey?"

Darcy sighed. "Yes. It's the Garden State, remember? Cape May's a stopping point for birds heading up or down the country. At this time of year we'll have our pick of places to stay."

"How many birders look like us?" She raised an eyebrow as she scanned over Darcy's headscarf and drab coat.

"Not many, but we could … take off the scarves."

Tess stabbed her fork into the remnants of Darcy's salad. After taking a bite she made a face. "No dressing?"

"I used dressing. Just not much."

"You're a strange one. Everyone knows iceberg lettuce is just a bed for a few ounces of dressing to lie in."

"I was going for healthy."

"Then don't get into situations where mobsters want to kill you. That's gotta be more dangerous than a few hundred calories."

After they were back in the car and started to drive again, Darcy said, "I hope you know how much I tried to keep you out of this. You were never in my escape plan."

"I figured as much." Tess turned and their eyes met. "I don't blame you, Darcy. Really."

"I don't have a great plan to get you out of this, but the obvious one is for you to bail. You can call the police and tell them I'm … heading back to New York or something."

"No way. I'm *not* going to help the police catch you. That's off the table."

"I should have had more plans. I should have thought it through better, but I screwed up, and now *you're* stuck."

"No, I'm not. I'm here because I want to be."

"You do?" Darcy's heart skipped a beat.

"I do. I'd never help them find you, but I could just go back to Brooklyn. The police probably don't know about me, right?"

"Right. I ... I guess you could just walk away."

"I thought about it when we were at the diner, but decided against it. If we work together, we'll get you cleared. I'm sure of that."

Struggling with her emotions, Darcy kept it together to say, "You're the best kidnap victim ever."

Darcy used her disposable cell phone to call her uncle as they approached Cape May. "Hi," she said. "Speaker phone."

"What's up?"

"The guy who beat me up might still be lying on the floor of an apartment building in Park Slope. I'm hoping he dies, but my luck hasn't been that good lately."

Danny's voice was higher than normal, and as tight as a bowstring. "Details, Darcy. Now."

"I was looking out the window and saw him come out of the building next door. Someone must have let him into Tess's building, and he walked up past her floor. On the way down, he tripped or something and fell against the door. Knocked himself out cold."

"Where are you?" He sounded like he was about to hyperventilate.

"Driving. I rented a car. With my own license and credit card."

"Oh, shit."

"Yeah," she agreed. "Not the smartest thing I've ever done, but we had to leave. I wanted to blow Sergei's brains out, but I knew that would lead the police to Tess, and I couldn't do that."

"Blow his brains out!"

"He would have done the same to me. After torturing me for a while. Fair's fair, Danny."

"Darcy," he said, his voice getting up to a register she'd never heard from him. "The guy was just sniffing around. You can't kill a man for knocking on your door!"

Wincing, she told the truth. "I would have, Danny. He was coming to *kill* me."

"So you just ran?"

"Yeah. We grabbed a cab and went to rent a car."

Silence reigned for a few seconds. "Wait … what? Tess is with you?"

"I am," she said. "We're in this together."

"Wha …"

Darcy jumped in. "She committed a felony just by letting me stay at her apartment. I'm not sure how many more she's added for driving me out of state."

"I appreciate you helping Darcy and all, but … that's just not smart, Tess."

"I know that. But sometimes you have to do what's right." Tess met Darcy's gaze. "And helping her stay alive is the right thing. She'll never make it alone. She's injured too badly."

It was damned strange having this talk with Danny on the line. It felt too—intimate was the only word she could think of.

But Danny wasn't affected by the emotion she felt welling up in her chest. He was all business. "What are your plans?"

"We're going to hide, and hope to fuck the cops can't track us. God knows how Sergei found me."

"The police must have triangulated your location from that one call you made with your smartphone."

"Then why didn't they just come get me?"

"They can't get an exact spot, just a few block area. They probably shared that location with the mob and they've been pounding the pavement, looking for you ever since."

"If that's true, they won't know Tess is involved, right?"

"Probably not." He cleared his throat and put on his somber, police officer voice. "I'm sorry you're involved in this, Tess, but I hope you know how grateful I am that you're sticking with Darcy. She needs all the help she can get."

"We'll get out of this one way or the other—together."

As they continued down the road, Tess could see Darcy's posture begin to change. When her ribs were aching she got very rigid and stopped speaking. She hadn't said a word in over twenty miles and was doing a very good impersonation of a statue. "Aching?"

"Yeah. The Parkway was in better shape."

Sometimes it was hard to remember that everything—from breathing to clearing her throat to twisting slightly—was tough for Darcy. Hitting large potholes in a small car was jarring for Tess, who didn't have a scratch. It must have been torture for the relatively stoic woman. "Bet you're glad we're not driving to Oregon."

"I would have gladly gone," Darcy said. "I'm truly sorry we can't."

"I am too, but messed up travel plans aren't the worst thing, right? Having guys shooting at you is much worse." She thought a little joking might pull Darcy from her glum mood. No dice. "I figured I'd go in to get a room. Is that cool?"

"Yeah. Even in my costume you can tell I've been in some kind of fight. I don't want to call any more attention to myself than I have to."

"Your scratches are getting better every day. You're a good healer."

"Tell that to my ribs," Darcy said, wincing audibly at a minor bump in the road.

It was almost ten when they rolled into town. "This place is cute," Tess said, noting the abundance of Victorian-era homes now mostly turned into B&Bs.

"Yeah, it's a nice place. It's got some style. It's not all cheap motels and chains."

"Should I just try the first place with a vacancy sign?"

"Let's look for a place that seems homey." She plucked at her coat. "Do we stick with our costumes?"

"I'm not sure. What's your gut instinct?"

"I'm torn. The costumes worked in Brooklyn, but here …"

"Then let's drop them. It's probably good to look different than you did when you rented the car, right?"

"Right. But how do we do this? It's hard enough for me to change in a bathroom."

"Mmm … let's just take off the scarves. The rest of the stuff is odd, but not too odd."

"Sounds good." Darcy immediately whipped off her scarf and started to fluff her hair out.

Tess cruised up and down a few streets, then pointed at a stately Victorian painted a creamy yellow with dark blue trim. "How about that one? Tasteful Christmas decorations, nice garland on the porch columns and a big wreath on the door."

"That looks fine. But don't park in front. I'd like to be at least two blocks away. If they've identified the car, I want to make them work to find us."

"Then you should get out now with our bags. I don't want to carry everything myself, and you're in no shape to lift a thing."

Darcy rolled her eyes but did as she was told. Tess got the car parked then nearly jogged back. "How do we do this? I'm going to have to tell them we're together. But it's not good for anyone to see you more than necessary."

"I'll sit on the porch," Darcy decided. "Tell them I'm shy or that I'm making a phone call."

"Got it. Be right back." Tess strode into the front door, which was unlocked. That wasn't ideal, but a sleepy town like this probably prided itself on its low crime rate. A little bell rang when she closed the door and in a few seconds a middle-aged man came out from a door at the rear of the parlor.

"Hi there. Can I help you?"

"I hope so. My—sister and I are looking for a room for a couple of weeks."

"Weeks?" He raised an eyebrow. "Not many people stay for more than a long weekend. Visiting family?"

"No." She spoke quietly, trying to look distressed—which wasn't too damned hard. "My sister's husband is abusive. We're going home to Chicago, but that's where he'll look first so we want to stay someplace he'll never think of, then move on after he's stopped searching."

He pursed his lips, looking like he might turn them away.

"She lived in Connecticut. He will never, ever guess we're here. We just want to stay in our room while she heals. We're very quiet people."

"Is it just you two? No children involved?"

"Oh, no. Neither of us has children. My sister's only been married for a year." She lowered her voice, trying to sound angry. "The bastard might not even look for her. You think you know someone ..."

He stuck his hand out and she shook it. "I'm Aaron. My wife Helen and I own the place. She was a social worker, so she's seen more of this kind of thing than you can imagine."

"Oh, I'm so glad you understand," Tess said, filled with relief.

"Do what you can to keep her from going back. If he hurt her once ..."

"He'll do it again." She nodded. "She knows that. I'm sure she'll file for divorce as soon as possible."

"I hope so." He walked over to a big reservations book. "I think we can find you a room. But we're going to be busy this weekend. Are you okay with sharing a bed? We only have one room with twins, and it's booked."

"We're grateful for anything you have. I can give you my credit card, but I'd prefer to pay cash if that's all right."

"No problem. Just let me keep your card on file."

Tess took out her card and he scanned it. "Here you go, Ms. Keller."

"Thank you so much. I'll go get my sister."

"Let me help you with your bags."

"No, no, she's embarrassed about her injuries. It's going to take her some time to realize she should be proud of herself for leaving, not ashamed she didn't see it coming."

"I understand," he said, empathy showing in his dark brown eyes. "You'll be in Painted Bunting."

"Pardon?"

"Painted Bunting. The bird."

"Oh, yes. This is a good place for birding. Maybe we'll get to see some pretty ones."

"Not much around but the overwintering birds at this time of year. But I guarantee this will be a good place to relax and take your minds off your troubles." He cleared his throat. "I'm sure my wife could help you find a social worker nearby to talk with."

"Thank you. That's very thoughtful of you." He exited the same way he'd come, leaving her to fetch Darcy, who was shivering in the cold. "Got it," she said. "Follow me to Painted Bunting."

"What?"

"Don't ask. Just follow along. I gave him a story he bought."

They hadn't thought to pack pajamas, but they each had a set of long underwear. Darcy got undressed first, and emerged from the bathroom feeling a little strange in her silk underwear. It was dark blue, hiding more than the white would have, but she still felt like she was almost naked.

Tess went into the bathroom and came out a while later, wearing just a white top and her panties. If Darcy hadn't still been terrified, she would have had to devote all of her powers of concentration to avoid looking at Tess's generous breasts straining against the snug, thin silk. "I can't stand to be hot in bed, and I have a feeling you're going to be thrashing around all night, heating the place up."

"Maybe we should have gotten two rooms."

"They only had this one available. And I'm just teasing you. I'm used to your nocturnal fits and starts. We've been together for a week now."

"Has it only been a week? It feels like I've been bruised and battered for months."

"Just a week." Tess started to gather all of the pillows and cushions from the sofa, arranging them to support Darcy. "I'll go out tomorrow to buy a lawn chair, some more pillows and an elastic bandage."

"That won't look too odd. A woman in a B&B in the middle of winter who brings a beach chair with her."

"I told him you were badly battered, Darcy. I'll tell him about your ribs. He can be an ally." Tess patted the bed. "Time to get in."

Darcy got into the high bed with Tess's help, then she settled down against the padded headboard. Her neck was going to bother her, since she didn't have her head pinned down, but the bed was soft and cushy. Tess got in and turned off the lights.

Her voice was gentle and warmly comforting when she started to speak. "Two years ago, I was in the South Seas. It was a very rustic village, with everyone living in huts. Imagine my surprise when a young couple asked me to join them in their hut. I tried to explain I wasn't into three-ways, but they said there was no alternative. No one slept alone, so there wasn't an extra hut for guests."

"I would have paced around all night, imagining what they really wanted me for."

Softly, Tess laughed. "I think it's clear that I'm a little more adventurous than you are. So I went in and saw a couple of small kids lying on mats. I lay down and in just a few minutes one of the kids was cuddled up next to me, then the wife tossed an arm around me when she fell asleep."

137

"I'd be waking up every two minutes, trying to figure out who was touching me," Darcy said.

"I certainly didn't get eight hours of uninterrupted sleep, but it felt very natural. We slept in cycles, sort of half waking then going back to sleep. I didn't know these people at all, but I felt connected to them in a very meaningful way." She scooted a little closer. "I'd been going through some stuff back home and hadn't realized how much I needed comfort. Some reassurance."

Darcy turned to see her staring into her eyes.

"I need some tonight. Would you mind?"

"You want—to cuddle?"

"As much as we can."

Tess didn't seem embarrassed in the slightest to ask for comfort. What freedom that must have given her!

"It's okay if you don't want to. I'm just … raw."

"I'm a little raw too. But how do we do this?"

Tess scooted even further over, then curled into a ball and draped an arm across Darcy's legs. "How's this?"

"That can't be comfortable. Put your head in my lap."

"Really?"

"Yeah. Really."

Tess gently lay her head on Darcy's lap, then stretched out and added an arm across her thighs. "Is this okay?"

Darcy looked down at her, seeing a vulnerability, a real need that she'd never seen Tess display. They'd had a horrible day. Just horrible. And there was something very soothing about touching each other. Reminding each other that even though there were bad people on the planet, they would look out for each other through the long night. She put her hand on Tess's head and slowly worked her fingers through the strawberry blonde locks. "It'll be all right. I'll take care of you. Promise."

"And I'll take care of you. It's mutual," Tess murmured.

Darcy felt centered. Calm. Humans needed touch. Especially when things were tough. It just took some folks from the South Seas to remind her of that.

CHAPTER SEVEN

LYING IN A REGULAR BED hadn't been a good idea. Darcy hadn't gotten more than a half-hour of sleep at a time. And having Tess lying either on her or next to her hadn't helped. But that was just the physical side of things. Emotionally, she'd never been so glad to have someone touch her. Tess had been right. They'd both been through a hell of a week, and snuggling while they slept had been the perfect cure for Darcy's jangled nerves.

They'd left the curtains open, and dawn was just starting to break, with the sky streaked pink mixing with the violet of the night now skittering away. As Darcy craned her neck, she could see the moonrise in the dark blue, the sunrise over the ocean. It was going to be a good day. She could just tell.

Tess was lying on her side, facing away from Darcy. But she'd stayed close—very close. Darcy could feel her warmth all along her side. She ached to touch her again, to play with her hair or stroke her skin. But she didn't have the nerve. Just because Tess had asked for touch last night didn't mean Darcy had the green light any time she wanted it.

Even though she couldn't give in to her need, Darcy relished lying close with Tess. She was very cuddly, something Darcy didn't have much experience with. Her lovers hadn't been standoffish, but none of them were particularly tactile. Emily needed so much personal space, she often got up and went home after they'd made love, always making Darcy feel rejected. Looking at Tess lying there, she mused that she wouldn't be the type to vanish after sex. She'd probably be all over you … a very nice fantasy.

A door closed loudly and Tess jerked. "What was that?" she asked, clearly groggy.

Darcy put a hand on her back and patted her. "Nothing. Go back to sleep."

"No one's here to kill us?" Her words were grim but her tone was light, close to a tease.

"Not a soul. I can smell bacon cooking so they might be trying to kill us by clogging our arteries. But that'll take a while."

Tess straightened out and rolled onto her left side, facing Darcy. "You look wide awake—and exhausted. How gruesome was it to sleep on your back?"

"On a scale of one to ten?" She thought about that. "About an eight. But I liked it." She screwed up her courage and said what was on her mind. "I liked being close to you. You were absolutely right. Sleeping next to someone can help calm you down."

Tess rested her head on her hand and looked at Darcy for a minute. "I've really missed a woman's touch. There's something so soothing, so calming to it. When you hugged me back at the apartment I believed I had an ally, someone who'd do everything she could to protect me."

"I know what you mean. I wish we could have gotten to Oregon so you could have that again. I know I'm a poor substitute, but I'm glad it helped."

"Oregon?"

"Yeah. So you could feel your mom's touch again."

Tess looked at her blankly.

"You were talking about how soothing it is to have your mom hug you."

Both eyebrows lifted. "I don't sleep with my mom. And even though she does give a nice hug, it's nothing like you get from a lover. Sam and I fought way, way too much, but she could always calm me down with a good hug."

"Sam was a … woman?"

"Of course. You knew that."

"I did not!" Darcy scrambled to free her feet from the covers then yelped in pain as they hit the floor. "You had a relationship with a woman?"

"All of my relationships have been with women." She blinked, clearly surprised. "That wasn't clear?"

"No!"

Obviously puzzled, Tess spoke slowly, like she was trying to piece something together. "I purposefully didn't tell you the night you told me you were gay, since I thought you'd freak out—"

"Why would you think that?"

"Because you acted like you were admitting to being a bed wetter. I thought I'd wait until you were a little more comfortable sleeping together." She frowned. "But I'm *sure* I told you about Sam."

Darcy stared at her. "You might not know this, but Sam is a man's name."

"Oh, shit!" She started to laugh. "I say Sam and think of this really sexy, really difficult woman. But I guess you can't see my mental image."

"I was one hundred percent sure you were straight. One hundred percent!"

"Well, I'm one hundred percent gay. Why is this freaking you out?"

"I don't … I don't know, but it is!"

"Uhm … is this a good time to tell you I'm attracted to you?"

"No!" She started to limp into the bathroom, then stopped and stared at Tess. "You are?"

She bit her bottom lip, looking both shy and devilish. "Uh-huh."

"Later. We'll talk about this later. I've got to … think."

Darcy grabbed her bag and went into the bath, determined to stay there until she had her feet under herself again. This was past strange. It was really tough to switch from being sure the woman you were crushed on was straight to not only learning she was gay but that she was interested in you!

Tess lay in bed, thinking about Darcy. She was drop-dead pretty, and as thoughtful and generous a woman as Tess had ever met. Those were damned nice qualities. Qualities Tess hadn't sought in her past slate of lovers. Maybe it was time to try something new—if Darcy could loosen up and have an affair. God knew, they had nothing else to do. If they couldn't explore the world, they might as well explore each other.

It took a long time to collect herself, but Darcy finally opened the bathroom door. To her relief, Tess was gone, but she'd left a note. "I'm bringing breakfast up."

That was thoughtful of her. But not surprising. Tess was consistently thoughtful. Darcy was just about to try to sit on the Victorian-style love-seat when someone knocked on the door.

"Yes?"

"Open the door."

Darcy opened it to find Tess laden down with a tray full of food, coffee and juice. "Damn, I wish I could help you," Darcy said.

"You can help by getting out of the way."

Darcy did, moving over to a table where a pitcher of water and glasses lay. "You can put it here," she said after whisking the things away.

"Whew! I'm questioning every part of my lesbian identity. I can't muscle a tray upstairs without panting, I can't hold it in one hand to get the door, and a woman I've been with for a solid week had no friggin' idea I was gay. And flirting with her!"

Darcy's mouth dropped open. "You've been flirting with me?"

"Not at first, but for the last couple of days I sure as hell have been. I was starting to think I'd read you wrong, so I amped it up last night. If you'd said you didn't want to cuddle, I was going to cut bait."

Inelegantly, Darcy dropped to the love-seat, then cursed quietly when the pain hit her. "I had no idea." She looked up at Tess. "But you didn't read me wrong. I've been telling myself to knock it off, but I haven't been very successful." She swallowed. "I'm very attracted to you."

"Well, cool. Wanna ..." She twitched her head towards the bed.

"No!" Darcy was so flustered she could barely form a sentence. "Not right now, that is. We have to"—her eyes scanned the room —"have breakfast."

"Okay, then. Let's eat."

Tess was trying not to laugh. That was clear. She'd probably been kidding about going back to bed. She must have thought Darcy was a true dunce.

"I'm not the type of person who rushes into things. You've got to be patient with me."

Tess was busy taking off the metal domes that covered the plates. "I'll do my best. But there's nothing I love more than rushing into things. Right now, I'm going to rush this French toast down my gullet. And if you don't finish that healthy bowl of oatmeal, that's gonna follow along."

"I'm starving," Darcy said, feeling a little more comfortable now that they were teasing about it. "I think I can handle my oatmeal all by myself."

Tess finished her French toast in record time. Being on the run had made her hungrier than normal. Or maybe stress was the culprit. If she didn't start getting some exercise, the pounds were going to start piling on, and buying a new wardrobe wasn't in her plans.

"Hey," she said, as Darcy finished her oatmeal. "I talked to Helen, the innkeeper, when I was downstairs. She seems like a nice person. Not the suspicious type."

"That's good. But she wouldn't have any reason to be suspicious of you. It's me who's been all over the news."

"Not down here," Tess said. "I asked about the weather and she turned on a TV to check the local forecast. They get Philadelphia stations, not New York ones."

"Mmm. Nice to know. But I still think I'd better stay inside."

"That's not a good idea. We've got to keep busy, Darcy. Exercise will help you heal, and it'll help you sleep."

In the blink of an eye, her expression grew anxious. "But—!"

"I know," Tess soothed. "You're worried someone will spot you. But it's been a week, and people don't have great memories for things that don't affect them personally. No one's going to remember you, even if they saw your face a week ago—which they probably haven't down here."

Soberly, she said, "We've gone through an awful lot just to get turned in for going on a walk."

"I wouldn't suggest this if I wasn't confident," Tess insisted. "And if the worst happens, they'll turn us in to the local cops."

Her gaze shifted around, like she couldn't relax enough to settle on anything. "I guess that's true. No local cop would be involved with the Brooklyn mob, so they wouldn't have any reason to gun me down in the street."

"Such a cheerful outlook!" Tess reached over and tickled under her chin.

"I used to be cheerful." She hesitated, then amended. "More cheerful than I am now, that is."

"That's what I thought you meant." Tess watched her get up, her body still very stiff and balky. Darcy hadn't had many reasons to be cheerful recently. But if there was a way to change that trend, Tess was going to go for it.

Because it was a crisp, cold, windy day near the ocean, they each wore their long underwear under their clothing. A modern ski jacket would have been much warmer than the old-fashioned cloth coats they wore, but, all things considered, it wasn't too awful.

Tess had begun to feel more protected when she wore her dated, unfashionable coat. It was almost as if the vague invisibility it gave was some minor super-power.

They'd been out for a while, plenty long enough for the innkeeper to have alerted the cops. As the minutes passed, Darcy started to loosen up. Tess could see by the set of her shoulders that her pain lessened as her muscles warmed up. But she was still a little withdrawn. Once she wasn't as worried about being shot, she had to deal with Tess's confession that she was attracted to her. Tess looked at her profile, realizing Darcy had barely looked at her while they walked. That spoke more of shyness than fear. It was time to try to loosen her up. "Hey. Wanna hear my coming-out story?"

"Sure." Darcy turned and finally met her gaze, but the connection only lasted for a second. Then her head dipped a little and she looked down at the path. That was discomfort, not fear. Tess was sure of it.

"It's not the most common coming-out story, but I think it's funny."

"I haven't heard too many funny ones. Most of my friends had a tough time."

"Not me. When I was about twelve, my mom said, 'Glen and I have been wondering if you're starting to think about dating.' I clammed up immediately, since I'd been thinking about somehow making Kimberly Jacobs my woman."

"Your woman?" Darcy asked, letting out the first laugh of their walk.

"Well, I didn't know what I wanted to do with her yet, but she was all I thought about."

"Who's Glen? Your step-dad?"

"No, my real dad. My parents wanted to be called by their first names."

"They did?" Darcy looked like she was about to swallow her tongue.

"Uh-huh. I went along with it until I brought a friend home, and she informed me that was weird." She laughed at the memory, thinking of how outraged she'd been to learn she was the only kid around who didn't use the usual terms for her parents.

"That wouldn't have flown at my house," Darcy said, her smile now looking genuine and relaxed. "So what did you say to your mom?"

"I said I'd been thinking about dating, but hadn't done anything. But then she said, 'We were wondering if you were starting to be interested in girls or boys.' Could have knocked me over with a feather!"

"Did you admit how you felt about Kimberly?"

"Of course. My mom asked. That meant she wanted to know."

"Amazing," Darcy said, rolling her eyes. "I couldn't admit that when I was thirty."

"Different situations," Tess reminded her. "My mom said that's what they'd guessed. Then she told me that not all girls would feel the same way, and that I should dip my toes in the water before I made a play."

"Did you take her advice?"

"Of course not. The next time I saw Kimberly I told her I thought we should be together, and she acted like I'd asked her to commit a double murder. It took me three long years to find a willing victim."

"At fifteen?" Darcy stopped and stared, wide-eyed. "I didn't get my first crack at a woman until I was twenty-one!"

"Late bloomer," Tess teased, while taking Darcy's arm and tucking it under her own.

"I was plenty bloomed. But I didn't have the nerve to ask anyone out. I dated guys … just to not look like a complete loser … and finally, *finally* a woman showed some interest in me."

"I don't get it. You're pretty as the day is long, you've got a great personality, and you're as nice as pie. Nicer, actually. Pie's jealous of you."

"Maybe I sensed that it wouldn't go over too big with my mom. Or maybe I was just too shy to make the first move. Either way, I could buy a drink in a bar before I had my first meaningful kiss."

"Have you ever made the first move with a woman?"

"Uhm …" She smiled, looking a little embarrassed. "No. I've had three girlfriends and each one basically told me we were going to start dating."

Tess squeezed her arm. "Play your cards right and you might make it four in a row."

After stopping at a medical supplies store for several new products to conquer the sleeping problem, they went back to their room. Darcy was dragging a little, so Tess set her up with the wedge pillow they'd bought, then went down to the parlor to write to her parents while Darcy took a nap.

It was hard to figure out exactly what to say. They didn't expect to hear from her for another three weeks, but if there was a glimmer of a chance the mob knew about her, she couldn't keep this a secret.

Tess couldn't imagine how she'd feel if her daughter wrote to tell her she was on the lam with a suspected murderer. But her parents were such anti-government, anti-authority hippies that she figured they'd give her the benefit of the doubt. What she wouldn't tell them though, was that Darcy had kidnapped her. That would be, in their terms, "not cool," and she didn't want them to dislike Darcy before they had the chance to meet her.

Tess sat in the sunny living room, watching a fire crackle in the stone fireplace. It was strange to think of taking Darcy to meet her parents, but she could somehow see it in her mind. Darcy would be nervous, of course, and she wouldn't know what to make of them. But she'd try hard to make them like her, and Tess knew she'd be successful. She was as likable as a basket of puppies.

The living room was nice, but with no one to talk with, Tess grew bored. After heading back upstairs, she poked her head in the room to find Darcy sound asleep. Her lips were lifted into a half-smile, and she seemed as peaceful as she had at any time since her injury. Assuming she'd be out for a long time, Tess got her coat and went out shopping. Darcy hadn't brought her pajamas, and she really did seem to prefer wearing them. Her long underwear probably made her feel too exposed. After poking around in every store in the pedestrian mall, just wasting time, Tess made one last stop, then raced back to the B&B. When she entered the room, Darcy was still asleep, but the creaking of the door woke her. "What …?"

"Shh," Tess soothed. "Go back to sleep if you can."

"The sun's setting," she grumbled. "How long have I been out?"

"A few hours. But that's okay." She slid off her coat, sat on the edge of the bed and stroked Darcy's head. "Close your eyes. Come on. Keep them closed."

"But I don't want to sleep the day away. You'll be bored if you don't have someone to talk to."

"Shh." Tess knew she could knock her out again with just a little more comforting.

Darcy was right, of course. Tess would much rather have her awake and talking. But now she could drink the cocoa she'd brought for Darcy guilt-free. Not a terrible trade-off.

When Darcy finally woke it took a long time for her to get back to her normal sharp self.

"I don't do well with long naps," she said, her eyes still droopy, "but it felt so good to be at that angle I couldn't make myself wake up. It probably didn't hurt that I'm less worried about being arrested too. Best nap I've had in a week." She patted her belly. "If I hadn't been so hungry, I might have slept through the night."

"You're trying to make up for a week's worth of sleep deprivation. That's gonna take a while."

"I guess. Uhm, I'd rather not risk taking the car out if we don't have to. Do you mind walking to find dinner?"

"Not a bit. I've checked the whole town out, and it's pretty sleepy. I guess people don't flock here when the birds are scarce." She paused, waiting for Darcy to catch her pun. Nothing. She was *really* out of it.

Darcy was so groggy, she easily accepted Tess's offer to help her dress. *That* was new. Especially since they'd talked about Tess's growing attraction. The poor thing was too tired to remember how nervous she'd been just a few hours earlier.

After a longish walk, they found a little place that looked inviting, and when Tess saw it specialized in Italian food, it got her vote.

"Are you Italian?" Darcy asked. "You sure do seem to like their food."

"Half German, half English/Scottish mix. Not a drop of Italian blood. But I could eat Italian food for every meal. No problem."

"I like it too," Darcy admitted, "but I grew up in an area where every other restaurant was Italian. I had so much of it that I search out different things when I can."

"I doubt your sincerity when you say you want difference. You turned up your nose when I told you about my Japanese meals."

"I think my different and your different are different," Darcy said, smiling a little.

No one came to their table, and every time Tess tried to make eye contact with a server they looked away. "I think your black eye and the scratches on your face are freaking people out," she said. "You're so good looking they probably feel like I would if someone knocked the arm off a gorgeous statue."

Darcy looked up, a shy but interested look on her face.

"I'm telling you. If you weren't so damned good looking we wouldn't have this problem," Tess said, frowning playfully. She reached across the table and gently patted Darcy's cheek. "Lucky for me you don't have 'pretty girl' syndrome."

"I can't wait to hear what that is." Darcy dropped her chin into her braced hand. "I'm all ears."

"Pretty girl syndrome is when a woman looks great, knows it, and wants you to remind her every two minutes that she's the best-looking woman in the room. When pretty girls don't get constant praise, they're miserable. But no matter how much you praise them, they're still always checking out the competition."

"It sounds like you've been intimately involved with a sufferer."

"Yeah. The girlfriend before Sam. She was a big pain in the butt." She let out a laugh. "But she sure was pretty."

A gangly-looking teenager came over and gave them hesitant glances. "Do you need menus?"

Tess gazed at him, puzzled. "Well, I could just tell you what I'd like to eat and see if you have it, but I bet we'd save time if we looked at menus." He handed them over, then scampered away. "They're treating us like we're from outer space."

Darcy gave the kid a look, then turned her attention back to Tess. "Have you had many girlfriends?" Her eyes grew wide. "I'm not asking about anything intimate, of course. I'm just interested in you."

"I don't mind." She looked into Darcy's inquisitive gaze. "How many have you had? Total."

"Three."

"Then that's how many I've had." She took a sip of her water, then folded her hands primly in front of herself.

Darcy grinned, shaking her head. "Why do I get the feeling you're lying?"

"I learned this lesson long ago. If you've got fewer than the person you're dating, they worry that you're a loser. If you've got more, they might think you're a slut. So I always try to figure out the other woman's number and get really close to it if she asks."

"Uhm … you just told me your trick. I don't think tricks are effective when you've stated you use them. And … are we dating?"

Tess waved her hand in the air. "You're not the type to judge me, so I can be honest. And, yes, I think we are."

"Interesting. Do I want to date?"

Tess smiled at how cute Darcy looked when she asked questions like this. As though she was genuinely curious about her own thoughts and actions. "Yes, you do. You've been single a long time. It's time to get back in dating shape, and I think I can help."

"I think I've always been out of shape when it comes to dating."

"Then we've got work to do." She reached over and took Darcy's hand. "We're in a strange position here. It's like we're on vacation, but we both know that's not so. One of these days you're going to get your life back—and I'll get mine back too."

"Mmm, the way you say that makes it sound like that'll be it between us. Our dating life might last one day."

"That's true," Tess said, trying to take the sting out of her cold assessment. "I travel for a living, Darcy. There isn't much opportunity for a nomad CPA, is there?"

"Not that I've heard of. So … you're not considering settling down … maybe in Brooklyn … with a nice woman who wants her girlfriend home for dinner every night?"

"I don't mean to brag about my perceptive nature, but that's just what I thought you wanted. And no, that's not me. I love what I do, and I have no interest in stopping."

Darcy looked down at their linked hands. "I had a feeling that was true. But … you'd still like to date?"

"We already *are* dating," Tess said. "And I see no reason to stop before we have to."

Darcy wasn't as amenable to accepting help in getting undressed as she'd been in getting dressed. That had clearly been an anomaly—probably because she was groggy.

Tess had to remind herself to give her some space. The woman definitely had a modest nature. But what they discussed earlier was absolutely true. Tess had been careful not to state the obvious while they were at the restaurant—they might only have a few days together. Of course, there was a chance Darcy might get a pass from the DA, but it was much more likely that she'd be arrested … or worse. It seemed silly to let too many days pass if they could be enjoying each other physically. You had to take pleasure when and where you found it.

Darcy emerged from the bathroom, wearing the new red plaid flannel pajamas Tess had bought her earlier in the day. Damn, she was a pretty woman. Even roomy pajamas didn't hide her many attractive features.

"Ready for bed?" Tess asked.

"I'm ready to try, I guess. I'm not too tired, given my long nap, but I do need sleep."

"Come on then." Tess patted the bed. "I'll help you in." She took Darcy's arm and supported her while she sat, then Tess hoisted her legs in. "Okay?"

"Yeah, I'm good," she said, giving Tess a grateful smile that warmed her heart.

"Be right back." She went into the bathroom and put on her long underwear top, then brushed and flossed her teeth. When she emerged, Darcy was wide awake.

"I'm not sure I can even try to sleep. I might keep you up with my fidgeting. Should I get dressed and go downstairs?"

"Don't be silly. I go right back to sleep when you wake me up. And even if you're not sleeping, you've got to be more comfortable in bed than you would be on those stiff Victorian pieces they have in the parlor."

"That's true. I'll just lie here quietly. Maybe tomorrow we can buy some books to keep me occupied when I'm awake in the middle of the night."

Tess got into bed and lay on her side, facing Darcy. "We'll do whatever you want." She gentled her voice and put her hand on Darcy's belly, gently rubbing it. "Can you feel how fond I am of you?"

Darcy nodded, looking more skittish by the moment.

"This is more than attraction, even though I'm very, very attracted to you." She scooted over a little more, her hand gently moving. "I care about you. And I'm so sorry you're hurt. I hate to see you in pain." She moved so their heads were close together, then kissed her cheek. "I hope we're able to get closer. I'd really like to." She moved again and lay down, leaving a respectful distance. Gazing at Darcy's profile in the dim light, she knew she was making the right decision by taking it slow. Darcy didn't seem like the type to have a true fling. Even though she was tempted, Tess wasn't going to push things until she knew her better. On top of every other pain, she wasn't going to take a nick out of her heart.

"Goodnight."

Stunned, Darcy lay there, looking down at Tess from her elevated position. Last night they'd cuddled. *Then* Tess admitted she was gay. *Then* that she was interested. *Then* that they were dating! So why were they lying with inches and inches of space between them? They were going backwards! And what was that comment about waiting to see if they could get closer? They could get closer right that minute!

But even though she longed to burst from her usual wait and see tactic, Darcy didn't have the guts. She hoped that she'd measure up to whatever standard Tess wanted to achieve before they could get closer. But how could you reach a goal when you had no idea what it was?

CHAPTER EIGHT

AFTER BREAKFAST THE NEXT day, they went out for their morning constitutional. Once again they were the only people out on the boardwalk. Apparently, people didn't like to go to the shore when it was fifteen degrees and cloudy. Tess noticed that Darcy was walking with more confidence. She seemed able to move pretty well at the start of the day, but as the day went on, her energy lagged. Tess wanted her to keep up a good pace, since expanding your lungs was supposed to help insure you didn't get pneumonia. That was the *last* thing they needed. Getting caught because of illness would have sucked bad.

As they walked along, Tess said, "Tell me about your life before your mom got sick. I don't have much of an image of you as a hot, young CPA."

She gave Tess a wry smile. She clearly didn't have pretty girl syndrome. "I was young, but the hot part is purely personal perspective." She paused. "I was …"—her brow furrowed—"I was closer to my mom than I should have been when I was young. She was clearly my mom, not just my friend, but neither one of us had many outside friends. When she was home, we spent time together."

"Who watched you when she wasn't home?"

"Day care. A lady in our neighborhood watched a bunch of kids. She was pretty nice, but her own kids were older and didn't want to play with me."

"You were with her for years?"

"Uh-huh. Until I went to school. But she never watched a kid I clicked with. They always seemed to be the wrong age."

"I spent a lot of time with my parents too. But I had some pals who lived pretty close. And I made more when I joined some clubs and played soccer."

"Not me. I didn't have time for friends. I was either in school, taking a class or hanging out with my mom." Her furrowed brow grew more prominent. "If I'd had kids, I wouldn't have done that. Kids need to be with other kids. Just playing, not learning every minute."

"I'm with you on that. My parents let me have a ton of autonomy. I never felt like they depended on me to hang out with."

Darcy seemed a little bristly when she spoke. "I'm not criticizing my mom. At all. But she worked a whole lot and when she was free, she wanted to spend her time with me. I got a lot from being with her so much. But … by the time I was ready for college, I knew I needed a little space. So I lived in the dorm at Rutgers, even though we only lived about a half hour away."

"Could your mom afford that?"

"I cobbled together a few little scholarships and some grants. And Rutgers is a state school. It wasn't too bad." She cleared her throat, probably embarrassed to admit she'd won scholarships. "After I graduated, I'd fallen in love. But I didn't want to face the music and tell my mom. So I stayed at Rutgers for another year and got my masters in accounting. By then, my girlfriend had moved on to greener pastures—"

"Not possible," Tess interrupted. "You're as green as grass."

A slight blush colored her cheeks. "I was very, very tentative back then. Always worried about what other people thought. Olivia wanted someone more forceful. She tried to change me, but I was a hopeless case."

"I bet she'd kick herself if she saw you today," Tess said, meaning the compliment sincerely.

"Yeah, I'm at my best right now." Darcy laughed. "Damn, I can't even laugh without feeling it."

156

"Tell me more about your golden youth. I'm getting a better picture of you."

"It's not very exciting," she warned. "I studied a lot in college, then worked a lot once I got my license. My second girlfriend came and went because I worked too hard. Then I met Emily. I was doing well at the firm, I could afford to fix up my apartment, and I was able to take Emily into the city—to go to plays and out to special restaurants. My mom was already sick at that point, but we thought it was something they could cure. But even then Emily wanted to help. To share my life rather than be stuck in the closet. That was the biggest mistake I've ever made," she said quietly. "I lost someone I cared for because I was too worried about my mom's reaction."

"You must have been pretty sure it wouldn't have gone well."

"Pretty sure. The TV was on Fox News all the time and she agreed with most of what they had to say. She particularly hated it when any group wanted what she called 'special rights.' But I can't be certain she would have reacted badly. I sure didn't give her a chance."

"That's water under the bridge. From now on you can be yourself."

"I was starting to be myself back then. I had a fire in my belly to be good at my job as well as a good partner. Emily and I even talked about having kids. I hardly recognize myself now."

She turned her head and met Tess's eyes, her sadness nearly glowing in its intensity. "I squandered my youth, and I don't mean by taking care of my mom. It wouldn't have been nearly so bad if I'd brought in other people to help. Emily offered repeatedly, some of my mom's co-workers did too, and her cousin was ready to move from Long Island to live with us. But I was locked into doing it all, mostly because my mom was skittish about letting people see her when she wasn't at her best. I chose to give up my girlfriend, my social network, my job … everything that gave me pleasure. Now I feel like I've got very little left."

Tess stopped her and put both hands on her shoulders. "Nothing could be further from the truth. You might not see it, Darcy, but you're an awesome woman. You're kind and thoughtful and smart and pretty. Did I mention pretty? 'Cause that's the most important thing." She gently wrapped her arms around her and kissed her chilled cheeks, putting as much feeling into the embrace as she could. "You know I'm teasing. It's your sweet soul that's most compelling."

"I've never been hugged in public," Darcy said, not even trying to move away. "By someone I'm dating, that is."

"Super! I want to be with you when you experience all sorts of firsts. All of them good."

"Don't get your heart set on feeding me eyeballs and organs," Darcy said, her eyes glittering in the winter sun. "That's not gonna happen."

On the way home, they stopped in the local post office, where Tess dashed in to pick up forms to have their mail held at their local post offices. Leave it to Darcy to think of something like that. And to have thought of all of the possible repercussions from filling out the forms, but finding none of any significance.

Once they returned to the B&B, Tess set Darcy up in front of the computer in the parlor. "No one comes in here during the day. You can spend a good, long time poking around, trying to find your father."

Darcy looked up, clearly surprised. "Do I want to find my father?"

"You do." Tess leaned over and kissed her head. "No more secrets. If he's alive, you deserve to know him. Now get busy." She ruffled her hair and started for their room. "I'm going to write a piece on Cape May on spec. Maybe I can make a few bucks off this little detour."

Not ten minutes later, Darcy trudged up the stairs, a gnawing feeling in her gut. The dread didn't ease even when she saw Tess's sunny smile as she looked up from her computer.

"What's wrong?"

"Is it that obvious?"

"Yeah. Now what's wrong?" Tess was beside her, looking into her eyes.

"While I was on the internet I went over to *The Times*. There was a story, posted today, saying that Harry's wife tried to get his body released for an independent autopsy."

"That's great!" Tess was beaming a grin. "That means she either believes you or has doubts that you killed him."

"Yeah, yeah, I guess that part's good. The bad part is that the coroner's office said they made a mistake and cremated him."

"Oh, shit!" Tess sank to the love-seat, like her legs couldn't hold her up. "That means the coroner's office is dirty too."

"It sure does look like it. If the mob and the cops and the coroner's office are all conspiring against me …"

"Fuck." Tess dropped her head into her hands. "I'm so sorry, Darcy. I kept hoping this was an isolated few guys."

"That's what I hoped for too. But it's a little hard to believe the coroner's office cremated a murder victim by accident."

Tess looked up, her expression a little brighter. "True. But if they don't have a body, that's not going to look good when they're trying to make a case against you, right? Won't they have to admit they cremated him before your side could have an expert dispute the findings?"

"Yeah, I guess that's true. But they've got the coroner's report, which obviously says I did it."

"True. But if I were on that jury and they tried to convince me they just made a simple clerical mistake—I'd smell a rat."

Darcy couldn't stop herself from laughing, even through her anxiety. "I love it when you talk like we're in an old gangster movie."

"Speaking of gangsters, why don't you call your uncle and see if he's got any fresh info on ours."

"Good idea. I'm sure he read the news today." She dialed his disposable phone and he answered on the second ring.

"I've been hoping you'd call," he said, sounding relieved.

159

"I guess you read the news?"

"Wish I hadn't, but, yeah. I was hoping just a few guys had turned bad but …"

"It's more than a few," Darcy agreed. "But when I was thinking about it, I decided it might not be too many guys."

"How do you figure that?"

"It's like having a dirty referee in a football game. You've got twenty-two guys playing the game straight-up, but just one can make it crooked. I'm hoping that's true here. That there are only a few key guys screwing up the whole place."

"I'm more than willing to hope for the best."

Darcy looked at Tess's anxious features and forced herself to ask the question that had been nagging at her. "Any word on Sergei?"

"Nothing. I obviously can't ask, but no one's mentioned him."

"Is that good news or bad news?"

"It's good news. If they'd connected him to you or Tess, they'd be over here questioning me. That's one sleeping dog I'm happy to let lie."

The internet was a pretty amazing tool. In just two days of searching, Darcy thought she had her man. It took a good amount of digging, but she'd found a photo of the graduating class of her mom's law school for the year she should have graduated. There were, surprisingly, two Benjamins in the class, but only one had her cheekbones, her deep-set eyes and her coloring.

With shaking hands, she looked further, finding that Benjamin Miller was alive and well and practicing commercial law in Manhattan.

Once again, Darcy went upstairs, this time nervous about good news. But Tess couldn't tell the difference. "What's wrong?" she demanded the minute Darcy entered.

"I think I found him. I'll show you his photo and you can tell me if you think my guess is right."

"Okay," Tess soothed, gently stroking Darcy's cheek. "You sure don't look happy."

"I am. I guess. But I don't know what to do now."

"You call him!"

"Oh, no, I couldn't do that. That's too abrupt. Too fast. I couldn't." She moved away from the disposable phone, as though it would jump into her hand and dial itself.

"Come on, Darcy. You've wanted to know who your dad was since you were a child. Don't waste time! You never know when …"

"I'm not *that* old. He's still practicing if this is the right guy."

"I wasn't implying that he'd drop dead of old age. But you know you can't predict how long someone will be around. You've got the chance. You've got to take it."

"I'll … think about it. First I want you to look at the photo and make sure you agree. Then I'll … think about it."

They were sitting in their room that afternoon, and Tess was itching to do something—anything.

"Helen told me about a Christmas Parade in town, and I think we should go."

"I don't think that's—"

"I know you don't want to be in a crowd, but when you're out and about you move more easily. I think walking around takes your mind off your pain."

"It's been ten days and I'm still miserable," Darcy grumbled. Her mood had turned dark, and Tess was sure they'd both perk up if they went out.

"Let's walk over to where the parade starts. If there are too many people, or you're not feeling it, we'll go have an early dinner."

"Dinner," she groused. "I'm so sick of having to eat every meal in a restaurant. Everything's covered in butter or sauce. And they cook the life out of every vegetable."

"Come on," Tess urged, sticking out a hand. "Let me help you up. After the parade, I promise we'll get something you really want for dinner."

"I want some vegetables that still look like they did not long after they were pulled from the ground." She glared at Tess. "Find me a place where I can have that, and I'll be happy."

"That's a tall order ... but I can do it."

Once they were dressed warmly, they started to walk. Tess held Darcy's arm, just to give her a little confidence along the dark streets. So many inns were decorated with tiny white lights that the sidewalks seemed darker than usual. They'd only gone a few blocks when Tess heard a sniffling sound. She looked over, surprised and dismayed to see tears running down Darcy's cheeks. "Do you hurt that bad? We can go home right now."

"No," she murmured. "It's ... it's ..." Her eyes closed tightly and she stopped to wipe her eyes. "I miss my mom. I've been thinking about her all day and"—she sucked in a breath—"it's hard. She really loved Christmas, and not being with her or even at home ..." Another shaky breath seemed to hurt her ribs. She grabbed at them and pressed for a second. "I feel so rootless."

"I'm so sorry," Tess soothed. She reached up and captured a few tears with her gloved hand. "I know it's hard for you. You're in pain, you don't have any of your routines, and you've got to get through the holidays alone."

"Yeah," Darcy said, nodding. "I feel all alone."

"But you're not." Tess held her hand firmly. "You've got me."

"No, I don't." She sniffled harder. "You're just here until I'm caught or turn myself in."

Tess grasped her arms and looked deeply into her eyes. "You should know this better than most, Darcy. Every relationship is temporary. We might have a few days, a few weeks, or even longer. But we can't *guarantee* either of us will be here tomorrow. I know this is hard, but try, just try to focus on the moment."

"That's not what I do," she admitted. "I'm always planning, thinking about the future."

"You can't control the future. But you can truly experience the present." She closed her eyes, tilted her head back and took in a deep breath. "Do you smell that? Fireplaces, fir trees, maybe a hint of snow about to fall. Let your senses open up. Experience the now." She touched Darcy's cheek, removing the last of her tears. "I know that sounds pretty New Age, but it works. If you're in the present, you don't have as much room in your head for thinking of the past or the future. The moment you're in takes up your mind."

Darcy closed her eyes and took in a deep breath. "I smell something savory being cooked." She sniffed the air for a few seconds. "I think it's coming from that house."

"This is fun," Tess decided. "Let's see what we can smell as we walk."

"I'll be good at this. My sense of smell is really sharp."

Tess took her hand as they started to walk. "It's not a competition. No winners or losers. Just focus on this moment and experience it through scent."

"That was some kind of stew," Darcy said, nodding towards the house they'd just passed. "Makes me hungry."

"I've got dinner covered. And I guarantee you're going to like it."

Darcy slid her hand up to grip Tess's arm. "Sorry about earlier. I don't get grouchy very often, but when I do it can be bad."

"You've got plenty to be grouchy about, so you get a pass."

"Thanks. I do feel better being outside, even though it's cold."

"Do you think the air smells different when it's cold?"

Darcy seemed to consider her answer. "You know, I think it does. I wonder why?"

163

Tess snuggled closer. She could almost see Darcy's dark mood lift. *Success!*

The Christmas Parade was remarkably charming. Everything about it was perfectly representative of a small town, from the fire trucks lavishly decorated with lights to groups of kids dressed in Christmassy costumes. Darcy's mood continued to climb, and within fifteen minutes she was excitedly pointing out every cute tyke who wandered past. "I love this," she said, her bright smile making her look completely carefree. "I'm so thankful you forced me to come."

"Forced you, huh?" Tess tucked an arm around her and gave her a very gentle hug, making sure she didn't squeeze any broken part.

"Encouraged me," Darcy amended. "I need to be outside as much as I can be, and being around kids always makes me happy. This was a perfect combination."

The parade didn't last long, and Darcy stared into the distance as the last group moved down the street. "I almost jumped in with that church group dressed in Victorian era clothes. I think I could have fit in with this coat."

Tess took her arm to help protect her from the jostling crowd as they dispersed into the street. "Have you ever been in a parade?"

"Yeah. A couple of times. My town had a Fourth of July parade and different groups I was in as a kid would march."

"No Pride parades?"

Darcy frowned as she turned her head to gaze at Tess. "You're kidding, right?"

"No. Why would I kid about that?"

"I must not have made myself clear. I wasn't out to my family. Or at my job. I never could have marched in a parade." Her expression slowly changed into a grin. "But I bet you have. Probably dozens of them."

"Not dozens," she demurred. "My favorite is still the first one I went to. In Eugene when I was about sixteen."

"That's really young. How'd your parents feel about you doing that."

She thought about that for a moment. "I don't think they knew. I met a girl who was going to UO, and she took me."

"A girl from your town?"

"Uh-huh. Well, not my exact town, but close enough. Willow was my first real girlfriend."

Darcy smiled. "An older woman, huh?"

"Yeah. I'd gotten a few local girls to fool around, but no one wanted to pair up. Willow was actually gay."

Darcy stopped abruptly, forcing a few people to move around them. "What were the girls who fooled around with you?" Darcy looked around, realized she was inconveniencing people, and pulled Tess over to the sidewalk.

"Straight, I guess." She shrugged. "Slightly open-minded. I don't really know."

"But they agreed to make-out with you?"

"A few. Yeah. If you ask enough, you're going to get a yes once in a while. My batting average sucked when I was a kid, but I'd bet I was hitting .300 by the time I was in college."

Darcy's mouth dropped open. "You're saying that you asked girls— girls you didn't know to be gay—to kiss you?"

Laughing, Tess said, "I wasn't that blunt. You scare people off if you make it into a big deal. I'd just go for it."

"You'd *go* for it?" Darcy looked like she'd taken a thunk to the head.

"Yeah. You know what I mean. I'd be talking to a girl at a party or in a car and I'd go for a kiss. Once in a while, I wouldn't get pushed away." She laughed harder, thinking of how many times she'd gotten shot down. "That's what guys do, right?"

They started walking again, with Darcy continuing to give her puzzled sidelong glances. "No discussion? No trying to make sure she was gay too?"

"Oh, god no! I never would have gotten a kiss if I'd asked. This was more than fifteen years ago, Darcy. Girls weren't as open-minded as they are now."

"And you didn't mind having them reject you?"

"Of course I minded. I wouldn't have tried to kiss a girl I wasn't interested in. But I never let that stop me."

"I'm …" She looked absolutely stunned. "I wouldn't do that today, much less when I was fifteen."

"Why not? You can't have what you want if you don't ask." She slipped her arm more tightly around Darcy's. "My tactic was to get the rejection out of the way as soon as possible. Then I didn't have to worry about it."

"Good god," Darcy said, sighing heavily. "If I added up all of the hours I've spent longing for women I was afraid to approach … I could have learned a new language with the time I wasted."

"No way. I like the interval between desire and action to be as short as possible. If you ask before you're invested, the rejection doesn't even register."

"I'd give a lot to have just a little bit of your nerve."

"I'd give you some if it was transferable," Tess said, truly wishing that were possible.

They stopped at a small grocery store, with Tess confidently moving up and down the aisles, mumbling to herself. "Worst spice selection I've ever seen. Only one kind of curry powder."

"Maybe it's not native to New Jersey."

Tess turned and stared, then chuckled. "You got me. I thought you were serious."

"What are we going to do with curry powder? Drink it?"

"No," she said, carefully scanning the racks of spices. "We're going to make dinner. I just have to figure out what I can make given how few things this store has."

166

Darcy looked at the racks, seeing every spice she'd ever used. They were obviously going to be making something unique … using a heat source yet to be named.

As soon as they returned to the B&B, Tess tossed off her coat, letting it land on the dining table. Then she pushed open the door to the kitchen with her hip. Darcy followed, tentatively. "Are we allowed to be in here?"

"Sure." Tess turned on the lights and opened the cabinets under the stove. "I told Helen that you had all sorts of food allergies and were a strict vegan. She said I could use the kitchen, so long as I cleaned it up when I was finished."

"You just … asked?"

Tess winked at her. "They can't say no if you don't ask." She chuckled softly. "I don't know what I was thinking when I was looking for Indian spices. They'd kill me if this place smelled like garam masala in the morning."

Darcy took off her coat and glove, then folded everything and settled it on a stool. "What can I do to help?"

"Mmm …" Tess looked at her. "Not much. You pretty much need two hands to cook." She started to pull the items she'd bought from the bags. "I've missed cooking. This'll be fun."

"Given how your kitchen cabinets looked, I assumed you didn't know how to make toast."

"Don't mean to brag," Tess said, a confident grin covering her face. "But I'm a good cook. I can take whatever you've got in the refrigerator and make a meal out of it."

"I don't think I've ever eaten a pomegranate, and I don't even know what that big bulblike thing is, but I'm very willing to eat anything you come up with."

"This is fennel," Tess said, picking it up and waving it in Darcy's face. "And you're going to love it." Darcy watched, transfixed, as Tess

167

quickly assembled a salad with orange slices, arugula, pomegranate seeds and slices of fennel. By the time Tess added a light orange-based dressing, Darcy's mouth was watering.

"That's the freshest thing I've seen in ten days," she said.

Tess had made a big bowl of the salad, and she stuck a fork into it, spearing a bit of everything. "Taste." She put the fork near Darcy's lips and smiled when her work was greeted with an appreciative moan.

"That's soooo good!"

"Good balance? Not too tart?"

"No, no, it's perfect."

"I like to have a little sweet, a little savory, a little tart and a little spice in everything I make. This is a little light on the spice, but I think the balance is good."

"Very, very good. I've been citrus deprived." Darcy took the fork and put another big bite into her mouth. "I'm claiming this. What are you going to eat?"

"Given that you wanted a vegetable that looks like its former self, I was going to make another salad. Roasted beets over some chèvre, walnuts, tarragon, a bit of oil and red wine vinegar. Want me to eat that?"

"No, I want that too. I love beets." She reached into her pocket to extract her wallet. "I'll give you twenty bucks. You can go get a hamburger."

Tess grabbed her nose and tugged. "I know you think I just eat junk, but I really don't. I love a good vegetable as much as the next woman. But if they're not good, I'd rather get a hamburger. An uninspired burger tastes better than bland, overcooked carrots any day of the week."

"There's nothing uninspired about this meal," Darcy insisted, her dark mood now completely evaporated. "Or you, for that matter."

They stayed down in the parlor for a long time after dinner, enjoying the fireplace. "If I ever have a real house," Tess said, "I want a fireplace."

"You didn't have one growing up?"

"No, we didn't have that kind of house. We had bonfires, though. My uncle Rick is almost a pyromaniac."

"I don't know much about your extended family. Is it large?"

"Biological? No. My dad has a sister, but we're not close. Our family of choice is big, though. It was a rare night that we didn't have a few people over for dinner."

"Really? I thought you lived way out in the sticks."

"We did. But that didn't stop people from dropping by."

"Mmm, that sounds like fun. It was just me and my mom unless we did something formal, like a birthday party."

"Not at my house." Tess chuckled softly. "My mom would make enough for ten. I used to wish more people would show up so I didn't have to eat the same thing for lunch all week."

"These were just what … neighbors?"

"Some. But also people passing through. Our close friends knew where we stashed a key. If we weren't home, they'd just come in and wait."

"People would be at your house when you were gone?"

"Uh-huh. If we were out trekking, we could have people there for a few days or a week."

"I'm … stunned. Even my grandparents didn't come over unless they were invited. My mom didn't like to be surprised."

"My parents thrive on surprise, but the bigger issue was being hospitable. You know, when I think of it, from the time I was a little kid, I was taught that you opened your home to people who needed it."

"I guess we did the same. My mom didn't hesitate to take my grandparents in."

169

"That was nice of her. And you, of course. We didn't take in any family members, but my parents always stressed that people didn't have to be related to you to have them be members of your family. I've got two aunts and three uncles who are like second parents to me."

"I wish I had that," Darcy said, feeling the longing sharply. "I just have my uncle."

"You can expand that," Tess said as she reached over and took Darcy's hand. "I've made friends all over the world. People I know I can rely on." She turned Darcy's hand and kissed the back of it. "You can rely on me."

Touched and unable to speak, Darcy just nodded. "You can rely on me too."

"I already do."

They went upstairs, and Darcy got ready for bed first. Tess spent a few minutes in the bathroom brushing her teeth and putting on some moisturizer. When she opened the door, Darcy was standing at the bookcase just a few feet away. As Tess started to move past her, Darcy put out a hand, stopping her.

Suddenly, the air was charged like a thunderstorm was about to break. Darcy moved to stand right in front of her, then put her hands on Tess's waist. It felt funny to have the casted hand on her hip, but the bare hand was gentle and warm through Tess's silk top. She almost spoke, but when she saw the determination in Darcy's eyes, she held her tongue.

Slowly, Darcy pulled her closer, then tilted her head and placed a soft but meaningful kiss to her lips. Tess nearly cheered for her. This was the first time in her life Darcy had made the first move, but now wasn't the time to make a big deal about that. They could talk later.

As they broke apart, Darcy stayed close. "Is this … okay?"

"You shouldn't ask that," Tess said, a quiet laugh bubbling up. "Just do what you want and see if it flies." She almost bit her tongue. Darcy wasn't asking for dating advice, she was making a move! Her first, no less.

It was like the reins had fallen from a spirited horse. Darcy immediately increased the pressure of her kisses, pushing so forcefully into Tess's body that she was soon backed up against the wall. It took her a second to get used to this new, assertive Darcy, but she wanted to know her well and soon. Gently, the soft tongue tickling Tess's lips chased sensation up her spine. Even though Darcy didn't have experience in making the first move, she knew how to kiss. Really well. Tess opened her mouth and growled when Darcy's tongue entered.

Thoughts started to flood her mind, interrupting her growing desire. She wasn't a hundred percent sure they were on the same page, and she had to be sure in order to let go. Purposefully pulling away, she put her hand on Darcy's cheek and looked into her eyes. "Are you sure this is the day you want to start having casual sex?"

Surprisingly, Darcy didn't falter. "This is the perfect day," she said firmly. "I promised myself I was going to be more experimental this year. It's time to start."

"Sure?" She searched Darcy's calm gaze for any sign of doubt.

With a teasing smile, Darcy said, "You're being a little presumptuous. Does every kiss lead to sex?"

"With *those* kinds of kisses?" She chuckled. "Yes."

"I'm nervous," Darcy admitted. "Can you tell?"

Anyone could tell. The hand on Tess's hip was trembling, and Darcy's breathing was much faster than normal, like it was when they were walking at a really good pace. But no one wanted to hear that they seemed nervous. Tess's protective instincts took over. "My heart's racing. That's all I know." She took Darcy's hand and put it over her heart. "Feel that?"

Darcy's mouth was open slightly when she nodded. "Yeah." Then her arms tightened around Tess's waist once again and she caught her lips in another searing kiss.

As the seconds passed, Darcy's nervousness seemed to evaporate. Her movements grew much more decisive, more focused. Tess could feel her start to act like she probably did when she knew a lover well—and this more surefooted Darcy was making her heart really race.

Possessively, Darcy grasped her face with her good hand and held her still as she hungrily devoured her, letting out a low purr that gave Tess goose bumps. "Your body is …" She looked like she'd been hit on the head. "I've never been so attracted to a woman." Her hand slid up Tess's side, and as it brushed against her breast, Darcy let out a whimper.

Grasping it, Tess pressed it against her flesh, smiling in satisfaction when Darcy's kisses grew even more fervid.

Slowly, Darcy started to back her up, moving towards the bed. When the backs of Tess's legs hit the frame, she said, "Let me help you get into bed." After guiding her to her preferred side, Tess urged Darcy to sit, then lifted her legs and swung them onto the bed. While extending an arm for Darcy to hold onto, Tess gently lowered her to the wedge pillow. "Are you okay?"

"Yeah, I think so." She looked embarrassed, probably at being tended to like a child. Tess's desire plummeted like a stone. If this had been their longstanding routine, she was sure she could keep up her desire while tending to Darcy like a nurse. But this was a swift seduction, all instinct and drive, and both were getting pummeled by having to be so careful.

Tess dashed around to the other side of the bed and climbed in. Being treated like an injured person seemed to dim Darcy's momentum too. She turned to look at Tess intently, but didn't move.

Tess slid her hand up under her pajama top, feeling warm, soft skin. "Are we moving too fast for you?"

Darcy blinked slowly. "No, I think this is my new normal. Warp speed."

"It probably feels just like that for you," Tess soothed. "I don't want to push you. But if you'd like to keep going …" The sheets rustled as she settled onto the big wedge pillow with Darcy. Their faces were just inches apart.

"You're not pushing me," Darcy said. "At all. I want to keep going." But again she didn't move. It seemed like she wasn't quite sure what she could do, how she could move. Trying to keep from hurting herself had to be on her mind constantly.

Tess put her hand on Darcy's cheek and kissed her again, sliding her tongue between moist lips. *Divine.* Was there any sensation better than kissing someone you were very attracted to? Those first kisses were filled with such meaning, such potential. Like the world was theirs to explore together through each other's bodies.

Darcy let out a frustrated grunt as her ungainly left hand tried to pull Tess closer. "Argh! I can't use the left and you've got the right one trapped."

"Just lie there and let me touch you," Tess whispered. "Close your eyes and feel my hand." Her hand slid back under the roomy top as Darcy's eyes closed.

"That feels so good," she murmured. "But I wanted to …" Clearly frustrated, she raked her teeth over her bottom lip. "I can't move like I want to."

Tess pushed her top up and gazed at the huge circle of bruising. With a whisper-soft touch she bent her head and kissed all around the vivid pastel bruises. "I wish I could make you better. I'd do anything to fix this."

"I know." Now that Tess had moved away from her shoulders, Darcy could put her right hand on her back. She stroked her as Tess continued to kiss her belly and side.

"Does this feel good?" Tess asked between kisses. "Not too much pressure?"

"Perfect." Darcy started to giggle. "First time I've felt like laughing when something touches my ribs. I'm a little ticklish."

"How about down here?" Tess lowered her pajama bottoms a few inches, then kissed along the soft skin.

"Not ticklish," Darcy murmured, her voice growing tight.

"Does this turn you on?"

"God, yes." Her eyes opened and she stared at Tess. "Someone I'm really attracted to is kissing some pretty sensitive skin."

Tess chuckled. "That was a rhetorical question. I like to talk during sex, but I don't expect answers."

"Oh." Her brows rose. "I'm not used to talking. But it's … nice. I'll shut up."

"You don't need to. I'm just telling you that you don't have to talk back—unless you want to."

Darcy took her literally, nodding her agreement this time.

"This is going to take some experimenting. You've got so many sore spots, and they're on different sides of your body. Tell me if I hurt you, okay?"

"I will. So far you're doing great. Really great." She took in a breath and seemed to settle down.

Tess took the opportunity to sit up and scoot over to straddle her, now able to use both hands. "I love to kiss breasts," she said as she unbuttoned the top. "I hope you like that too."

"I do." Darcy's voice was higher than normal and it sounded like she was struggling to get out words.

"I'm really, really glad to hear that," Tess said as she put a hand under each breast and hefted it. "Because these are spectacular."

Putting her hands next to Darcy's shoulders, she lowered herself, careful to keep every ounce of her weight off her chest. Then she sucked a hard pink nipple into her mouth, and they both growled in pleasure. "Luscious," she murmured when she pulled back to barely lick the quivering flesh.

174

Darcy was trying to talk, but all she got out was a low moan which sent Tess's arousal up to another level. She had to kiss those beautiful lips again. She straightened up, then leaned in to kiss her. Her eyes widened in surprise when Darcy captured her tongue and suckled on it. *Very* forceful. *Very* nice. But Tess couldn't hold herself up long enough to really do what she wanted. Her entire body craved Darcy's lips and tongue and she had mental images of them rolling around on the bed, devouring each other. But that would have to wait—for months. Months they might not have.

Gently, she disengaged and moved back to lie beside her. Using her hand, she once again rubbed Darcy's body, the skin noticeably hotter than it had been just a few minutes before. Tess longed to see that toned, muscular body laid bare in the golden light. But she couldn't possibly get her clothes off without a production. *Damn the mob!*

Despite all of the impediments, Darcy moaned and whimpered every time Tess's gently moving hand touched a sensitive spot. Finally, she let her hand slip below the fabric and skim along her pubic bone. "Can I touch you? I *really* want to."

"Touch me," she murmured. "I'm so ready for you." Her eyes were smoky with desire, and her beautiful lips were slightly parted. She was the sexiest woman Tess had been close to in a very long time, and that surprised the hell out of her.

There was nothing hotter than a woman who showed how much you affected her, and Darcy wasn't at all shy about that. Tess slid her hand down as Darcy's legs opened. But she whimpered and her eyes snapped shut, with Tess quickly realizing it was from pain rather than pleasure. Holding her legs open like this had to put pressure on her ribs. As quickly as she could, Tess grabbed all of the pillows and stuffed them under Darcy's knees.

"Thank you," she said softly. "That helps a lot."

Cuddling up against her, Tess spent a few minutes kissing Darcy's tender lips. This was *not* the smoothest she'd ever been in bed, but that didn't matter. She wasn't intent on *doing* her. This wasn't even primarily about sex. What she needed was to show Darcy how much she cared for her, and she was confident that was getting through. They continued to kiss and nibble on each other's lips, and after a few minutes Tess slipped her hand down inside Darcy's pants again. The heat radiated from her, and Tess felt a jolt between her own legs as she parted Darcy's swollen skin and let her fingers slide all around her wetness.

"*Jesus*," Darcy whispered as her legs opened even wider.

"You feel so good. So hot. I'm going to touch you until you can't bear it." She suckled on Darcy's tongue while her fingers explored her depths.

Minutes passed, with Tess getting more and more aroused. But Darcy wasn't making the same pleasured noises she'd made at the start. "Are you okay?" Tess asked while nibbling on her ear.

"Yeah." Darcy grunted. "I just can't get into the right position. I'm so turned on, I ache, but I can't get to the next level."

"What can I do? I'll do *anything*," she promised.

"Uhm … your mouth?"

"Great. Love to. Let me at it," Tess said, chuckling. This was the least elegant sex she'd ever been involved in, but it was still a load of fun. She clambered down to sit between Darcy's legs, then tried to pull her pajama bottoms off without Darcy having to lift her hips. She'd probably have rug burns from the fabric rubbing against her butt, but at last she was free. Tess's mouth watered as she looked at her glistening pink skin just waiting for her tongue. She *loved* going down on a woman, and was focused on making Darcy feel just how much she relished the opportunity.

From the first taste, Tess knew they were a match. Something about Darcy's flesh appealed to her at a cellular level. It had happened before, but not often. It was just a damned shame they couldn't really let go.

Both of Darcy's hands settled on Tess's head. The one with the cast couldn't do much, but Darcy clearly needed to touch. Her right hand threaded through Tess's hair, stroking and urging her on as she gently probed all around Darcy's slippery flesh.

Learning a woman's cues was a big part of the fun of sex, and Darcy gave off a ton of them. She kept trying to thrust herself against Tess, but her ribs would not let her. Each time she tried, she let out a yelp of pain. And each cry hurt Tess as well. Listening to someone you cared for moan in pain made you hyper aware of every movement—which wasn't ideal for pleasurable sex.

Tess's tongue had grown heavy and numb when Darcy finally stroked her shoulder. "I can't get there," she said, frustration coloring her words.

Shifting away, Tess took Darcy's hand and settled it between her legs. "Touch yourself. I'll help." She slid her fingers inside, softly asking, "Do you like this?"

"Yes. A lot," she whimpered. "But it's not … right. I can't relax enough to respond the way I want to."

Gently, Tess slipped from her and moved up to cuddle against her side. "I'm so sorry. I didn't want to frustrate you, I wanted to comfort you."

Darcy twitched, then grunted, "Damn! I can't even put my arm around you."

"It's okay. You'll start feeling better soon."

"I'm getting a little cold. Can you cover me up?"

"Sure." Tess reached down, noticing when she did that Darcy had shaved her legs. *That's* why she'd been in the bathroom so long earlier. Apparently they'd both hoped for some connection. She snuggled against her, sharing the wedge pillow. "Are you okay?"

"Yeah, yeah." But even though she claimed to be fine, there were a few lines on her forehead. "I'm just … I'm pissed. I've got a woman who turns me on like I've never been, and I can't even show her how hot she makes me."

"I can tell," Tess assured her. "You're just not well enough yet."

"Parts of me are perfectly fine. I'm sure I could get there ..."

Her cheeks were flushed and Tess guessed it wasn't from arousal. Embarrassment was the more likely culprit. "Do you need some mechanical help?"

Now she was sure of it. Darcy was seriously embarrassed. Her eyes shifted away to look at the darkened window. "I've never ..." Her gaze traveled back to lock on Tess. "I've never talked about this with anyone."

"You can talk to me," Tess said, reaching over to hold Darcy's hand. "You can't shock me. Really. I've been ..." She started to chuckle, even though she tried to stop. "If I admit how hard it is to shock me, you're not going to believe I've only had three lovers."

Darcy's smile seemed to whisk away some of the tension that was making her body stiffer than usual. "You didn't sell that very well in the first place." Taking their linked hands, she brought them to her mouth and kissed Tess's fingers. "I like that you have experience. Really. I'm not judgmental about things like that."

"That's what they all say," Tess teased. "Until I talk about my career in porn. It was fun for a few years, but once I finished *Lusty Lesbians Volume Fifty*, I hung up my strap-on."

Even though she still seemed uncomfortable, Darcy laughed. "I like that you can cheer me up even when I'm tense. *Especially* when I'm tense."

"Come on," Tess urged, putting her hand back onto Darcy's belly and rubbing it soothingly. "Tell me what's stopping you from getting off. Whatever it is, we can figure out a workaround."

"I'm not sure," she said slowly. "I assume it's because I can't truly relax. I need a ... little help to push me over. Your tongue can't replicate what I'm used to."

"Try not to be embarrassed at needing a vibrator, Darcy. I use one too." She pinched her cheek as a memory hit her. "You've seen mine!"

"I know," she said, clearly still flustered. "I'm just not used to talking about things like this."

"It's good to be able to talk about sex. That's the only way to make sure the sex you're having is good." She increased the friction of her hand. "We can practice. Come on."

"All right." Darcy let out a big sigh. "If I had my vibrator I would have had a few dozen orgasms by now." She slammed her eyes shut, then let the right one creep open just enough to meet Tess's gaze. "Can you ever look me in the eye again?"

"You're silly." Tess gave her a quick kiss. "Top this one. When I was about sixteen, I was in the backseat of a car with another girl"—she paused and smiled—"a fire and brimstone minister's daughter."

"Wow," Darcy said, her eyes widening. "You were clearly not risk averse."

"Never have been. Anyway, we were really going at it in her dad's car, and I'd finally gotten her jeans off. I tossed them into the front seat and they must have landed in a weird way. The panic button locked the doors, made the lights flash and set off an alarm."

"You must have wet your pants!" Darcy cried, then added, "You were probably prone to that even then."

Tess slapped at her arm. "Funny girl. So her dad came running out of the house in his underwear, but we were so tangled up it took a minute or two for her to climb in the front seat and get the keys. Her whole family was outside by then, all of them staring at Faith's sweet ass as she slithered between the seats to grab her jeans and turn the darned thing off." She wiped her forehead with the back of her hand. "Thank god I wasn't a year older or Reverend Garland would have been able to convince the sheriff to arrest me for sodomy."

"He called the sheriff?"

"Oh, hell yes! It was a scene. Blue police lights spinning around. Neighbors from all sides clustered at the property line, waiting to see what horrible thing I'd done. My parents had to come get me, and they hadn't known I was even out of the house."

"You snuck out?"

Shrugging, Tess said, "Not technically. I didn't have a curfew or anything. Faith called to say she could sneak out and my parents were in bed … so I just left."

"Oh, my god. My mom would have grounded me until … her death."

"Not mine. They said I should probably stay away from girls whose fathers were nutjobs, but they didn't have another thing to say about it."

Darcy leaned close, whimpered in pain, but managed to remain long enough to place a long kiss on Tess's lips. "Your story made me feel better. Confessing to using a vibrator's pretty small potatoes to having a crowd see you …" She stopped. "Were you dressed?"

"Shirt open. Bra unfastened. Jeans off. Panties off. I might have had my socks on …"

"Of having a crowd see your everything!" Darcy laughed, her eyes closing against the pain of her shaking chest.

"I've been mortally embarrassed many times, Darcy. I'm always going to win this contest." She let her hand slip down, then gently patted between her legs. "Do you *need* a vibrator to come?"

It took her a second to answer, but she finally did. "I didn't know it, but maybe I do."

"You didn't know …?"

"It's been a very long time since a woman's touched me, remember?"

"I do. But you touch yourself, don't you?"

"I'd normally be embarrassed to admit this, but you've probably touched yourself in the Sistine Chapel." She took in a breath and let it out. "All the damned time," she admitted. "For the last eight years I put myself to sleep most nights with a quick orgasm. I kind of soothed myself that way."

"That was probably the only time you had to yourself."

"Just about."

"And you always used a vibrator?"

Darcy seemed to think for a minute. "Not at first, but in the last few years I was so tired at night I just wanted to get to sleep. A vibrator let me come in a minute or two."

"Hmm … could you use the shower?"

"No handheld," she said. "I checked." When Tess pinched her she admitted, "I'm starting to get my mojo back. I thought I might have to take care of business so I could lie next to this incredibly hot woman and not dive for her."

"Ha! Your diving days are on hiatus."

"Yeah, but yours aren't." She turned and looked into Tess's eyes. "Don't tell me you're not turned on."

"Way, way past that," she admitted, laughing a little. "But I'm not so much into merely having orgasms. I'm into connecting with a partner. Let's wait until we can really do that." Tess patted her again. "I'll try to find a sex toy store and buy you a new vibrator. That'll help."

Laughing, Darcy said, "It might be fun to go in wearing your costume. I'd like to be there just to see the look on the clerk's face." She shook her head. "But I don't want you to do that. I'm going to go cold turkey. I used to be able to come like a pro with just a hand—mine or another woman's. I'm going to hold out until I can do that again."

"We'll keep practicing … if you want to."

Darcy smiled. "You're too perceptive a woman to have to ask that question." She twitched, then cursed again. "God damn it, I really, really want to put my arm around you."

"Could you use your left?"

"Yeah, I guess I can. But you're on my right."

"Is it worth the pain of getting up and changing places?"

"It's worth more than that." Without help, she sat up. Tess could see her gritting her teeth, but she got her feet to the floor and moved to the right side of the bed. "I wouldn't mind a little help in getting back down. That took a lot out of me."

Tess got to her knees and supported her as she settled back down. They had to share the wedge pillow to cuddle, but when Darcy wrapped her arm around her shoulders, they both sighed. "This is nice," Tess purred.

"You're on my left for the duration. This is perfect."

"So are you." Tess lifted her head and kissed Darcy, trying to show with a single kiss how much she cared for her. "I was very impressed by your showing me that you wanted to have sex. Was that fun?"

She seemed to think about that. "Fun? No, that's not the word I'd use. But it was good to act rather than wish. I'm going to try to keep doing that."

"Let's sleep and dream about the day you can toss me around and rattle my senses." She gently tickled Darcy's chest as she buttoned her top back up. "I bet you're awesome in bed when everything's working."

"Given that we probably won't be together when that happens, I'll confidently assure you that's the gospel truth."

CHAPTER NINE

THE NEXT MORNING, TESS was very, very grateful that Darcy seemed not only fairly well rested, but she also didn't show any signs of embarrassment or unease about the night before.

Darcy gave her a shy look. "Will you cook for me again tonight?"

Tess wanted to high-five her. Darcy had not only refused to get tied up in worrying about sex, she'd come right out and asked for something she wanted. That was progress. "I'd be happy to. Very happy."

After breakfast, they braved the windy, cold day to walk around the neighborhood. Darcy seemed to be affected by the cold more than normal, and Tess idly considered getting her a parka so she could ditch the cloth coat.

"How are you feeling today?" Tess asked as Darcy stopped to look at a lavishly decorated hotel.

"Not bad. I'm a little disappointed in myself for not handling the pain better, but I don't know how to change that."

"You needed more pain meds. I was reading stories on the internet and some people get a prescription that lasts for a month or more. They were very miserly with you. But I'm worried about taking you to see another doctor."

"No more doctors. The last one tried to file a report because she thought I was battered. If I tried to get more drugs, they'd probably think I was a junkie. It's not worth it."

"Well, how's the rest of you?" She squeezed her arm. "No regrets about last night?"

"Regrets?" Darcy stopped and stared, her eyes wide. "No! Do you have any?"

"I don't regret much," Tess admitted. "And being affectionate with you is something I'll never look back on with anything other than pleasure."

"You scared me for a minute. If you get sick of me, it'd be tough to have much distance in a little room."

"I'm glad you showed me what you wanted. I was a little hesitant, but not because I'm not into you." At Darcy's raised eyebrow, she continued. "From what you've told me, you've only had sex with people you were committed to."

"Yeah, that's true. But I think I would have grown out of that in the last eight years. I need more experience. I just didn't have the opportunity."

"You understand that I'm not in a position to be in a long-term relationship?"

"I am," Darcy said. She waited a second, then laughed nervously as she added, "But I can't guarantee I won't try to worm my way into your heart."

Tess stopped her and looked deeply into her eyes. "You've already done that. Even though we won't be together for a long time, you've gotten inside, Darcy." She patted over her chest. "Right in here." Tess took her hand and they started to walk again. "I've had some very meaningful relationships that didn't last long. That doesn't mean they weren't important."

They were quiet for a few minutes, just looking at the houses festooned with holiday greenery. "I don't know much about your past relationships," Darcy said. "I assume Sam was really important, since you were together for three years, but I'm not sure of that."

"Mmm, yeah, she was important in some ways." Tess looked at her. "But neither of us ever thought we'd be together for the rest of our lives."

"You weren't in love?" Darcy's head cocked like an interested puppy's.

"I loved her," Tess said carefully. "But we weren't good together. I didn't make her happy—at least not consistently."

"Because you were gone so often?"

"Oh, god, no. If I'd been home all the time we wouldn't have lasted six months."

"Then why …?"

"It's funny when you travel all the time. You can ignore things. A whole lot of things. If you have something that keeps drawing you back, you can just remind yourself you're leaving again in a week or two and gut it out."

"What drew you back?" She smiled. "I bet I know."

"Yeah," Tess admitted, a little embarrassed. "Sam and I got along great in bed. She was the sexiest woman I'd ever been with. Her … well, some of her parts made me ignore the fact that she was on the crazy side."

"Crazy? Really?"

"Volatile's probably a nicer term. She picked fights with me over next to nothing. Then we'd make up and have really emotional, passionate sex. That kept me coming back much longer than I should have." She met Darcy's eyes. "I would have left much sooner if I'd thought I was making her … volatile. But hearing some of her other lovers talk, I realized she was acting true to form."

"And that was enough for you?" Darcy sounded like it definitely wouldn't be enough for her.

"It wouldn't be enough if I'd thought we were building something. But we weren't. In retrospect, we were just sex partners who kept things going for quite a while." Images of Sam, her beautiful face lighting up when Tess returned from a trip filled her mind for a few moments. "But it was still hard to break up. You can't be intimate with someone—at least I can't—if you don't care for them."

"No, I couldn't be either. But I need to be more extemporaneous when it comes to sex. Historically, I go through a pretty extensive due diligence before I get naked."

"Accounting term?"

"A general business term. If you really dig into a company's books, you're supposed to be able to avoid mistakes. I've tried to figure out a woman's weaknesses before I take a chance."

"To avoid getting hurt?"

"Yeah. I hate to get hurt. I … I avoid it like the plague."

Tess pulled her closer and bent her head to speak into Darcy's ear. "I've got a secret to share."

"Yeah?"

"You can't avoid pain. It hurts to love, it hurts to refuse love, it hurts to avoid love. Don't let your fears stop you from taking risks, Darcy. I guarantee you'll regret it." She stopped, put her hands on Darcy's arms and held her still. Then she tilted her head and kissed her, lovingly. "Open yourself up to whatever experiences come your way."

A slow, shy smile bloomed on Darcy's lips, making her even lovelier in the gray light. "My first kiss in public."

"Let's make it two," Tess decided, leaning in for another long, sweet touch.

They were almost home when Darcy gripped Tess's arm so fiercely she had to swallow a cry. But the tension in Darcy's body made her force herself to act normally. A man was walking down the other side of the street. He didn't quite fit in, but he didn't look particularly dangerous to Tess. Darcy obviously thought different. Instead of going to their B&B, they kept walking, quickly. On the next block they turned and Darcy stopped to take in a breath.

"I didn't like the way that guy looked. All in black. Alone …"

"He wasn't that odd looking," Tess insisted. "Lots of guys wear black leather jackets and black pants. That's not a mob uniform."

"I don't like it." She started off again, almost dragging Tess with her. After another block they were at the car. "I want to find a new place. I'll drive you by and you can pack up our stuff—after I make sure he's not on our street."

"Really? You're that frightened?"

She frowned, staring into Tess's eyes. "No, I'm not very frightened. But I'm not going to ignore anything that raises my hackles. Are you with me?"

"I am."

After settling the bill and gathering all of their things, they sat in the car and tried to decide where to go. "There are dozens of small towns around here," Darcy said, her eyes twitching to look at the rearview mirror every two seconds. "But I think we need to stay somewhere with a lot of B&Bs or hotels. The more tourists, the less people will remember us."

"We've been fine here. Why upset the apple cart? Let's just move to another B&B."

"All right," Darcy said, shrugging. "But I want to cross every walk and every store we've been to off our list. All new everything."

Their new B&B was as far from the old one as they could get. It was in a less fashionable part of town, closer to the lighthouse, but farther from the ocean. Tess didn't care for the neighborhood, especially since there were no sidewalks, but she didn't want to make Darcy any more skittish, so she went inside to rent a room.

Once they were settled, Tess could see that Darcy was jumpy. She sat by the window that faced the street, her eyes locked on every car that came by. Trying to distract her, Tess said, "Hey, I've got an idea. We've got a great tub here. Why don't we try it out? Once your muscles get loose, we can take a walk."

"I guess it couldn't hurt," she said, indecision showing. "But what if I can't get out of the tub?"

"I can help you. I think it's worth the risk." She put her hand on Darcy's cheek and pinched it. "And if I can't, I'll go get our hosts. The three of us can surely pick you up."

Chuckling, Darcy said, "If that happens, I'll be dead—of embarrassment—so you might as well wait for the fire department to drag my carcass out."

"Come on," Tess said, tugging on her hand. "Don't assume the worst. You'll have a nice, long bath and you'll feel better afterwards."

"I'm going. I'm going," she said, getting up with a decided wince.

When they were both in the bathroom, Tess sat on the edge of the tub and started to fill it. "Bath salts or bubbles?" She opened both and sniffed. "The bubbles smell better."

"Bubbles it is." Darcy started to take her clothes off, seemingly more at ease about showing her body. She was moving very slowly, and by the time she'd shimmied out of her panties, the bath was ready. Tess gripped her hand firmly and stood next to the tub, letting Darcy figure out how to enter.

"If I hold onto your arm, can you help lower me in?"

"I can. I'm stronger than I look."

They moved very slowly, but Darcy eased herself into the tub without too many curses and whimpers. As the water rose to cover her, she let out a long sigh. "I love a good bath. So do my ribs." She looked up and Tess returned her grateful smile. "Thanks."

"No trouble at all. Do you want to soak alone? Or would you like a pedicure? I assume you can't bend down to clip your nails."

"I don't have a nail clipper. And if I did, I wouldn't be able to use it."

"I've got one. Be right back."

Tess returned and sat on the edge of the tub. After pushing her sleeve up, she slipped her hand into the water, grasped Darcy's leg and lifted it. "I figured you'd have trouble doing this on your own."

A sweet smile was her only reply.

"Yep. Your nails need some tending. Why didn't you ask?"

While wrinkling up her nose, Darcy said, "That's a pretty big favor to ask."

"You asked me to go down on you," Tess teased, then laughed at the look of horror that flashed onto Darcy's face. "I'm kidding," she insisted. With one more sidelong glance, she added, "But you did."

"I guess I don't have to wait for the innkeepers to come up to die of embarrassment. I can get it out of the way right now."

Tess gently stroked the pink foot that lay in her lap. "Why does that embarrass you? We were having sex. You ask for things when you have sex."

"I know," she mumbled. "But I don't generally talk about them when I'm not actively having sex."

"That's part of the fun. At least for me it is." Tess opened her clippers and carefully nipped Darcy's nails, then switched feet and did the other. "I don't think I ever did this for a girlfriend."

One brown eye popped open. "Really? Why?"

"Mmm … I've never been in a long term relationship where I … what's the right word …" Thinking hard, she finally landed on, "Nurture? Yeah, that's it. I've never nurtured a girlfriend."

"Never?"

"I can't think of an instance. Maybe that's because I've never been attracted to a woman who wanted that." She looked over and saw Darcy's wide eyes. "But I like it. I like caring for you."

"You do a very, very good job of it." Her earnest gaze locked onto Tess. "I've never had a girlfriend who was very nurturing." As she continued to speak her eyes shifted downward, like she was embarrassed. "But it's really nice. God knows I need it right now."

"You do." Tess put Darcy's foot back into the water, then she moved over and knelt next to her head. Cupping her cheek in her hand, she leaned forward and kissed her, savoring the softness of her lips. "But this is temporary. When you're feeling better you'll get back to your old self."

A shy smile bloomed on her mouth. "I might prefer my new self. I like having you care for me."

Tess fussed over Darcy's hair, smoothing flyaway strands back into place while she thought. "My mom's a very caring, loving woman. She's the one everyone goes to when something bad happens. I can't count the times I went into the house to see her feeding someone a piece of pie while she lent a shoulder to cry on." She met Darcy's gaze. "Maybe I'm getting to be a little bit like her. I sure hope so. She's a fabulous person."

"So are you," Darcy said, her voice low and soft. "You're one of the kindest people I've ever met, Tess. That's what's so compelling about you."

"Really?" She leaned forward and placed a gentle kiss on the scratches still marring Darcy's cheek. "I'm sure none of my exes thought that. They liked my adventurous side."

"I like that too. But it's your heart that's irresistible. From that first night when you offered to walk me home … Your kindness shines through."

"Thanks." She had to look away. Sometimes Darcy's eyes seemed to go right through her.

"I think we're both going outside of our comfort zones here."

"Yeah?" She placed another quick kiss onto Darcy's cheek, then moved back to give her feet some more pampering. "Like how?"

"I've always been attracted to women who were pretty much like me. Practical, organized, predictable." When Tess looked up Darcy met her gaze with a smile. "Not like you at all."

"How do you see me?"

Eyes narrowed in thought, Darcy hesitated for just a few moments. "You're spontaneous, and surprising. Very independent, but also able to be very connected."

"Hmm … that's funny. It sounds like you're describing my mom. But I can't argue with the description." She couldn't help but smile.

"You see me differently than my past girlfriends did. I'm not sure if I've changed or ..."

"Maybe I just appreciate different things about you."

"Yeah. Maybe that's it. Whatever it is, I like being thought of as caring and connected." Chuckling, she added, "Sam said being with me was like being at the top of the roller coaster. It seemed like fun, but it was actually terrifying."

"I know we've only known each other for a couple of weeks, but I don't recognize that woman."

After pondering that for a minute, Tess said, "I always felt like I was chasing Sam or being chased. We were hardly ever in the same place emotionally. It was a struggle," she added, letting a little of the sadness she still carried reach her. When she looked up, Darcy's warm brown eyes gazed back at her, so full of empathy and concern they almost took her breath away. She reached out and took Darcy's hand, bending to kiss it. "If I were in this situation with Sam, she'd have me in such a state I wouldn't be able to think straight. But with you ..." A big smile lit her face. "I forget we're on the run. How is it possible to sleep like a baby when ..." She trailed off, not needing to state the obvious. "I feel centered when we're together. That's really, really nice."

"And I feel cared for and supported." Darcy laughed softly. "And like I can't predict what's going to happen—which is a very nice change for me."

Tess leaned over and took a playful bite from Darcy's instep, making those big brown eyes pop wide open. "That's going to continue. Count on it."

After ten days at the Lighthouse Inn, things were eerily, blessedly normal. It had been three weeks since her pummeling, and Darcy was starting to make progress. Sleeping was still tough, and she couldn't begin to think of rolling over in bed, but her wrist no longer ached and her ribs were less painful—so long as she didn't jar them.

She and Tess had grown more comfortable with each other, cuddling as best they could, kissing whenever the urge struck, always holding hands on their walks. But they hadn't tried to make love again. Darcy was sure she couldn't move well enough to get into it, and being turned on but unable to climax wasn't her idea of fun. They hadn't explicitly talked about sex again, but Darcy was pretty sure Tess was waiting for her to make a move. She wanted to. More than she could say. But fumbling around, unable to move like she wanted would have been nothing but frustrating—for both of them.

Nothing had broken their routine except periodic, unproductive calls from her uncle. Even though they were bored, neither of them was ready to move. Mostly because they didn't have a single good idea of where to go.

That morning, Darcy stood waiting by the front door in her coat. Tess came scampering down the stairs and they called out a goodbye to Elsa, the cleaning woman. "They're gonna miss us when we're gone," Tess said, taking Darcy's arm.

"I'm sure that's true. We don't ask for a thing—other than to use the kitchen at night—and we're paying in cash."

"Where to? Back to the lighthouse?"

"Let's go to Rehoboth Beach. It'll give us something to do for the whole day and let us make sure the car hasn't been ticketed."

"That's a pretty gay place, isn't it?"

"Uh-huh. If we're still hiding in June, we should move over there. It'd been a good place to learn how to be gay in public."

"You're doing pretty well," Tess said, smiling at her. "You're only partially like a statue when I kiss you when we're out walking."

Their car was parked to the south, so Darcy had insisted they go in every other direction on their daily walks. Given that the car was the most likely way they'd be caught, that seemed wise. But getting a ticket was nearly as dangerous, and her worry about that had been growing.

She let out a relieved sigh when she saw that the car was ticket free, and that made her loosen up about going exploring.

Darcy decided to drive, one more small step on the road to recovery. It took her a moment to get her seat belt on, and she giggled when Tess finally grabbed it and managed to get it snapped into place.

Because Tess had driven the last time, Darcy adjusted the side-view mirrors to her satisfaction, but when she tinkered with the rearview mirror, she yelped from shock. A very big, very menacing-looking Cadillac Escalade pulled away from the curb and zipped up the street, heading right for her.

"Fuck!" she cried as her hand grasped, clumsily, for the keys. By the time the car was on, she'd gunned it, almost clipping the rear bumper of the car in front of her. The Escalade was clearly coming for her, and her blood ran cold when she saw Sergei's ugly mug zero in on her. Snatching a quick glance at Tess, she saw her face, now bone-white.

"Sergei's following us. I'm sure of it."

"He's two inches from our bumper, Darcy," she said, her voice quavering.

"I'm going to floor it, stop when I can, and you're going to get out."

"What?" Her voice, normally so confident and melodious, was barely a whisper. A terrified whisper.

"You have to get out," she said, trying to sound like she had control, which she didn't. "He's after me, not you. He'll follow me. I'm sure of it."

Tess grabbed at her arm, her grip so strong it hurt. "I'm not leaving you!"

A loud "pop" took out the rear window and Darcy nearly ran off the road when a bullet lodged into the roof—right above her head. She stomped on the gas, the car rocketing as well as its small engine would let it. After blowing through a stop sign, she shot a look at Tess. "Get out now!" Then she jammed on the brakes, holding her breath, hoping that Tess would, for once, just follow instructions. Blessedly, she did, leaping from the car while it was still moving. She rolled as she hit the ground, and Darcy let out a sigh of relief when Sergei slowed but didn't stop. Another, louder "pop" fractured the windshield, the bullet coming so close she heard it whiz past her.

She flew down Lighthouse Avenue, serpentining so he wouldn't have a clear shot at her. Despite the cold wind blowing in her face, she thanked god it was winter, with no pedestrians and far fewer cars than clogged the roads in summer. If she was going to die, at least she wouldn't accidentally take anyone else with her.

On Sunset, she took the turn so fast the car almost spun out, but the little sedan managed to hold onto the pavement. The Escalade shimmied behind her, but hung on as well.

Sunset was a major road, right up against the bucolic, tree-studded state park. But it was empty today, and Darcy continued to use whatever evasive maneuvers her little car was capable of. Another round zipped past her, this one coming in when she'd jerked the car to the right. Her window blew out, and she almost vomited from tension. The bullet had missed her by inches. Her nose caught the scent of burning fabric and she glanced at her shoulder to see it had gone through the padding of her coat.

Her hand itched to grab her weapon and fire back, but it was impossible. Driving with one hand was hard enough as it was. Trying to draw her gun and fire it behind her at a speeding car was a foolish dream.

The road curved a little as they hit the more populated part of town. Darcy purposefully slammed into a curb, screaming in pain as the car jumped into a parking lot and shot down an aisle. Sergei followed, but his car's greater weight made it skid when it landed and she saw it bash into a compact. A cloud of dust hovered over the cars for a second, but the Escalade paused for only a moment. That moment was barely long enough for her to zip out of the lot and make it through a stop light before he could follow. Cars blocked the intersection, making the

Escalade wait precious seconds before it blew through the red and started to gain on her again.

Driving this way in the business district during Christmas would surely get someone killed and she couldn't live with herself if she allowed that to happen. She was about to jump out of the car and take her chances when she remembered she was almost at the pedestrian mall. As soon as she was close, she slammed on the brakes and got out, running as fast as she could. Her speed wasn't what it had been three weeks ago, but she was still in decent shape. The mall wasn't filled with people, but there were small groups and couples slowly sauntering along. Every person she passed stared or gaped at her, and when a shot rang out, no one seemed to notice. Her mom had always told her people not used to the sound never correctly identified gunfire—usually thinking it was a car backfiring or something equally harmless. But she knew the sound all too well, and knew exactly why the plate glass window in the knickknacks store next to her shattered.

"Gun!" she shouted, hoping people would take shelter.

She turned to see Sergei lumbering after her, his left arm in some kind of brace that held it close to his chest. He was too big to be very fast, but he was skilled enough to come very close to her on the next round, which exploded another window with a bang. Darcy careened down an alley, determined to keep innocent people out of harm's way. She squeezed into a tiny space between two buildings, right behind a dumpster. Stealthily, she reached into her pocket, and extracted her weapon. Sergei followed her down the alley, his heavy gait slowing as he must have realized she could be hiding anywhere. But his labored breathing gave him away as the sounds of his gasping for breath echoed off the brick buildings.

His weapon caught the sun as he poked it around the dumpster. On instinct, she grabbed it with all of her strength, twisting it from his hand. As it clattered to the ground she grabbed him and pulled him towards herself then hit him as hard as she could with the gun in her hand. She caught him right on the chin and his eyes rolled back in his head as he crumpled to the ground. Darcy grabbed his weapon, then yanked from her pocket the handcuffs she'd started to carry, managing to snap them onto his left wrist and an ankle, effectively hobbling him. A moment of pleasure rolled down her spine when she thought of the pain he'd be in when he woke. The cruelest part of her wanted to jump onto his shoulder with all of her weight, re-breaking whatever he needed the brace for. But she hadn't yet lost her humanity. She took off again, trying to get out of the alley before the police could get to her.

She headed for the street, hoping no one recognized her. Her mom had taught her that people generally had poor recollection of details when they were afraid. Seeing those windows shot out and having people run past them shooting at each other would probably wipe out every other detail.

When she got to the street, her stomach fell—her little car was blocked in by police cars with their flashing blue lights. But the Escalade was in the clear and still running. Darcy jumped in and pulled away slowly, just trying to blend in. She was halfway down the street when she allowed herself to take a breath and feel the pain that shot through her body. Her chest and ribs hurt as much as they had the first minutes after Sergei had beaten her. If they'd gotten displaced there was a chance they could puncture a lung. But she couldn't think of that now. All she could think of was Tess.

It only took a few minutes to get back to the B&B. As Darcy slowed down, she saw her, sitting on the top step, bags in her hands. Tess ran to the car and got in, her face so pale it hurt to look at her. She bent, hugging herself as she gasped for breath. "I was sure you were dead. God damn it, Darcy. I was *sure* of it."

"I almost was," she admitted, hearing how her voice shook. "But I'm not. We've got to get out of here. Any ideas?"

"I can't think." She sat up and grasped her face with her open hands. "I've just been trying to figure out what to do if you were—" She started to cry, her whole body shaking.

"Shh," Darcy soothed, forcing herself to think clearly—for Tess's sake. "We're both okay. Stay in the moment, right?"

"The moment sucks!" Tess whimpered.

"No, the last half hour sucked. Now, we're okay," she soothed. "We just have to get out of here."

"Whose car is this?"

"Sergei's."

Gasping, Tess sat up straight. "Did you kill him?"

"No. I knocked him out, and handcuffed him. He'll be fine."

"Fuck," she murmured. "I thought you were crazy to carry those damn handcuffs you got from the sex toy store. Shows what I know."

"We've got to ditch this car. Fast."

"There's a car rental place way out on Washington. Do you think we can go that far?"

"We're going to have to," Darcy said grimly as she continued to drive.

They argued all the way, but Tess finally won the battle. Darcy let her out a block away. "I'll leave the car on a side street and walk over. Are you *sure* you want to use your credit card?"

"You can't use yours, so we don't have any other choice. Let's just get this done." She jumped from the tall SUV and walked determinedly towards the car rental agency. Darcy watched her go, sick with worry. If they connected them—Tess was in a world of trouble, and every bit of it was Darcy's fault.

It took much longer than she thought it would, but Tess finally emerged from the shop and went to the lot to get into a car that looked almost exactly like their last rental.

She pulled up and Darcy got in, throwing their bags over the seat to land on the floor.

Tess gave her a wan smile. "Thank god you made me put that money in my account. My credit card bill is deducted automatically, and it would have bounced if you hadn't done that."

"Yeah, I'm a real genius. I'm so smart I don't have any fucking idea where to go next."

"We can't go to Oregon now, even if the police aren't looking for us," Tess said quietly. "I can't risk getting my family involved in this."

"God damn it!" Darcy yelled, making Tess flinch and put a hand over her ear. "I'm sorry. I'm not usually a yeller."

"I know that, Darcy. You're frustrated. But we've got to get out of here. I'll just drive until we get to that tollway." She let the car start down the street, slowly.

"Fine." She reached up and yanked the transponder from the windshield. "We'll pay as we go."

"Is it safe to go through the tollbooths? They can't read the thing?"

She rooted around in the glove box and pulled out a metallic lined bag. "They left the package it came in. This'll shield it."

"Positive?" Tess asked, sparing one final look.

"Yeah. We're good." She closed her eyes, still so filled with anxiety her hands were shaking. "How in the fuck did they know we were in Cape May?"

"They probably did what they did before—sent a bunch of goons to find us. They knew the license number of the car, and that's plenty if you throw enough manpower at it. There have probably been low-level grunts checking every street between Atlantic City and the end of the state."

Sick with dread, Darcy said, "I can't outrun them. I need to turn myself in."

"No." Tess's voice was low and firm. "We're in this together. And we're going to keep running until the pressure gets too heavy on the NYPD."

"That could take years!"

"No, it won't. It might take months, but not years. I've got faith in the system. It's slow, but we can wait it out."

Darcy wasn't willing to admit how her faith had been shattered. Instead, she nodded and said, "We'll go to Newark Airport, then turn in the car. That'll be easier than driving into the city."

"The city? We're going to the city?"

"We are. We're going to meet my father."

"Your *what*?"

"We need help, Tess. I know it's a long shot, but he might be able to help. He *is* an attorney."

"He's an attorney who doesn't know you exist!"

"I know that. And I know it's dangerous. But it's just as dangerous to wander around waiting for the mob to catch me."

"Darcy, he'll turn you in," Tess said, her voice filled with fear. "You can't show up and announce to a stranger that you're wanted for murder!"

"I'll figure something out," she grumbled, not at all sure of what that would be. "Stop at a fast food place so we can use the bathroom. It's time we got back into our costumes."

Since they barely spoke, the long trip up almost the entire length of New Jersey seemed even longer. Finally, when they were about ten miles from Newark, Darcy said, "Here's the story you need to memorize."

"What? Why do I need a story?"

"Because we might get caught. If we do, you need to protect yourself."

"That's not possible at this point, Darcy. Don't fool yourself."

"I'm not," she said firmly. "I've concocted a viable story and you need to learn it."

"Fine," she said, sounding resigned. "What's my story?"

"You and I met a few weeks before the … incident. We hit it off and started dating. One night I showed up at your apartment, battered. You freaked out and wanted to call the police, but I told you I couldn't do that. I hadn't known it, but my boss had been doing business with the mob. Some hood had beaten us both up and told me to disappear. We cowered in your apartment for a few days, then the guy who beat me showed up. He tripped and hurt himself, but we knew they'd send another guy if they sent one. We bought disguises and went to Cape May. But the bad guys found us and we're running again. That's *your* story."

"My story? What's yours?"

"The truth. Except I'm also going to say we met a few weeks before the incident. I knew Harry had been killed, but I didn't want you to know because I wasn't sure you'd believe me. I shielded you from finding out."

"Darcy," Tess said gently. "No one will believe that. Your face was all over the neighborhood. All over TV and the newspapers."

"You don't have a TV and no one can prove you read the paper since you don't have it delivered. And I know it's a sucky story, but it's all that I can think of. You're *not* going to jail for this, Tess. You're not!"

"Okay, okay. I'll try to sell it. But we're not going to need the story. We're going to be fine," she said, her voice shaking. It was clear she didn't believe that one bit, but Darcy truly appreciated her acting like she did.

Once they'd dropped the car off, they waited on an exposed platform for the next New Jersey Transit train to Penn Station. It was beyond nerve wracking, but there were many people around them who'd just flown into Newark and a few of them were dressed at least as uniquely as they were. They sat apart on the train, then met up again on Thirty-fourth and Sixth Avenue. "Ben's office is about ten blocks away," Darcy said. "Pray that he's at work today."

They started to walk, with Darcy carrying the small bags and Tess hefting the large one on her back. By the time they'd gone a few blocks they began to fit in. There weren't many observant Jewish women on the streets, but as they passed the jewelry district, every other man was wearing religious garb. It was strange, but she began to feel like she belonged with this group. Clothing gave you an identity much faster than she would have thought.

It was around three when they entered the narrow, old office building where Benjamin Miller had his practice. Darcy stood there, momentarily befuddled when the guard at the desk asked her to sign in. "Go wait for me at the Starbucks on the corner," she said to Tess. "I need to do this alone."

Tess started to protest, but when the guard took a long look at her, she turned and left the building without another word. Darcy signed in, using the name she'd decided upon during their drive. Then she got into the ancient elevator and rode up to the sixth floor. When the doors opened, it was like she'd entered a different building. The office space was bright and airy and seemed very prosperous. "Miller and Keating" read the name above the desk where a receptionist sat. She looked up, must've thought Darcy didn't look threatening, and buzzed her in through the glass panels. "Hello," the woman said. "Can I help you?"

"I need to talk with Benjamin Miller."

"Do you have an appointment?"

"No, but he'll want to talk to me. It's a private matter."

"Well …" the woman looked at her for a long moment. "I'll see if he's in." She turned and spoke into the phone, lowering her voice so that Darcy couldn't hear. She stood there, cooling her heels, until a middle-aged woman came out.

"Hello. I'm Mr. Miller's secretary. Can I help you with something?"

201

"I need to speak to Mr. Miller. It's private … personal."

The woman shrugged, clearly not in the mood to argue. "Give me your name and I'll see if he can make time."

Darcy cleared her throat and said, "Karen Morgan. We went to law school together."

It hurt just a little bit when the woman wrote her name down and disappeared behind a wood panel. Darcy knew she looked bad in her costume, but her mother was sixty-five when she died. A few minutes later, the secretary returned. "He can see you. Follow me." She led Darcy to a small, but well-appointed conference room. "It'll just be a minute. Can I get you something to drink?"

"Water would be nice."

The woman opened a small refrigerator hidden in the credenza. "Here you go." She handed her the water and left the room. Darcy went over her first words, but she had so many thoughts fighting for supremacy, she was struck mute when the door opened and a tall, handsome, silver-haired man strode in with a big smile on his face. That smile faded immediately. "Who are you?" he demanded, remaining in the doorway.

"I'm Karen Morgan's daughter."

His deep-set eyes, so like her own, narrowed. "Then why did you tell my secretary you were Karen?"

"Because you wouldn't have recognized my name. I needed to meet you and I couldn't think of any other way to do it."

He inched into the room, clearly curious. "Why do you want to meet me?"

She swallowed, her nerves so bad she almost vomited. "Because I think you're my father."

Ben dropped into one of the comfortable high-backed leather chairs. "What did you say?"

"I think you're my father."

That gave him a burst of energy. "I most certainly am not. I think you'd better leave." He stood and grasped the door handle, but then hesitated. "Why do you think that?"

"My mom died a few months ago and when we went through her things we found a letter you'd written to her."

"A letter?" he asked sharply. "Why would I write to her? We lived ten minutes from each other."

She swallowed. "You wrote when she broke up with you." He still stared, unblinking, but didn't refute that, so she went on. "I searched until I found a photo of your law school class and decided you were the Ben who looked most like me."

His eyes scanned her face carefully. She could almost see glimmers of recognition dawn. "So you found a picture of me and thought we looked alike. What kind of evidence is that?"

"It's not good," she admitted. "But I'm not trying to prove anything. I'm simply asking if you think you might be my father."

His scowl slowly eased. "Your mom's dead?" he asked quietly.

"Yes. This past April."

"I'm sorry to hear that," he said, looking down at the floor. "But … I still don't see how that's relevant."

"It's not." She got up and dropped two small, square boxes in front of him. "These are paternity test kits I bought at the pharmacy. I used one. If you're interested, use the other and send it in. If you want to know—you'll know." She started for the door.

"Wait! You can't leave now!"

"I have to. If you want to find out if you're my father, do the test. I'll call."

Ben stood and for a moment Darcy thought he'd block the door. But he held it open as she passed through.

"I don't even know your name!" he called out as she walked quickly to the door.

"I'll be in touch soon," Darcy said. She knew several sets of eyes were on her as she waited for the elevator in the glass-walled lobby. But she didn't turn around. All she wanted was to get out of public view as quickly as possible.

Her heart started to beat more slowly when she went into the coffee shop and saw Tess, sitting at a table, having a mug of cocoa. "Thank god," she said when she touched and squeezed her shoulder.

Tess looked up, clearly a ball of nerves. "Is everything okay?"

"I think so. Ready to go?"

"Do you know where we're going?"

"Yeah. There's a big hotel on Thirty-Fourth by the train station. They get all kinds of people there. We won't stand out." As they started to walk, Darcy said, "Can you use your skills to convince them to let you pay cash? We really need to lie low."

"I'm sure I can. Leave it to me."

When Tess told the desk clerk that it was sinful to use a credit card on the Sabbath he didn't blink. He made a copy of her card, just in case she bolted, but he didn't mention that it was Wednesday, not the Sabbath in any religion she could think of.

They went up to their room, not speaking, but as soon as the door closed, Tess demanded, "Tell me everything!"

"There's not a lot to tell. I gave him the DNA test, and told him to use it and send it in if he wanted to know." She shrugged. "Then I left."

"*What*? Why'd you leave? The whole point was to get his help!"

"I know that. But I've got to be sure of him. Once he gets confirmation we're related, he might be more willing to go to bat for me."

"Do you think he's the guy?"

"I'm sure of it," Darcy said, a slow smile forming. "There's not a doubt in my mind. Every part of me that doesn't fit in with my family was right there in front of me."

Tess threw her arms around her, holding her the same way she usually did. But this time Darcy whimpered and pulled away. "I had to do a few things that aggravated my ribs today. They've got to settle down again."

As Tess moved back she gasped when she saw the neat hole that cut right through the shoulder of Darcy's coat. "Is this …?"

"A bullet hole? Yeah, it is. Luck was on my side."

"I have to hug you," Tess said, but this time she held her much more gently. "Thank god you're all right," she murmured as she nuzzled her face against Darcy's neck. "You mean so much to me. So very much."

"Me too," Darcy said, her voice shaking.

They'd had a pretty awful day, but when Tess held her she could convince herself that things would, eventually, be all right.

CHAPTER TEN

THEY HIBERNATED IN THE hotel that night, ordering room service with prices that made Darcy gag. But she was so skittish, she couldn't even bear for Tess to go out.

Sleep evaded Darcy most of the night. Once the weak winter sun began to show around the tall buildings that surrounded them, Darcy used Tess's computer to scour the local newspapers. It took a long time, but she finally found a mention of her escapade in the *Cape May County Herald*. "I got a hit," she said, waking a startled Tess.

"What?" She struggled to sit up, then blinked slowly. "What did you say?"

"I found something about our latest adventure."

Immediately, Tess scrambled across the bed to lean over Darcy's shoulder. "Read it to me."

"You could read it to me from that angle," Darcy teased, but she continued, "Cape May police are holding thirty-seven-year-old Sergei Zahorchak on an unspecified weapons charge. Zahorchak allegedly fired upon an unidentified woman during an incident at the Washington Street Mall on Wednesday morning. Witnesses claim the woman ran down the mall, warning people that Zahorchak had a gun. Several shots were fired, with two local businesses suffering the loss of their display windows. Both the woman and Zahorchak ran down an alley next to Cape Collectibles, where Cape May police later found Zahorchak, with his hand cuffed to his ankle. The police are not commenting on what transpired." Darcy turned her head and met Tess's eyes. "I love being called an unidentified woman. I hope my name never appears in a newspaper again."

For a few seconds, Tess lovingly cradled Darcy's cheeks. "You didn't tell me you tried to warn people. But, knowing you, I'm not surprised."

Blushing, Darcy tried to shrug it off. "A heartless jerk was taking pot shots at me. The least I could do was tell people to look out."

"You're a good person, Darcy. And one day I hope your name's in the paper … as the hero of this really messed up story." She placed a gentle, soft kiss on her lips. "You're my hero."

"Mmm. Well, the police know your hero was involved, given that they found my car with the windows shot out. I'm not sure why they're not identifying me—but it's probably bad news."

"Sounds like it's time to write to Eliza, our reporter, again."

"I'm already thinking about what to say. Will you help me draft something?"

After four days, Darcy couldn't convince Tess to stay in their tiny, cramped hotel room any longer. "If you insist on going out, would you buy me another disposable phone?" she asked. "I want to call Ben today, and I'd like to throw the phone away after I do."

"Sure." Tess stood by her chair, the small, uncomfortable one where she'd been sitting for what seemed like years. Leaning over, Tess got very close, close enough for Darcy to smell the citrusy soap the hotel supplied. "You know I hate to leave you, but if I don't get some fresh air, I'm going to get bitchy, and you don't want that."

Darcy ran her fingers along Tess's jawline, loving the way she always got goose bumps on her arms when she did that. "I've never seen you bitchy. It might be fun."

"Not so much. Now I'm going to be gone for a while, so try not to worry. I promise I'll be back by seven, and I'll bring dinner. Something both nutritious and flavorful."

"I don't want you to leave, but as long as I've got to worry, I might as well get a good meal in return." She gave her a kiss and rubbed their noses together. "Miss you already."

While Tess was gone, Darcy tried to keep busy, but she couldn't think of anything other than talking to Ben. Finally, she gave in to temptation and called him at his office. "Hi, this is Karen Morgan calling for Mr. Miller."

"Oh, right, please hold on," the woman said, snapping to attention. In just seconds, Ben's deep voice said, "Hello?"

"Hi. It's …" She realized she still hadn't told him her name. "It's Karen's daughter."

His voice took on a funny quality, making him sound wistful. "You're my daughter too, and I don't even know your name."

"What? How did you get the results …?"

"I wasn't going to trust some internet outfit I've never heard of. So I went to a lab here in New York and had my blood drawn. They checked my sample against the one you gave me and … you were right."

"Wow." It took her a minute to let the information settle. Even though she'd been sure, it was a shock to finally know who her father was. "How do you feel about that?"

"Sad," he said, and she realized that was the tone she'd noticed. He sounded like his heart had been broken. "Your mom was a heck of a woman. The one who got away. Do you know what I mean?"

"I think I do."

He sighed audibly. "I never knew why she left so abruptly. I couldn't get a word out of her mother or any of her friends. It's like she disappeared off the face of the earth."

"She almost did."

"Where did she wind up?"

"Six months after you wrote that letter, she'd already moved to New Jersey, taken the test to become a peace officer, and given birth to me. She wasn't the kind of woman who let the grass grow under her feet."

"Why was I such a bad guy? What terrible thing did I do to have her take off without a word? Did she tell you I was some kind of jerk?"

"She never mentioned you or told me a single thing about my father or my conception. It's like our life started in New Jersey when I was born."

"Good god," he grumbled. "You think you know someone. You think you have a chance to build something ..." He sounded so sad her heart went out to him. But in the course of five seconds his voice sharpened. "What do you want?"

"Nothing. I just wanted to meet you. My mom made it clear she didn't want me to know you, but I couldn't live with that."

"You want nothing more than to meet me," he said, suspicion coloring his words.

"Nothing at all."

"Well, you're a little old to ask for child support." His voice grew even more sharp. "And don't think about asking for back support at this point. Your mother chose to go her own way. There isn't a court in—"

"I don't want your money," Darcy interrupted. "I swear that."

"Then what *do* you want?"

"I just wanted to meet you. I ... I've wanted to know you since I was a child, but my mom didn't want that."

A long silence settled between them, and when he spoke again he sounded weary. "God damn it, I would have loved to have had a daughter."

"You would have?"

"I really would have. A child is the one thing I've always wanted, but never came close to getting."

"I wanted a dad so badly," she admitted, feeling tears well up in her eyes. "I used to dream of you all the time. But I never pictured you like you are." She felt a smile break through her sadness. "You're really handsome."

"Thanks." he said, his voice betraying some embarrassment. "Your mother thought so. Or at least that's what she used to call me. Handsome Devil."

"You don't seem devilish to me. You seem like a very nice guy. I wish … I wish we'd known each other many, many years ago."

"Me too. So … what do we do now?"

"Well, we can … meet. If you want to."

"I do. I'd like to get to know you."

"I'm not sure you'll think that when I tell you my whole story …"

His voice took on the suspicious tone he'd had earlier. "What's the whole story?"

"I'm … well, I'm in trouble and I could use some advice."

"Look. I'm glad to know about you. Really, I am. But I'm not a soft touch. You've got to have some relatives on your mom's side of the family—"

"I don't want money," she insisted. "But I could really use some advice."

"I do real estate law," he said, sighing in what was probably frustration. "Are you buying a house?"

"No, I'm not. I'll tell you my whole story if you've got a few minutes."

"Why would I be in a rush at this point? But I'm not the kind of guy who throws money around because of a sob story. Don't waste your time if that's what this is."

"I've cried a lot over this, but it's not a sob story." She took a breath, and began …

When Tess returned, she found Darcy sitting on the wide window sill. "Hi. I brought some good-looking Thai food. Lots of veggies for you."

Darcy stood and came over to give Tess a gentle hug. "Thanks. I missed you."

After taking off her coat, Tess grasped her chin and looked into her eyes. "You don't look right. What happened?"

"I talked to Ben. Told him the whole story."

"Shit! He believes you're his daughter?"

"Yep. He had a test done at a lab he trusts."

"You don't seem happy. Why not?"

"Mmm …" She sat on the desk chair, looking very contemplative. "We're going to meet. But I'm not sure I can trust him. He could easily turn me in."

"Where are you meeting him?"

"I'm going to go to his office on Monday morning."

"Not good. Make it … Bryant Park. By the Gertrude Stein statue. Ten o'clock. Trust me."

On Monday morning, Darcy, clad in her costume, stood as far away from the Stein statue as she could while still keeping Tess in view. At ten o'clock Ben walked over to the statue while Tess carefully strolled around the perimeter of the park, checking for cops. When she'd scanned the whole place, she waved and Darcy made her way across the square, smiling when Ben saw her and seemed to light up.

"I was afraid you were going to stand me up," he said, extending a hand to shake.

"I'm not the type to do that. But I wanted to make sure you didn't bring a dozen cops with you."

His eyes opened wide, almost like she'd slapped him. "Why would I do that?"

"The police say I killed a man. A lot of people would trust them over a stranger."

"I'm not most people," he said. "How about going for a cup of coffee? We'll freeze out here."

They crossed the park and sat in the corner of a coffee shop. He waited in line, finally delivering plain black coffees for each of them. "Here's the bottom line," he said, gazing into his cup. "I have no reason to believe you, but I do. Your mom was honest and loyal and a heck of a good woman. I … did some research on her and confirmed everything you told me. So … I want to … I don't know … pay you back for not being there when I should have been. I want to help, Darcy."

"You don't owe me a thing," she insisted. "But I could really use the help."

"First off, we've got to get you out of the public eye. I have a weekend house in Westhampton that I'd like you to use."

"Westhampton? Really?"

"Really," he insisted, now looking into her eyes. "I hardly ever use it, so it's just sitting there empty. Once we get you to a safe place, we'll work on the details."

"The details are pretty big."

"True. But we'll nip away at them until we've got this figured out. That's how you solve problems … by being dogged." He frowned briefly, then said, "I hope I'm not asking you to do something you're uncomfortable with, but if you could wear … regular clothing you'd fit in a lot better. My neighbor across the street will see you come in and she'll …"

"That's not a problem," Darcy said. "We have regular clothes."

"Are you … Orthodox?"

She could have explained the whole thing, but Tess was sitting on the other side of the coffee shop, looking like she was about to burst. "In some ways, yes. I'll tell you all about it when we meet again."

As soon as Ben walked out the door, Darcy walked over to Tess and sat next to her. "Apparently, my father earns more than my mother did. We're going to hide out in his spare house in Westhampton."

"Westhampton? Is that *the* Hamptons?"

"It is. Tonight we're going to see how the one percent lives."

That night, dressed in their normal clothes, Darcy and Tess emerged from the eight-o'clock train, where a big, dark BMW waited. "That's him," Darcy said. "Remember your story. Don't change a single thing—except for the fact that I just told you the whole truth about Harry's death today. You're angry and a little in shock."

"I'm a lot in shock!" Tess stammered as Darcy led the way to the street.

Darcy opened the passenger door and met Ben's eyes. "I've brought someone," she said. "My girlfriend, Tess."

Tess nearly swallowed her tongue, but she played along gamely. She reached her hand through the seats and shook his. "I'm pleased to meet you. I guess we've both had a pretty big shock today."

His brow furrowed. "Should I know about your shock?"

"I'll tell you the whole story when we get to your house," Darcy said. "Is it far?"

"About ten minutes." He put the car in drive and Tess felt like her head was on a swivel. She looked in every direction, but didn't see a single police officer, FBI agent, or hit man. No one spoke on the drive, and Tess could feel the anxiety pouring off both Darcy and Ben. They reached a pretty, ranch-style home, set on a corner lot, with a separate two-car garage. Ben hit a button and the garage door opened. After he pulled in, they all exited via a side door, then entered the house through the front. "Here we are," he said. "Would either of you like a drink?"

"I'll take a double. Of whatever you have," Tess said, glaring at Darcy.

"None for me thanks," Darcy said.

Ben made drinks for himself and Tess, then came back into the living room, where he turned on some lights. "My god," he said when he caught a full look at Darcy in her regular clothes with her hair exposed. "You're just as pretty as your mother."

"But with your cheekbones," Tess said, unable to stop herself.

"Thanks," Darcy said, blushing. "I think I look a little like my mom, but she was smaller, and more delicate than I am."

"You've got nothing to complain about, Darcy." He cleared his throat. "Well, I suppose you have a lot to complain about." He took a sip of his drink. "If you're anything like your mom, you're as honest as the day is long, so this must be very hard on you."

"She's exactly that," Tess said. "Unless she's trying to protect someone she cares for. Then she lies without a second thought."

Ben shifted his gaze from Tess to Darcy. "Do either of you want to tell me what that means?"

"I will," Tess volunteered. She could feel the tension rolling off Darcy's body, but she thought she was the right person to tell the story. "We'd only been dating for a few weeks when Darcy appeared on my doorstep, battered and beaten. I ran to call the police, but she told me she'd just found out her boss had been working for the mob. A gangster had beaten both her and her boss at their office, then told her to disappear. From that day until today I thought that was the whole story. But today," she said loudly, glaring at Darcy, "today she told me her boss died during the beating and the police think she did it!"

"And that's protecting you … how?" Ben shifted his gaze to Darcy. "Sorry, but that sounds like you lied to protect yourself."

"She's not the type," Tess insisted. "She knew I'd believe she was innocent, since she's as gentle as a lamb and had no motivation to kill her poor boss, but she guessed I could be charged with harboring a fugitive if I knew the truth." With her voice rising, Tess added, "I would have happily harbored this particular fugitive, and I'm pissed as hell that she lied to me!"

Ben smiled, as he gave Darcy a long look. "They say girls tend to marry people who remind them of their dads, but in your case, I think you went for a carbon-copy of your mom."

They talked until almost eleven, with Ben finally standing to say, "I've got a very big day tomorrow, so I've got to turn in. Let me show you to your room."

"Are you sure about this?" Darcy asked. "You could lose your license if the police find out you're hiding me."

"No one will look for you out here. Most of my neighbors are summer people, and the old couple across the street will believe anything I tell them. Very few people on the block know me. They won't notice a couple of young women coming and going."

"I don't want to do that to you," Darcy insisted. "I have some money, I can afford to stay in a hotel."

"Nonsense." He walked over to the sofa and put a hand on her shoulder. "Let me help you, Darcy. I can arrange for representation for you, and I'll gladly pay for it."

"You don't have to do that—"

"It'll be less than the child support I should have paid your mother." He gripped her firmly. "I hope to god you didn't go without."

"We were fine. I had everything I ever needed."

"That's good to hear. I know how strong-willed your mom was, but there's no excuse for short-changing a child."

"She did a great job," Darcy said, her hackles rising as they always did when her mother's judgment was called into question. She stood and glared at him, with Tess watching in amazement. "She sacrificed her career to have me. Then she gave up any chance of having a love life." Her voice was rising and Ben looked like he was very sorry he'd brought the whole topic up. "Everything she did was for me. Everything! Even when she retired, she took a lower pension so I could get a check for the rest of my life. I was her sole focus, Ben. There's never been a woman who short-changed her child less than my mom."

"I didn't mean to imply she did," he said gently. "I bet she was a great mother."

"She was," Darcy said, starting to cry. "When people criticize her it breaks my heart. She tried so hard."

"I'm sorry," he said. "I can see how much you loved her, and I really didn't mean to criticize."

"It's all right." She took in a shaky breath. "She was hard-headed, and rigid, and suspicious of people. But god, she was devoted to me."

He nodded, looking like he might tear up too. "You've had a tough time of it. You'll be able to rest and recuperate here. Pick either of the guest rooms. The village is only a few blocks away, but if you want to drive, there's a spare car in the garage. Can you drive a stick?"

"I can," Tess volunteered.

"Great. I'll take off early in the morning, so I probably won't see you. But I'll call when I get a break."

"Is there a land line?" Darcy asked.

"Of course. I have all of the latest gadgets, but I like to be able to hear the person calling me."

"Great. Thanks, Ben. You've been a lifesaver," Darcy said.

"Not yet, I haven't. But we'll get there. Trust me on that."

With that, he headed to the master bedroom, on the other end of the house. Darcy let out a sigh. "He's too good to be true. He's probably figuring out who'll pay more for my head."

"Such a pessimist," Tess said, leaning close to kiss Darcy's cheek. "I say we trust him until he proves he's unreliable."

"I guess we don't have any other options. I think we're at the end of our trail—for better or worse."

They lay in bed together, with Darcy propped up on all of the spare pillows Tess could find. She was clearly in pain, and Tess wished she'd asked Ben if he had any industrial-strength pain killers lying around. But she'd let that opportunity slide by, and now she had to simply feel bad that Darcy hurt. Sometimes it took Darcy's mind off her pain if she talked. It was worth a try.

"I'm not complaining," Tess said, "but why did you come out to your dad today?"

"Shouldn't I have?" she asked, brow rising.

"Of course you should have. But … you didn't come out to your mom or your uncle …"

"I know. That was a mistake." She took a breath, her frown showing her determination. "If I'm going to have a relationship with Ben, it's going to be an honest one. I might have to hide from the police and the mob, but I'm sick of hiding the fact that I like women."

"Aww ... that makes this woman very happy. It's your first coming out day."

Darcy smiled, her grin so cute Tess nearly swooned. "You said you wanted to be with me when I did all sorts of firsts. This was just one more in a series." A troubled look clouded her expression. "I'm sorry I said you were my girlfriend. I just ..." She shrugged, looking uncomfortable. "It's pretty unbelievable that you'd still be with me if we weren't pretty committed to each other."

"That's fine, Darcy." Tess leaned close and kissed her cheek. "If I could be happy living in one place, I'd be trying like mad to get that girlfriend title."

Darcy woke early, unable to fully relax in the strange house. Oddly, the B&B had seemed more home-like. Ben's house was nice—very nice. It wasn't huge, just three bedrooms and a den, but it was filled with light from the all-glass east-facing side of the house. Even though it was ranch-style, the ceilings were very high in the great room, with exposed beams throughout.

Standing in front of the glass wall, Darcy looked out on the pool, now covered. She had a brief sense of longing at the thought of having a place like this to cool off in the humid Northeast summers of her youth. But more than the nice house, she wished she'd been able to have a relationship with her father. Now, as a middle-aged adult, she knew it was too late to create one.

She was so lost in her thoughts she hadn't heard or felt Tess come up behind her and gently hug her.

"Hi," Darcy said, patting Tess's hands.

"Hi. Did you sleep poorly again?"

"A little. But not too bad." Darcy turned in her loose embrace. "Hungry?"

"Very. We skipped lunch and dinner."

"You had dinner," Darcy teased. "A double Scotch, right?"

"Yeah, that was smart." Tess chuckled. "I had to stop myself from getting up on the table and dancing. But I didn't think that would make a good first impression."

"I would have liked it."

"I bet you would have." Tess leaned in and kissed her. "I'm going to run to the store. Anything you'd like for breakfast?"

Darcy blinked. "You're going alone?"

"Yeah. We should keep you out of sight as much as possible until we're sure we're safe here. No one's seen a picture of me."

"I've got to get outside at some point," Darcy warned. "I'll go crazy stuck in here."

"We're just a few blocks from the beach. We'll go for long walks. I just want to ease into things."

"All right." Darcy put her arm around Tess's shoulders and walked her to the bedroom. "I've gotten very used to having someone make breakfast for us. I'm not sure I remember how to make up my own mind."

"Then I'll decide for you." Tess shimmied into her jeans, then put on socks and shoes. "Passable?" she asked, after fluffing her hair.

"Beautiful. Hurry back."

Tess came back with two bags filled to the top with groceries, along with another wedge pillow. "Thank god we have a suitcase full of cash. The prices here are criminal!" She maneuvered into the kitchen, then turned and gave Darcy an excited smile. "Your dad's spare car is awesome! A really cute Alfa Romeo. If we're still here this spring, I'm going to drop the top and cruise the Hamptons."

Darcy couldn't stop herself from returning the smile, even though the thought of being stuck there through the winter made her stomach grip. "You'll fit right in. Was the town nice?"

"Oh, hell, yes! Don't you know the Hamptons? Your uncle lives not too far from here, right?"

"Yeah. My grandparents did too. There wasn't a huge distance in terms of geography, but there was a massive one in class. We went towards Brooklyn when we went out to do things, not Montauk."

"Then we'll have lots of things to explore."

"Super. Just the way I've always dreamed of traveling—ducking every pair of eyes that land on me for more than two seconds."

Despite Darcy's claim that she needed to be outdoors, Tess couldn't lure her out, despite trying several times. "I want to let a day or two pass. I'm still not convinced there won't be a cop car parked just down the street, waiting for me."

Tess stood close and looked into Darcy's eyes. They were filled with fear. "Why would that happen? If your dad was going to turn you in, why wouldn't the cops have been crawling all over the place while we slept?"

"Mmm, maybe he wants to turn me in, but doesn't want me to know he did it. It might look like a fluke if they caught me when I was out walking."

"I understand you're frightened," Tess soothed, "but I think you're imagining things."

"Even paranoids have enemies, and I have more than I can count."

The phone rang that afternoon, and Darcy picked it up and answered, "Miller residence."

"Hi, Darcy." Even though she'd only heard it three times, she immediately recognized her father's voice.

"Hi, Ben."

"I was thinking of coming back out if that's okay. I could pick up something for dinner."

"Uhm, sure. That'd be great."

"What kinds of food do you two like?"

"Just about anything. Tess is more experimental than I am, but I'm not picky."

"Great. I'll get Italian if that's okay."

"That's Tess's favorite."

"I'll see you about six. Oh, how closely do you follow Kashrut?"

"Cash ... what?"

"Don't you keep Kosher?"

"We eat everything, Ben. I'll explain more when you get here."

Right on time, Ben knocked on the door. Darcy opened it, and stood there for a second. He looked like he wanted to hug her, but unsure if she was reading him right, she just smiled and moved back so he could enter.

"Hi," he said, smiling back at her. He took a quick look at her clothing. "Feel free to wear your usual clothes here at home, Darcy. I want you to be comfortable."

She led the way over to a round table close to the kitchen area. "I ... are you Jewish?"

"I am. But your mom wasn't, so I've been wondering ..."

"Neither am I. When we started to run, Tess thought we needed to change our look so we'd be less noticeable."

He raised an eyebrow. "That was a costume?"

"Yeah." She winced, thinking of how their choice might come across. "I hope we haven't offended you or your faith ..."

He started to laugh. "I didn't even make my bar mitzvah. You're not offending me in the least. But that was a strange choice—"

Tess came out of the bathroom just then. "Blame me for the idea," she interrupted. "It helped render us fairly invisible in Brooklyn, but I don't think it's going to fly out here."

"No, this isn't a hub for observant Jews," he agreed. "If you want to fit in, you'll wear very expensive jeans that don't look expensive, and ski jackets that weigh about an ounce."

"We can do that," Tess said as she went into the cupboards to pull out dishes and flat wear.

They sat at the dining table, and Darcy was both pleased and surprised to feel an easy camaraderie develop among them. Ben had a ton of natural charm, which had to help in his career. But he seemed like a genuinely nice guy, not just a poser. He was a healthy eater too, avoiding the pasta dishes to pick at the broccoli rabe and grilled vegetables. He pushed his plate just out of reach when he was finished, and Darcy smiled to herself. Could that habit be genetic?

"So, Darcy, tell me more about your mom. I know she didn't marry, but was there anyone special in her life?"

"No," she said, shaking her head. "Dating was never on her list of things to do."

"Why not? She was a heck of a catch."

"Yeah, she was. But she concentrated on her job and on me. That didn't leave much time."

"No, I suppose not." He sighed, looking melancholy. "I still can't make sense of her not telling me about you. We were really solid."

"I don't have much to add, since we never talked about you. I always …" She hesitated just a moment before speaking her mind, "I always thought you might have been a jerk. Or that she told you and you wanted her to have an abortion."

"Absolutely not," he said, his voice rising. "Well, I was twenty-two, so I might have had some jerk tendencies. But I would have married your mom if she had told me. That wasn't my plan … but plans change."

"What was your plan?"

221

"To finish school, get my career started, and get married after I'd practiced for a few years. I'd seen too many guys marry early and then have trouble when they had to work eighty or ninety hours a week."

"Did my mom know that plan?"

"Sure. She agreed with it. As a matter of fact, she was always the one putting the brakes on when I wanted to spend time with her rather than study."

"That sounds like her," Darcy said fondly. "No one followed through on her obligations more than my mom." She looked at Ben for a moment. "Maybe that's why she left. She felt I was her obligation, and she didn't want you to get pulled in if you didn't want to be."

"But I would have wanted to be!"

"Yeah, but if you knew her well, you'd know she couldn't stand having anyone pity her. If she thought you were stepping up to the plate out of obligation …"

"But she didn't even give me a chance! Everyone has plans, but you change your plans based on circumstances."

"She wasn't very extemporaneous," Darcy said, recognizing the same trait in herself. "If she was convinced you weren't ready to be a dad, I can easily see her leaving without telling you." She nodded thoughtfully. "On top of that, she might not have wanted to share the decision-making with you. She clearly liked to go her own way."

"I'm like that too," he said, looking abashed. "Maybe we wouldn't have been able to get along." He met Darcy's gaze. "But I still wish I'd known about you. You don't happen to have any kids, do you? I missed being a dad, but I know I'd be a great grandfather."

"No," she said, sighing. "I wish I did, but I wasn't in the right situation when I was young enough."

"Hey," he said, playfully. "You're a very young woman. Don't contradict me because, if I have a daughter who's too old to have a child, that makes me a *very* old guy!"

"She's not too old," Tess said, giving Darcy a very fond look. "She's the perfect age."

"Okay," Darcy said, standing to collect their plates, "enough talk about my reproductive capacity. Would anyone like dessert? Tess bought some scrumptious-looking cookies."

"None for me," Ben said.

"More for me," Tess said, grinning like a kid.

They went to sit by the glass wall, with a plate of cookies much closer to Tess than to Darcy or Ben. "Let's talk about our strategy," Ben said.

"I'd be happy to have one," Darcy said. "Right now we're just going wherever the wind takes us."

"That's not wise," he said. "You need to be proactive."

"I think we need to put more pressure on the NYPD," Tess offered.

Ben shook his head. "I don't know how effective that will be. But a good criminal defense attorney will be able to give us an opinion on that. If it were my call, I'd try to strike a deal with the DA."

"My uncle, my mom's brother Danny, is on the police force here in Suffolk County. He's trying to find out whatever he can from his contacts in the NYPD, but he's basically found nothing that helps us."

"You need an attorney," Ben stressed. "Let me make some calls. I'll find you someone topnotch."

"I want someone great," Darcy admitted, "but I don't want you to be involved to that extent. If you can give me some names, I'll make the calls."

"I don't mean to brag, but I pull a little weight in the New York Bar. People will take my call."

"Get me some names," Darcy insisted. "If I can't get anyone to nibble, then I might need you to get involved—but only as a last resort. Okay?"

"She wants to protect everyone she cares for," Tess said, giving Darcy a very fond look.

"I hope I'm on that list," Ben said. "I'll do my best to earn my place."

CHAPTER ELEVEN

TESS WANDERED OUT INTO the hall the next morning, looking for Darcy.

She was sitting on a modern, curvy, mid-century-style chair when Tess saw her. Struck by how pretty she looked, Tess stopped in the hallway and observed her. Even though she was in her flannel pajamas, Darcy looked like a captain of industry. The tortoiseshell reading glasses Tess had picked up for her at the drugstore made her look super smart. And the graceful way she inhabited the chair, with the paper held wide open while her chin tilted up and down as she scanned the page, made Tess's libido spark. She'd been waiting for a signal that Darcy was ready to rock, but she wasn't averse to giving her a kick start.

Darcy lowered the paper as Tess crossed the room. "Hi, there."

"Hi. I heard Ben leave. Been up long?"

"Nope. My coffee isn't even ready yet."

Tess grabbed the top of the paper and whisked it from her hands, then knelt on the edge of the chair before sitting on Darcy's lap, facing her. "Too heavy?"

"No"—she patted Tess's ass—"but you're right at my limit. One more cookie last night and …"

"Funny." Leaning over, Tess removed Darcy's glasses and kissed her, tasting her minty toothpaste. "You taste good."

"You too. I like that you brush as soon as you get up. I love clean teeth."

"I like to please you," Tess murmured as she leaned in for another, longer kiss. "Actually, I'd like to please you right now. What do you say?"

Darcy's eyebrow lifted. "Really? Right now? Before breakfast?"

"Uh-huh." She rocked back and forth on her lap, grinding against her. "I'm hot for you."

"How hot?" Those big brown eyes locked on Tess as a smile quirked the corner of her mouth. "I haven't been getting much of a sexual vibe from you. I thought maybe you'd … lost interest."

Tess leaned back, staring at her. "Are you kidding?"

The smile grew. "Little bit. But I've also been waiting for you to give me a signal."

"How's this?" She put her hands on Darcy's shoulders and leaned close, kissing her with every bit of enthusiasm she could muster. She smelled great. Minty and fresh, with the clean, springtime scent of her pajamas just reaching Tess's nose.

"That's a pretty nice signal," Darcy murmured, her voice turning sexy and low.

"Got another one for you." Tess tilted her pelvis and slid onto one of Darcy's legs. Slowly, she worked herself over the muscular thigh, grinning as sensation shot through her. "Mmm, I'm not sure you need to do a thing. Just sit there and let me go."

"Lazy woman's foreplay. Love it." Darcy put her hands on Tess's hips and closed her eyes as she gently moved her body. "I could grow to like this a whole lot."

Tess leaned forward and kissed her again, sucking her tongue into her mouth as Darcy purred with pleasure. "What's your favorite view?" Tess started to nibble on her neck, something she'd learned drove Darcy to distraction.

"View?"

"Uh-huh," she said between licks and bites of Darcy's soft skin. "Front or back?"

"How can I pick one?" Her hands slid up and down Tess's body and she closed her eyes as if deep in thought. When the back of her hand glided across Tess's breasts she said, "If I look at these, I can't see

226

this." The hand slithered down to cup Tess's ass possessively. "And I *love* this part."

"How about this?" Tess stood, turned, then sat back down, straddling Darcy's leg. While twitching her ass, she ground herself against the muscle. As soon as Darcy groaned in pleasure Tess grasped her hand and clamped it to her breast. "I'm gonna ride you," she growled, then started to snap her hips back and forth, letting her pussy press into Darcy's muscular leg. "Ooo," she murmured. "I'm so hot for you I could burst."

Darcy wrapped her injured arm around Tess's waist, holding her tightly as she continued to glide back and forth. Then she slid a warm, soft hand under Tess's top and slipped across her breasts, teasing them with a whisper-soft caress. Her fingers grasped and pinched a nipple, then cupped and squeezed until Tess felt the sensation right between her legs. "Oh, yeah, do that," she begged, her hips never stopping.

"You're as hot as a firecracker," Darcy murmured, with her hand sliding around Tess's body to slip into her panties and grab a handful of her ass. "I've never, ever been so into a woman." She bent forward until her face was pressed hard into Tess's back.

Either Darcy's ribs were much better or lust was a great analgesic! Tess pressed a hand atop each knee, allowing her to push harder and rock her hips into Darcy's body. The pulsing between her legs made her growl; she needed just a little more to go over the edge.

Darcy pulled her in tighter, then her hand grasped and tugged at Tess's nipple, sending chills down her spine. "So close," she gasped. Bending at the waist, she thrust herself hard against Darcy's leg as a hand threaded through her hair and pulled just hard enough to tilt her face towards the ceiling. Her body opened up, with a cry rising from deep inside as sensation thrummed through her. "Ohhh ..." she moaned, sure she was going to fall. But Darcy's strong arm held her tightly, pinning her in place.

"Good god, where did that come from?" she gasped as she began to laugh. "See what happens when you let me go too long without sex?"

"I hope that's the longest you ever go," Darcy murmured, rubbing her face all across Tess's damp back. "If I could move the way I want to, we'd be having sex right about … now."

Tess wiped the perspiration from her forehead and rose on shaky legs. Turning, she sat astride Darcy's lap, their faces just inches apart. "Tell me about this moving you want to do."

"I've *got* to be able to move. That's what was wrong before. I get turned on by moving against a lover, and I'm not I'm able to do that yet."

"You need to move, huh?"

"More than that," Darcy said as she wrapped her arms around Tess and kissed her hard. "I want to rub my body against yours from the top to the bottom. I want to feel your skin touching mine."

"That's all you need? Really?"

"It would help—a lot."

"Then walk this way. I've got the solution."

They walked hand in hand to the sumptuous guest bathroom. "Either your dad or his decorator is a hedonist," Tess said. "Luckily."

"This is a darned nice bathroom. I thought about pulling you in here with me yesterday, but I was too tense."

Tess turned to her and gave her another long kiss. "You don't seem tense today. I think you're starting to trust your dad. That adolescent defiance only lasted one day," she said, laughing.

"If he was going to rat me out, he'd have done it by now. And he clearly doesn't need the ransom the mob would pay for my head." She looked around. "You could hose down a whole football team in here."

"Mmm, I'd rather have a women's softball team, but that's my kink." She started to slowly unbutton Darcy's top. "I've never fully undressed you. Can't wait."

"I've never even gotten your top off. What kind of lesbian am I?"

228

"The semi-cautious kind."

"Semi?"

"Uh-huh. You haven't gotten my top off, but you pinched the heck out of my nipples." She leaned forward and gave Darcy a big, wet kiss. "Love that, by the way." Tess finished with the buttons, then slid the top from her shoulders. "You have such a nice build. I love the way your shoulders are so square." She smacked the flats of her hands against the tops of Darcy's arms. "Shit! Did that hurt?"

"No," she said, looking down in amazement. "It didn't hurt a bit." Their eyes met again. "But don't keep testing me. I'm sure you could still get me to cry without too much trouble."

Tess put her head on her shoulder and hugged her gently. "I got carried away. I really love your shoulders."

"Let me take a peek at yours. They're always covered up."

"Well, it is December. I don't wear many tank tops when it's below thirty."

"Tank tops?" Darcy said, her eyes wide. "Did you say tank tops? My favorite part of summer is tank tops and shorts on cute women." She placed a kiss on Tess's lips. "You're definitely on the cute women list."

"I probably shouldn't, but I rock a bikini when I go to the beach."

"Mmm, summer can't come soon enough." Darcy touched the hem of her top and whipped it off with one sharp tug. Her hand started at Tess's shoulders, then roamed up and down her torso. "Who's the dunce who said you shouldn't wear a bikini? This body was *made* for one."

"I'm not model-thin, but women with a curve to their hips shouldn't be locked away in a dark room."

"I love curves," Darcy said, looking positively stunned as her hand dipped into Tess's panties, feeling every undulation.

"Let's get in the shower. I want to play with you." Tess reached in and turned on the big rainfall shower head. "I hope your dad has a huge hot water tank. I normally conserve, but today I want to be a glutton."

She grabbed the roll of plastic wrap they'd used the day before to wrap Darcy's casted hand.

Then Darcy pulled the tie on her pajama bottoms and they dropped to the floor. With one hand she tugged Tess's panties down and they let their bodies touch all along their lengths for the first time. "Maybe we should go back to bed," Darcy murmured hotly into Tess's ear. "I'm not sure I'm going to be able to stand for much longer."

"No way. I'm testing a theory." She took Darcy's hand and pulled her into the steamy shower. "Work with me here." She used her hand as a cup to wet Darcy down, then squirted liquid soap all over both of them. "Now show me how you move." She draped her arms around Darcy's neck and stood there, waiting for the fun to begin.

With a devilish gleam in her eyes, Darcy put a firm grip on her shoulder and rubbed their wet, slippery breasts together, grinning happily when their nipples hardened.

"Nice," Tess breathed. "I love that."

Darcy turned her around and whispered into her ear, "We haven't even begun." Holding her tightly, she started to move, with her wet body plastered to Tess's. "You had some great moves against my leg. I just need a bigger canvas."

"Oh, yeah," Tess purred. "This is gonna be good."

Darcy cupped a breast and squeezed as her body slipped and rubbed all over Tess. "You feel so good," she murmured. "So firm and springy. Like a teenager."

"How would you know? You've never been with a teenager," Tess teased.

"I feel like I'm with one now. A sexy, sensual teenager." Darcy's body hadn't stilled for a second. She rubbed and skimmed her flesh against Tess's, touching every place her hand or body could reach. It was amazing when Tess considered that just two weeks ago she could barely laugh without shuddering in pain. But now she was moving again, and things were getting interesting. Darcy clamped her mouth onto Tess's neck and bit down as her hand slipped between her legs.

"Really good," Tess growled. "Perfect." She tilted her hips, making her clit glide over Darcy's fingers. "Come inside me," she begged. "I need to feel you."

Wet fingers slid inside and Tess let out a hiss of pleasure. "Ooo," she moaned. "More of that." The fingers started to move, probing deeply as she ground herself against Darcy's hand. "Good, good," was all she could get out.

Darcy didn't need a bit of instruction, but Tess loved to talk, to communicate with more than just her body. "Bite my neck again. Yeah … just like that," she groaned when Darcy's teeth pressed hard against the skin.

A hand lifted to pinch and tug on her nipples, then slid back down to fuck her in a perfect rhythm. "I've got to touch myself," Tess panted as her fingers skimmed over her clit. "Keep it up, baby. Do it … do it." She thrust her butt against Darcy, the changed angle making gentle fingers press against a sensitive spot. "Oh, god, that's so good," she moaned as spasms rolled through her body, making her shiver. "Slow … slow … but don't stop. That's it. Nice and easy." Another climax followed the first, this one slow and gentle. "Jesus, I've got to sit before I fall." Darcy turned her around and let her slide to the heated bench that ran along the wall.

Tess longed to pull her down and kiss her until her lips hurt, but she had the presence of mind to know that would kill her. But Darcy sensed what she needed and sat on her lap, mirroring the pose Tess had adopted earlier. They kissed; deep, soulful kisses that left them both panting.

"That was awesome," Darcy murmured. She looked so sexy, dripping wet with her hair a mess and her eyes shining with desire. "We have to do that every day. Every single day."

"I'm in. No question. Make me a part of that team."

"A small team. Just me and you." Darcy bent her head, then lifted it, gazing into Tess's eyes. "This doesn't hurt!" Smiling, she let her head drop again as she placed kiss after kiss on Tess's lips.

"You're getting better," Tess said, bubbling with happiness. "I bet every part of you is getting back to normal." She let her hand move along Darcy's back to slide down and explore between her legs. "I bet this little part's ready to rock again."

"I'm not sure …" A furrow in her brow showed she was starting to think about their previous attempt.

"It's no big deal. I've got nothing but patience. If not today, then tomorrow or the day after." Tess threaded her fingers into Darcy's hair, being careful not to pull her down too far. "You like being touched even if you can't have an orgasm, right?"

"Yeah," Darcy said with a warm smile. "I really like having you touch me."

"Then let's focus on that. We don't have to concentrate on the ending. The journey's the fun part, and it lasts longer."

"How should we …?"

"You look chilly. Why don't you stand under the water and I'll…" She grabbed a towel and rolled it up. "I'll do what I like best."

"Really? But how will you reach …?"

Tess slapped the heated bench. "One foot up here. Let me do the rest."

"If you insist," Darcy said, grinning slyly. "I hate to disappoint you."

She put her foot on the edge of the bench, then leaned against the wall, with the warm water cascading down her body. Tess knelt on the towel, then had to work on the angles, but she maneuvered herself and Darcy until they were both comfortable. Then she looked up and gazed at Darcy's luscious body, feeling her desire flare again. "You're so freakishly hot," she said, her eyes unable to move away from Darcy's breasts, which looked even better from below. "When you're completely healed ... Whew!"

Darcy looked down at her, and for just a second a veil of sadness took the spark from her eyes. Her hand went to Tess's head, and she tenderly moved some strands of hair from her face. "I hope we're together then." Those big brown eyes blinked slowly. "I really hope that."

Tess wrapped her arms around Darcy's slippery body, hugging her hard. There wasn't a scratch on her below the waist, and Tess didn't have to control herself. She held on tightly, then burrowed her face into Darcy's belly. "You'll be free soon. It's all going to work out."

"I'll try to catch some of your optimism."

Looking up at her, Tess forced herself to smile brightly. "I'm optimistic about many things." She placed a kiss on the pale, soft skin. "I'm damned sure you're going to love this." Concentrating, she nuzzled against Darcy's body, loving her scent and the way her muscles tensed when she stood this way.

Using her hands to gently open her, Tess slid her tongue inside to lick and tease every inch. Almost at once, Darcy started to shake. She was *so* responsive. Tess's body shivered when Darcy's did, like they were sharing a nervous system. "That feels wonderful," Darcy murmured. "So sweet and gentle."

Tess nuzzled against her in a sensual fog. She loved using her mouth on Darcy, only disappointed that she couldn't speak to express how much she was enjoying herself. But Darcy seemed to know. Her hips started a slow back and forth motion, positioning herself exactly where she wanted to be touched.

Tess let her move, staying in one place to let Darcy have control. In just a few seconds they were on the same wavelength, and Tess let her mind wander briefly to how easy that was for them. Almost from the first she'd been able to guess what was on Darcy's mind—anything from how she was feeling to what was worrying her. In three years, she and Sam had never gotten to that place, almost always guessing wrong —often hurting each other's feelings in the process.

Looking up, Tess saw Darcy's eyes shut tightly, her head leaning back against the wall. She was such a beautiful woman. With such a modest ego that she seemed surprised every time Tess complimented her. She was a gem, and Tess hoped some sweet homebody would sweep her off her feet and give her the stable life she longed for—and deserved.

"Put your fingers inside me," Darcy said, her voice soft and sexy.

Hurrying to please her, Tess growled when her fingers slid into that warm, slick skin. Darcy still controlled the pace and the pressure, moving around Tess's tongue. Tess was able to concentrate on fucking her, which she did with gusto. Darcy didn't say a word, obviously focused on her pleasure, but her body shook harder as Tess moved inside, plunging her fingers into her wetness again and again.

The casted hand landed hard on Tess's shoulder, while the other one slapped against the wall. "Almost," she cried, her body shivering roughly as her pussy contracted firmly around Tess's fingers. Darcy panted out nonsense when her foot slid from the bench and her knees started to buckle. But Tess was able to put a hand on each thigh to hold her up.

"Hold on, baby," she said, scrambling to her feet to press against her hips. "I've got you."

"Fantastic," Darcy murmured, her body heavy against Tess.

"Sit," Tess directed as she moved her to the bench. When she was certain Darcy wouldn't slip off, she went to fetch bath sheets for them both. Then she turned off the water, wrapped the big towel around Darcy and sat next to her on the bench. "Happy?" she asked, leaning her head onto Darcy's shoulder.

"Very. Relieved, too. I've been worried that it wouldn't work."

"Aww …" She reached down and gently patted her. "You're back in business. You can have fun even if you run out of batteries or there's a power outage."

"That's the longest I've gone in my adult life without having an orgasm. I hope my dry spell is over."

"There wasn't an inch of you that was dry," Tess teased. "I foresee hours of fun in the shower until you're fully healed. We'll be the cleanest women in Westhampton."

"Not a bad fate. I'll eagerly take it."

Tess was still drying her hair when Darcy went into the kitchen to get breakfast. Darcy often got a headache when she didn't have a caffeine jolt in the morning, but her romp in the shower had given her such a boost caffeine was incidental today.

Tess liked something sweet in the morning, and Darcy decided to try to make her pancakes. It wasn't going to be easy with one hand, but she'd learned to make accommodations. She was tired of being limited by her injuries.

While trying to recall the proper proportions, images kept invading her mind. Thoughts of Tess's incredible body wouldn't give her a moment's peace. But it wasn't just her body that Darcy found so appealing. The whole package was so desirable, she had to hold onto the counter for a few seconds to get her balance. Tess had knocked her off her feet, just as surely as if she'd tackled her.

Darcy poured a cup of coffee and leaned against the counter for a minute, trying to put things into perspective. Tess was her ally, her friend, her partner in crime. But she wasn't her girlfriend, and she never would be. This was one more area where Darcy had to control her desire, to tamp down her needs. Tess was like a big, gooey hot fudge sundae. Something you wanted—badly. But sundaes weren't a meal. They were a rare treat. If you were going to have one, you'd be a fool not to savor it. But you were a bigger fool if you thought empty calories would sustain you. That was a harsh way to think of Tess. But it was accurate. She was a treat. A delightful, mesmerizing, intoxicating treat. Nothing more.

After breakfast, Darcy picked up reading the paper where she'd left off when Tess had so nicely interrupted her. On the first page of the Metro section was another update from Eliza, her reporter. "Hey, Tess," she called out.

Tess emerged from the study, where she'd set up her temporary office. "Yeah?"

"Update. Eliza must have gotten confirmation on my story."

"Read it!" She dashed over to sit next to Darcy, as alert as a cat watching a mouse.

"Sources have confirmed that Darcy Morgan, wanted for the murder of an accountant in Brooklyn last month, was involved in a bizarre incident on Wednesday in Cape May, New Jersey. Morgan was chased through the Washington Street Mall by one Sergei Zahorchak, who fired at her at least three times. Zahorchak is in custody on a weapons charge, but Morgan escaped both the attempt on her life and the Cape May police. In a letter to *The Times*, Morgan again states her claim that members of the NYPD have conspired with organized crime in attempting to frame her for the murder. In related news, shopkeepers in the Gravesend section of Brooklyn claim widespread police corruption. Several residents state that organized crime figures control the whole neighborhood, and that repeated complaints to the NYPD have been ignored." Darcy looked up and saw a spark of hope in Tess's pale eyes. "There are a number of Russian-owned businesses in the neighborhood, and one man stated that the situation is no different than it was in Odessa. He moved his family here to start fresh, but the criminals moved right along with him."

"Good," Tess said. "Not good that the mob's hurting people, of course. But good that Eliza's keeping on it."

The phone rang, and Darcy got up to answer. "Miller residence."

"Hi, Darcy, it's Ben."

"Good. You're the only person I want to hear from."

"You're not taking calls from reporters?"

She laughed. "No, I'm only communicating with that reporter by mail. I'm more than a little skittish."

"It's working so far, so why change? I called to tell you I've got a few attorney recommendations for you. Can you write them down?"

"Sure. Let me get a pen. Oh, I had a question. Tess needs to keep in touch with her parents. Do you think it's safe for her to use this phone? I've heard it's tougher for the government to put a tap on a landline."

"Hmm … They can't know about me, so that's not an issue. Is there any chance the police know her name?"

"Any chance? Sure. But it's not a big one."

"You have to decide how much risk you're willing to accept."

"Who am I kidding?" she said. "I worry about Tess slipping in the shower. Any risk is too much."

"Then have her write and arrange for them to call her from a relative's house or an office."

"Okay. I'll do that. I just want her to be able to reassure them." She turned and met Tess's affectionate gaze. "I'll get that pen."

After lunch, Darcy got busy, calling each of the three attorneys Ben had suggested. She knew she was being overly careful, but she didn't use Ben's landline. Her disposable phone was going to have to do, even though constantly spending so much money on new ones annoyed her.

One of the attorneys called her back quickly. "Hi," she said when he'd identified himself. "My name's Darcy Morgan, and the NYPD is trying to pin a crime on me that I didn't commit."

The guy chuckled. "That's a pretty common complaint, but in your case, you might be telling the truth."

"Why do you say that?"

"Because I've read the stories in the paper. I also saw the photo they posted of you. First time I've ever seen a killer who looks worse than the victim."

"He looked pretty bad," Darcy admitted, still seeing Harry's lifeless body in her dreams.

"Maybe, but it's hard to figure out how you broke your own ribs and your wrist while beating a guy. You don't look like you've got that kind of wallop in your punch."

"No, I don't. But I've learned it's not hard to break a woman's wrist if you're a massive guy who gets off on hurting people."

"Are you calling from a safe line? I don't usually worry about that, but I've heard the police are leaning on everyone they can to find you."

"I'm calling from a disposable phone. And as soon as we hang up I'm going to throw it away and buy another."

"Good idea. So … what do you want to know about me?"

"I'm not sure. I've never needed a criminal defense attorney before. Why don't you tell me why I should hire you?"

"That's a good question. I'm not cheap, and I'm not the most fun guy to hang out with. I'm very argumentative. My wife says I'm a huge pain in the ass, if I'm gonna be honest. But I love to win, and I love to help the few innocent people I run across who've been charged with crimes. From what I've heard, you couldn't have killed your boss, and I'm itching to dig into the dirt and find out why the NYPD wants you to go down for it."

"Those are pretty good answers, Mr. Cullen."

"Call me Ned."

"Okay, Ned. I'm going to talk to a couple of other people, then I'll get back to you."

"I'll clear my calendar tomorrow afternoon if you can meet."

"Uhm, I don't think that's a good idea. I don't want you to be put into a bad position with the police, so I want to stay as anonymous as I can. I plan on using disposable phones to call you, and I don't want to tell you where I am, either."

"That's not how I usually do business, but in this case I understand. If you're going to call me, do it between six and eight a.m. I'll give you my home number."

"Really?"

"Yeah, really. I don't leave the house until eight, and no one'll be competing for my attention."

"Got it. Thanks, Ned. I'll get back to you."

"No problem. Hey, who recommended me?"

"Can't say. But you came very highly recommended."

He chuckled. "I'll tell my wife not everybody cuts me down." His voice took on a sober tone. "You're going to have to figure out how to cover my retainer if you hire me. Like I said, I'm not cheap."

"Will you take a check?" She briefly wondered how her mother would feel about using her life insurance proceeds to pay for a criminal defense attorney.

"If it's good I will."

"It's definitely good. I might be wanted for murder, but they'll never get me for check kiting."

Late that evening, after Darcy had spoken to all three attorneys, she and Tess discussed the merits of each of them as they walked to the deserted village.

"I think I'm going to go with Ned. He seems like a straight shooter, and Ben said he has a reputation as a bulldog."

"That's what you need. Someone who grabs on and won't let go."

"Each of them agrees on the basic strategy. My best hope is to work out a deal with the DA. I'll have to testify about Sergei and Viktor, and in return, I'll get immunity."

"I don't like that. It implies your guilt, and I don't want that hanging over your head. It might affect your ability to get a good job."

"That's the other reason I like Ned. He agreed that working out a deal for immunity would be easiest, but he wants to get the DA to drop the charges. He wants to make it clear to them that we're not playing around, and that I'll hide for as long as I have to."

"Will you?" Tess gazed into her eyes after pulling Darcy to a stop. "No time limit?"

"Hmm. I haven't thought about that yet, but I don't think I have a limit. I'm innocent and I want to prove it. But I'm not dumb enough to give myself up just because I believe the justice system is always right. It's not," she said, her vehemence surprising even her.

"I think that's the right choice." Tess took her arm and they continued to walk down the street, with the Christmas lights that brightened all of the trees and shops lighting up their faces.

"What about you?" Darcy asked, trying not to sound as tentative as she was. "What's your time limit?"

"We're in this together, Bitsy. I'm never going to turn on you, so I can't give up before you do."

Darcy stood in front of an old-fashioned store front, looking at the astoundingly expensive children's shoes. "Maybe that's not a good idea." She took Tess's hand, peeled off the new glove Tess had bought, and brought the warm hand to her lips for a kiss. "If the police don't know about you, you could just walk away. Even if they've connected you to me, you might be able to get away now if you told the story you told Ben. You could say that as soon as you found out what I'd been charged with you told me you were going to the cops. Then I snuck out of the hotel and you haven't seen me since." She kissed the soft skin again, relishing the feel of any part of Tess.

"You're going to have to actually do that if you want to get rid of me." Tess put her now chilled hand on Darcy's cheek and gazed into her eyes for a long time. "I know you're trying to protect me, but I don't want you to do that. Focus on yourself, Darcy. You're the one they're after. I'm an afterthought."

"But you might be able to walk away from this and get back to your life."

"I'm young," she said, smiling. "Hopefully I've got a lot of life left. I can afford to blow a few months."

Overcome with feeling, Darcy wrapped her arms around Tess and held on as tightly as she could. "I want you with me. You *know* that. But it's going to get harder and harder for me to let you go." She knew her smile was not convincing, but she had no way of making it perk up. "We probably shouldn't have let ourselves get this involved."

Tess fondly patted her cheek. "We were involved the minute you showed me your big gun. It's too late to turn back now, so we'll just take it one day at a time and try to have as much fun as we can. That's my life motto."

"Mine is to be careful, and double check everything."

Tess placed a gentle kiss on her lips. "Then I'll be in charge of having fun and you be in charge of"—knitting her brows in thought, she stopped—"just let me be in charge. You're running a fun deficit that I think I can make a dent in."

When Tess walked into the living room the next morning, Darcy was speaking on her disposable phone.

"Yeah, I think that's true," Darcy said, offering a little wave to Tess. "I know it's strange, but so far he's surprised me in very nice ways." Darcy nodded, "Yeah, of course, I'll keep you posted. Thanks, Danny. I'll call you in a few."

As she hung up, Darcy said, "I didn't tell him my father's name, I didn't say what he did for a living, and I didn't tell Danny we're twenty minutes from his house. I'm doing my best to keep him in the dark."

"Good morning to you too." Tess gave her a quick kiss. "What else did you two not talk about?"

"Nothing. He has nothing new." Darcy moved to her favorite chair, the curvy modern one. "It was a little odd, though. I thought

241

Danny would be happy about me finding Ben. But he … he kept bringing up all sorts of things. The DNA test might not be accurate. He was probably a jerk if my mom didn't want me to know him. He might turn on me. All sorts of bad stuff like that."

"He might be jealous." Tess straddled Darcy's lap.

"Jealous? Of what?"

"Of losing his place." She put her hand under Darcy's chin and lifted it. "He's been your *de facto* father forever, right? Having the actual guy enter the picture might mean he gets squeezed out."

"That's ridiculous! I'm *crazy* about my uncle. I'd *never* let Ben take his place."

"Maybe I'm wrong. Maybe Danny's just being super cautious. That *is* in the Morgan DNA, from what I can tell." She placed a tiny kiss on Darcy's forehead.

"Yeah. Maybe. But you might be onto something. If you're right, it won't help to tell him about Ben's two houses, sexy sports car, big BMW, or his prestigious job. Danny's never been a big fan of lawyers."

"Have you celebrated father's day with Danny?'

"Huh?" She looked up in surprise. "No, it's never been like that. He's been more like a big brother. He was still in high school when I was born, and my mom always treated him more like a kid than a peer."

"Good. Because I have a feeling you're going to want to spend a certain Sunday in June with Ben, and I don't want Danny to get his feelings hurt."

"Ooo, the thought of June is nice. I just hope I'm able to get into the water this year. The women's facility in Bedford Hills doesn't have a beach."

"You're not going to jail," Tess said firmly. "And if you are, I'm going with you. It wouldn't be fun, but I bet I could write a killer book out of the experience."

CHAPTER TWELVE

THE WEATHER HAD BEEN so unpredictable, they never knew when they'd be able to go out. But one morning, Tess was already lacing up her shoes when Darcy woke. "Going somewhere?"

"I'm antsy," she admitted. "This is a gorgeous place, don't get me wrong, but I'm not used to being in one place for more than a few days."

"Then we'll go somewhere. We've got a car no one knows about, and the police aren't looking out here. Name it."

"No, that's risky. I'll just go for a long walk on the beach."

The phone rang and Darcy answered it. "Hello?"

"Hello?" a woman's voice said. "Is this … Darcy?"

"I'm afraid you have the wrong number."

"I'm looking for Tess. This is her mom."

"Oh, gosh, I'm sorry, Mrs. Keller. Yes, this is Darcy. I'm so sorry to have gotten your daughter involved in this—"

"You can't get Tess involved in anything she doesn't want to be a part of, honey. There's no need to feel guilty about that."

"But I do," Darcy said, meeting Tess's eyes. "I feel very guilty about it."

"Let me talk to her. I know her inside and out. If she's unhappy about being involved, we'll think of a way to get her out."

"I've offered her ways, Mrs. Keller. But she's not interested."

Tess walked over and snatched the phone away. "Will you two stop talking about me like I'm not here? Hi, Mom. Miss you." She laughed. "Yes, I'll tell her."

Darcy gave her a quick hug and left her alone. If her mom could talk her into giving herself up that would definitely be the best thing—for Tess.

The Keller women were both pretty gabby. Darcy was desperate for her coffee, but once she'd decided to leave Tess alone, she felt odd going back in. Maybe she could just listen for a minute …

"No, being idle isn't bad at all. I worked too hard this past year. I really needed the break."

Tess's laugh made the hairs on the back of Darcy's neck stand up. The woman had the most attractive laugh in the world.

"If I could do anything, I'd go into Manhattan and look at the Christmas lights. But that's too dangerous for us, so I'll satisfy myself with our little village." She listened for a moment. "Yeah, I know. But there's a chance I'll still be in New York next year. I can do it then."

Darcy went back into their bedroom and considered how they could go into the city. Because they *were* going.

They argued all during breakfast, but Darcy thought she was winning the point. Tess sat on her lap, staring into her eyes. "I've never seen the Christmas lights, but I don't celebrate the holiday, so it's not a big deal. It was just an item I wanted to tick off my list."

"You don't celebrate Christmas? Why not?"

"Too commercial." She shrugged. "My parents aren't into things like that."

"That's really swimming against the tide."

"Oh, they do that," Tess agreed, chuckling. "They're pretty unique. By the way, my mom isn't Mrs. Keller."

"She's not?"

"Nope. And my dad isn't Mr. Keller. His last name is Becker."

"You … were named after your mom?"

"Uh-huh. We're matrilineal."

"I think you're the first person I've ever met who was named after her mom. That's really cool."

"We weren't always viewed as cool, but that's probably more because we didn't celebrate Christmas. People think you're really out there if you don't."

"But you seem to really like the decorations."

"Uh-huh. I like exuberance. Any kind."

"Well, that's double the reason to go. We'll go look at the lights and the store windows. Let's take the train, and plan to be in Manhattan around six. We'll wear our costumes."

"After we wear them, can we burn them? Now that I have a spiffy new lightweight jacket the thought of wearing that heavy wool coat is really off-putting."

"We'll give them to a charity. They're always collecting coats at this time of year."

"They'll make good blankets for a homeless person," Tess agreed. "Great idea."

Darcy was fidgety all day, but Tess let her be. It was hard to talk someone out of being nervous—especially when she had good reason to be. They'd talked to Danny and he said things were calm. He also confirmed that the NYPD was looking for Darcy alone. That was a *huge* relief. Tess wasn't worried about herself, but having the police looking for just one of them made being together a benefit. If you were on the lookout for one woman, seeing a pair of them strolling down the street wouldn't jump out at you.

Even though things hadn't gotten more dangerous, she still would have refused Darcy's suggestion to go to the city—but she was starting to go stir-crazy. And she knew she would only remain helpful if she was in a good frame of mind. Being with Sam had taught her that. When she felt hemmed in, she got bitchy, and Darcy certainly didn't deserve that.

As they had before, they sat apart on the train. Two women in headscarves and shin-length skirts drew a little attention when everyone else was dressed in modern clothing, and being together for a long ride let people stare. Staring was bad.

When they got to Penn Station, they met up again and walked directly to Macy's, just across the street. The streets were jammed with commuters, tourists, people checking out the displays and … cops. Lots and lots of cops. Tess hadn't considered there would be extra patrols in Herald Square, but it made perfect sense. A big, distracted crowd was a great place for pickpockets and purse-snatchers. Still, she wasn't too worried. The throng didn't allow for a clear view of anyone unless you were right on top of them.

It took a while to wait in a slow-moving line that snaked along the windows. Now that they'd been out of the house for a while, Darcy seemed more at ease.

The windows themselves were pretty cool, with lots of moving parts and snow and cheery fires with pink-cheeked children gathered 'round. Very Dickensian. But her parents had a point—Christmas was all about moving product. The window-display artists had to go back a hundred and fifty years to find families celebrating in a way that was aesthetically pleasing, and that was pretty sad.

They reached the main store entrance on Sixth Avenue and got caught in a scrum of people trying to enter or exit the building. A Salvation Army kettle was parked right at the curb and Darcy almost took a tumble when some jerk pushed her from behind. Tess yelped as she rushed to grab her arm, then the cop who stood next to the kettle stared at her for a second. Tess watched, in horror, as Darcy did the worst thing possible. "Run!" she cried. "Get home!" Then she yanked her arm away from Tess and disappeared into the crowd.

Tess stared at the cop, who grabbed a device from his shoulder and started to speak into it. In slow motion, his hand reached out and without thinking she ducked behind a big guy, then dashed into the street. It was a mass of cars and buses, most of them at a standstill. But a big, lumbering crosstown express came flying down the dedicated bus lane and she found herself vaulting over the barrier that kept other cars from using the lane. A few kind-hearted pedestrians screamed when it looked like the bus would mow her down, but she made it over and kept moving.

Picking her way through the stopped cars, she ran for Penn Station, her heart racing faster than her thoughts. The police would definitely be on the lookout for her *if* they were looking for her. Given how Darcy had behaved, a good police officer would check to see if there was an alert for someone matching their description, even if he didn't recognize them. But Tess couldn't allow herself to believe the officer was just being careful. She had to act on the worst possibility—that he'd recognized Darcy and had the ability to disseminate information about her sighting quickly.

If she were looking for a fugitive, she'd check the damned train station. And right now being dressed oddly was doing her no favors. If the cop called in the description "youngish woman, long skirt, long coat, headscarf," she would stick out like a very sore thumb. She was standing on 35th street, trying to decide what to do when a yellow cab—empty —stopped right next to her. Maybe that was a sign. After jumping in, she said, "I need to get to Long Island."

"Get a private car," the cabbie said, glaring at her in the rearview mirror. "That's too far for me."

"How much?" She stared right back at him. "Name your price."

"Where you going?"

She couldn't afford to tell him the exact address. "JFK," she finally said.

Dismissively, he grumbled, "That's not Long Island." He gave her another surly look, then logged the destination and pulled away from the curb. Tess sank down in the seat, trying to disappear. Her heart hammered in her chest, and she fought the urge to be sick. Darcy was lost … either caught or running … and she couldn't do a damn thing to help her.

Stupid, stupid, stupid! Darcy slid into Macy's, using large people to hide behind as she would a tree in the woods. By the time she'd gone fifty feet the crowd thinned out. Off came the headscarf. With her one working hand she tried to fluff her hair out to look a little different. Her coat was a distinctive shade of brown, so it had to go too. She got between two tall guys heading for the customer relations desk on the mezzanine. There were dozens of people crammed into the relatively small area, all trying to get a free shopping bag. A few couches bracketed the space, and she walked over to one and said to the woman on the end, "Watch my coat for a second, okay?" Then she threaded her way past the group at the desk and walked back down the stairs to the first floor.

Now she just looked dowdy. Having not bought any more clothes, despite Tess's prodding, she wore a white blouse tucked into her long skirt. Even though no one would mistake it for fashionable, she didn't look too different from some of the salesclerks. But she couldn't afford to stay in the building—or the neighborhood. The store was designed to make you stop and look at all sorts of merchandize, so it was always hard to move quickly. She exited, finally, on Sixth Avenue. Despite her skyrocketing anxiety, the cold shocked her. Walking around New York without a coat in December was a sure way to draw a second look. So she ducked into the first clothing store she spied. It was one of those places that sold very trendy clothes for young women, not the kind of place a woman who looked like her would ever go. But she didn't have many options. Without trying anything on, she bought a dark blue ski jacket, a black turtleneck, a pair of jeans and a dark beanie with matching gloves. Thank god she'd tucked a wad of cash into her skirt pocket.

A relatively upscale chain restaurant was right on the corner and she went in and made eye contact with the hostess. "Table for one. But I need the restroom first."

"It's in the back, on the right," the woman said.

Darcy went into a stall and struggled into her new clothes, finding the sizes on the tags weren't what she'd expected. The jeans were way too big, the sweater much smaller than she would have chosen. But when she exited and looked at herself in the mirror, she breathed a sigh of relief. She looked different. Very different. That was all that mattered. Her old clothes wouldn't fit in the trash receptacle, so she stuffed them into the shopping bag and left it on the floor. On the way out, she breezed right by the hostess, who didn't seem to notice her. *Success!*

Now that she didn't feel she had to slither down the street, she stopped at a shoe store and bought socks and a pair of sneakers. She planned on walking a lot and the orthopedic shoes she'd been wearing weren't up to the task. After asking the clerk to put her old shoes in the box, she went out and dumped it into the first trash can she found.

Getting away from Herald Square was her first priority. She started to head northeast, trying to get to a less crowded neighborhood. As she walked, her entire body thrummed with only one thought. *Tess.*

As soon as Tess was dropped off at terminal two, a spot she chose for no logical reason, she went inside and found the ground transportation desk. "I need a limo," she informed the clerk.

"Where are you going?"

"Montauk." The word jumped out of her mouth without much help from her brain. Montauk was the furthest eastern spot on Long Island, and from the poking around she'd done on Ben's computer, it was a long way from Westhampton. But maybe her brain had made the right choice. From there, she could catch a westbound train back to Westhampton, then walk home from the station. No one would expect her to be on the Long Island Railroad coming from the east—given that she herself hadn't expected to be doing that.

Darcy walked along Lexington Avenue, going further north for no good reason. She hadn't given any thought of how to get to Long Island. Her only instinct was to distance herself from Herald Square. But now that she'd done that, she needed a plan. Taking the train was too risky. Even though the trains were crowded, it wouldn't be hard to send a cop through each one. She was fairly confident she looked different enough from her photo to fool anyone but the most careful searchers, but, given how she'd reacted when the cop had made eye contact with her, she couldn't trust herself. As she walked along, she considered that she wasn't normally the kind of woman who overreacted like that. But she'd grown so protective of Tess that she hadn't given it a second thought. The cop looked at her—she thought there was a small chance he recognized her—and she lost it. It was as simple as that. Her mom had always told her the way to catch an escapee was to go to his mother's house. Sooner or later, everyone went home to mom for comfort. She'd never believed any of her mom's truisms more. All she wanted was to be in Tess's arms. But her stupidity might have Tess locked up at that very moment, and the mere thought of her beautiful spirit confined in a cell made her sick.

It took forever to travel across Long Island. Traffic was heavy, a light rain had started to fall, and parts of the road were icy. Darcy had a rule that Tess was damned glad she'd followed. Whenever they went out, they each had to carry a thousand dollars in cash. She patted her pocket to reassure herself that she still had over nine hundred dollars. "Any idea of how long it's going to take us?" she asked after an hour.

"Maybe another hour," the driver said. "There aren't any shortcuts."

"Where are we now?"

"Almost Amagansett."

"Could I get out there and take the train the rest of the way?"

He looked in his rearview mirror. "If you wanted to take the train, why didn't you connect from JFK?"

"Uhm, I've never been here before. I didn't know it would take this long."

"It takes what it takes, lady. I'm not crazy about going to the end of the earth myself, so if you want out—be my guest. You're paying for the whole trip, though."

"I can pay," she said, trying not to sound too testy. This was yet another person she didn't want to remember her well. "Let me out at the train station."

"Bad choice," he said, shrugging. "You'll probably wait at the station for an hour. The train doesn't run very much."

"I don't mind. I like trains."

After paying nearly two hundred dollars, Tess got out and walked through the bitterly cold wind to find there was no real station—just an elevated platform. There wasn't another soul around, and when she climbed the steps on the westbound side she saw why. It was just after nine and the next train wasn't until a few minutes before eleven. A two hour wait. In a cold rain. With nothing to do but obsess about Darcy.

Years of travel had given her the tools to figure her way out of this. She'd been stuck, far out of town, with few options, several times. But she'd never been quite so far out of town or quite so ill-dressed for the weather. Standing on the platform might give her frostbite, and she wasn't going to waste over a month on the lam only to be cut down by pneumonia. With no other viable ideas, she decided to walk around town. Maybe there was a bar or a restaurant open, even though she couldn't see much of a town from where she stood. But people, even people in the middle of nowhere, needed a good, stiff drink once in a while. She fervently hoped.

It took over thirty minutes to find a bar, but it was a good one. Dark, nearly empty, with a young guy running the place. Before entering, Tess had taken off her headscarf and given some sense of order to her hair, then opened her coat to show her relatively normal blouse. Now she amped up her personality, trying to seem friendly and lost. "Hi," she said when the bartender looked up. "I had some car trouble and I think my batteries are dead."

"You've just got one battery," the guy said, his gaze running up and down her body briefly. For once, she hoped a guy liked what he saw.

"Two." She shrugged, trying to look hapless. "My cell phone's dead too."

"I guess it's not your night." His smile was a little flirty, but she had to admit her competition wasn't very strong. Two guys sat apart from each other at the bar, each in his sixties, each in his cups.

"You don't have a phone I can use, do you?"

He reached into his pocket and extended his cell.

"Oh, I don't want to put you out," she said as she grabbed it before he could change his mind.

"No problem."

Once again, Darcy's planning was worth its weight in gold. Wrapped around her cash was a slip of paper with three phone numbers. Darcy's latest disposable phone, Danny's disposable, and Ben's cell. Her fingers trembled as she dialed Darcy's number. It rang and rang, with Tess willing Darcy to pick up the damn call. Finally, she cut it off and tried Danny's. It rang twice, then went to voicemail. There was no sense in leaving a message only to worry him, so she cut that one off too. That left Ben. Tess turned so no one could hear her. Relief flooded her when he picked up on the first ring. "Hello?"

"Ben? It's Tess." She could feel her composure start to fall apart. Hearing a familiar voice made it feel like someone had tossed her a life-ring after she'd been treading water for hours.

"Tess? What's wrong? Where's Darcy?"

"I don't know." She lost it, starting to sob.

"You don't know?" He was clearly trying to be gentle with her. His voice got softer and he spoke more slowly. "Where are you? Do you know?"

"Yes … yes, I know. I'm in Amagansett. Don't ask how I got here. It's a long story. But I lost Darcy in Manhattan. She's not answering her cell phone and she's probably been ar … ar … arrested."

"Give me your address," he said, a model of composure. "I'll send a car to take you to my house."

"But … what about Darcy?"

"She has my cell number, doesn't she?"

"Y … yes, she does."

"She'll call it if she can. If not … we'll just have to find her. I'm going to leave now. If I drive like hell, I might get to Westhampton before you do. Just try to stay calm, Tess. We'll find her. I promise."

It took a half hour before a man entered the bar, startling everyone. "Somebody call for a limo?"

Tess slid off her stool, and waved her hand. "I did." She dropped a twenty on the bar, paying for her glass of soda water as well as conversation. If she hadn't had Gerry to talk to, she might have lost her mind. "See you," she said as she headed for the door. "I'll try to come by this summer when there's a little more action."

"What little we had is leaving," he said, chuckling.

Tess got into the car and let out a sigh of relief. Having Ben take charge let her delude herself into believing everything would be all right.

It took a full hour to get to Westhampton. That was some *long* island. She was planning on having the driver leave her at the train station, but Ben had given him the proper address. That might not have been smart, but she was damned glad she didn't have to walk another couple of miles in the cold.

Darcy had the keys to the house, so Tess had planned on walking around rather than have someone catch her lurking. But as they pulled into the drive, her heart skipped with joy at seeing the lights on. Ben came out as she opened the car door. "The car's paid for," he said, throwing his arms around her for a long, very much needed hug.

"Thank you," she whimpered. "Thank you so much."

"Hey, don't act like I'm doing you a favor. It's long, long overdue, but this is what fathers do when their kids are in trouble."

"She is in trouble, isn't she?" Tess hadn't cried on the long trip, but now that she was with someone she trusted, she started to lose control again.

"I don't know," he said, giving her another hug. "But I sure hope not."

"I'm going to go change. I never want to see these clothes again."

"Can I make you something to eat?"

"No, thanks. My stomach's too upset to risk it."

"Would you like another Scotch?"

"No, thanks. I want all of my limited resources sharp. Darcy might need me."

The clock struck two. Tess looked up, squinting to make sure the time matched the chimes. It felt like four or even five. Ben was dozing next to her, having nodded off after looking at Darcy's childhood photo album. Tess couldn't identify anyone except Darcy and her mom, but Ben remembered Karen's parents. A few times during the long night he'd stop and stare at a photo. It hurt to watch a guy who'd so wanted to have a child be faced with the incontrovertible proof of her existence—yet completely out of his reach.

Darcy might defend her mom like she was without fault, but Tess was developing a streak of animosity towards the woman. No one understood the need for autonomy more than Tess, but it just wasn't fair to keep a child from her father, or vice versa. Karen had been selfish—

pure and simple. But Tess knew Darcy would never agree with that assessment. She bet Ben would though.

A key jiggled in the lock, and Tess jumped up and ran for the door. Throwing it open, she found the most welcome sight of her life. A nearly frozen Darcy, shivering but intact.

"Oh, god," Tess cried as she put her arms around her and hugged her until Darcy whimpered in pain. "Where have you been?"

"Everywhere."

Tess immediately pulled her inside and removed her hat that was stiff with ice. Then Darcy shrugged out of her jacket.

Looking a little dazed at first, Ben got up, then walked purposefully to the door and hugged Darcy almost as hard as Tess had. "Hurts," Darcy squeaked.

"I'm so sorry," he said, clearly embarrassed. "I'm just so glad to see you."

Darcy's pale face broke into a smile. "You've got my pajamas on," she said to Tess as she tugged at the flannel. "I thought you didn't like pajamas."

"I don't. But I felt closer to you when I put them on. Come on," she said, taking her by the hand. "Let's go get you out of these wet clothes."

"I'm getting into the shower," Darcy said. "I've got to warm up."

"Uhm," Ben cleared his throat. "Do you girls mind if I stay over tonight?"

"I'd steal your car keys if you tried to leave in this weather," Tess said. "We'll be back soon. I know you want to hear what happened."

"You can tell me in the morning." He started for his bedroom. "My days of staying up past two are well behind me."

"Will you be here in the morning?" Darcy asked. "We could have breakfast together."

He took out his cell phone and started to dial a number. "I'm leaving a message for my secretary to clear my calendar. Wake me if I sleep past lunch." He met Darcy's gaze and said, "I'm very, very glad you're all right."

"Me too," she said as she took Tess's hand and headed for the shower.

Tess had to peel Darcy's clothes off, even though the jeans she wore were awfully large. "Where did you get these clothes?"

Darcy looked at the discarded jeans like she wasn't sure of their provenance. "Want the whole story?"

"No, I'd rather hear if the Knicks won. Yes!" She slapped her on the butt, knowing her ribs wouldn't hurt from a blow that far down.

"Okay, okay. You don't have to get violent." She stepped into the warm water and in just seconds her body stopped shivering. Tess leaned against the glass door, listening intently. "I ran into Macy's, circled around until I was fairly sure no one was on my tail, then went back outside. The first store I saw had almost everything—from hat to jeans. Then I found a place for socks and shoes and started walking."

"Why didn't you call Ben? Or at least leave a message here at the house?" Tess was glad they had a little distance, for she'd never wanted to shake someone so badly.

"I was afraid to use the phone. I know I'm paranoid, but I didn't want to use anything they could possibly use to trace me."

It was hard, very hard to keep the anger from her voice. Tess spoke slowly and carefully. "Did you stop to think of how worried I'd be?"

Darcy nodded, then Tess saw her chin begin to quiver. "All I thought of was you." Her body shivered and her head dropped as she cried. "I wanted you to be safe. No matter what, I wanted to protect you."

Tess whipped the pajamas off and went into the shower. She wrapped her arms around Darcy and murmured in her ear. "You've got to think about yourself, too. Where have you been, baby?"

"I wanted to make sure no one could possibly follow me. I took cabs, but only for a town or two. It's so fucking far!"

"I know. Believe me, I know. I was in a black car for hours and we'd only gotten half way across Long Island."

"What?" Darcy looked up, her eyes red and swollen.

"I took a cab to JFK, then hired a car. They asked where I was going and I said Montauk for some reason. After I decided we'd never get there, I got out in Amagansett. I borrowed a guy's cell phone and called Ben."

"And he drove all the way out there to get you?"

"Better. He had a car pick me up, then he drove here. He beat me to the house." She laughed a little. "He must have driven like a bat out of hell."

"He cares about us," Darcy said, sniffling again.

"He does. He loves you, Darcy. Even though he's only known about you for a little while. You're his girl."

She nodded. "It feels that way. I didn't … I didn't guess a guy would be that interested in being a dad, but he sure is."

"Many men have a great fathering instinct. My dad wanted kids more than my mom did."

Darcy let out a long sigh. "I'm so glad to be home."

"I'm so glad to have you home. Let's stay inside for a while, okay?"

"How about March? Is March good for you?"

"Let's not rush. I'd like to go swimming in the ocean. As soon as it gets above seventy degrees, we'll go out."

Smiling, Darcy said, "We might never leave the house. This isn't the Caribbean."

Darcy was surprised to find Ben up making coffee when she emerged from her room in the morning. "Hi," she said.

"Good morning. And it's a *very* good morning since you're both safe and sound."

"I think so too." She clapped him on the back, still skittish about being too affectionate. "Thanks so much for taking care of Tess last night. She said she was on the verge of losing it."

"It was nothing. As I told her, this is what parents are supposed to do."

She poured a cup of coffee, watching him measure oatmeal and water into a rice cooker. "I hope this doesn't sound funny, but I'm … puzzled or maybe just surprised at how you're jumping right in. I really didn't expect this."

"What did you expect?" He gave her a quizzical look.

Darcy thought about her expectations, but had to admit she'd never been that specific. She closed her eyes. She had to say this the right way. "I've had fantasies about you my whole life. But they were fragments. Just a flash of a guy smiling at me when we met."

"Then I guess I've already surpassed your expectations. It's all downhill from here, right?"

"Right. I guess that's true …" She was troubled, but couldn't, even to herself, say what was bothering her.

Ben got back to his oatmeal preparation. When he was finished, he leaned back against the counter, one ankle crossed over the other. Today he wore casual clothes—a blue oxford-cloth shirt and a navy sweater over dark jeans. The dark suede driving moccasins seemed out of place for the season, but they were probably something he wore in the summer when he used the house more often.

"You don't trust me yet. I can tell."

Wincing, she shook her head. "It's not that …" Thoughts flew through her mind. Random snatches of images and projections. But one stayed with her. An image of her mother, her mouth set in a hard, thin line. "I was thinking of what my mom would do if she were in your place. I mean, it's not possible for a woman to be in your position, but if she were …"

"What would she do?"

"She'd tell me to screw off. Maybe in so many words." She started to chuckle, then realized it wasn't very funny. "She wasn't a mean person. At all. But she'd be too suspicious of me to take a chance." Shrugging, she added, "I'm not sure what I would do, but I think I'd be somewhere between the two of you. I could be supportive, but I'd have to do a lot of prep work to get past my suspicions."

Ben tilted his head towards his oatmeal. "Mind if I eat?"

"No, go ahead. We can sit down."

"I can make a bowl for you. No problem."

"I'll wait for Tess. But thanks."

They sat at the dining table, where Ben ate a few bites in silence. Darcy didn't know him well enough to guess if he was going to continue the conversation, but waiting made her anxious.

After taking another bite, he pointed his spoon at her. "Why would you be so suspicious of a woman who wanted to meet her father?"

"I wouldn't be suspicious of a girl, or even a young woman. But someone my age?" She shook her head dismissively. "I'd assume she was only looking for me because she'd run through everyone else. She'd probably be a user—at best."

"But you're not," he said gently "I can tell."

Her cheeks flushed slightly, and she fidgeted in her chair. "Not technically, but all of a sudden you're involved with a woman running from the police."

"Don't forget the mob," he added with a grin.

"Oh, I don't ever forget them. So ... I come with a lot of baggage too. Baggage that most people wouldn't be able to ignore."

"Mmm." He focused on his cereal for a few minutes, eating quickly. Then he stood and took his bowl to the kitchen, where he rinsed it and placed it in the dishwasher. When he came back, he stood near Darcy and put his hand on her shoulder.

"If I'd gotten any indication you wanted money, you wouldn't be here now. And I'll admit you surprised the hell out of me at first. I couldn't figure out your angle. But once I did ..." He moved back to his seat, still gazing into her eyes.

"What's my angle?" she asked, puzzled at the way he'd stated that.

"You're frightened and you need someone on your side. You're sure no one can know I exist, so you don't mind getting me involved. But only a little. You're still testing me."

She laughed, having to admit that was true. "I've got a lot of nerve, don't I?"

"You're cautious. Just like your mom. And a little bit like me. Maybe it's genetic."

"For a cautious guy, you're jumping in pretty quickly, Ben. That's what's puzzling me."

"What are my options?" He stared hard, his eyes penetrating. "I've always wanted to be a father. If I don't get involved now, I'll miss my chance."

"But I'm pretty persistent. I'd probably come back around if you weren't ready now."

The hint of a smile dropped from his expression. "You might not be alive to come back around. And if I rejected you only to ..." Shaking his head, he got up to refill his coffee. "I don't want to think about the bad outcomes. I'd much rather get to know you. And Tess."

"You're okay with my being gay?" she asked, feeling strangely proud of herself for her boldness.

He looked completely befuddled. "Why would I even have an opinion?"

"Uhm ... a lot of people have very strong opinions about it."

Chuckling, he said, "People have strong opinions about a lot of things that are absolutely none of their business. I try to keep out of other people's personal choices. I'm not always successful, but I try." That pointed gaze landed on her again. "How do you feel about my being Jewish?"

She started to laugh. "I can't imagine why I'd have an opinion."

"Then we're even."

"Can I be even too?" Tess asked as she walked into the room. "I love to be part of a team." Warm, gentle hands settled onto Darcy's shoulders. She looked up at the bright, expectant look on Tess's face.

"Sure. We were just agreeing that we don't care about other people's religion or sexual orientation."

"I guess I can get behind that," Tess said. "Make me a part of the team."

Darcy stood up and placed a kiss on her cheek. "Breakfast?"

"Sure. What can a one-handed woman make? Will we have another demonstration of how much flour a person can toss onto her flannel pajamas?" She sat down and rested her chin on her hand, watching Darcy.

"I guess pancakes were a little beyond my reach. Ben did the work this time. But I can handily put some oatmeal into bowls."

"I'll accept that. Thanks, Ben," Tess said, giving him one of her guileless smiles. "I need honey on mine. I assume yours will be bare of all ornamentation."

"A banana is sweet enough for me."

"A banana and a tablespoon of honey and you've got yourself a deal."

After breakfast, Darcy and Ben took another spin down memory lane as she added context to many of the photos Ben and Tess had looked at the night before.

"I see a lot of pictures from the Jersey Shore," he said. "Did you go down there every year?"

"Pretty much. My whole family would rent a big house in Seaside Heights. Everyone would take a week off in August and soak up the sun. We had some good times down there."

"I can't provide the boardwalk or the rides, but I've got a nice boat that I keep nearby. I'd love to take you two out any time you want to go."

"I've *always* wanted to be on a boat out in the ocean," Darcy said, almost embarrassed by her excitement. "When I was a kid, I'd sit on the beach and watch the boats zip past, just wishing I knew someone who owned one. Tess?"

"I love to be on the water. I'm in."

"Great! This will all be over by then and we'll get out there every chance we get." He stopped, almost mid-word. "I have no idea what your normal life is like. What do you do for a living?"

"I'm a CPA. An unemployed one."

"Tess?"

"Travel writer. Vaguely employed at the moment."

"If you need help, Darcy, I've got contacts at quite a few corporations in New York. I'm sure I could get you an interview." He gave Tess a long look. "I don't know a single person in the travel biz. But I can try to—"

"It's okay," Tess interrupted. "I'll be fine once I'm able to travel again. It's Darcy who'll need a full-time gig."

"I'm sure I can help if you need an introduction." Ben stood and went to the counter to get his keys. "I'm going to run by the office. My partner's in Colorado this week, and I can't let things slide too much."

Darcy and Tess walked him to the door, where he took his coat from the coat tree and slipped it on. Darcy said, "Thanks again for helping so much last night. We both appreciate it."

"We're family, even though it's a recently formed family." He put his hands on Darcy's shoulders and looked in her eyes. "I'm very, very happy to have found my daughter"—he turned to smile at Tess—"and her partner."

Darcy knew she'd cry if he didn't stop looking at her so intently. Thankfully, he pulled her close and placed a kiss on her forehead. "Call me any time."

"We will," she said, putting an arm around Tess when she moved to stand beside her. "The same goes for us. Maybe you can come out this weekend? I can cook. I mean, Tess can cook."

"It's a date. See you girls then."

As he left, Darcy leaned her head on Tess's shoulder. "What I would have given to have him around when I was young." She sighed, then stood up straight. "But we've both been given a second chance, and I'm going to make the best of it."

CHAPTER THIRTEEN

THE NEXT MORNING, DARCY had just finished reading Eliza's latest follow-up in *The Times* when Tess emerged from their bedroom.

"Eliza's still digging," Darcy reported, "but they're not going to keep giving her column space if she doesn't uncover something significant."

"Nothing big today?"

"No," she said, her shoulders slumping. "Everything's unsubstantiated. We need a break, but there's no indication we're going to get one."

When Tess smiled, her expression was so cheery Darcy had to return it.

"Then we wait. It's not so bad living in a great house and not having to put your eyeshade on, is it?"

Darcy went to her and put her hands on Tess's hips. "Being with you makes everything good. But I'd really like to see some progress. I need resolution."

"I don't know how to rush that. I don't think we can."

Shrugging, Darcy started for their room. "I'm going to get dressed and go call Ned. If I rush, I can make his morning deadline."

"Can't you just … call him?"

"Yeah, I'm going to. But I want to call from another area. I don't want to give them any info they can use against me."

"But it's a disposable phone …"

"I know." She kissed Tess. "I'm overly cautious. But I sleep better when I'm more careful."

"Then by all means …" She stood aside and let Darcy continue. "Hey, we need to get to bed early tonight. I want to be up before dawn tomorrow."

Darcy stopped and looked at her, puzzled.

"It's a surprise," Tess said. "And I'll bet it's a new experience for you."

"Good. I'm trying to expand my universe. I will happily await your surprise. Meanwhile, if I don't leave now, it'll be too late to call Ned."

Darcy drove towards the city, heading west. Intending to go all the way to Bayshore, she was only able to get to Brookhaven by 7:25. Traffic on the LIE was a real mess, and she didn't want to waste her time and not get to speak to Ned. He answered after a few rings. "State your business," he said brusquely.

"Ned? It's Darcy Morgan."

"Hey, how's it going?"

"Okay. I'm not disturbing you, am I?"

He laughed. "You're the first client I've ever had who's asked that. And no, you're not."

"Good. I know you're trying to get to work, but I wanted to check in and see if you've made any progress with the DA."

"If by progress you mean they're getting more and more pissed, then yeah, I'm doing great."

"Pissed? Do we want them pissed?"

"I'm not sure. Sometimes that means the guy's at the end of his rope and he's trying not to have to cut a losing deal. But other times it means he's dug in and we're wasting time by dragging this out."

"How do you know which it is?"

With a chuckle, he said, "When I figure that out, all of my clients will walk free." His laugh grew louder. "Trust me. *No one* wants that."

"So … we just wait?"

"That's up to you, Darcy. They say they're not going to negotiate unless you turn yourself in. I told them that's not going to happen.

From what I can tell, the rat squad is looking into your claims, but they're doing it on the down-low. My guess is that they know you're right about the corruption, but they either don't want a scandal or they can't prove anything yet."

"So I wait."

"Unless you want to surrender. But we're in a weak position right now. And I never like to negotiate when I'm down."

"But this could go on forever!"

"I know. And I might be imagining this, but I get the feeling they wouldn't mind that. If you're hiding, they can ignore the corruption charge to some extent. Every criminal says he's innocent, so you're just another whiner. But if you come in, they'll have to defend themselves against a woman who, I'm certain, is going to be a very formidable witness."

"You haven't even met me."

"You're articulate, thoughtful, hard to rattle and, most of all, innocent. That comes through when you speak. And if you turn yourself in, I'm going to have you sitting down for long interviews with every legitimate interviewer I can book you with. We'll win the PR battle before it's even begun."

"I think you might be overselling me. I don't have any experience in things like that."

"You don't need experience to convince people you've been framed. You just need believability—and you've got that in spades."

Darcy didn't have much to keep her busy, so she'd started to read. In the last few years she'd been too busy or stressed to focus, but now, even though she was in hiding, she was calmer than she'd been when her mom was so ill. When her mom was well enough to concentrate, they'd read crime novels together. One of them would start, and when halfway through she'd cut the book in half and the other would begin. Darcy was the faster reader, so she'd usually dive in first—then they'd discuss plot points as her mom caught up.

Over the years, she'd gotten pretty good at guessing what would happen and even figuring out things the writer could do to tighten up the story. Now, she tried to apply those same skills to Tess's work, trying to figure out what point she was trying to make, or what market she was trying to appeal to. It was fun testing her theories with the actual writer, and she found her appetite for Tess's work to be nearly insatiable.

She was just starting an article about a dude ranch in New Zealand when Tess came into the living room. "How about a long walk on the beach? It's cold and cloudy, but not awful out."

Darcy lowered the laptop and gave Tess a smile. "You're quite the saleswoman. Who would refuse such an enticing invitation?" She got up and put her arms around her. "Not me."

Tess lifted her hand and slid her fingers down Darcy's cheek. "I can't even tell where the scratches were on your face." A gentle finger pressed a spot on her chin. "This doesn't still hurt, does it?"

"Not a bit. You can slap me hard any time I get out of line."

"That'll be the day. Only kisses go on this pretty face."

"Let me put my sweater on. I have a feeling you're downplaying how cold it is."

Tess gave her a sweet kiss. "Not too much. But I do want you to go with me, so I might be lying just a little."

"I'm learning that about you. So far you only have two faults. You're on the messy side and you lie a little. Not bad."

As they walked to the bedroom, Tess took her hand. "You have the same number. You're overly neat and you could stand to loosen up a bit. Also not bad. Maybe we'll meet in the middle. We'll be fairly neat."

"Yeah," Darcy said, smiling. "That's not gonna happen. My need for neatness is absolute."

Darcy also had a need to know where she was in the world, so she'd used the internet to get an overview of the area and plan their walks. They sometimes headed inland, but the beach always lured them back. They usually flipped a coin, then headed East or West for two, five, seven or ten mile loops, depending on the weather and their stamina. Her ribs had improved to the point where she could do ten miles one day, then cut back to five the next. But that was good progress.

There were usually a few people walking along the beach near sunset, but on a gloomy day like today that number diminished. They walked at a good clip, with Tess talking about the article she was writing. Given that she wasn't traveling, Darcy had a hard time understanding how she could write, but Tess said that wasn't a problem. She'd write a thoughtful piece about an experience she'd actually had, then make a quick trip to the area to add current hotel and meal listings.

Tess might be messy with her things, but she was rigorous about her work—a trait Darcy admired without reservation. She spent anywhere from five to seven hours a day writing and researching on Ben's computer. When she was really feeling creative, she got absolutely bubbly, the ideas just flowing from her as she talked through them with Darcy.

Tess was quieter today, not speaking much … for her. They'd completed about nine miles, and were in the home stretch. It was almost dusk—Tess's favorite time of day. The waning sun cut through the heavy cloud cover to appear just before it set. Tess grasped Darcy's hand and they stood, watching it. "Tomorrow's Solstice," Tess said quietly. "The shortest day of the year."

"Mmm. I hate winter. The first day of spring is when the world starts up again."

Turning away from the sunset, Tess gazed at Darcy. "That's not how I think of it. To me, the shortest day is the beginning, not the end. From now on every day will get a little longer. It's the earth's rebirth."

She leaned forward and kissed Darcy, slowly and sweetly. "What's your wish for the rebirth?"

Darcy thought for just a minute. "To build a better, more extemporaneous, more honest life for myself. And to find a partner." She made sure to make her smile appear lighthearted. "I'm still accepting applications ..."

"Those are damned good wishes," Tess said, ignoring Darcy's last comment. "My wish is for you to be exonerated, and to find love. You deserve to be loved, Darcy."

"That's more than one wish. You're cheating."

"I'm known to cheat. I am, after all, an inveterate liar."

"You know I was teasing when I said that, right?"

Tess patted her on the butt. "Yes, Darcy. I know you don't think I'm unable to tell the truth. I can take teasing. All you want to give."

"I've never been much of a teaser. But it's fun to do with you."

"I can rattle off a hundred things that are fun to do with me. Why don't we go home and do one of them right now?"

"I thought you'd never ask." Darcy took her hand and they picked up the pace. The night was young, and long, and they had plenty of time to bid the day goodbye.

For dinner, Tess cooked a hearty stew with lots of root vegetables and barley. "This is the kind of thing we always had on Solstice Eve," she said, working around Darcy, who was sitting on the counter. "A vegetable stew, and some brown bread my mom would make." She grabbed a loaf of French bread she'd bought earlier in the day. "We're skipping that part because it's a pain in the ass. Then we'd make wassail or some other spicy drink and build a bonfire."

"I can do that," Darcy said. "No problem."

"Where ...?" Then she nodded. "Your dad has that chiminea out by the pool. Good idea."

269

"I didn't know what it was called, but it looks like you can build a fire in it. I saw some firewood under a tarp by the garage. If I don't burn the house down, we'll have a warm place to sit and eat our stew."

"I'd tell you to break a leg, but you might actually do it." She firmly grasped Darcy and placed a long kiss on her lips.

Darcy loved how she invaded her personal space, staying just a couple of inches from her mouth.

When Tess spoke, her voice was low and sexy. "I know I should be satisfied after you chased me around in the shower for a solid hour, but I could go again."

"It's a long night. We can multitask. As long as the water heater doesn't blow, we can go at it as many times as your racy heart desires."

After eating too much, sitting by the warm fire, and sharing tales of past holidays, Darcy could feel herself starting to slump in her chair. "It's only nine o'clock," she said as she looked at the clock, "but I'm done."

"I could sleep," Tess agreed. "You're always tired early when we take a long walk." She stood and helped Darcy to her feet. "But you're moving so much better than you were even a week ago. I think you've turned the corner."

Darcy stood with very little pain. Just a twinge that she could easily ignore. "I think so too. In another week or two I'm going to be able to have sex in a real bed."

Tess gazed at her, a half smile on her face. "Will you still be attracted to me if my skin's not all pruned?"

"We'll just have to see. But I think the odds are in your favor."

Tess opened her eyes and saw that she'd beaten the alarm clock by fifteen minutes. She could tell that Darcy didn't understand the importance Solstice had in her life, but that was fine. It honestly didn't matter if other people shared or even understood her beliefs. They were intensely personal, and solid as a rock.

After sneaking out of bed, she gathered the candles she'd bought and placed them in a circle on the dining table. In the center, she added a taller, bright yellow pillar-style candle. Then she stuck a couple of metal ornaments into it, a tiny sun and a moon. Nothing like the carefully hand-crafted things her mom made. Tess loved the celebration, but she hadn't inherited a bit of her mom's handiness, nor her aversion to feeding corporate coffers.

Even though she wasn't very handy, collecting pinecones in the neighborhood had been a snap. And Ben's neatly tended garden—neatly tended by a service—had a big rosemary bush that she'd used to make a decent-looking wreath. After placing it over the big candle, she went to wake Darcy.

She was so pretty when she slept. Now, that is. At first, she'd tossed and turned and moaned most of the night. But now she slept like an angel, barely moving. Tess leaned over and kissed her on the forehead. "Wake up, sleepy head."

Darcy's beautiful brown eyes fluttered as they opened. "It's dark out."

"I know. That's part of the celebration. We're going to greet the dawn."

Wincing just a little, Darcy stood and wrapped her arms around Tess, holding on as they swayed together. She was as cuddly as a puppy when she first woke, always needing a long hug before she could get moving. "Give me five minutes," she murmured, then kissed Tess's cheek.

"Okay. But Darcy?"

"Yeah?"

"Don't turn the lights on, okay?"

She paused, then continued on her way. Tess loved the fact that she'd do as asked—no questions.

As promised, five minutes later she was back, dressed and clear-eyed. "I feel good," she said. "Sleeping through the night is making a huge difference. I think I'm ready to try lying on my side. I'm *really* looking forward to that."

"Bundle up," Tess warned. "It's clear and cold out."

Darcy pulled up her sweater, showing she had on her long underwear. When she added the coat, that was everything she owned, except for the three blouses they'd bought online. The woman needed some more clothes!

When they went into the great room, Tess led Darcy to the dining table. "Hey, what's all of this? Not that I can really see in the dark, but it looks like a nice display."

"Just some things nature didn't mind my taking." Striking a match, she lit the first candle, closed her eyes and let her heart speak. It took a few seconds for her wish to form, then she handed the box of matches to Darcy. "Just think of your intentions for the year."

"Uhm …" Darcy lit a match and held it to a candle.

Tess could see she was confused, but she was game for almost anything. Darcy's eyes closed and she nodded after a second or two. "I think I'm finished."

Tess smiled at her while she lit another candle. "We've got a few more to go." They took turns, lighting candles and silently setting their intentions to words. Taking a final match, Tess struck it, then held her hand over Darcy's. Together, they lit the large candle. "We welcome the day of the earth's rebirth. Each day will add a little more light, a little more warmth into our lives."

She turned to Darcy and said, "Now we'll go greet the dawn." She blew out the thin candles, leaving the large one burning. "I'd like it if we can go without electricity today and just focus on this one light source."

"Uhm … can we cook?"

"Of course. I just like things to be simple on Solstice. It's a good day to slow down and read and reflect, maybe write a long letter to my parents. I like to be connected to the people who matter most today."

"Sounds great. Let's go greet the day."

They walked quickly along the deserted, dark streets. There were few lights on in the houses they passed, and Tess relished being up before the town came to life. By the time they reached the ocean, a tiny line of pink was barely visible on the horizon. Tess grasped Darcy's gloved hand then leaned against her when Darcy shifted to tuck her arms around Tess's waist. The sky grew lighter and lighter, with the pink haze quickly illuminating the entire horizon. The waves quietly lapped at the shore, a few seagulls cried as they circled overhead, and the warmth of Darcy's body infused Tess with peace. It was going to be a great year.

On Christmas Eve, Ben was scheduled to come for dinner, and Darcy spent the day making a very complex Mexican casserole. Her hand wasn't painful any more, and she was able to use her fingers to a good degree, which made things so much easier. By the time Ben arrived, she had roasted peppers, sliced jalapeños, pickled some onions and braised a chicken. Now all she had to do was construct the layers.

Ben stood in the kitchen, sipping on a glass of Scotch, while Darcy worked. "How are you keeping yourself busy?" he asked. "I know Tess is working on a number of articles, but CPAs can't just find audits lying around."

"I'm doing all right. I've been reading Tess's archive." She chuckled. "That woman has been to places I didn't know existed." She lowered her voice. "I'm a little worried about her. She's used to a very active life, and I'm afraid she'll get so bored she won't be able to stand it."

"I don't think I've asked how long you've been together."

"Not long," she said, freezing a bit. "It's been a whirlwind romance so far. Being together every minute has let us get close very quickly."

"I'd bet that's true." He lowered his voice a little and added, "I'm not sure how committed to each other you are, but she's very fond of you. She was heartbroken the other night when she didn't know where you were."

"That's mutual," Darcy said. "We're a pretty good team."

"Where is she now?"

Darcy laughed, then spoke in her normal voice. "I don't know why I'm whispering. She wanted some sour cream for the casserole, so she ran to the store to pick some up."

"Hmm. I wish I could think of something to keep you two busy. I thought people your age watched TV constantly. No?"

"We watch some things in the evening. But neither of us likes it on during the day. I guess we should binge-watch a good series, but we'd have to find someplace local that sold DVDs."

"Just order whatever you want from Amazon or iTunes."

"Can't. I know the police have flagged my cards by now, and I'm too paranoid to let Tess use hers. She's going a little crazy because all of her music is on her phone and I don't want her to have it on."

He moved over to her and put his hand on her shoulder. "You're being silly. Just go onto the computer and log into Amazon. My password is on a note right next to the machine. Order whatever you want, Darcy. Really."

"I'll see if Tess wants to watch anything. Thanks," she added. "It's tough to be in a cashless society and not have a credit card you can use."

"How have you gotten by so far?"

She could have, should have told him about the money. But she didn't want anyone else to know about it unless absolutely necessary. If you didn't know the facts, you wouldn't have to lie about them later. "I had some cash stashed away for emergencies. And Tess had the use of her bank account for a while. We're fine."

He reached out and held her casted hand. "What about this? How long has the cast been on?"

"Five weeks."

"This seems awfully loose." He gently moved the cast, which could turn about a half inch.

"Yeah. The swelling's gone down. I should see a doctor ..."

"But you're afraid to go."

"Yeah. Very much."

"I've got a friend who's an orthopedist. I'll get you in to see him."

"But I can't use my name or my insurance," she said, her anxiety picking up at the thought.

"Not a problem. I'll figure out a way around that."

The next morning, Darcy and Tess went into the living room to find a cache of presents lying on the table. "Santa came!" Tess cried, giggling like a little girl.

"Hey, no fair," Darcy said, going into the kitchen, where Ben was making coffee. "We don't have anything for you."

"You couldn't have given me a better present than you did the day you showed up at my office. And I didn't buy you much. Just a few things to get you through the winter."

"Still ..." She crossed her arms over her chest. "Just for that I'm going to have to make you a nice breakfast. No complaints."

After they ate, Tess dashed to the table by the sofa. "Let's open our presents!"

"You act like you've never had a Christmas present," Darcy teased. Then her expression sobered. "Maybe you haven't."

"No, I have. I've lived in the normal world all of my adult life, Darcy. My former girlfriends were Christmas people."

"Normal world?" Ben asked.

"Oh. My parents didn't celebrate Christmas. They're unreformed hippies."

"Wow. That takes me back. I haven't talked to a hippie in forty years."

"With luck, you'll get to talk to a pair of them. I'd love to have them come here and stay for a few days when this has all blown over—or visit me in Alcatraz."

Ben gave Darcy a look. "Is she always so upbeat?"

"Pretty much. Nice, isn't it?"

"It really is. Do you have any older sisters, Tess?"

"No. I'm an only. Just like Darcy. How about you?"

"I've got a sister, but she lives in Florida."

"I've got an aunt!" Darcy could feel herself perk up. "What's her name?"

"Sylvia. I think you'll like her. She sells real estate in Palm Beach."

"Do I have cousins?"

"Two," he said. "Both boys. David runs an upholstery shop and Jerry's a dentist. Good boys, both of them. Jerry's wife's pregnant, so you'll soon have a … what would that be? First cousin once removed, or second cousin?"

"I have no idea, but I really want to meet them." She stopped abruptly. "After this is all resolved, of course."

"I've told no one," Ben said. "Not even my secretary, who knows every one of my secrets."

"I hate to be so cloak and dagger …"

"You've got good reason, Darcy. Don't give it another thought." He clapped his hands together. "I can see Tess champing at the bit. Let's open some presents!"

As he'd promised, Ben had only bought them some things to keep them warm; down mittens, earmuffs and very nice cashmere scarves. Both Darcy and Tess kept thanking him, but he waved them away. "You can't be out walking for as long as you two do and not have the right clothing."

One small gift was left and he picked it up and gave it to Darcy. "I hope you don't think this is strange, and I know it's a few decades late, but I saw this the other day and knew it belonged with you."

Puzzled, she opened the wrapping paper and pried the top off the box. Inside was a small, silver cup. The type they sold at fine jewelry stores—for babies. She cocked her head, then looked carefully at it. As she squinted to read the inscription, Ben said, "My great-grandfather's is the first name. That cup's been given to the first-born son in each generation of Millers, or Mueller, as the name was back in Germany. I offered it to my sister when David was born, but she was thoroughly convinced I was going to find a young wife and have my own family." He took in a breath. "I didn't think that would ever happen, and I'm so glad to learn that it did."

Tess reached over and put her hand over Darcy's. "I know you can't read this small type, but it says Isaiah, Solomon, Aaron, Benjamin, Darcy." She looked up at Ben. "This is beyond thoughtful."

Darcy blinked away her tears, then got up and embraced her father. "Best gift I've ever gotten. Really. The best."

"Right back at you, Darcy. No comparison. And one year my wife gave me that car in the garage." He chuckled, but Darcy could see he was forcing it. What he wanted to do was cry, and that touched her nearly as much as the gift had.

When Darcy woke two days after Christmas, Tess was sitting up in bed, looking at her. "I've got to get my e-mail," she said, a frown on her normally sunny features.

Struggling to get the cobwebs out, Darcy said, "Is there something … Did I miss …?"

"No, not really. I just realized I should be back from my trip now. I'd put a few people off, telling them I'd get back to them when I returned …"

"Okay. Got it." Darcy sat up, pleased to feel just stiffness and mild pain. "Well … I suppose we could put a virtual private network on Ben's computer, but I don't want to do that without asking him. Or we could go to a public library and use their computers. That would also let us go for a drive." She tried to sell that option, which made her feel safer. "What do you say? We could go anywhere you want."

"Mmm." Tess's eyes narrowed. "I want to go … someplace pretty. And I want to have lunch in a restaurant. Can you satisfy me?"

"Let's get in the shower and we'll see," Darcy said, her libido waking up. "Then we'll go to a library."

They drove for a very long time to get to Oyster Bay. Darcy spent much of the drive apologizing for the lack of entertainment options. "I had no idea Teddy Roosevelt's home had such limited hours in the winter."

"Don't worry about it. We can go another day."

"I guess the truth is that Long Island is all about the beaches." Tess could see her wracking her brain. "We could have gone on the wine trail, but I didn't want to go all the way up there and have everything closed."

"This is fine. It's a nice, clear day, not too cold. I'm loving being out on the open road with you in this cool car." She winked. "Your pops has nice taste."

"Didn't he say his ex-wife gave it to him for Christmas? Maybe she's the one with good taste."

"Once we clear our names we can look her up. Maybe she's always wanted an adult step-daughter."

"I'm sure everyone wants one of those," Darcy joked. "What do you want to do first? Hike, check mail, or eat?"

"Mmm … Check mail, then eat, then hike."

"Great. That would have been my choice too. We think alike."

"I'm not sure that's true," Tess said, grinning. "You're just really agreeable."

Darcy watched as Tess put a fake name on a list of people waiting for a computer. They had a twenty-minute time limit when there was a line, but there were only two people in front of them. As soon as Tess got the go-ahead, she was all business. She got to her mail account, mumbled to herself, then started sorting things. "Wish I could print some of these off."

"I don't think they have that capacity. Can I take notes for you?"

"No," she said, distractedly. "I'm good. I'll just jot a few things down." She jotted a lot more than a few things down, giving Darcy a tiny glimpse into what it must be like to work independently. Tess needed to find her own jobs, negotiate her compensation for each project, and juggle her calendar to make sure she could physically do the best-paying gigs, while keeping the others as back-up in case something fell through. Then she often had to hire a "fixer"—a local who'd guide her to the best-kept secret spots. All in all, she had to organize an awful lot of things to do her job, and given how messy she could be, it surprised the heck out of Darcy that she was so successful. Her brain obviously ran on two tracks: personal and professional, and the professional track ran like a Swiss watch.

There were other people waiting for the machine, but Darcy nearly had to pry Tess's fingers off the keyboard when the twenty minutes was up.

"We've got to go," Darcy whispered. "But we can sign up for another session if you need to."

"No, it's okay. I just need to keep this one thing straight." She made a few more indecipherable notes, then let out a breath and stood. "That was fun. I knew I should have taken a speed-reading course."

As they left, Darcy said, "How many messages did you have?"

"Over six hundred. But only about ten of them were things I have to seriously consider."

Darcy's heart started to race. "Job offers?"

"Yeah." She put her hands in her pockets as they walked to the parking lot.

Darcy wasn't sure what was bothering Tess, but she clearly wasn't in the mood to talk. She drove by a burger place and pulled in without even asking if that's what Darcy wanted. That was *not* like Tess. Darcy's stomach was in knots.

Once they were seated at a table, Tess rearranged her silverware nervously. "I hate not being able to get my mail My reputation's going to take a hit if I let messages lie there unanswered." Their eyes met. "We need to use a VPN or an anonymizer. If you want me to ask Ben about it, I will."

"I'm sorry," Darcy said, reaching across the table to capture her hand. Thankfully, it wasn't pulled away. "I should have gotten on this right after we got to Ben's. I just let myself get into a worry cycle about the police tracing me through a computer."

Tess let out a long sigh. "I should have asked for what I needed. It's my career."

"We'll do it as soon as possible. Promise."

Tess picked up her menu and started to scan it. "I need something lethal to cheer me up. Think I can eat a burger, a malt, fries and onion rings?"

"I certainly hope not!" Darcy laughed as she looked at the menu, finding very few healthy choices. "I might just watch you eat. This place is a heart attack waiting to happen." She looked over the menu more carefully. "Did I tell you that Ben had a heart attack when he was barely fifty?"

"No, you didn't. Is he okay?"

"Yeah, I think so. He watches his diet and took a lot of steps to reduce his stress."

"I'm glad to hear that. I want him to baby you for a very, very long time."

"Me too. And now that I know I have a family history of heart trouble, I'm going to be even more annoying about my diet."

"Not possible," Tess said, sticking out her tongue. "You're already as annoying as a woman can be."

That night, Darcy sat on the edge of the bed, looking nervous.

"We'll give it a try," Tess assured her. "If it hurts too much, you'll use the wedge pillow for another few days. You're almost home free. I'm certain of that."

"How do I do this? Just try to lie down and hope for the best?"

"No, that's not a good idea. Let's put all of the pillows down, then I'll lower you onto them. Can you sleep on your left?"

"Yeah. Either side's good. I usually turn during the night no matter which side I start out from."

"I'd advise against that for a while. I think you'll want to stay off your right until you're fully healed."

"Yeah, the thought of pressing my ribs into the mattress actually makes me sick to my stomach." She shivered, probably imagining the pain.

Tess had caught her looking up various sites where people offered suggestions for fellow sufferers. All that information seemed to make her more skittish rather than less.

"I don't know how people tolerate it when they've broken all of the ribs on one side. That's not uncommon," Darcy added earnestly. "And most of them have a broken clavicle to go with it."

"You don't have that. This is going to work." After taking all of the pillows from both guest bedrooms, Tess lay them in a stripe down Darcy's side of the bed. Then she knelt at the head, waiting to help lower her gently. "You can do this," she said, trying to sound confident. "I can help."

Looking very unsure, Darcy started to lie down, letting Tess help guide her. "Not bad."

"Almost there." Tess had one hand under her head, the other gripping a shoulder.

As Darcy's head touched the two fluffy pillows she let out a long, relieved sigh. "I can't believe how happy I am to lie on my side. Other than to remember to always wear body armor, this incident has taught me to appreciate the small things."

"It's no small thing to be able to spoon." Tess slid off the bed, then ran around to her side and climbed in. "I've been wanting to do this for a month." She snuggled up against Darcy's warm back, purring as their bodies molded together. "Good?"

"Great. Really great. I'm sure this is going to be the best night's sleep I've had in six weeks." She grasped Tess's arm and tucked it around her waist. "Thanks to you."

CHAPTER FOURTEEN

ON NEW YEAR'S DAY, Darcy sat on her second favorite chair, a cushy leather one in the study, watching the Rose Parade. Tess was puttering in the kitchen, and when a sharp knock sounded through the house, Darcy started to get up. But Tess beat her to the door and, in a few seconds, Ben poked his head into the room. "Happy New Year," he said, sounding great but looking a little worse-for-wear.

"Happy New Year to you too." Once again she started to get up, but he moved over to her chair and bent to kiss her head.

"I'm going to go see if I can scare up some coffee." He checked his watch. "Then we're going to go on a little trip."

"We are?"

"We are. It won't take long. All I need is for you to be compliant."

"She's good at that," Tess said as she stood in the doorway. "I'm not as good though. Do I have to be compliant too?"

Ben looked at her critically. "No, you've got a different job. You're going to be the local woman she's fallen in love with. No one would question her moving from England to be with you."

"*I'd* question it," Darcy said, completely flummoxed. She looked at Tess. "Not *that* way. But … what?"

"I'll explain on the ride over. I think Alan's punishing me by insisting we do this at the crack of dawn, but he's always trying to get the upper hand."

"Did you have too much to drink last night?" Darcy asked, "Because nothing you're saying is making sense." She took a look at the clock. "And it's almost noon."

"Dawn is in the eye of the beholder. I'll tell you the whole story on the way. But I *really* need a cup of coffee first."

A half hour later, the three of them sat in an examining room in East Hampton. Ben's friend and golfing buddy Alan stood at a display, looking at the X-ray he'd just taken of Darcy's wrist. "How long have you lived in London?" he asked as he studied the film.

Darcy shot Ben a look. He shrugged but didn't add a word. "A few years," she said.

"Did someone in the NHS take care of this for you?"

Tess nodded, so Darcy said, "Yes. How'd they do?"

"Very well." He moved back to her and picked up her bare, pasty white, flaky-skinned left hand. "Grip my hand."

She did, finding her hand stiff but not painful. Her grip was awful, but he didn't seem to think so. "Good. Ideally, you would have had another cast put on after a couple of weeks, but I suppose you had other things on your mind." He gave her a sly smile. "I'm not sure how it healed so well, to be honest."

"She's a quick healer," Tess said.

"She must be." After turning Darcy's hand over he instructed, "Try to move it up and down." She did, but only convinced it to move an inch or two in each direction.

"That's not bad. You'll need physical therapy." He looked at Ben. "Who are you going to coerce into doing that?"

"I didn't coerce you," Ben said, laughing softly. "You're getting the best end of this deal and you know it."

"True. But that's only if you really know how to do a real estate closing. When's the last time you did one?"

He seemed to think. "Interest rates were around fifteen percent. I guess it's been a while."

Alan poked Darcy in the shoulder. "Your uncle's a funny guy. Can't play cards or sink a putt, but he's hilarious."

"We think so." She knew she wasn't carrying her end of the conversation, but the less said, the better.

"We're going on a trip soon," Tess jumped in. "I travel for a living and Karen's going to tag along. Is there anything she could do, at home, just until she gets back to England?"

"How long will that be?"

"A few weeks," Tess said.

"Hmm." He studied Darcy's wrist, moving her hand a few degrees in every direction. "I'd go to PT if it was mine. I've never met anyone who will do the exercises without someone forcing them to."

"Karen's very determined," Tess said. "And I'm a real nudge."

Alan looked at Ben. "I think your niece is as hard-headed as you are. It must run in the family." He moved over to write on a chart. "I'll ask my physical therapist to print off the usual exercises for a distal fracture. If you're religious about it, you should be fine."

"She's very religious," Tess said.

Darcy couldn't help but comment. "Another thing I've learned about myself today. I'm religious."

On the way back to Westhampton, Darcy said, "Your friend seemed to think it was odd that I didn't have an email address I was willing to give him."

"Only a little. He's not a very curious guy. Heck of a golfer though. And he always follows through. You'll have those exercises in the mail in a couple of days."

"Thanks so much for taking care of this," Darcy said. "I was really beginning to stress over it."

"Just be glad it healed properly. When I think of what that guy did to you …" His lip curled in disgust. "I wish I'd gotten a crack at him."

"I would have gladly shot him," Tess said. "*Gladly.*"

Ben looked in the rearview mirror and smiled at her. "You don't look like the type."

"Neither does Darcy, but she was ready to blow his head off."

"Literally?" Ben shot Darcy a quick look.

"Uhm … yeah. I had my weapon aimed right where his chest would have been if he'd knocked on the door. I was going to answer with firepower."

"I wet my pants," Tess added cheerily, making Ben whip his head around to stare at her.

Darcy put her hand on the wheel, just in case. "Don't distract him when he's driving," she chided.

"I'm … I …"

"She's not as docile as she looks," Tess said, as she blew Darcy a kiss.

A few days into the new year, Tess was sitting at the desk in the office, staring out the window. Darcy entered the room, but Tess didn't hear her. Quietly, Darcy said, "You look like you're a million miles away."

"Oh." She turned and shook her head. "No. I'm right here. What's up?"

"Nothing much. I was planning dinner. Is there anything you're in the mood for?"

"Not really. You can surprise me."

Darcy put her hand on Tess's head. "Is everything okay? You seem a little down." Bending to kiss her, she added, "That's not like you."

"I was just trying to think of how to turn down a job."

"How …?"

Tess grasped Darcy's hand and pulled her around so she could see the computer screen. "Read this email, and you'll know what I'm talking about."

Darcy moved back a few inches to be able to read the small font. "Who's Melissa Hartwig?"

"A friend. Actually, more of an acquaintance. She's the editor for most of the East Coast editions of Global Traveler."

"Ahh … one of the big travel guides."

"The biggest at this point," Tess said. "They don't sell many hard copies any more, but they have a big internet presence."

"Uh-huh." Darcy carefully read the text. "Why do you want to turn the job down? I'd think you'd love to have a couple of weeks in the Catskills."

Tess gazed up at her, a funny look on her face. "Uhm … we're kind of involved here, Darcy. What with running from the mob *and* the cops …"

"I know that." She turned Tess's chair around, then leaned over to rest her hands on her shoulders. "You haven't worked in a month and a half. You've got to be going stir-crazy."

"No, I'm not. Really." Taking Darcy's left hand, she kissed it tenderly. "I've got plenty to do. I'm supervising your physical therapy, propping you up with pillows at night, keeping you from breaking anything else." Her eyes were bright when her gaze traveled up to meet Darcy's. "I'm employed full-time, taking care of you."

"I can take care of myself. We discussed this weeks ago, Tess. You need to travel. I *know* that about you. Don't act like it's not important."

Tess grasped Darcy's hand and stood. "It is important. But it's not important right now. Besides, you don't want me to use my credit card and I can't travel without one."

"Sure you can. Hotels and restaurants still take cash. We proved that in Cape May. You could use your credit card to make the reservation, then pay in cash. No problem."

"Are you trying to get rid of me?" She pulled Darcy close and stared into her eyes when they were nose to nose. "Is there a woman you'd rather be in hiding with?"

Chuckling, Darcy pulled away so she could see. "No. You're my number one choice for being on the run. But this job sounds perfect. It's an easy drive, and taking it will keep your name out there." She cupped her hand under Tess's chin and tilted it until their eyes met. "It's important to keep working. You've told me that."

"It is," she said, sounding unsure of herself. "And I've never worked directly for Melissa. It would be nice to let her see how flexible I can be." Rolling her eyes, she said, "Giving me five days' notice before a two or three week trip is cutting it awfully close."

"It doesn't sound like she had much notice herself," Darcy said. "It's kind of funny that the writer she'd assigned actually has appendicitis."

"Unless he's also on the run and that's the go-to excuse," Tess teased.

"Do you want to take the job? If we weren't in the fix we're in, would you take it?"

"In a heartbeat," Tess said without hesitation. "Global Traveler produces hundreds of city and region guides. And they pay well. Much better than any of the other guides I've worked for."

"Then write her back and tell her you're available."

Tess looked very unsure of herself—an anomaly.

"I don't think I should leave you." Tenderly, she touched Darcy's hand again. "I'm not sure you'll do your exercises if I don't reward you for being a good patient."

Smiling, Darcy said, "I love your rewards, but I'm very motivated to build up the strength and flexibility in my wrist. I'll be fine. Promise."

"How will we stay in touch? I'll worry if I don't talk to you."

Darcy could see her resolve crumbling. "You can call the house. Every night before you go to bed." Just saying the words—that they'd be apart for a couple of weeks—made her stomach hurt. But this was the right choice for Tess and her career.

"You're sure you're ready for me to get back to work? You're sure?" Her eyes bore into Darcy.

"I'm sure. Act like you used to—before this carefree vacation you've been on."

"Okay. I'll write to her right now." Tess grasped Darcy and gave her a sound kiss—one that probably signaled her relief at the thought of seeing something other than the grocery store and the beach.

Darcy tried to stay busy, to keep her mind off Tess's leaving, but she didn't have much to keep her occupied. Finally, she sat down and spent a few hours looking at various job sites. At some point she was going to have to get on with her life, and a decent job would be the cornerstone of her new start. But nothing caught her interest. Maybe because no one was looking for an accountant/travel writer combo. A new life without Tess hardly seemed like a life at all.

Over dinner, Tess acted a little more bubbly than normal. Like she was trying to sell Darcy on something. "I did what you said and acted like I normally act when I get a job."

"What's that?" Darcy asked, her anxiety starting to build.

"I never do one job if I can do two at the same time. A few months ago, a magazine asked me to do a piece on a destination spa. They wanted it for January, when a lot of people go to places like that. I didn't take the job at the time, and … You know what happened next. But I did some searching and found a health and detox spa in the Catskills. I wrote to the editor who'd brought it up months ago, and she seems interested. She's going to get back to me."

"That's fine," Darcy said, working hard to make her voice sound calm and cool. "How long would you need to stay?"

"Well …" Her eyes darted around evasively. "The detox special's a week. My pitch is that this would be a great place for people trying to look good in their swim suits, so I'd need to play along with the program. I guess that means I'll be gone three weeks."

"Three weeks." It took all of Darcy's composure to smile encouragingly. "Great. You'll get your name back out there, and the offers will start rolling in." That was probably truer than she wanted to believe.

Tess tried hard to make her departure a non-event. But that was very tough to do. Ben had come out the night before and they'd gone to rent a four-wheel-drive car that would get her through any snowy roads up in the mountains. And using Ben's credit card allowed her to be the second driver and not have her info go into an easily searchable database. All of that had been Darcy's idea, of course. Tess had been looking forward to driving Ben's Alfa Romeo along twisty, curvy mountain lanes.

Darcy had obviously gotten up hours earlier, since she'd made chicken salad sandwiches from freshly cooked chicken for Tess's lunch. Tess hefted the paper bag filled with all of the treats Darcy had packed. "You might not know this, but there are restaurants all over New York. I'm not heading into a vast food desert."

"I know." Darcy fussed over her, sweeping her hair out of her collar, then snapping it so it lay neatly against her neck. "But I don't want you to have to eat junk. You'll be more alert if you have good food."

"Thank you," Tess said, leaning forward to kiss Darcy. "This was very thoughtful of you. I'll think of you with every bite."

"You'll pull over and get out of the car to eat, right? It's safer that way."

Looking into Darcy's eyes, Tess could see how anxious she was. Gently stroking her cheek, she said, "I promise I'll take care of myself. I might not do things exactly as you would, but I'm not reckless."

"So … you won't get out of the car?" Darcy was clearly trying to appear cool, but Tess could see the tension etched across her face.

"It depends. If I'm tired, I will." She took a breath. It was time to set some rules. "We have to give each other room, Darcy. Room to be who we are. I'll never be like you, and you'll go crazy trying to make that happen." She kissed her, holding the embrace for a few long seconds. "Don't make yourself crazy. Try to trust me."

"I do," she said, her eyes searching Tess's. "I don't want you to be like me. I just ..."

"You're worried," Tess soothed. "I understand that. But I'm probably safer in the Catskills than you are here. Especially alone," she stressed. "I'm the one who should be worried."

"Are you?"

"Yes," Tess said, biting her lip to keep from crying. "I'm very worried about you." She leaned in, relishing the feel of Darcy's arms encircling her body. "I don't want to go."

"I'll be fine," Darcy murmured. "I'll only have to worry about myself. That reduces my job by fifty percent."

Tess tilted her head back so she could gaze into Darcy's eyes. "Do you worry about me all of the time?"

"*All* of the time. I don't think that's going to stop just because you're away from home." She smiled. "I'll have different things to worry about, but I'll still worry. It's who I am."

"I know." Tess patted her side. "I wasn't much of a worrier—until I met you. It must be contagious."

"Yeah." Darcy put her arm around Tess's shoulders as they walked to the front door together. "I'm sure it doesn't have anything to do with people actively trying to kill us."

"That's been weeks," Tess teased. "You're so dramatic!"

Darcy pulled her to a stop and gave her a long hug. "I'm going to miss you, but I'm glad you're going. You can get back into writing shape for when we're free."

Tess gazed at her for a second, letting herself think about the future. She'd intentionally stopped doing that, but now, with a long trip ahead of her, she let herself get back into work-mode. This was going to be interesting.

Darcy spent her first day alone cleaning the house. Since she neatened up all the time it didn't need it, but washing the cabinets in the kitchen let her focus on something other than Tess driving in the mountains. The possibly snowy, icy, treacherous mountains.

Once she'd finished, she put on her coat and went out to the patio behind the house, just to get a breath of fresh air. With her hands stuck in her pockets, she looked up at the gray, leaden sky.

She'd have to go outside for her walks, but she thought she could wait for a day. Even though she hadn't admitted this to Tess, she was skittish about walking around by herself.

Looking past the pool, she noticed a covered area with some things wrapped in black. Curious, she walked over and found various pieces of exercise equipment. The stationary bike caught her interest. She removed the cover fully and sat astride the seat. She gasped in surprise when she put her hands on the grips and found all of the pressure taken off her ribs. Stunned, she focused on her body, realizing she hadn't been in such little pain since the moment her ribs were broken.

Gleefully, she went back inside and got her gloves and earmuffs. She loved walking, but she loved working up a sweat even more. And with Tess gone, no one would tell her she was doing too much. *Score!*

Her body was still in decent, but not great shape, but her hand could only take a half hour of pressure. But a half hour of working her body up to its max, then pedaling at a moderate clip until her heart slowed down let her brain clear in ways it hadn't for over a month.

She *needed* this kind of exercise. Tess could maintain her focus and her mood just by walking, but Darcy wasn't made that way. She had to get her heart rate up for sustained periods to think clearly and reduce her stress. As she pushed herself for one last maximum burst, a thought hit her so hard she almost fell from the bike. She hadn't checked the balance on her bank accounts since the day Harry died. That was over fifty days!

As her heart rate slowed, nerves made her extremities tingle. Ever since she'd had a checking account she'd checked her balance every morning, making sure checks were clearing properly and that no unexpected withdrawals had been processed. She'd caught bank errors several times, but she had to admit it was now just an obsessive habit. A habit she'd let drop without a thought.

After going back into the house, she stripped, wiped her sweaty body down, then put on her pajamas again. Using her disposable phone, she called Danny's, relieved when he picked up. "Hello, my fugitive niece," he said. He'd lightened up quite a bit since she'd first gone on the run.

"Hi, Danny. Will you do me a favor?"

"Name it. I've got the day off."

"This won't take long. I need for you to call my management company and make sure the auto-pay for my co-op assessment went through."

"Will do. Give me the info and I'll call you right back."

A few minutes later, Danny called. "Bad news, Darce. Your assessment was due on December twenty-second. You're way overdue."

"Shit! If that auto-pay didn't go through, neither did the ones for my health insurance, credit card, cable, electricity, gas …"

"Ease up now. You sound like you're going to pass out."

Darcy *was* ready to have some kind of fit. She'd never admit this, but letting her bills go unpaid was as upsetting as being chased by the mob. "Can you help me out, Danny? I can pay you back—easily—once I get sprung. But until then …"

"Sure. Sure. Just calm down. Do you have the info for all of your bills? Or do you want me to go online and look at your checking account?"

"Won't that get you into trouble? I know they're still watching you."

"Nah. You're my niece. Having my name on the title to your house shows how close we are."

"All right. Are you sure you can front me the money? It's a total of about a thousand dollars."

"Yes, Darcy, I can front you a thousand dollars," he said, chuckling. "I don't live hand-to-mouth."

"This sucks," she grumbled. "And you know how I hate to pay for things I don't use."

"Speaking of things you don't use …" He paused for a second. "You're fooling yourself if you think you're going to be able to move back to your co-op. The mob knows your address, Darce. They have long memories."

She let out a sigh. "Yeah, I guess I might as well get rid of it. The market's still really strong, and inventory's low. I might be able to sell without a loss."

"I'll call the agent you used when you bought and see what she thinks you could sell it for. It can't hurt to have information, right?"

"Right. Thanks, Danny. Let me know what you find out."

"Will do. Are you doing okay with Tess gone?"

"Yeah. Pretty okay." It was silly to put on an act with Danny. "I'm lonely."

"Aww, now you're making me feel worse. Is there any way I could come see you?"

"I'm not going to put you into that kind of position. The less you know, the better." She took a breath and tried to sound perky. "I'm fine. It's just hard to have my routine disrupted." She almost spit it out. Almost told him how close she and Tess had gotten. But the words didn't want to come. Damn, what in the hell was there to be afraid of?

In Tess's mind, freedom had always been a given. From the time she was a child, she'd had fewer constraints put on her than just about anyone she knew. Her parents let her make her own choices from a very young age, and once she'd grown, she'd chosen women who were equally independent.

Giving yourself exclusively to one woman had always seemed so limiting, as well as a recipe for heartache. It was hard to have a committed relationship when you shared a home. Making one work when you were away for six to nine months of the year was asking for trouble. And staying in one place was never going to work for her. The essence of life was new experiences, new people, new places.

As she drove, Tess cracked her window to let fresh, cold air in. Tall pines with snow hanging heavily off the tips of branches hugged both sides of the road. The air was bracing, with the hint of wood smoke wafting upon it. She hadn't been in this part of New York, and she briefly wished Darcy was with her to explore. Then the truth—the truth she'd been evading crept into her consciousness. Darcy might enjoy spending a day or two driving around aimlessly, looking for a good place to eat or sleep. But she probably wouldn't get the same thrill that Tess experienced from exploring. That was the difference—the very big difference between them.

Tess lusted to get into a car or a train or a plane and take off. To see a part of the world she'd never laid eyes on. It didn't have to be any place particularly unique. But the variety was addictive. And she'd never met anyone less adventurous than Darcy. Yes, she'd adapted to their current circumstances very well, moving around as needed. But she didn't have that spirit of wanderlust. If she'd had it, she would have pulled it out by now.

She thought of Darcy. The kindest, most sincere, open-hearted woman she'd ever met. She thought of how well they meshed sexually. Even emotionally. But she knew she couldn't plant herself down in a city and flourish. And Darcy would never be able to wander along the streets of an isolated village in Japan, looking for the best place in town for soup that looked back at you. And that was a damned shame.

That night, Tess called the land line from the new disposable phone that Darcy had insisted she buy before she left.

"Hi there."

"Nicest sound I've heard all day. How's my favorite traveler?"

"I'm good. I quickly checked out four hotels, had lunch at a very good place and dinner at a fairly good place, so my travel needs are being satisfied. *But* … I keep having moments of …" She struggled to find the right word. "It's not loneliness, but it's something. I guess being with you nonstop for fifty days is a harder habit than I thought it'd be to break."

"That's true for me too. It's been hard to find anything to keep myself occupied. Especially at night. It's no fun to watch TV alone."

"Did you talk to Ben today?"

"Uh-huh. He's coming out tomorrow night. He hinted that he might stay for a few days and take the train in to work."

"Oh, good. I really hope he does that. You need someone to keep you from talking to yourself."

"I'm a long way from that. Although you might have heard a string of profanity this morning."

"Did you hurt yourself?"

Darcy laughed. "I'm really not accident-prone, Tess. Someone hurt me, I didn't hurt myself."

"So why were you cursing?"

"Because I found out my checking account's been frozen. All of my automatic debits have bounced."

"Oh, shit! I haven't even thought of my bills!"

"I'll have Danny check your stuff if you want. He thinks I should sell my apartment, and I can't argue if I'm being logical."

"You're always logical. Do you think you'll do it?"

"Yeah, I guess I will. I hate to let it go, but I'll never be able to go back."

"My lease is over in another month. I guess I should … What should I do?"

"I'll have Danny hire someone to pack your things up and put them in storage. How's that?"

"That's good. But that means some other stranger's going to find my sex toys."

"Ha! You weren't even slightly embarrassed when I found them. Don't act like you're easily shamed."

"I'm shameless," Tess admitted. "Why lie?"

CHAPTER FIFTEEN

TEN DAYS LATER, DARCY sat by the glass wall of the living room, staring out at the snow that covered most of the swimming pool cover. Bits of black poked out from the whiteness, straps and tethers holding on against winter. Idly, she pictured herself holding Tess's hand as they cannonballed into pure, blue water. Just the two of them in what would be an idyllic scene once the Summer Solstice arrived. Unless she was in a women's prison, of course. The delightful scene evaporated. Every time she tried to picture the future, she was slapped into the present by the noose she felt tightening around her neck.

The stress assaulted her gut and her stomach spasmed painfully. Being in prison would be awful. No doubt about it. But a close second was being without Tess. When then next Solstice arrived, she'd be long gone.

The usual antidote to her stressors was planning and preparation. If she had some idea of how things might shake out once she was free, some of her anxiety might fade.

She'd checked out a few job sites, but hadn't been very serious about it. Just to give herself something to do, she went into Ben's den and did a more careful search.

There were more jobs than she thought she'd find, many that demanded her level of experience. Some even paid better than she'd gotten at Harry's firm. But not a single one interested her enough to bother to write down the details.

Idly, she pulled up her profile on a dating site she'd registered with not long after moving to Brooklyn. Her cautious nature compelled her to block other members from pinging her, but she could look at other profiles. Her requirements weren't very strict; women, thirty and up, physically active. Since she'd cast her net so widely, there were literally thousands of women who qualified.

Taking a glance at the clock, she decided to devote an hour a day to finding someone to date once Tess took off for her next great adventure. That wasn't much of an investment, and trying to convince herself she could find a woman to match Tess was a nice fantasy. A delusional one, but it made the time pass.

That evening, the phone rang and she moved quickly to pick it up. "State your business," she said, imitating Ned.

"Or what?" Tess chuckled.

"Or nothing. Just trying to sound funny. How are you?"

"I'm okay. But I just found out I'm not going to be able to call you for a few days."

"A few days?" Darcy braced herself for the bad news. Had she always been like this? Or had her mother's illness turned her into a person who was always anticipating the next catastrophe?

"Yeah. I'm not going to have cell service for a few … like seven … days."

"I don't mean to be picky, but I'd call that a week."

"I guess it is," Tess said, her voice soft. "Will you be okay?"

"Yeah, but I won't like it," Darcy said, finding herself being uncharacteristically honest about a disappointment. "I understand, though. You're at work."

"This is true." A silence settled between them, then Tess said, "I'm very glad you understand that I'm at work. A lot of people—most people—think I'm on vacation. But it's not like that when you're visiting a place to write about it." She lowered her voice, like she was revealing something she didn't want bystanders to hear. "I wouldn't have chosen to come to the Catskills for two weeks—alone—as a vacation."

"Three weeks," Darcy reminded her.

"Right. But for two weeks, I've been driving from place to place, trying to digest everything these small towns have to offer. The spa's going to be a different experience. I assume I'll be with a group of people the whole time. That'll be nice. I've missed having long talks with you. Now I can annoy strangers."

Darcy's imagination flashed to Tess, naked, with a group of other women, also naked. Tess had given her the impression she didn't sleep with people she'd just met but … "Can I send you an email? Just in case I need to get in touch."

"No computer, either. But I wrote the number of the place on the itinerary I left you."

"You're not going to be able to use your computer to write?"

"I'm going to have to rely on a pen and a notepad. Very twentieth century." Her voice grew warmer, more caring. "If you need me—even if you just need to talk for a while—call the office. They can find me. Promise?"

"Yeah, I promise. But I shouldn't have to bother you."

"You're not a bother, Darcy. I'm serious. I miss talking to you."

"You do?" Just that little bit of encouragement brightened her day.

"Of course I do. We've been together for weeks now. I feel like a puppy taken from my littermate."

"That's a good way to put it. The house seems so empty." She wanted to say so much more. To tell Tess how nothing was the same without her. Even the normally cheery house seemed dull and gray without Tess's sunny smile to brighten it. But she didn't have the nerve. They were close. They had great sexual chemistry. But Tess had made it crystal clear she was going back to her old life as soon as this detour was over. Darcy was going to be one more person Tess thought of fondly—and infrequently.

Darcy had worked out hard, very hard, despite the snow blowing in her face. Exercising on a cold day was a joy. And standing in the shower, working out the stiffness was a close second. A rustling noise caught her attention, but she dismissed it. With the wind blowing like it was, all sorts of tree limbs hit the house. She'd jumped so many times that day that she was finally able to relax and convince herself that houses made noises.

A shadow passed by the bathroom window, propelling her from the shower to the vanity, where she grabbed her weapon while she tossed her head to get the hair from her eyes.

Naked and dripping wet, Darcy ran for the front door and braced herself against the jamb. From there, she could see the sliders that led to the back patio. And she could easily hear any of the bedroom windows being forced open. Her weapon was aimed at chest height. If someone forced the door open, she'd have a clear shot.

A sharp rap on the door nearly made her wet herself. "Open the damn door, Darcy!" Tess yelled.

Stunned, she threw the door open, and a blast of frigid air hit her bare, wet body.

"Put that gun down!"

"Shit! I was in the shower and ..."

Tess walked in and kicked the door closed with her foot while wrapping her body around Darcy. "Missed you, missed you, missed you," she murmured into her shoulder.

Fighting against a multitude of sensations—Tess's ice cold hands, the frigid zipper of her jacket, the fluffy slickness of the material and her very reassuring scent—Darcy carefully placed her weapon onto a table, tucked her arms around Tess and hugged her tightly. "I missed you too. Every minute."

Tess tilted her head, a beatific smile lighting up her face. Ignoring her wet hair, wet body and the frosty air that had settled in the room, Darcy slid her hands into Tess's hair and held her still. For long moments she gazed into her clear blue eyes. Then she dipped her head and kissed Tess, trying to show with that one kiss how every day had dragged on without her to brighten it.

"Mmm," Tess murmured. "You *did* miss me."

After another passion-laced kiss, Darcy let herself get lost in her feelings. She'd missed Tess more than she could express, and now that she had her in her arms she was going to make up for lost time.

Without pause, she started to unzip her coat, then whipped her sweater over her head. Tess looked a little stunned, but she didn't resist. Instead, she grasped Darcy's head and kissed her while her jeans were being pushed down her legs. Together, they clumsily got her boots off, then Tess stepped out of her jeans and took Darcy's hand. When she made the turn to go into the bathroom, Darcy tugged her in the other direction. "To bed," she said, her heart hammering with desire.

Tess simply raised an eyebrow, then followed along compliantly. Once in the bedroom, Darcy sat on the bed, then pulled Tess down until they were lying side by side. Showing off, she pressed up onto her hands, hovering over her. "I'm better," she said, grinning lasciviously.

"So am I," Tess said, a massive smile making Darcy's heart clutch with emotion. "Much, much better than I've been in three weeks."

Darcy closed her eyes and moved over Tess's body, finally feeling their skin touch in exactly the way she'd dreamed of. This was the moment she'd been waiting for, and it was well worth it. Tess purred like a kitten as Darcy's nipples caught on her own, her breasts jiggling as they moved past.

Strong legs wrapped around Darcy's thighs, caressing her, but not restricting her movements. Tess clearly realized that moving this way was a vital building block to Darcy's arousal, and she encouraged her by palming her ass and squeezing. "So good," she growled. "Your body feels so good against mine." Tess's hands went to her shoulders, gliding over the muscles she'd developed over the past weeks.

Darcy bent to kiss her again, finally unleashing some of the pent-up desire that had been growing day by day. Her body shivered with sensation as she continued to move, to press into Tess's heated skin until her muscles shook with fatigue.

The legs that wrapped around her now started to contract, to pull her harder into Tess's body. Eyes glassy with desire, she murmured, "You're the sexiest woman alive."

Darcy kept moving, gliding then pushing into Tess, responding to her cues, following her moans with renewed energy. It was as if they were conversing, but Tess had stopped speaking, only communicating with her body as her hips thrust against Darcy. Sweat covered them as they ground against each other, their bodies slipping and sliding across the bed.

Tess threw her head back as she panted, "Let me …" Then she grabbed Darcy hard and held her still. A quick shift of her body had her positioned against Darcy's hip and she ground against it while gasping in pure pleasure. "Jesus!" she cried as her muscles gave out and her legs dropped heavily onto the bed.

Still lying atop her, Darcy gently smoothed some of the damp blonde hairs away from her flushed face. "I love you," she murmured. "With all my heart."

Tess slapped at her weakly. "That was my line, damn it!"

Darcy just stared, unable to say a word. "That just came out!" she finally gasped. "I … I hadn't planned on … What?"

A delighted grin covered Tess's face. "I'm in love with you. And I'm so damned proud of you for saying it first that I have to give you a big, big reward." She gently rolled Darcy onto her side, then started to kiss her, the heat turning up so fast Darcy had to forcefully pull away.

"Say that again," she demanded. Her heart was pumping so hard her chest hurt. But she had to make sure she wasn't just dreaming the words she'd longed to hear.

Tess's smile faded, her gaze sharpening as their eyes met. "I said that I love you, Darcy. And I do." She slid a hand behind her head and pulled her close for a long, tender kiss. "I do."

"Love me … how?" That sounded so stupid. But she had to know exactly what she meant.

303

Now the teasing smile came back. Tess couldn't stay serious for long. "Uhm … really well, I hope."

Darcy sat up, pushed the still-damp hair from her eyes and drew the covers up to cover her breasts. "You've got to tell me more," she insisted. "You've made it clear all along that we're just together while we wait to resolve this."

Tess's smile was absolutely guileless. "I was wrong." Tess sat up as well, then leaned forward and placed another gentle kiss to Darcy's lips. "I knew something was happening … something good. But I'd been able to put it out of my mind, thinking we were growing close at least partially because we were together so much."

Darcy's mind was able to stay right with her. To let Tess tell her story. But her body was racing ahead, heart hammering with excitement. "Go on," she urged, desperate for more.

"Remember Solstice? Our intentions?"

"Sure."

"Mine was to open myself to love."

She smiled, such a gentle, open expression that Darcy's stomach flipped. "Mine was to be less predictable," Darcy admitted, a little embarrassed.

"There's nothing wrong with being predictable," Tess assured her. "I think of you as reliable, and I consider that a really nice trait."

Ducking her head, Darcy nodded. 'Thanks. Uhm … I like hearing you think I'm reliable, but I'm going to do something crazy if you don't say more about loving me!" She grasped her by the shoulders and gave her a playful shake. "I'm at the end of my rope!"

Soothingly, Tess petted her head, then wrapped an arm around her and lowered them both to the bed. "I've been daydreaming of lying with you just this way. Holding the woman I love in my arms." Her hand continued to stroke along Darcy's cheek. "I missed you—a lot—the first two weeks. It was actually kind of annoying," she admitted, a soft chuckle bubbling up. "I'm used to being able to focus. To just be in the moment, enjoying whatever I'm doing. But I kept thinking everything would be better if you were with me."

"I thought that every day. Every minute."

"Yeah. It was about that often for me too. But I thought it would lessen as the days went on." She turned her head and tenderly nibbled on Darcy's ear, making her squirm. "You've gotten inside, baby. I can't just put you away like I have other women I've been with."

"I'm so happy to hear that," Darcy whispered, on the verge of tears.

"I spent the last week doing yoga and meditation and guided imagery and all sorts of things that made me think. And the one thing I couldn't avoid was acknowledging that you've become part of me." Their eyes met again, with Darcy feeling like her heart would explode at the tenderness she saw in Tess's beautiful eyes. "I love you, Darcy, and I want to build a life with you—somehow."

"We'll figure it out if we're meant to be together." She snuggled close, burrowing her face into Tess's chest, filling her lungs with her delightful scent. The scent she'd missed more than she'd ever be able to put into words. "I hope to god we are."

"We are," Tess insisted, her impish smile growing. "We've got the big things locked down. We get along great and you're freakishly attractive. Everything else is negotiable."

Tess was able to joke, but Darcy couldn't get there. This was too important. Not just important—life changing. "I've been feeling closer and closer to you," she admitted. "I've tried to tamp my feelings down, but it's been hard. Really hard."

"Let them go," Tess urged, tightening her embrace. "Let me know how you feel, baby. Trust me."

Darcy looked into her eyes. She'd never experienced such a sure, welcoming look in her life. This was such a gift—a woman who Darcy could trust with her secrets, her fears, her dreams. "I want to touch you," she whispered. "To show you how much I've longed for you."

Tess didn't bother responding in words. She just shifted her body until they were nose to nose, then closed her eyes, waiting.

Darcy grasped her face, forcing herself to be gentle. But the feelings were so strong, so overwhelming, she was afraid she'd be unable to control herself. When their lips met, some of the drive, the tension lessened. Tess's tender lips centered her, made her consciously slow down so she could let her body speak for her heart.

They'd had sex often, each time trying something a little different, pushing boundaries in various ways. But today Darcy didn't need to show she was versatile. She only wanted to show Tess her love. Her devotion.

Tenderly touching her silky cheeks, Darcy placed long, soft kisses to Tess's lips, repeatedly moving away to be able to meet her fervent gaze. This was love. It hardly mattered if they went further. Opening up their hearts to each other, and sharing this intimacy was the sexiest thing she'd ever experienced.

Tess grasped her hand and closed her eyes as she placed delicate kisses across it. "You have the kindest hands I've ever felt," she whispered. "You're so tender with me." Her eyes opened and their gazes met. "I can feel your love by the way you touch me."

Biting her lip, Darcy could only nod. She took a breath to try to tamp down some of the emotion that threatened to overcome her. "I've never cared for anyone like I do you. I can't …" She blinked back the tears that wanted to come. "I can't imagine loving anyone more than this."

"Oh, yes, you can," Tess said, her voice full of certainty. "We're both going to love each other more and more. We've just barely started, Darcy. This is the beginning of a very long journey."

"And you love to travel," Darcy agreed, smiling when Tess reached up to wipe a tear from her cheek.

"This is a journey for the two of us." She pulled her close and delivered an achingly tender kiss. "Only the two of us."

Darcy hadn't spent much time in church, but she had some idea of what it meant to worship. Every part of Tess captivated her, and she spent hours expressing her devotion, kissing and caressing every part in turn. "I'm certainly not glad we're stuck here, but I'd lose my job if I had one," Darcy murmured. Her eyes roamed down Tess's thigh, enthralled by its contours, its softness. "Making love is so much better than having sex. I'm going to keep you in bed for hours every day."

"If you think I'm going to try to talk you out of that, you're sadly mistaken." She reached down and scratched behind Darcy's ear, making her giggle. "Every day is precious."

Tess's playful gesture didn't match her tone. There was a sadness there that caught Darcy's attention. She scrambled up to meet her gaze. "Are you okay?"

"Sure." She ruffled her hair, then carefully arranged it across her shoulders. "I could use a bite to eat pretty soon, though. I've been living on green drinks and lean protein for a week you know."

"I must have read your schedule wrong. I was sure you weren't going to be home for three more days."

"I jammed three days of work into one, and went to the spa early. I was at the reception area when I called you last. They were about to take my cell phone away, but I held them off."

"Why didn't you tell me?"

"Because I wanted it to be a surprise. I stopped by and asked if I could check in early, then I stayed the whole, horrible week."

"But you had a slew of restaurants to review. How'd you get them all in?"

Tess laughed. "I ate two dinners three days in a row."

"You did?"

"Sure did. When we talked about ten days ago, I found myself missing you so damned much"—she leaned in and kissed Darcy

307

tenderly—"I had to figure out a way to get my work done and get home sooner."

"How do you eat dinner twice? You must have been sick!"

"It wasn't too bad. You don't have to eat a whole entree to tell if it's cooked well. Given how I have to order, the kitchen either knows I'm reviewing them—or I'm some kind of lunatic. Either way, they tend not to comment when I order two or three items for each course and only eat a bite or two." She patted her belly. "I just had to do that twice a night."

"You did that three nights in a row to get home to me?"

Tess nodded. "I had to take antacids to get to sleep, but you're well worth it."

"I think you really love me," Darcy said, her grin covering her entire face.

"I do." Tess took Darcy's left hand and kissed it. "I also love that you've been doing your exercises. I saw how easily you moved when you were tossing me around."

"Twice a day, every day. And when I'm just sitting around I grip that rubber ball obsessively."

"I'm so proud of you," Tess purred. "I should have known you'd be a perfect patient."

"I had a big goal." Darcy put her arm around Tess and hugged her hard. "I wanted to touch you while we lay in a real bed. Mission accomplished."

They'd decided they desperately needed a shower, but Darcy had to get a drink first. Tess's suggestion that she drink from the shower head was dismissed with just a puzzled look. She lay in bed and watched Darcy's adorable butt twitch as she rushed down the hallway. It was *so* good to be home. She'd intentionally underplayed how unhappy she'd been on her trip, not wanting Darcy to know exactly how dependent she'd grown. There was a real chance they'd be separated for a long time.

Maybe a very long time. And the last thing Darcy needed was to worry about that.

A few seconds later, Darcy burst into the room, radiating good health. "Miss me?"

Tess swallowed, feeling like she might cry. "I'm so happy to be home."

"No happier than I am." She slid back into bed, wrapped an arm tightly around Tess's waist and gave her a gentle kiss.

Tess moved so they were almost nose-to-nose. "I feel like I'm home when I'm with you—even though we're not in a place we chose." A finger gently traced down Darcy's chest. "You're home to me."

"Yeah. That's it," Darcy agreed, her voice catching in her throat. "Home isn't a place. It's a feeling." Tenderly, she kissed Tess's welcoming lips. "It's a feeling I get when I look into your eyes."

"You're a very poetic CPA," Tess teased. "I love that about you. You're the perfect blend of pragmatic and poetic."

"Don't forget sex-crazed."

Darcy looked so beautiful, so content, so satisfied. *That's* how you knew you were missed. The unconscious expressions that your lover didn't even know she was making showed what was in her heart.

"I love you so much," Tess whispered as she threaded her fingers through Darcy's hair and pushed thick strands from her face. "Why don't we stay here ... permanently? We have money, and I know Ben wouldn't mind. My parents could come visit. After a while the police would forget about us." Her words tumbled against each other in the rush to get them all out.

Darcy gave her such a sympathetic look that Tess lost it. "I kept having nightmares that they'd find you while I was gone. And I ... I didn't even get to say goodbye."

Darcy's warm body encircled her as Tess cried.

"I can't bear to think of losing you. Don't let that happen."

"Shh," Darcy soothed as she rocked Tess in her arms. "It'll be all right. Sooner or later the truth will come out."

"It's the later I'm worried about. It might take years to prove how those cops conspired with the mob."

"Yeah, it might. But it might not. That's what we've got to keep hoping for. We've got to stay optimistic."

"I'm sorry," Tess whimpered. "I lectured myself the whole way home. I was determined not to dump my anxieties on you, but I blew it."

"Hey …" Darcy pulled away and smiled when their eyes met. "I like knowing how much you care. Don't feel like you have to hide that."

Tess gripped her by the shoulders. "I will never hide how much I care for you. I just don't want to add to your stress." Pulling Darcy close, she kissed across her forehead. "You have too many things on your mind already."

"Knowing how much you care for me isn't stressful," Darcy insisted. "It's calming. Knowing that lets me sleep at night."

"I will *always* be there for you," Tess said, her voice cracking with emotion. "Always."

Darcy cradled Tess in her arms and murmured, "Has this been on your mind a lot?"

"Yeah." Sniffling, she added, "I can keep a lid on it when we're here, but it's on my mind when we're outside. It was much worse when I was away, and it got out of control when I couldn't use my cell phone. The last week was really bad."

"I'm so sorry, Tess. I'm sorry I've gotten you into this whole mess. It would have been better for you if you'd never gone to that diner."

"What?" Tess wrenched out of Darcy's embrace and sat up to glare at her. "What an awful thing to say! What if …" She wracked her brain for an example. "What if I got sick? What if I got cancer? Would you regret falling in love with me?"

"Of course not," Darcy soothed. "But this is different. I dragged you into this. Literally."

"That's true. For one full day. But from the moment I went downstairs to welcome you back into my apartment, I've chosen to be here. I've *chosen* to be with you, Darcy. I've chosen to love you."

"And I'm so very happy you have." Gently, Darcy put her arms around Tess and pulled her back into an embrace. "I would have given up that day if not for you—and I'd probably just be a stubborn red stain on the sidewalk if I had."

"Don't talk like that," Tess murmured with her face pressed into Darcy's chest. "Don't. Please."

"Let's get off this depressing topic." Taking Tess with her, Darcy settled back down onto the bed. "I think you need a nap more than a shower."

"I really missed being in your arms. Will you hold me?"

"Any time." Darcy tucked her arms more fully around Tess, who rested her head on a significantly stronger shoulder. "We'll stay in bed all day."

"I'm in." Tess filled her lungs with Darcy's scent, finally able to relax. If they could just stay right where they were, everything would be fine. But getting the rest of the world to leave them alone was going to be tougher than she cared to think about.

Tess hadn't realized how much stress she'd been under. But when she woke, hours after they'd fallen asleep, she felt better—much better, than she had while she was in the Catskills. As she turned her head, she saw Darcy's big, soulful eyes gazing at her.

"What's that look?"

"I think it's time to put this behind us."

"What?" She sat up, trying to knock the cobwebs out. "Where in the hell did that come from?"

"I want to get on with our lives," Darcy said, her eyes glowing with determination. "I want to be able to go where we want, when we want. We've been stuck here long enough."

"Darcy," Tess soothed, touching her face. "We don't have any control over when we can leave. They'll *arrest* you, baby." Her heart was thrumming so heavily in her chest, she felt like she'd been running.

"I know." Darcy's voice was soft but there was a firmness to it that caught Tess by surprise. "I know exactly what might happen. But we're not getting anywhere. The DA's made it clear he won't negotiate with Ned. I don't see that changing. And I can't ask you to live like this for much longer. I just can't."

"I want to." Tess grasped her by the shoulders and shook her. "I'd live in a box under the highway to keep you out of jail." She stuck her hand out, pointing at the lovely room they shared. "Staying here isn't a sacrifice." Throwing her arms around Darcy, she hugged her tightly. "Losing you *is*. That's a sacrifice I'm not willing to make."

"Look." Darcy slithered out of bed, grabbed her pajamas and put them on. Then she started to pace, anxiety rolling off her. "We have to look at reality. I think there's a chance—maybe even a good chance—that the DA's office will eventually ferret out the corruption in the police department. It might take a while, but I think it can happen."

"I do too," Tess interrupted. "So we let them grind away at glacial speed while we stay right here."

"No." Darcy stopped and looked at her. "If it takes a year ... or two ... your career will be over. You can't just stop working, Tess. There are too many people who want to be travel writers. If you turn down enough jobs, people will stop calling—permanently." Leaning over the bed, she stared directly into Tess's eyes. "Convince me that's not true."

"I can't," she admitted. "So I'll do something else. I'll ..." She shook her head, frustrated with her inability to think of any other source of income. "I don't *need* to work at all. We haven't counted it, but we've got a shitload of money in that bag we've been dragging around."

312

"And you'd be happy? Just hanging out until everyone's forgotten about us ... probably for a couple of years, then doing basically nothing for the rest of your life?"

"Don't be so dramatic! I won't lose my ability to write. I'll just figure out different ways to market myself."

"But you love traveling, Tess. I know you. I see how your eyes light up when you talk about the places you've been, the people you've met, the foods you've sampled. You'd miss that."

"You're right," she admitted. "But I'd miss you more. Meeting strangers isn't as important as being with you, Darcy. It just isn't. I found that out on this last trip. It *sucked* being away from you."

Darcy stood by the bed and took both of Tess's hands in her own. "I know that. And no one wants us to be together more than I do. But we need to be free too. We'll go nuts if we're stuck here for much longer."

"Then we'll move around. There are thousands of places we could visit. And no one would be looking for us once we were outside of New York."

"I don't want to spend my life visiting places," Darcy said, her voice rising. "Because we wouldn't be visiting ... we'd be hiding. I'm sick of it. I need some resolution. God knows I don't want to go to jail, but at least I'd have some resolution."

Tess wrapped her arms around Darcy's legs and held on tightly. "I don't want you to do this." She looked up and met her eyes. "But you have to do what you think is right."

CHAPTER SIXTEEN

THREE DAYS LATER, BEN, Danny and Tess sat in the living room, all staring at Darcy, who hadn't been able to stop pacing. "I know it's crazy to turn myself in," she said. "But I can't live this way anymore." She took a deep breath, willing herself not to cry. "I was locked away in a nice, suburban house in New Jersey for over eight years. I know what it's like to feel the walls closing in on you more and more as the years pass. The fact that it's a nice place, and you're with people you love doesn't take away the reality. You can't leave." She wrapped her arms around herself, shivering from the memory of those pre-dawn hours when she'd lie in bed longing for a day she could call her own. "I need my freedom. And if I have to go to jail for a while to get it … I'm resigned to that."

Danny, who'd been ill-at-ease ever since he arrived, spoke, his voice strained with tension. "Don't trust them, Darce. The NYPD wants to make you their stooge. Once they get you into custody who's going to protect you? How do we make sure you don't wind up with a knife in your back? If they want you gone, they're not above getting another prisoner to do it for them."

She stared at him, annoyed that he'd bring up something she hadn't been worried about.

"We'll demand they put her in protective custody—if it comes to that," Ben said. He shot Danny a harsh look and Darcy saw he didn't like his speculating either. "But I agree that it's too risky. If you want to leave the country, I'm sure I can help. If you have the right documents, you can live abroad for the rest of your lives."

"As a different person! We'd be like deposed royalty. Wandering around, looking for people to take us in."

"It wouldn't be like that," Ben insisted. "You'd pick a country you liked and settle down. If you're not working, any country in the Western world would welcome you. I could buy you a house and Tess's parents and Danny and I would all visit. We'd keep you busy."

"That's not true. Danny would never be able to visit me. The second he left the country, they'd track him. And if you don't think the Feds know where you are, you haven't been paying attention to the news."

"I know they can track people, Darcy. But we don't know the federal government is involved here. It's very possible that only the NYPD is interested in you."

"Not true," she insisted. "They couldn't get my bank accounts frozen without some arm of the federal government getting involved."

"But we don't *know* that," Ben said.

"We don't know anything. Because the DA's office won't tell us a damned thing!"

"We do know one thing," Tess said quietly.

Darcy stopped and looked at her, realizing Tess hadn't spoken for most of the night. "What's that?"

"We know you're at the end of your rope." She got up and walked to Darcy, and wrapped her in a hug.

Darcy wanted to squirm out of her embrace. She hadn't explicitly told her uncle about their relationship, and she could feel her cheeks coloring. But this wasn't the night to have that talk. He'd just have to assume the obvious. She sighed as she focused on Tess's love, letting it reach deep inside to soothe her. "I am," she admitted. "Today is day seventy-five. That's all I can take."

"Did the DA promise *any*thing?" Danny asked.

"No," she admitted. "But he's agreed to meet with me at Ned's office, which we both think is encouraging."

"That's it? That's not much."

"No, it's not. But Ned says they've hinted they'll let me go on my own recognizance." A headache that had been building for the two days Ned had been having his fruitless discussions flared again, making her a little sick to her stomach. "But they'd probably arrest me first."

"Great. You'll be stuck with an arrest record," Danny grumbled. "Good luck getting that expunged, even if they decide not to charge you."

"I can't focus on that right now," Darcy said. "I've got bigger things to worry about. Like what will happen to me if the mob tracks me down. I'm much more worried about them than I am in having an arrest record."

"Think about going abroad," Ben insisted. "Living in Switzerland, or Italy, or France … It would be like a full-time vacation."

"No, it wouldn't," Darcy said. "I'd still be hiding. And I'm *done*."

Later that night, Tess and Darcy lay in bed, holding each other in a loose embrace.

"This was a strange night," Darcy said. "I couldn't tell if Danny was acting weird because he was uncomfortable around Ben or us."

"Us …? Oh. You mean *us*. Maybe you should have had a talk with him before he came over, baby."

"I've been so preoccupied, I didn't even think about it until you stood up and put your arms around me." She leaned over and kissed Tess's temple. "I'm glad you did that, by the way. It helped calm me down."

"He has to have known. Not many kidnapping victims voluntarily go into hiding with their captors."

"Hmm … I'm not sure that's true. He might think you have Stockholm Syndrome."

"Oh, yeah, that's me," Tess said, chuckling. "I admit I'm under your spell, but it's not a psychological defense. I'm with you because I want to be." She sat up. "I very much want to be." Stroking Darcy's face, she murmured, "Take care of yourself for me. No matter what happens tomorrow, know that I'm behind you."

Darcy swallowed around the lump in her throat. Blinking back tears, she nodded. "I know that. So … you'll wait for me if they arrest me?"

"For the rest of my life." She lay back down and took Darcy in her arms, smothering her with kisses. "I don't agree with what you're doing, Darcy. I don't want you to turn yourself in. But I support you. You know that, right?"

"I do. And that gives me the strength to do what I think is right." She closed her eyes and whispered, "I hope to god I'm right."

Leaving Tess was like ripping off a piece of herself, but once Darcy and Danny were in his car, driving into Manhattan, she switched her focus to what lay in front of her. The DA was going to meet with her and Ned in his office. She prayed she'd be going home with her uncle at the end of the meeting. If not … she still had faith in the system. There were pockets of corruption in every major organization. But overall, she believed the government would do the right thing by her.

When they reached the building, a high-rise in Midtown, Danny said, "I'll go park. I don't want you to be late."

Darcy grasped the door handle, then leaned across the car and kissed Danny's cheek. "Thanks for everything. Uhm … if I don't … if I'm not able to go home … will you look out for Tess?"

"I will," he said, staring straight ahead. "And so will Ben. He's a good guy, Darce. I'm really glad you found him."

"Me too. Now get going before the cabbie behind you loses his mind."

"See you in a bit," he said, his voice cracking a little.

Darcy got out and stood on the crowded street, taking in the freedom her decision had given her. Even though she might be going to jail, at least she wouldn't have to worry about being caught—and having something bad happen to Tess in the process. For weeks now she'd been tortured by the thought of someone shooting at her and catching Tess

317

in the crossfire. That was something she couldn't let happen, no matter what.

As soon as she gave her name, Ned came out to the reception area and grasped her hand. "Damned nice to finally meet you," he said. He was surprisingly short, and a little overweight, but his personality made him seem like a much bigger man. "I knew if I practiced long enough I'd eventually get a good-looking client." He turned and said to the receptionist, "Marilyn, take a picture of us. A client my wife can be jealous of."

Marilyn was obviously used to his joking, since she just chuckled. Then she shifted her gaze to the door. "I think this is the DA," she said quietly.

Ned turned, and immediately scowled. "Maybe the DA's grandson." He walked over to the door and caught the young man as he entered. "When were you elected DA?" he demanded.

"Uhm … I'm Assistant District Attorney Nate Greene," the man said. "I don't know who told you the DA himself would be here, but they were wrong. This is my case."

"What bureau are you in?"

"I'm in the trial division," he said, nervously shifting his weight from one foot to the other.

"How many years experience?"

"Three."

"Three." Ned leaned in close, like he was trying to see his pores. "Three years. That's bullshit. Utter bullshit."

"No it's not! I have three years of experience. This is only my second homicide, but I've earned the right to prosecute this case."

"The trial division shouldn't be involved at all," Ned growled. "The investigation division should be handling this. Darcy's stuck in a load of bullshit that you people can get to the bottom of if you'll leave her alone and start digging!"

"Your client is being charged with murder, Mr. Cullen. The trials division handles murder cases."

Ned turned and started to walk towards a conference room, grasping Darcy by the arm and taking her with him. "You'd better have more authority than it looks like you have," he grumbled as the young ADA followed along. They all sat down, and Ned continued his questioning. "Why'd they send you? That's showing no respect at all for my client."

"You're client's being charged with murder. We don't generally roll out the welcome mat to murder suspects who've evaded law enforcement for over two months." Nate was clearly a polite guy, as he reached across the table and extended his hand. "Nate Greene. I assume you're Ms. Morgan?"

"I am." Having Ned next to her gave Darcy more confidence than she thought she'd be able to summon.

"I'm sorry to tell you this, Ms. Morgan, but I have two police officers downstairs. They're going to arrest you when we've finished talking."

"Bullshit!" Ned leapt to his feet. "Your boss led me to believe Darcy wouldn't be charged if she came in voluntarily."

"No one told me anything close to that," Nate said, his voice quiet but firm. "When someone evades arrest for a few months we don't give them another chance."

"Listen, kid," Ned said, leaning over and slamming his hands against the desk. "Darcy's been keeping her mouth shut, hoping you'd be able to figure out the bullcrap that's going on in that piece of shit precinct where her boss was killed. But if you think you can arrest her, and she'll just go along quietly, you're sadly mistaken. A reporter from *The Times* is very, very anxious to hear her speculate on how she wound up here. And given what's going on today—I'll bet Darcy thinks the corruption runs all the way to the DA's office."

"We'd prefer she didn't do that," Nate said quietly, not looking up from his notes. "This is a simple murder case. We'll let a jury decide her guilt or innocence."

"No, we won't," Ned boomed, his voice reverberating off the walls of the conference room. "We'll bombard the media with her side of the story." He reached over and grasped Darcy's cheeks with one hand, squeezing them tightly. "Look at this face. Have you ever seen a less guilty looking defendant? She's never had a fucking parking ticket! And you're going to convince the people of New York that one day she decided to kill her boss … for what, exactly? I haven't yet heard what her motive was. Did she want to take over the whole place? To be the *lead* accountant in a two-man office?"

"We haven't begun our investigation yet," he admitted. "I'm sure we'll dig something up once our investigators get to it."

"Call your supervisor," Ned said, sounding almost weary. "Tell him I want her to walk—no charges. If she walks, we'll cooperate fully. She'll show up every single time you want to meet with her—to tell you fuck all—which is what she knows."

Nate stood up and nodded. "I'll be right back."

As he left, Ned sat back down. "They're fucking with us," he grumbled. "But there's no way they want us to go blabbing to the press."

"Uhm … how will I blab to anyone if I'm in jail?"

"I'll have as much access as I need. I'll bring that reporter along with me. I'll tell them she's my paralegal."

"Am I going to jail?" Darcy started to tremble.

"I sure as hell hope not." He turned and gave her a gentle smile. "If they take you in, I'll move mountains to get you released quickly. I promise." He got up and went to a credenza where a few urns sat. "Coffee? I didn't want to have to offer any to that little pissant."

"No, thanks. My stomach's upset enough without adding more acid to it."

He poured some for himself, then added cream and two sugars. "Don't worry, Darcy," he said. "We'll fight them with everything we have."

A few minutes later, Nate re-entered the room. He sat down and shuffled his papers, then said, "We have an optics problem."

"Optics my ass," Ned growled. "Speak English."

"It doesn't look good for our office if we let a woman accused of murder …" He turned to Darcy. "A woman who has evaded arrest for over two months … walk. It would look best for us if she was in custody while the investigations continue."

"Investigations … plural?"

"Yes. There are two other bureaus working on various aspects of the case."

"Fina-fuckin'-ly!" Ned said. "That's the first time anyone's confirmed that."

"That doesn't help your client," Nate insisted. "At least not today. My supervisor wants her brought in."

"Well, she doesn't *want* to be brought in." He jumped up, a habit Darcy was sure would give her a heart attack if he kept doing it, then walked over to refresh his coffee. "How about this?" He moved to stand behind Nate, then put his coffee down and began to massage his shoulders, like they were friends or … intimates. "You've got an optics problem. Darcy has an incarceration problem. I can solve both of them."

Nate looked up, trying to see Ned's face. "Okay. Let's hear your solution."

"Go for a grand jury indictment. That'll let you look like you're doing your job, while still keeping Darcy at home."

"I don't think my supervisors will go for that. Ms. Morgan's a proven flight risk. If things aren't going her way she'll probably take off again. That would look very bad for the office."

"Fine." Ned slapped him hard on the shoulder, picked up his coffee and moved back to sit by Darcy. "Chew on this. We volunteer to have her wear a GPS device. We'll use the most reliable service out there. They'll ping her every hour. If she moves out of the area—you'll know."

"Mmm, I don't think that's good enough. How about house arrest?" he said, a hopeful tone to his voice.

"No way. She's been shut up in a house for months."

"That was her choice," Nate warned. "Entirely her choice."

"What if I give you my location, and return home every night by … ten o'clock?" Darcy asked. "You'll know I'm in the same spot every night. And I doubt I'll go far during the day. I just … I'm going crazy trapped in one spot."

"It's better than jail, isn't it?" Nate asked, arching an eyebrow.

"We're offering to have her wear a monitor. She'll sleep in the same place the whole time. That's good enough," Ned insisted. "And for your troubles, she'll keep her mouth shut. No more talking to the press. Right, Darcy?"

"I won't say another word. To anyone."

Nate put the pen he'd been twirling onto the table. "Let me make another call."

As he left, Darcy leaned her head back and exhaled. "This is taking an awful lot out of me."

"Best part of my job," Ned said, grinning. "I love trading horseflesh."

"I've never been referred to in quite that way, but I'll admit you look pretty happy."

"We've got him by the …" He shut his mouth. "We've got him," he continued, obviously thinking Darcy was too innocent to hear course language. "Bet you a hundred bucks."

"I don't think I want to bet about my own future. I'm just relieved he hasn't mentioned Tess. I was afraid they'd pull her into this as leverage."

"Don't mention her name," he advised. "This kid doesn't seem like the brightest bulb in the pack. He might have heard about her and forgot."

The door opened again and Nate took his chair. After clearing his throat, he said, "Here's the agreement. Ms. Morgan wears a GPS tracking device. The service will ping her every minute. If she leaves the New York metropolitan area we're going to pick her up. If we do that, she's in jail for the duration." He met Darcy's gaze. "No exceptions. In addition, we'll want her to remain at her place of residence from ten p.m. until six a.m. Agreed?"

"Agreed," she said, trying to get her answer in before Ned asked for something and ruined the deal. "Happily."

"Great. Where will you be?"

"Uhm … what do you mean by the metropolitan area?"

"Commuting distance. You know. The city, Jersey, Long Island, Southern Connecticut."

"That works, but I'm not sure yet where I'll go. I'm selling my apartment in Brooklyn, since the mob and a few cops are still looking for me."

"What are you going to do about that?" Ned demanded. "How will you protect her?"

"We can protect her if she's in custody," Nate said as he made a few notes. "Outside … she's on her own." He looked up. "Sorry. But we don't have the resources for that."

"It's okay," Darcy said, putting her hand on Ned's arm. "I'll be all right."

"Not if the police know where you are," he growled, glaring at Nate. "And I bet the DA's going to tell anyone who asks."

"That's not true," Nate said. "But we have to tell the NYPD not to enforce the warrant. Unless you want her picked up."

"That's putting a target on her back!"

Nate shrugged. "I don't have any other solution. We do *not* want her arrested. *The Post* will have a field day with that."

"I'd rather be free to walk around," Darcy said. "My uncle can help protect me."

"I don't like it," Ned said, his face stretched into a dark frown. "I'd rather not tell the NYPD where you are and take our chances with one of the boys in blue recognizing you."

"No deal," Nate insisted, bristling.

Darcy didn't have as much experience as Ned did, but she could tell Nate wasn't going to budge on this. "I'll be fine. Until I get my own place I'll be at my uncle's house." She wrote down his address on a slip of paper and handed it to Nate. "Could you get someone to take the hold off my bank accounts? I'll need to write some checks when I find a place to rent."

"Sure. I can have that done today." He looked up. "Anything else?"

"I'm happy," Darcy said. "But … didn't you have any questions for me?"

"Oh! Right!" Nate opened his folio again. "Thanks," he mumbled as he looked for his notes. Darcy turned to see Ned rolling his eyes. Maybe he was right about the dimness of Nate's bulb.

An hour later, Darcy emerged from the office, rushing across the reception area to fall into Danny's embrace. "I'm so glad you're free," he murmured. "I've been a nervous wreck."

"I've got to make a call. Tess has probably worn a path in Ben's carpet by now."

He nodded, then moved away to give her privacy.

"Tess?" she said when the phone was answered. "I'm coming home, baby."

"Yeow!" Tess yelled, making Darcy's ear thrum with very welcome pain.

At four o'clock, Darcy and Danny went to pick up Tess. She was out the door, running for Darcy before the car stopped.

Kisses rained down on her face as Darcy stood there, mortally embarrassed. "Shh," she soothed, as she caught her uncle's expression. He looked almost as embarrassed as she did. No matter the sexual orientation, they weren't physically demonstrative people.

"I never thought you'd get here."

"It took forever to get the ankle monitor fitted," Darcy said.

Tess grasped her pant-leg and tugged it up. "Nice look. Does it have to be as big as a can of tuna?"

"I don't know. But it's a lot better than being in … wherever they put women pending trial. I was too afraid to look it up before I went in."

"I'm all packed," Tess said. She looked at Danny. "Thanks so much for taking us in." Giving Darcy a hug, she said, "Your dad called to try to talk us out of leaving."

"You've got to move," Danny said, his expression glum. "My complex is much more secure than this."

"I think my uncle's right," Darcy said. "Besides, I don't want Ben brought into this. No one knows about him and I'd like to keep it that way."

Late that night, Darcy sat at her uncle's dining table, gazing at her bulky, uncomfortable ankle monitor. "I guess I'll get used to this," she said. "But it's really unwieldy."

"Better than jail," he reminded her. "Although I think you two should stay inside until the grand jury meets."

"I've been thinking that too," she said. "I can't imagine the dirty cops want me alive."

"I'm *sure* the mob doesn't. You fucked them out of money, Darcy. That wasn't the smartest thing you've ever done."

325

"I'd give it back if they'd leave me alone, but I think you're wrong about it being a dumb move. If I had given that thug the combination, he would have killed me. And if I hadn't had ready access to cash, I couldn't have escaped. But now? Hell yes I'd give it back."

"I don't think it works like that. They're not a live-and-let-live kind of group."

"No, I don't think they are." She leaned over and rested her chin on her folded arms. "But we can't stay here for long, Danny. We'll drive each other nuts."

"No we won't. You're really easy to live with."

Darcy fixed him with a look. "Your girlfriend won't agree."

"Oh, shit. I didn't even tell her you were coming."

"Better call," she said, going into the living room to wake up a dozing Tess and take her to bed. "Women don't like surprises."

Darcy lay in bed the next morning, happily playing with her phone. She hadn't realized how much she relied on the device until she'd been forced to live without it. Now, she scrolled through all of her apps, then settled on one to read the newspaper.

Tess woke a while later, lazily stretching out her body. "Why does my back hurt?" she grumbled.

"Because my uncle bought the cheapest mattress ever made. I don't think he planned on ever having guests. It's like a rock, isn't it?"

"Don't insult rocks," Tess said, thumping the bed with her fist. "I felt like I was lying on the ground." She sat up and fussed with her hair. "Can we go out to breakfast? I want pancakes."

"I can make pancakes. No problem."

"I'd rather go out. Now that you're free …" She slid out of bed and tried to drag Darcy with her.

"Uhm … I'm free … technically. But I'm not totally free. My uncle and I think we should stay inside. At least until the grand jury meets."

Tess's face fell. "That could be weeks!"

"Or … months," Darcy said, wincing.

Tess dropped to the bed. "I don't …" She looked around the small, utilitarian room with a view of the adjacent apartment building filling the window. "I might have some trouble with that, baby. This is a fine apartment, much nicer than mine, but …"

"I know," Darcy soothed. "But once the police know where I am, it will be very, very easy for the bad guys to tell the mob the address. I really don't think it's safe—for either of us—to leave." She took Tess's chilled hand. "But only for a while. Maybe the grand jury will meet really quickly."

Tess turned and looked at her skeptically. "Why will you be safe then?"

"Uhm … I'm not sure. I guess I hope that if the grand jury doesn't indict me the bad cops will assume I won't …" She flopped down on the mattress. "We're screwed."

Darcy didn't suffer from PMS if she could exercise. But when she was stuck inside on a cold, snowy day, she got a little bitchy. Tess had responded with good humor all day, but she'd obviously had enough. It was barely nine when she said, "I'm going to bed. Why don't you … do something to make yourself feel better."

"I'll be better by tomorrow," Darcy promised. "I'm just …"

"I know." Tess leaned over and kissed her. "I'm not angry with you. I just want to give you some space."

"My uncle will be home soon. Maybe I'll stay up and annoy him."

"You're not annoying." Another quick kiss followed the previous one. "Well, that's a lie, but you're not annoying very often."

"Thanks for being honest."

"That's what I'm best at." Tess ruffled her hair playfully, then walked down the hall to the guest bedroom.

The Knicks were playing, and even though Darcy was more of a fan of women's college basketball, it was fun to watch the big guys play once in a while. It was a good game, and she found herself getting into it. When she heard Danny's key in the lock she called out, "Fourth quarter. It's the Knicks' game to lose."

The door closed and Darcy turned to see her uncle standing in the entry way, his expression grim. "I've got news."

Already weak with anxiety, Darcy got up and walked to him. Danny wasn't the kind to get rattled easily, and he was rattled. "Tell me!"

"Viktor Gibazov and Sergei Zahorchak were murdered this afternoon." Their eyes met and for the first time in her life she could see that her uncle was frightened.

"They think a cop did it," Danny added. "Separate locations, about an hour apart. Same car was seen speeding away."

Darcy grabbed for the half-wall that set the entryway apart from the living room. Her legs were ready to give way. "Oh, fuck. I'm next."

Danny grasped her by the arm and guided her to a dining chair. "No, you're not." He whipped off his coat and hat and tossed them onto the table. "I've been thinking about this all day, and there's a chance … a good chance, I think, that this is good news for you."

"Sure. This is great news!" She dropped her head onto the table. "The mob and some dirty cops are after me, and the dirty cops are bold enough to murder two of the mob's top guys. What could be better?"

"No, no, you're looking at it wrong. Try this." Darcy lifted her head and looked at him. "The cops are dirty *because* of this Viktor guy. Everybody I've talked to says he's the main guy in that area. You screwed Viktor out of some serious cash. But the cops probably don't know that."

Her gaze sharpened. "Why wouldn't they? I'd think he'd tell all his hired muscle so they'd understand how important it was to kill me—as painfully as possible"

"No way, Darce. That's not how those guys think."

"Which guys are we talking about? The cops or the mob?"

"The mob, primarily. A guy like Viktor can't afford to look weak—to anyone. Having a civilian—especially a woman—rob him makes him look stupid. And having you dance away and hide for over two months makes it worse."

"But Sergei found us down in Cape May. He could only have done that with the cops' help."

"Oh, they're working together. That's not a question. But I don't think Viktor told the cops about the money. In fact, I bet Sergei's the only guy who knew about it. The boss doesn't want lower level guys to know he's got buckets full of money stashed all over town. The grunts would spend all of their time looking for the money instead of doing what he tells them to do."

"Why do you think the cops killed them now?"

"They must have been afraid your testimony would lead the DA to one of them—the only guys who know the names and faces of the dirty cops."

"But I wouldn't know Viktor if he bit me!"

"Exactly!" He smiled as he slapped his hand on the table. "Which makes me more certain that the cops don't know about the money or the real reason Viktor wanted you found. I think he was playing coy, and it cost him."

"So I'm in as much, if not more danger from the cops."

"Yeah," he said, his head dropping. "I guess that's true. But I bet the mob's not interested in you any more. That's an improvement, right?"

"Sure. Of course it is," she said, patting him on the arm. "You're absolutely right." *And I'm absolutely dead!*

Darcy and Danny stayed up until three, debating and guessing about every detail of the police and mob involvement in her case. She was dead to the world when Tess shook her early the next morning. "Ned's on the phone. Do you want me to answer it?"

Darcy got to her feet, stumbling as she banged into the wall on the way to the living room. Ned's voice echoed through the answering machine. "Pick up the damn phone. Pick up. Pick up. Pick up. Pick up. Pick up."

"Yeah," she said, slowly getting her bearings as she grabbed the phone. "I was up half the night trying to decide what planet I can hide on."

"I'm calling that pipsqueak ADA as soon as he gets his lazy ass into the office. You're not going to be a sitting duck."

"There's no way they're going to let me walk away, Ned. They made that clear."

"That was before witnesses saw a guy who looks a lot like a local cop gun down this Sergei guy in the street."

"Witnesses?" Darcy sat down hard.

"Yeah." He chuckled. "You can never get anyone to make a statement about anything mob related—unless it's against a cop. I guess the idiot who pulled the trigger didn't understand people fear the mob more than the cops."

"They really think they've got the guy who did it?"

"If the witnesses hold up, the guy who shot Sergei was a detective third grade named …" He paused for a minute. "Named Hardison. He drives an older gold Lexus that was also spotted blowing away from Viktor's house when he was killed. "Ever heard of him?"

"I don't know a single person in the NYPD."

"Good. Let's keep it that way. For now, get your stuff packed up and decide where you want to go." His voice took on a more serious tone. "Make it some place safe, Darcy."

"It will be." Her sleep-deprived brain wasn't working as quickly as it normally did, but a very big issue finally floated to the surface. "How will it help to move? The police will still know where I am."

"That deal's over. I talked to the monitoring company already. They have the ability to keep your location secret unless you leave the metropolitan area. As soon as I can get hold of the ADA, that's going to be the new normal."

"So I'm supposed to drive around until you get them to agree?"

"I guess so." He paused for a few seconds. "Yeah. Do that. Get in the car and keep moving. As soon as I get the okay, I'll call you."

"You've got the number of my disposable phone, right?"

"I do. Next time we talk, be moving."

"Even before you talk to the DA's office?"

"Before we hang up. Go!"

Darcy hung up, then looked at a very agitated Tess. "We've got to move. Right now."

Given that the NYPD knew his car and license number, Danny arranged to borrow a neighbor's car for the getaway. Darcy and Tess lay down in the backseat, hiding until Danny was sure they weren't being followed.

They drove around Long Island, staying on small, local streets, with Darcy holding her weapon in her hand. She knew it made Tess jumpy, but keeping them both safe was a higher priority than Tess's nerves. If anyone made a move, she was ready. Finally, just after eight, Ned called with the all clear.

Darcy called Ben, catching him before he left for work. "It's Darcy," she said when he answered. "How do you feel about us moving back into your house?"

"I feel great about it. But I thought you'd all agreed you'd be safer with your uncle nearby."

"There's been a change in plans. Two of the mobsters who were after me were murdered yesterday, and it looks like one of the dirty cops pulled the trigger on both of them."

"I'll be out there as fast as I can get there," he said, his voice tight with anxiety.

"There's no need for that. Danny's driving us over right now. We'll be fine."

"I can clear my calendar," he insisted.

"No, really. Come see us tonight if you want to, but go ahead and go to work. We're just going to hunker down and hope not to attract attention."

"Call me the second you get there. I'm worried, Darcy. Really worried."

She looked at Tess, whose normally pink cheeks had turned a sickly white over an hour ago. "So are we."

Danny had quite an arsenal in his apartment, and he'd brought pieces of it with him. He and Darcy sat at the dining room table, calmly loading guns the size of violins, while Tess paced. She was so nervous that she nearly shrieked when she heard an unexpected noise coming from the driveway. "Someone's out there," she whispered before going to hide behind Darcy and her huge gun.

Both Darcy and Danny got up quickly, then Danny pointed at the front door and Darcy moved to stand behind it. He went to the window, carrying the biggest of the guns, something that looked like he'd brought it back from Iraq. In a nanosecond, it was aimed right at the driver of a big, black sedan. Tess could look through the sidelight windows of the front door, and to her the guy looked exactly like a cop. Then his passenger got out and started to walk around the car. "That's a pretty calm hit man," Tess whispered. "Parking right in the driveway?"

Danny obviously didn't agree. "They aren't cops. If they draw their weapons—they're gone," he said quietly.

The phone began to ring, and Darcy twitched her head in its direction. "Answer it."

Tess tiptoed over to the phone and picked it up, her hands shaking so badly she almost dropped it. "Hello?" she whispered.

"Tess? It's Ben."

"Can't talk. The bad guys are in the driveway."

"No! I hired a security firm!"

"Security firm!" she yelled. "Ben hired them."

"Shit," Danny said, his posture loosening into its normal affect. "I was ready to blow this window out and send those two to meet their maker."

"God damn it," Tess groused. "I wet my pants again!"

After a civilized, non-weaponized discussion with the security firm, Darcy sent them on their way. She didn't want to attract one bit of attention that wasn't absolutely necessary, and two lunks sitting in a big sedan in the drive wasn't inconspicuous enough for her. But no less than ten minutes after they left, a Suffolk Police Department squad car pulled up.

"Your idea?" Darcy asked her uncle, her eyes narrowing.

"Two guys I trust with my life. They're gonna watch the house when I'm not here."

"Send them away," Darcy insisted. "The neighbors will know something's up."

"Okay, okay." He went outside, grumbling to himself.

Tess sidled up to Darcy and put her arms around her. "You're radiating tension," she soothed.

"That's what it feels like. I'm about to snap."

The phone rang again, and Darcy went to pick it up. "Hello?"

"Is Ben there?"

"No, he's not at home right now. Can I take a message?"

"Is this his niece?"

"Right. I mean, yes," Darcy corrected when she recalled that's what Ben had told his neighbors.

"This is Mrs. Gordon from across the street. Is everything all right? I see the police are there."

"Oh, sure, everything's fine, Mrs. Gordon," she said, rolling her eyes. "Thanks for looking out for us."

There was silence on the line. With flinty determination, Mrs. Gordon asked again, "Why are the police there, honey?"

"Well," she struggled to think of an excuse. "They know Ben's not normally here during the week. They saw us pull in and wanted to check to make sure we weren't burglarizing the house."

"Oh! That's very good to hear. Roger, my husband, always says the police don't do enough patrols around here. He'll be glad to hear that."

"Yes, ma'am. We're glad too. It's nice to feel safe."

"When it warms up, you and your friend should come by. Ben says you're writers. Is that right?"

"Sure. I mean, yes. Yes, we are. We're doing some research for our next book."

"Well, Roger and I would love to hear about it. You come by as soon as it's not so cold."

"We will. Thanks again for calling." She hung up and collapsed onto a chair. "We might as well put a sign out advertising visiting hours. Who else can come by?"

Tess looked outside as she saw a flash of white on the driveway. "Long Island Security Systems. Do you want to take this one, or should I?"

Darcy and Danny were outside for so long, Tess put her coat on to go check on them. Darcy was talking to a guy in coveralls when Tess found her near the corner of the house. When he walked back to his truck, Darcy said, "We're going to let them put motion-detection lights around the perimeter, cameras that will capture every window on a closed circuit, pressure strips that will sound an alarm on every window and door that's opened, and a backup power source if someone cuts the line. I'll be able to monitor the whole building on my tablet computer."

"You don't have one."

"Ben's bringing me one tonight. He said it's a graduation present—a few years late." She snapped her fingers. "Will you call and ask him to let his neighbors know he's making some changes to his system? I think Mrs. Gordon's probably better security than we're installing, but I'm pretty sure she doesn't stay up twenty-four hours a day."

Ben not only brought Darcy a computer, he brought top-notch sushi, making Tess fall just a little in love with him. Darcy suspiciously poked at anything even slightly exotic with the tip of a chopstick, making her stock fall as Ben's rose, but Tess was confident Darcy's would rally.

Given that Ben didn't know how to shoot a gun, he really wasn't much help in the security department. But just having him in the house made Tess feel safer. He gave off a very strong "I've got this" vibe, and when you added that to Darcy and Danny's calm temperaments and firepower, all seemed right with the world.

Danny had arranged to take a week of vacation and was going to stay with them. Since he was used to working a variety of shifts, he was going to stay up at night to keep an eye on things while they slept.

It was so nice to join a family with members who had practical skills. Tess's own parents would have been able to bake pies or find some nice mushrooms for the bad guys, but those skills weren't needed at the moment. She was thrilled to be in the Morgan/Miller clan, especially when one of them knew how to stay awake while she tried to catch some shut-eye.

After a week of nighttime vigilance, Danny reluctantly went back to work. He was retiring in March, and Darcy wanted him to get all of his unused vacation pay rather than waste it sitting up all night. It might have been wrong-headed, but she'd convinced herself the dirty cops would have moved fast if they were going to move at all.

Danny seemed confident that the trigger-man they had under arrest was the muscle for the whole enterprise. And given that they both agreed that smart cops would rather go to prison for taking bribes than murdering innocent women, he didn't argue much when Darcy demanded he go finish his final month of work.

On their first solo day, she and Tess dressed warmly and went to sit outside. It was far too cold to do that comfortably, but they'd been inside for a full week and were both itching to breathe some fresh air. As always when she was outside or near a window, Darcy had her Beretta in her hand, safety on, and a Smith and Wesson M4 rifle, borrowed from Danny, lying on the table next to her. "Do you have any interest in learning to shoot?" she asked Tess.

"Shoot?" Her eyebrows rose to their full height. "A gun?"

"Uhm … I guess you've answered my question already. I just thought you might feel better if you could defend yourself."

Smirking, Tess said, "I defend myself by hiding behind you. That's plenty."

Darcy held up her hands. "No argument. Just checking." She looked around the backyard; snow massed on the pool cover, lounge chairs neatly stacked in a corner, big barbecue grill and wet bar covered with black tarps. "I thought sitting out here might cheer me up, but it's just reminding me how long it's going to be until we can use any of this stuff."

Tess reached over and took her gloved hand. "I know what you need."

"You do? 'Cause I sure don't."

"Uh-huh," she said, her expression sly. "You need a job."

Nodding, Darcy said, "I guess I could do Ben's taxes. And yours. That would keep me busy for a couple of days."

"Not that kind of job. You need to do something to keep you on your toes. Something you don't yet know how to do."

Darcy smiled when she said, "That's a very big list. Should I just decide to be a ... biologist and try to figure things out? Maybe get one of those biology for dummies books?"

"Nope. I think you should work with me."

"With you ...? How would I do that?"

"Come inside." Tess took her hand and they went back into the house. She stripped off her coat and dropped it onto a kitchen chair, then Darcy did her usual, picking it up and taking it to the closet where she hung up both jackets.

"I'm going to train you eventually," she said, hoping her chiding sounded good-natured. She was sure she'd never get Tess to be as neat as she wished. Luckily, it didn't bother her to tidy up for both of them.

"While you're training me to be neat, I'm training you to be messy." Tess grasped her hand again, pulled her close and kissed her cheek. "I bet we're both failures." They went into the den, which Tess used as her office. She sat down at the desk chair, and opened the program she used to organize her notes. She compiled the notes and printed off a draft. When the printer spit out six pages of double-spaced lines she handed them to Darcy. "Why don't you read this and give me your opinion?"

"My ... opinion? Like ... what, exactly?"

"Your opinion," she repeated. "What you think of the article."

"I like your articles," Darcy said. "All of them."

"I know, baby, but you've read the things I've had published. This is my first draft on my spa experience, and I'm trying to get the tone right." She batted her big, blue eyes, a trait she probably didn't know she resorted to when she wanted something. "I'd love your help."

"Really?" Charmed, Darcy sat down and gazed at her for a second. "But I've never done anything like this. What makes you think I'll have anything worthwhile to say?"

"Because everything you have to say is worthwhile. You're very perceptive and you're a very careful reader. I can see that in the way you talk about other things you've read. Like your mysteries."

"Talking about the books we read and critiquing plots was just a thing my mom and I did. We didn't have any great insights or anything."

Tess got up and went to sit on the arm of Darcy's chair. "I don't think that's true. You're very thoughtful, and that's the reader I'm trying to reach. You're also in the perfect demographic for this article; an upper middle class, professional woman with enough disposable income to treat herself to a week's holiday."

Frowning, Darcy said, "I'm not sure I see myself that way, but I'm happy to help in any way I can."

"Just read the darned thing and we'll talk, okay?"

"I'm on it," she agreed, smiling when Tess slipped her reading glasses onto her face.

After Darcy had gone over the article three times, they spent a long time talking about it.

"You really think I sound snarky?" Tess asked. She looked so cute, sitting in her chair, her knees pulled up as high as she could get them, a red pencil stuck behind her ear.

"Just a little. You sound like you wouldn't have chosen to go to the place and you thought some of the treatments were a waste of time. Maybe that's what you're going for ..."

"No, it's not," she said, taking her pencil and moving it quickly along the lines of type as she read the section they were talking about. "Okay, I can see your point." She leaned back in the chair, assessing Darcy. "I didn't want to be there and I did think some of the treatments were utter BS. I think that's my built-in prejudice about places like this, but I don't want to let that show in my article." Taking her pencil and pointing it at Darcy she said, "I love the fact that you're willing to point out flaws. I was afraid you'd just say you loved it."

"I did," she agreed, smiling warmly. "I loved that you were snarky about it. That's you, and I like seeing your personality come out in your writing."

"I'm snarky? All of the time?"

"Of course not. But you're not afraid to say something's lame if you think it is."

"True. But I'm trying to sell this article to a publication aimed at women who love this kind of thing. I have to give my opinion, but I also have to have an open mind."

"Then say what your prejudices are," Darcy urged.

Laughing, Tess said, "If I did that, they'd never buy the article. No, I've got to be fair and try to reassess the place as if I liked this kind of thing. I'll give it another go." With a sly grin she took her pencil and pointed at the door. "I'll come find you when I've reworked it."

Darcy stood and started to leave. "If I didn't know better, I'd think you were kicking me out."

"Me? Never." She turned back to her draft and started to slash at it with her pencil. Hard workers were such a turn-on!

Late that afternoon, Tess went into the living room to find Darcy soberly reading something on her tablet computer. "Whatcha doin', good lookin'?"

"I found this book that got a lot of raves." She turned the pad around and Tess read the title.

"Editing Non-fiction?" Tess sat down next to Darcy, put her arm around her, and kissed her gently. "You're such a good partner."

"I am?" As always, she looked pleased, but also surprised to field a compliment. Her past girlfriends must have been real jerks!

"You are. It's adorable that you're jumping right into this."

She shrugged, her cheeks coloring slightly. "Well, it's …" She looked up and met Tess's gaze. "I wanted to major in English. I was never very good at writing, but when I learned you could make a living editing other people's work I thought I might like to do it."

"You did? But …"

"My mom talked me out of it, and I should be glad she did. It's really tough making a living as an editor since the major publishing houses cut back so much." A wistful smile settled on her lips. "The world will always need accountants. The tax code isn't as complex as it is by chance, you know. Accountants wrote it."

Tess slipped an arm around her and snuggled up to rest her head on Darcy's shoulder. "Know what I love about you?"

"I can make a few guesses, but you're the expert."

"I love your generosity," she said.

"Really? That wouldn't have been on my list."

"It's number one, baby. I'm so glad I've chosen someone who cares about me—and my career—and what's important to me. You don't just love my personality and how much fun we have together. We're working towards something here. Something lasting. Something that will benefit us both in the long term." She kissed her cheek again, finding she never tired of touching Darcy's skin. "We have a true partnership."

Darcy shifted so they were face to face. "I'd always wanted to be a partner in a big firm. But a two-man shop is what I needed. Me and you. Equal partners."

CHAPTER SEVENTEEN

AT THE END OF TWO weeks, Tess's jeans fit snugly again, and she decided she had to get outside and start walking before she had to buy a bigger size. Darcy seemed content staying inside to work out on the exercise bike and lift weights, but they couldn't hide forever. If they were going to live normal lives, it was time to start.

Their first long walks were almost comical. "We're acting like a pair of long-tailed cats in a room full of rocking chairs," Tess said when they'd both flinched at a seagull's squawk.

"It's hard to calm down," Darcy admitted. "I almost pulled the trigger that time. I'd hate to shoot myself in the leg."

Tess slapped at her. "Put the safety on!"

"It's on," she admitted, a slow smile showing. "I was teasing … kind of."

"Do you think we'll loosen up?"

"Yeah. Eventually. But I'll admit to being more comfortable in the house."

"If the evil cops are coming for us, they're really lazy."

"True." She turned and smiled. "Tell that to my central nervous system. It's still locked in on 'fight or flight,' and it thinks flight is the better option."

On the sixth of March, Darcy woke to the smell of something sweet. She lay there, sniffing the air, before jumping up, uncharacteristically alert. Once she padded into the kitchen, she saw her birthday present—Tess—who'd snuck out of bed early to make muffins.

"Happy birthday!" she said, practically squirming with delight. "Look what I bought you." From the microwave, she removed a very large Starbucks cup. "Cinnamon dolce latte." She froze for just a second. "You like that, right? They don't have the Christmas flavors any more."

Darcy grasped the cup in one hand, and wrapped the other arm around Tess. "I love it. And I love you for giving me such a nice treat."

"Don't forget the muffins." She placed a sweet kiss to Darcy's lips. "I haven't made them before, but once you told me you liked cinnamon chip muffins, I knew I had to make them for you."

Amazed and touched by her thoughtfulness, Darcy gazed at Tess. "It has to have been months ago I said that."

"Yeah, I guess so. And …?"

"You remembered," Darcy said, wrapping her in another snug hug. "You remember little things I say. Stuff I mention in passing. You make me feel so special."

"You *are* special." Tess pulled the tin from the oven and set it on the counter. "We'll let those cool for a few minutes, then demolish them," she said, giggling. "Three each. Okay. Four for you and two for me. It's your birthday."

"Four muffins? I don't think I've eaten four muffins in the last year! I'm certainly not going to eat four in one day."

Tess grinned slyly. "It's your birthday, so every wish you make will be fulfilled. Four for me. Two for you."

"Deal." Darcy put an arm around her and led her into the living area. It was a bright, sunny morning, with the big oaks in the side yard just starting to show some green buds.

They sat on the sofa together, cuddling while Darcy drank her coffee. "What's your birthday wish?" Tess asked.

"Mmm, I think you can probably guess. I want the phone to ring and have Ned tell me the DA's dropping the case."

"Yeah, that'd be mine too."

A little of her good humor faded, and Darcy wished she hadn't put a damper on things.

"I know!" Tess said, her perky mood returning with a vengeance. "Tell me what you'll do when the call comes. 'Cause it's going to come."

This had become Tess's new dogma. She was certain that the DA didn't have enough evidence to make a case stick, and was just moving slowly in dropping the charges. Darcy was equally sure that wasn't going to happen, but it was nice to act like it might. She blew out a long breath, her lips flapping as she let many possible scenarios parade through her mind. "I'd like to go somewhere far away. I got a passport a couple of years ago, and have never used it."

Tess's smile grew even brighter. "Done. Where do you want to go?"

"Hmm … That's a tougher call. What do you think?"

"How about Europe? You've never been, right?"

Darcy rolled her eyes. "Can you drive to Europe from New Jersey?"

Patting her, Tess said, "Just checking. I don't like to assume too much." Her eyes narrowed in thought. "I think your first trip should be someplace with a lot of history. I'm thinking … England, Scotland, Wales or Ireland."

"I sense a theme."

"I think you'll enjoy your first big trip if you can speak the language. Once you see the road signs in Wales and Ireland you won't think we're united in a common tongue, but we really are."

"Let's do England. My mom's family has been in America a very long time, but both of her lines came from England. I'd love to poke around a little and see if I can drum up any trace of the Morgan or Harris families."

"Let's start now," Tess decided. "We'll sign up for one of those ancestry search websites and get a head start. Then we'll chase down every lead during our long, leisurely trip."

"Long and leisurely?" Darcy asked.

"Yep." Tess snuck an arm around her shoulders and hugged her for a long time. "I want to be gone for quite a while. Our nerves need a chance to settle down. If we're bobbing and weaving around England for a few months, we'll both be able to get back to normal."

"And you might be able to shoehorn a job or two into our travels."

"Only if you'll help me. Having an editor at my beck and call is going to be fantastic!"

"I'm no editor," Darcy warned. "But I'm a very enthusiastic first reader."

Tess cuddled up closer and purred with delight. "We're going to have such a good time. No schedule. No rush."

Darcy chuckled. "I was just going to suggest we start putting a tentative schedule together. That's the part of travel I'm most looking forward to. Planning."

"We'll be a great team," Tess teased. "You do all the prep work and notify me a few hours before I have to leave for the airport."

"I hope it's soon," Darcy said, already dreaming of the day they could put some distance between them and the mess that had started over three months ago.

On a surprisingly warm Friday in late March, Darcy was sitting by the pool, reading a book. Her phone rang and she grabbed it quickly. "Hello?"

"It's Ned. We're on the docket for the grand jury on Monday. How do you feel about practicing your testimony this weekend?"

"Practicing?" she asked, feeling all of the blood leave her brain.

"Yeah. It's a pain, but we've got to be prepared."

"I'm here," she said vacantly.

"Uhm … I don't know where 'here' is, Darcy. How about an address?"

"Right. Right. Uhm … when are you coming?"

"Tomorrow morning. How about nine?"

"Great. Just great."

Tess got up early and made another batch of those delicious cinnamon chip muffins. She had a fresh pot of coffee brewing when Ned rang the bell right at nine.

Trying to be upbeat, Darcy smiled and said, "First time I've answered the door without a gun," before she opened it.

"Good to meet you," Ned said, taking Tess's hand as he burst into the house. "Ned Cullen."

Tess blinked in surprise, but she was very able to roll with the punches. "It's nice to meet you too, Ned. I have fresh coffee and homemade muffins just out of the oven. Can I get you one?"

He gave Darcy a look that questioned her sanity. "You have this great house and a girlfriend who makes you muffins. Yet you're in a hurry to give yourself up? What in the hell's wrong with you?"

"I ask myself that nearly every day," Darcy said, putting her hand on his shoulder as she led him to the kitchen.

After getting their coffee, they went into the dining room, where Ned opened his briefcase and took out a couple of legal pads. Notes were scrawled all over what looked like dozens of pages, but he also had a few file folders that were in much better order. "Okay. Here's the deal on the grand jury." He took a bite of his muffin, gave Tess a look then whipped his gaze towards Darcy. "You're insane."

"The grand jury?" she said, trying to keep him on track.

"Right. I don't know if you've read up on this, but it won't be like a regular trial. There's no judge, there's going to be a load of jurors, and I don't get to talk."

"No judge?"

"Nope. The jury hears evidence put on by the prosecutor only. If they think he's got enough to send you to trial, that's what will happen. If they don't—you're a free woman."

"Why can't you talk?" Tess asked.

"They're not trying to determine if Darcy's guilty," he explained. "Only if there's sufficient evidence to bring her to trial." His expression turned sober. "A judge once said the New York grand juries would indict a ham sandwich. But I'm hoping there are enough holes in the prosecutor's case that the jury tells him to shove it."

"How can we make sure the jury sees the holes? The prosecutor isn't going to bring them up, right?"

He winked at Tess. "You've got a real sharp one here." Thumbing through a legal pad, he paused and said, "You're a hundred percent right on that. That's why I requested some extra witnesses. Like the whole chain of command that allowed your boss to be cremated. I guarantee some of those folks don't want to have to explain how that happened."

"Great," Darcy said, starting to feel a glimmer of optimism. "I know you're on top of things, Ned."

"I am." He was frowning when he faced her again. "That's why I have to make sure you understand the ramifications of testifying."

"I think I do—"

Tess cut in. "I only know what Darcy's told me and I'm not sure she tells me things I might not like. Give me the whole scoop."

"There's only one downside," Ned said. "Anything she says can be used against her if she's indicted and goes to trial. Given that I assume she's only got one version of the truth—that shouldn't be a problem."

Darcy held up a finger. "I've got one solitary version of what happened. I'm not worried about being caught in a lie."

"Can I be there?" Tess asked.

"No," both Darcy and Ned said at the same moment.

He gave Darcy a quizzical look, then responded to Tess. "It's a closed proceeding. Darcy can only be there because she's going to testify. And she had to waive immunity to even get to do that."

"You waived immunity?" Tess looked like she was going to punch something.

"I didn't have any immunity to waive," Darcy said, soothingly. "I'm the last person the prosecutor would give immunity to."

"Yeah, yeah, that's just a technicality." He clapped Darcy on the back. "Don't worry. I won't let her do anything dumb."

"She's turning herself in voluntarily," Tess said, sparing a brief scowl for Darcy. "She's beaten you to the punch."

On Monday morning, Darcy walked up and down the marble hallway of a courthouse in Brooklyn, trying to keep her anxiety at bay. She and Ned had been there for two hours, but they had no way of knowing if her case was even being heard yet. So far, they'd watched four people come and go, and two of them, both men, one early middle-age and casually dressed, the other older, wearing a suit and a very world-weary look, were now standing at the other end of the hall. The door opened again, and Darcy's heart skipped a beat, the way it had every other time she heard the big oak door creak.

A harried-looking, middle-aged woman emerged, turned her head and took note of the men who now walked towards her. Suddenly, she put her hand up, like she was warning them to leave her alone.

Ned caught Darcy's eye and they watched, transfixed, as the woman snapped, "Thanks for all the help. It's really nice to know we're all in this together." Then she yanked open the door to the stairway and started down—fifteen floors. The two men spoke quietly, then the casually dressed one started after her. But the other guy grabbed him by the arm, said something, then led him to the elevator.

"I don't know what that means, but I'm always happy to see a prosecution witness look pissed," Ned said, a wicked smile on his face.

The door opened again and a huge man in a uniform pointed at her. "Darcy Morgan?"

"Yes." She had to swallow to get even that one word out.

"They're ready for you."

Shaking, she started for the door, relieved to feel Ned's hand grip her arm. They entered, and it took a moment for her to adjust to the set-up. It wasn't a regular courtroom at all. More like a big conference room. No bench, no judge, no jury box. Just a court reporter, a bunch of people dressed in business casual attire, and a rattled-looking Nate Greene standing before them.

Darcy had, for no particular reason, assumed the district attorney for King's County would prosecute the case, not a untested rookie like the assistant district attorney who'd questioned her in Ned's office. But he was clearly in charge.

Darcy took a chair and Ned sat next to her. Nate looked at his notes for a minute, then said, "State your name please."

"Darcy Morgan."

"Ms. Morgan, can you tell the jury what happened on the night of November the twenty-ninth, at 302 Avenue X, in Brooklyn, New York?"

She hadn't understood things would be so … free form. But she and Ned had rehearsed her spiel a dozen times, and she was ready. "I'd gone out for dinner, and stopped by my office to make sure my boss was going to keep his promise to go home early …"

Ned had his arm around her, but Darcy still almost stumbled leaving the room. "It's okay," he soothed. "You did a very good job."

"I know," she said, her tears continuing to roll down her cheeks. "It's still so hard to talk about it. When I think of how Harry looked …" She shivered roughly, her whole body stiffening when she let those horrid images assault her. "I don't think I'll ever get that picture out of my mind."

"I'm sorry it's so hard for you," he said softly. "But you had seventeen pretty sympathetic-looking faces absolutely enthralled. I guarantee you're the most compelling, believable defendant they've heard from all week. That's got to help."

"I told the truth. If they don't believe me ..." She shrugged, the helpless feeling she was often gripped by filling her once again. "That's all I can do."

"I think you were the last witness," Ned said. "With any luck."

Fifteen minutes later, the door opened and Nate emerged, his tie slightly askew. "Long day," he said, giving Darcy an anemic smile. He sat on the bench they'd been using, and stuck his legs out straight in front of himself.

Darcy looked at Ned, but he didn't comment on Nate's sitting in the hall. But Darcy found it too odd to let pass. "Why are you out here?"

"Just waiting. It won't take long." He took his phone out and started to swipe his finger across the screen.

"What won't take long?"

"It won't take long for the jury to make up their minds." He looked at her, and for the first time she didn't feel like he was her prosecutor. He seemed more like a co-worker or a neighbor. "I don't make predictions, but ..." Shrugging, he said, "I can't imagine it'll take long."

"Because ...?" Darcy said, trying to lead him to say something that would stop her stomach from filling with acid.

"I can't comment about the other witnesses. But you did very well for yourself, Ms. Morgan. You're a good witness."

"Thanks. I hope I never get another opportunity to practice."

"With any luck—"

They all looked towards the door when it opened again. The same uniformed officer signaled Nate, and he got up and entered. For the next three minutes, Darcy tried every relaxation trick she'd ever read. But none of them helped. A group of people who she'd never met were inside deciding whether her life could begin again—or take a very dark turn.

349

One last time, the door opened and Nate emerged, smiling. He shook Ned's hand, then said, "No true bill. You're free to go, Ms. Morgan."

"I am?" She didn't realize her knees had buckled until Ned's bulky arm was around her waist, holding her up.

"You are. No one in that room, including me, believed you were guilty."

"Then why'd you prosecute?" Ned demanded, his face turning an angry red.

"I had my doubts the whole time," Nate said. "Anyone would have. But I'm not the one who decides which cases we pursue."

Darcy stuck her hand out and shook Nate's. "No hard feelings. Someone should pay for what happened to Harry."

"A couple of fresh graves say two guys already have, but more indictments are coming. Some people are going to be back here soon, and next time they'll be defendants, not witnesses."

Ned got a fiendishly delighted look on his ruddy face. "I am so friggin' glad those idiots from the coroner's office were as dumb as I thought. I don't mean to brag, but you hired yourself a hell of a good attorney, Darcy."

Since he was still partially holding her up, she didn't have far to go to turn and give him a long hug. "You've helped me get my life back," she murmured. "I'll never be able to thank you enough."

"Don't forget that when I send you my final bill," he said, chuckling. "Remember, I'm not cheap."

Darcy stood on the top step of the courthouse and powered up her phone. But she didn't need to use it. A gorgeous strawberry blonde was striding down the street, the long steps showing off Tess's fitness. Danny and Ben either hadn't tried to keep up with her, or had surrendered, since they sat atop nearby concrete bollards meant to prevent cars from crashing into the building.

Darcy ran down the stairs, catching Tess just as she was about to turn and make another loop. A hopeful but frightened look froze on Tess's beautiful face. Her mouth opened, but words didn't come. Arms flew around Darcy, almost knocking the air from her. "You're free," Tess finally murmured. "You're coming home with me."

"I sure am," Darcy agreed. "Tonight and every night for the rest of my life."

"What happened?" Tess asked, her voice quavering.

"I don't know what happened behind those doors, but the assistant DA obviously couldn't convince twelve of the seventeen jurors that I might have killed Harry."

"Are you safe?" Tess pulled away and carefully scanned Darcy's face.

"I don't think anyone can tell me that. So let's get on the first plane we can book and start the English portion of our journey."

A smile started on Tess's face, it faltered, then grew until it was bright enough to light up downtown Brooklyn. "I booked the flight this morning. We leave tomorrow afternoon."

Darcy stared at her for a second, too stunned to speak. But she rallied quickly. "What if they'd indicted me?"

Tess's impish smile totally disarmed her. As it did every time. "No one could listen to your story and think you killed a man. No one. I didn't think twice about booking the flight."

It must have been wonderful to have that kind of certainty. Then it struck her. Tess was certain of *her*. She believed in her so totally, it wasn't possible for her to think other people wouldn't feel the same.

Darcy tilted her head and placed a long, emotion-filled kiss upon Tess's lips. If anyone had told her she'd one day be kissing a woman in public, she would have told them they were crazy. Of course, she wouldn't have believed she'd be doing it while her father and her uncle watched, either. And just moments after learning she wasn't going to be arrested for murder! Life was full of surprises. Some of them very, very good. Some of them utterly fantastic.

THE END

What comes next? Read the epilogue at:
www.briskpress.com/out-of-whack-epilogue.html

By Susan X Meagher

Novels

Arbor Vitae
All That Matters
Cherry Grove
Girl Meets Girl
The Lies That Bind
The Legacy
Doublecrossed
Smooth Sailing
How To Wrangle a Woman
Almost Heaven
The Crush
The Reunion
Inside Out
Out of Whack

Serial Novel

I Found My Heart In San Francisco

Awakenings: Book One
Beginnings: Book Two
Coalescence: Book Three
Disclosures: Book Four
Entwined: Book Five
Fidelity: Book Six
Getaway: Book Seven
Honesty: Book Eight
Intentions: Book Nine
Journeys: Book Ten
Karma: Book Eleven
Lifeline: Book Twelve
Monogamy: Book Thirteen
Nurture: Book Fourteen
Osmosis: Book Fifteen
Paradigm: Book Sixteen
Quandary: Book Seventeen

Anthologies

Undercover Tales
Outsiders

Visit Susan's website at
www.susanxmeagher.com

Go to www.briskpress.com to purchase any of her books.

facebook.com/susanxmeagher
twitter.com/susanx